Terror in My Heart

David Adams

Published by David Adams, 2025.

TERROR IN MY HEART

First edition. July 28, 2025.

ISBN: 978-0645361162

Written by David Adams.

Table of Contents

TERROR IN MY HEART

A President has been assassinated, a Prime Minister has been murdered. Who is next? Steve Wallace comes up against an international Assassin and the confrontation might costs Steve everything he loves.

by
DAVID ADAMS

Grief never ends.... But it changes. It's a passage, not a place to stay. Grief is not a sign of weakness, nor a lack of faith....
IT IS THE PRICE OF LOVE

Published by: DAVID ADAMS
   JULY 2025
   ISBN: 9780645361162

ABOUT THE AUTHOR

David Adams spends as much time as possible in the Australian bush, camping, fishing, gold and treasure fossicking, and hunting feral animals throughout Australia. He served as an Officer in the Australian Army Reserve during the post-Vietnam era. Dave has trained alongside members of the United States Marine Corps and Special Air Services SAS. Serving his last two years in the A.D.F as a Platoon Commander Military Police provided him with exposure to law enforcement working closely with his civilian counterparts in the Queensland Police Service. His experience and work with Child Safety as an Assessor / Investigator provides him with a depth of understanding and insider knowledge that is obvious to his readers who enjoy his Crime Genre Novels. Dave relies on this real-life experience to provide him with authentic characters, settings, and a knowledge of military equipment and procedures. He continues to travel the world in search of exciting settings and characters that he hopes will transport his readers to these exotic places while adding a reality to his books.

DEDICATION

I acknowledge that any gifts, skills or creativity I have come from God blessing me with them.

Thank you to Broni my wife who travels with me into places that have a reputation and sometimes the potential for being dangerous. My companion through life as well, putting up with my being distracted when in her company and spending hours locked up in my office. Thank you Hon for all your hours of editing and convincing me to make valuable changes, (another demonstration of her bravery). A life partner who puts up with me sitting facing the door in restaurants and searching for secondary and tertiary exits.

On this novel I especially want to thank Brenda Rudolph who is a good enough friend to have reminded me why I write and how to do it better.

I also want to thank Brenda's husband Ivan Rudolph an international author and blogger. He claims I'm the only Fiction author he reads, and that he loves my books. I value their friendship, encouragement and qualified contribution to my work.

Thank you Gus and Judy over there in Florida I have valued and incorporated your advice in the designing of my Book Covers.

I also thank all the readers and friends who also contributed towards my design of this book's covers, I love the result.

OTHER BOOKS WRITTEN BY DAVE ADAMS
GENRE: MILITARY/ TERRORISM
TERROR in OUR HOMELAND
What readers say!

- Everything you look for in a great thriller; action packed, authentic and intense.

- A compelling voice in action/thriller writing; characters are flawed but become real as every page makes them come alive.

- Explodes on the pages, twists and turns that coax you onward.

- Highly engaging characters, heart stopping scenes that keep you reading into the night.

- Authentic battle scenes from a soldier's perspective.

Linda Mapp[1]

- Scary to think that this sort of thing can actually happen. Captivating from beginning to end.

TERROR in PARADISE
What readers say!

- JUDY from Florida USA

This is Judy writing. I will be writing a review for you on Amazon about *Terror in Paradise.* I just finished reading the book last Friday. Not only was it great to meet you and Broni on our cruise but it was exciting to read your book! I loved it. I was reading in the middle of the night. When Ramone got killed I had to wake Gus up to discuss that chapter. Your research for the book was amazing. I learned a lot about self defence, baddies, and international antiques smuggling.

Prudence Bessant

---

1.   https://www.facebook.com/
mapp.l.1990?comment_id=Y29tbWVudDoxNTA0MDEyODgwNDM0NzIyXzgwODE1OTg5NzU0Mz
M2NQ%3D%3D&__tn__=R*F

• I love a mystery to be solved and plenty of intrigue and drama along the way, complete with an Australian hero in the essence of James Bond. I really enjoyed being taken to exotic locations and interesting details about smuggling and ancient artefacts.

• A book with a hero in the essence of an Australian James Bond. This was a thrilling read with plenty of drama and suspense. A wonderful mystery to be solved and intrigue along the way. Exotic locations and interesting details about smuggling and ancient artefacts to inform the reader.

GUS HOUGH Florida USA.

• *A terrific read! Can't wait for Adams' third novel. Both books blur the line between fiction and (terrorist organization vs Australian security) non-fiction. Can't wait to see what operation Steve Wallace gets into next.*

GENRE: CRIME. THE OTHER STOLEN GENERATIONS; A novel that takes you into the mind and world of the Paedophile and their Victims, and those who pursue them.

What readers say!

Ivan Rudolph[2] (International Non-Fiction Author)

• Well done tackling a fictional approach to raise awareness, Dave. Not a pleasant subject to have had to work in, on, or research.

CHAPTER 1.

It all begins with Osama Bin Laden's ghost.

THE BLUE MOSQUE
ISTANBUL

The prayer room had one door and no windows, and, much to the discomfort of the F.S.B. director, there was no Western furniture. Instead, there were several prayer rugs and a few large cushions. This was the first time the Director had been outside mother Russia since he was a field agent. It made him anxious on many fronts, and he was vulnerable to attack away from his castle, like Moscow HQs. On top of that, his President could never find out about this trip; he longed for the stale and smoke-filled office he called home. There was one strange item in the prayer room: a screen similar to that found in a hospital ward or perhaps a dressing room in an off Broadway theatre.

The voice that now came from behind that screen was somehow familiar. Maksimov had fought in Afghanistan initially as an Armoured Corps Officer and then in the more covert role of a KGB agent. As the man behind the screen began to speak, he recognised the familiar accent of a man born in Saudi Arabia, educated in the West, and having lived and fought for many years in the mountains of Afghanistan.

"Now, Aleksey, if you hire the Assassin Roza as I have suggested, the execution of the contract is a given. It will be done, inshallah. He has never failed," the anonymous voice behind the screen asserted.

"Yes, well, we haven't believed in God for a long time, so if this contract is 'his will' as you suggest, it won't be my prayers that have caused it," the Russian F.S.B. Director stated, cringing because the man hiding behind the screen had used his first name.

The man behind the screen hated Russians. He had fought them for decades; they had killed many of his family and comrades. He hated their godlessness, arrogant world ambitions and corruption at every level. The man squirming uncomfortably on the Persian cushions symbolised all these characteristics. He despised him. However, he hated the evil American, the Great Satan even more, if that was possible.

"We are well past debating faith or religion. Now you have the complete list of the HVTs I require, and in the spirit of a mutually beneficial partnership, I am happy to accept the order you desired for your purposes. The Russian President will go first as you wanted. Equal in importance to the mission, I must again emphasise the need for my involvement to be not just protected, but non-existent. I will leave the smoke screen to achieve that for you. I mean, you have to earn your twenty-five Million Dollar commission somehow," the smooth accented voice stated.

Thinking about the other twenty-five Million Dollars that the Russian Director was planning to hold back from the Assassin on top of his commission, he allowed himself a smile.

"Of course, I appreciate the importance of that mission component. I am anxious to return to Russia; I have a meeting with this Roza in less than ten hours," the Director said as he attempted to shorten this meeting. Between the anxiety of being exposed, lack of civilised furniture and the fact that he was about five smokes in debit, he wanted out of there. Now, whether it was arrogance, some primal need for comfort and nicotine, or just an attempt to assert his usual status, the F.S.B. Director made the biggest mistake of his life.

"You know, between having hundreds of millions of dollars and a hatred of Americans that is stronger than your hatred of me and my country, I think I might know who the mystery man behind the screen is. I never trusted Obama; here he was on TV celebrating the killing of Bin Laden. You don't have to believe in conspiracies to notice they shot the Target in the face and then quickly buried him at sea. I know they talked about a DNA match, but that's also easy to fake. You've gone awfully quiet behind there. Am I right?" the arrogant Russian asked.

"You have all you need; be on your way and be extremely careful," the cultured voice hissed. Bin Laden was astonished and had to admit impressed by this corrupt Intelligence Officer. His deductive powers were totally accurate, and to a terrorist leader such as Bin Laden, who had remained invisible and untraceable for so long, he was more than a little shocked at being identified. As brilliant as the Russian had demonstrated he could be, blurting out his deduction was incredibly stupid. Either way, he had signed his own Death Warrant.

Behind the screen, the older man turned to the one who had spoken to the stupid Russian and whispered, "I didn't believe it, but you were right. He actually believed that you were Osama bin Laden. For such a successful, devious man who has survived so long in this field, he is truly gullible."

As he turned his head slightly, the younger man's head and face caught a beam of sunshine falling through the intricate wooden privacy screens called Mashrabiya. The resemblance to the real Osama bin Laden was uncanny for anyone except perhaps the famous terrorist's son.

CHAPTER 2.

A second chance to stop the nightmares.

THREE MONTHS EARLIER.

Another gritty gust heated somewhere in hell hit my face. I turned away by reflex even though I was wearing the latest ESS desert goggles favoured by all the US Marines in country. This Ahl Alqarya was pretty much the same as every desert village in the region. Except for the visitors expected the next day. Situated just near the Syrian border, it had been chosen to host some very special training. Forty-eight hours before, Australian Intel, based in neighbouring Iraq, had overheard some coms about the little get-together, and for some unknown reason, never to be known to mere grunts such as me, I had been sent in to crash the party. A Marine Osprey, those weird planes that can rotate their props and operate as a helicopter, had dropped me ten klicks east of the village under the cover of a moonless night. I had a bitch of a headache from the NVGs and had tripped more than a few times, but it was worth it to be able to see my way in the inky black.

My SatNav told me that my new Forward Operating Base, FOB, for the next two days was over the next rise. I took a knee and allowed my breathing to quieten; I listened for anything out of the ordinary: a click, a metallic thunk, a rock kicked by a boot. All quiet. Like a good little boy, I told Mum how my walk was going. I had radioed Base each time I crossed the designated checkpoint. We had decided that my present Pos would be my last contact until my mission was completed.

"Grandad, this Sierra One, copy over," I radioed.

A reply came so quickly I imagined them all sitting around the planning tent waiting for my call.

"Sierra One, copy over," a female voice answered, probably Warrant Officer Evelyn Plater, one of the strategy planners.

"Grandad just crossed Murray over," I checked in.

"Sierra One, good copy. Have a good stay, over," The same female replied.

"Roger that out." I terminated the coms, knowing that total radio silence would remain until exfil.

Happy, I moved on. Sun up was in about four hours, so darkness covered my trek. Crawling to the forward edge of the ridge above the village, I carefully chose my hide and set up for a long wait. I was operating without a spotter so I made sure I had a wide line of sight to the Target building. Whatever happened with the plan, I had to be able to drop the hammer on the bomb maker if he tried to make a run for it. Waiting is the sniper's closest companion. I had to sit tight until this time tomorrow morning. I would make sure it was worth the wait.

Just after 0300 Hrs, I descended the stony ridge. A thick, cold fog now embraced the mountain all the way down to the village. My NVGs were useless in this cloud, but I would be happy to have them if some freak wind blew the dense fog away. This made the going treacherous but I was in no hurry. If it had been a clear night this would have been different as I would have stuck out like the proverbial. I hoped it would hide me from any sentries guarding the grey mud-wall house where they would hold the lectures the next day. The trouble with that is the same cloud could be hiding a platoon of baddies right in front of my trail.

So far so good, as the ground levelled out I had to approach the huts from memory the pea soup fog I couldn't believe my good fortune; no guards were a gift to my plans of my nocturnal visit going undetected. I took out my lock pick gun, and with a few clicks, the simple lock quietly opened. I made a mental note to lock it again as I left to mask my visit. The largest room was on the ground floor, with no windows and two entries. One opening probably led to the kitchen, and I stood motionless in the other, listening. In preparation for the next day's meeting, the smoky room contained several trestle tables along one wall. Grubby sheets covered each table and draped over something. Holding a small red lens torch, I gently lifted the corner of one of the covers. Drawing back a sheet, I could see several different types of SVs laid out like a chef would set up for a cooking class. I selected the SV that seemed to be holding the most Semtec. It probably didn't matter which Suicide Vest exploded, but it never hurt to go for a big bang. I knew the other belts and vests would go off in sympathy, vaporising the classroom of future jihadist students. Removing the original mobile phone, I inserted the one I had brought with me.

The ability to calmly wait was a given for a trained and experienced sniper. Under the cover of the friendly fog, I climbed back up the small ridge that overlooked the Syrian village. It was either pork or chicken MRE; I ate the roast chicken Meals Ready to Eat. I had figured that the suicide bomb class would be an all-day affair and wouldn't start before the devout group had said Salat al-fajr or pre-dawn prayers. I dozed until the sun had burned the fog off and which now burnt me through my hoochie. I watched the comings and goings around the deadly classroom. Several men arrived at the door that I had locked on my way out the previous night. I set my Military151 Spotting Scope to mid-range magnification of around X 25 and took photos of each militant as they approached the house. The images were then fed through to Intel at HQ for facial recognition and matching using six different systems. If the face was unknown, a new file would be started.

As I ate, I thought about the similarity of this mission to the failed Op that had haunted my sleep for so long. It wasn't my style to overthink stuff, but this Op might have some cathartic outcome. I was looking forward to ending a bomber's career. It had been a long time, but I was still plagued by a recurring nightmare. We had a local man undercover in the bomb class whose task was to mark the bomb maker/teacher. Once identified, I was to end the bomb-making teacher's career. I had a 7.62 168-grain Sierra MatchKing boat tail hollow point (BTHP) with his name on it. It all went pear-shaped, and the Jihadists beheaded the UC ally.

I hadn't identified the HVT up to this point, nor had I recognised anyone else for that matter. That was no surprise to me as this was the first Op in this massive sandbox for years. The other 'students' arrived in twos and threes.

All the men wore the unofficial uniform for Middle Eastern terrorists, baggy pants and farm clothes with a fighting vest probably of Russian origin. However, the next man arrived on his own; although dressed similarly, he was at least twenty years older than the earlier arrivals. My heart skipped a beat as I saw the bomb maker's face as I clicked the long-distance camera. The face from my nightmares filled my spotting scope's lens.

I didn't really believe in Karma, but this offering would be accepted with the greatest of pleasure. This mission just got personal. Not that anything would change. Emotion clouds judgement. I was too focused to let this revelation negatively affect my actions. The bomb-maker cum teacher entered the house without knocking. I waited an hour or so. Some movement near the house dragged me from thoughts about my nightmare coming true before my eyes. Two women arriving with baskets of food confirmed that the bomb-making lesson had started, and logically, the teacher and all his students were present. I assumed that the women were serving the food, and as I waited, I hoped they would then exit the house. A wave of adrenalin was surging through me. I was a little surprised by this. However, the nightmares had hammered me nearly every night since my last tour. A bit of biofeedback was only natural. Finally, the women left the house carrying the now empty trays and baskets.

I picked up the Sat phone I had laid out beside my spotting scope. I pushed the preset key for the only contact in the phone. The call didn't require anyone to answer. I smiled as I imagined the old terrorist who had murdered so many Soldiers and innocents turning towards the table behind him. He alone understood the deadly meaning of the ringtone, which was the theme of The Good, the Bad, and the Ugly, which interrupted his class, but only for a second. The thousands of screws, ball bearings and steel nuts filled every inch of the training room. The shrapnel was travelling at approximately four thousand feet per second and decimated everything in its path. Flesh and bone were separated to become bloody fragments as the projectiles from the Suicide Vests sliced them into meaty confetti as the balls and screws ricocheted off the walls.

I was already packing my rucksack when I looked down to see and hear five separate explosions as the various SVs and belts exploded. It was too dangerous to confirm any kills. However, nothing was left of the training room except for some low brickwork. I stood up, confident that no one in such a confined area as the training room could have survived. Slowly, I exfiled down the back of the ridge that had been my hide for the last forty-eight hours.

AUSTRALIAN NATIONAL
SECURITY CENTRE
CANBERRA
AUSTRALIA

Holding up the newspaper report, Colonel Goodrich laughed. He had been my Control at the Australian National Security Centre for nearly three years. The Colonel was the only one who believed in me when I was a nightmare-driven, half-drunk hermit. I had reported that Taliban terrorists had set up a training camp near my hunting property just outside the Queensland rural town of Roma. That was the first Op we had shared. Since then, I have completed numerous missions, including working with the CIA to shut down a worldwide ISIS banking system. Colonel Goodrich laughed again.

"So Steve, when we first met, even your friends weren't sure you were squared away. PTSD nightmares and never far from your old counsellor, Mr Jack Daniels. You never really told me what tipped you over the edge, what those nightmares were about."

I grimaced at the memory of how bad my life had been before I had a new mission in life: serving my country again and finding love with a local cop out Roma way. I laughed to hide the hurt that had just stabbed me as real as any USMC Kabar fighting knife.

"Well, Sir, it was all about an HVT bomb maker and losing a local who was brave enough to go UC," I stated calmly.

The Colonel was famous for his intelligence and deductive processes.

"You're kidding me, so this latest mission turned out to be the same guy? You got a second chance at him, hey? Maybe get some payback for that Under Cover local?" He asked.

"He sure is or was; I thought it was Christmas when I clocked him through the spotting scope. Completing a mission always feels great, but nailing that butcher was an absolute bonus." I said.

The Colonel looked up from some papers on his desk. Astute as ever, he continued, "I've never pushed you about how you're travelling these days. I figure that getting back in the green saddle and having someone love you at home has turned you around. Let's hope that ending this guy might end those nightmares for good," he stated.

Usually, I wouldn't appreciate this analysis, but Goodrich and I had developed a trust and brotherhood borne by watching each other's backs time and time again. I changed the subject at least a little, "Sir, don't you love it when the media get a true story so wrong?" I asked.

"Yeah, what do you expect? They nearly sound sorry; these murderers have bought it." Colonel Wallace replied. Remember what Mark Twain said; 'If you don't read newspapers, you are uninformed; if you do read them, you are ill-informed. It was true then, and it's even more so now, especially with the political agenda of most modern media. Colonel did you read the rubbish in that newspaper story?" I asked holding the paper up.

"Islamic Suicide Bomber Trainer Accidentally Blows Up His Entire Class

By: JACK MARSH, Canberra Times, **Time:** 4 days ago

In Baghdad, a terrorist who appeared to be in the middle of conducting a training session for future militants accidentally blew up an entire class, killing 21 of his students and himself.

The group was part of the Islamic State of Iraq and Syria, the terror group that has been participating in a string of attacks in the United States.

The report stated that the incident may be viewed as justice for the many lives lost in the wake of foreign and domestic terrorists' relentless attempts to convert the nation into an extreme-religious state. This turn of events will have spared many innocent lives.

According to recent reports, the instructor was in the process of showing his students how to use a suicide belt. As he was teaching, the live suicide belt appears to have detonated, resulting in mass fatalities.

"What's the plan, Steve, heading home for a while?" The Colonel asked.

"That's a definite Roger, Sir; spend some time with Chris and Jake, of course. Chris always accuses me of loving that dog more than her. I tell her that when she starts jumping in the air and wagging her tail when I get home, I'll be less confused about that." I said with a laugh.

"I know you are one of the bravest men I have ever worked with, but that's gotta be pushing your luck. Anyway, head home, and I hope I won't need you for a good while." Colonel Goodrich smiled as he stood and offered his hand. I shook it warmly and stepped back, a Major saluting his Colonel.

CHAPTER 3.

The Evil is unleashed.

F.S.B. H.Q.
LUBYANKA BUILDING
MOSCOW

The Russians weren't any different to the Americans, thinking that re-badging their notorious and murderous spy organisation, the KGB, would change the world's perception of it, but nothing had changed. Aleksey Maksimov, the current Director of Russia's Federal Security Service (FSB), lit his hundredth cigarette for the day using the one he had just exhausted. Once an iron-hard killer, he spent too much time behind his antique desk. Way too many cigarettes and bottles of Vodka had thickened his girth, causing his once handsome face to become splotchy and saggy. He knew Russia's current President had once sat in this same chair. And just like his predecessor, this ruthless Director believed he too, was destined to be the nation's next President. He was sure the highest office would be his if he pulled off this coup. Director Aleksey Maksimov had thought of nothing else but this call for days. He answered the burner phone: naturally, it was attached to a scrambler just to be sure.

"Yes, Dobre Utra," he said, attempting to hide his excitement at receiving the call he had anticipated.

"Good Morning, Director. Can we speak English, please?" the calm voice asked.

This ploy hadn't fooled the experienced Russian Intel Officer; even though it was feint, he placed the underlying accent as Serbian.

"Certainly, go ahead," the Director relaxed a little.

"You have an excellent C.V., but of course, we would not be talking if that was not the case, Dah?" the Russian said, more to regain his calm than to state the obvious.

The Assassin, all business as usual continued as if the Director had not spoken.

"From this point on, you can call me Roza. We need to meet somewhere safe, somewhere nice and public," it was a demand, not a request.

" I don't think that's going to happen. I like privacy," the Director countered.

"So, to make sure we both understand, as of this call I am in charge. I will guarantee the completion of the contract. However, I must have total control from this point," the Assassin asserted, leaving no room for debate.

"Alright, point taken," the Russian Leader said, unused to being told what to do.

"One hour, the Biblioteka imeni Lenina," Roza spat. The line went dead.

The F.S.B. Director smiled at the Assassin's choice of meeting places. A busy Moscow Railway Station made perfect sense. Unlike the more suburban stations that displayed better artwork and sculptures that many museums would envy, this big city station was a sterile, white-tiled tunnel crowded any time of the day or night.

Forty minutes later, riding in the leather luxury of his bulletproof Limousine, he swirled the cold Vodka and smiled contentedly.

"Viktor, I heard the name Roza, and I can not remember where I know it from; it feels like it's an important name. I just can't place it," the Director asked his chauffeur.

"Roza, the WW2 sniper, Sir. A famous war hero and inspiration to many, even us Spetsnaz guys. An amazing woman, sniper and comrade," the bodyguard cum tactical Driver stated passionately.

"Of course, of course. Now I remember. Roza Shanina, the Kindergarten Teacher, became a world-class sniper after the Nazis killed her brother. They named her 'The Unseen Terror of East Prussia'. Forty-nine confirmed kills, but you know there was probably twice that number," the Director remembered from the back seat.

"Dah, Dah. She wasn't the only female sniper, but she was the first to win an Order of Glory medal for her service," agreed the Driver.

He had forgotten how much he detested public transport. It hadn't crossed his mind for many years, the F.S.B. Director having his own high-security detail, including his Spetsnaz-trained chauffeur. The Security Detail Commander wasn't happy being told his Principal wanted to go out without his detail. It worried the Captain, but he was always a Soldier first and obeyed his commander's orders without discussion. Entering the busy Railway Station, the F.S.B. Director and his loyal chauffeur were met with a blast of cold, stale air coming from the depths of this man-made cave system that assaulted their senses.

To make matters worse, as with most railway stations in these liberal days, an amateur band playing old Beatles songs echoed around the tiled cavern. There was a wall of information posters, ticket booths on their immediate left, and a massive map of the Moscow railway system. The wall map resembled a flat Christmas tree, with every stop on every track represented by a bright little red light. This bulb would become green as the train entered that particular stop.

The chauffeur was arguing with the ticket seller, "We don't want any tickets we are not catching a train," he growled.

"That's is what they all say, Dah. You will buy a ticket, or you will not go down those escalators," the old railway woman said. Seeing his growing frustration and anger, she stood up behind the perspex screen to further assert herself. "One more word, and I will call Security. Is that what you want?" she asked threateningly.

The chauffeur/ bodyguard knew they wanted no commotion, publicity, or official reports placing the Director at the railway station. A scene would then mean questions about why he was there, and his many enemies would try to make something of it. He gave up.

"Two tickets to Aleksandrovskiy sad," he demanded, purposely refusing to say please as he paid to go to the next railway station up the line.

The heavy-set woman with a flat face and tobacco-stained teeth smiled in victory as she slipped the two tickets under the perspex.

"Spa-si-bo," she exaggerated her 'thank you' by emphasising the three syllables.

"OK, my friend, try to keep me in sight but be careful, this Roza has not earned that reputation by being sloppy.

That we can be certain of," the older man said in a tired voice. He then walked over to what could have been a cliff because the floor abruptly dropped away from where they stood. Eight escalators a hundred metres long fell away like a ski slope. Hundreds of people filled these moving steps, going both up and down. Unlike many Asian and some European countries where the habit of standing to the right to allow people to run up and down these escalators, this didn't apply here. The Director was immediately swept downwards as he stepped onto the moving incline. The chauffeur followed his Boss a few seconds later. It seemed to take an eternity for the escalator to reach the bottom and disgorge its writhing worm of passengers. Uncomfortable on about twenty different levels, the F.S.B. Director moved with the crowd of commuters. Towering tiled pillars supported the ceiling. As he walked, he was counting them. He just passed the fifth one on his right; it was covered in cigarette advertising and students leaning there acting cool.

"Don't turn around; just stand there like you're waiting for someone. You are very nearly late, my Director," Roza the Assassin said quietly.

The F.S.B. Boss froze. "Very nearly doesn't count. Let's get this done. I'd rather be just about anywhere else," the older man hissed through his clenched teeth.

"OK, that's good you've caught on, hey? Straight down to business, I like it," the Assassin said in a friendly voice.

"This contract, the HVTs, well they are the perfect definition of High Value Targets. Your Russian President, then the American President in that order, as per your requirement. Then you want me to remove two Prime Ministers that don't seem in the same class, the English and the Australian Head of State," the Assassin stated.

Showing more annoyance than he would have years ago and realising it, he hid his shaking hands as he lit yet another smoke. The F.S.B. Director smiled as he remembered the first time he evaluated this imposed order of events from the man behind the screen. Thinking back to that initial meeting the Russian bureaucrat remembered that he had become even more sure it was Bin Laden. When the unidentified man used the term the great Satan, one normally used by the Jihadists when speaking of America. The Russian Director knew that those ordering these high level hits hated Russia nearly as much because in Afghanistan his Comrades had become just another invader. Of course, this suited his ambitions. Was this a coincidence, or was he being manipulated by the possible Bin Laden? Either way, he would benefit, his next promotion was a massive one and all that money was a landfall. He didn't care if he was being pushed through a gate. It was the one with a sign saying WIN / WIN. Thinking more about the contract details, he assumed that the English and Australian Prime Ministers were being targeted because they had been both vocal and military allies of the USA.

The Director disliked being told what to do, so he took this opportunity to assert his position. Sounding more indignant than he felt, he demanded, "Surely you're not asking why. I was assured your professionalism would dictate that you wouldn't require an explanation of my motivation or any of the details regarding this contract."

Backed by his own F.S.B. army and the might of the entire Russian Military that he would inherit, he feared no man. However, the Director knew he must be careful. Upsetting the world-class Assassin standing behind him was as deadly as playing with a spitting cobra. He had mentally balanced the risks a thousand times. Any personal danger was outweighed. There was so much money at stake as well.

"I couldn't care less why, but it's a huge risk. What you are proposing is the biggest hit in the history of hits. If, and I say if I was to take this on, well, it would be the end of my career," the Assassin stated.

"With $250 Million in an offshore account, I think you may be able to buy a small country to retire to. I am certain that you will get by, my comrade," the Director said sarcastically.

CHAPTER 4.

A nice Russian river cruise.

Nearly four months had passed since Roza met the F.S.B. Director at the Moscow Railway Station. After taking an Uber from his hotel to the Kremlin gardens he wandered around Red Square and the surrounds of the Kremlin taking lots of photos as any tourist would. He had ended up sitting in the Kremlin Rose Garden going through the photos he had just taken. His concentration was interrupted when he was surrounded by a bus load of tourists filling the path between the rose bushes and a central fountain. Roza heard a woman with an annoying American accent ask the guide, Sasha a question that was redundant as he had just explained the answer a minute ago. He responded politely, in clear English with the slightest Russian accent. The Assassin listened to the guide's response and his repeated explanation of the gardens and the surrounding points of interest. Roza had already noticed and photographed the L.Z., that was at the base of a slope on the Eastern side of the garden. He had an inkling of the L.Z.'s function. However, he had no way of knowing it's true purpose. The guide's next story stunned the Assassin where he sat. He explained that the L.Z. was where 'our President's helicopter lands each day'. Roza couldn't believe his good fortune as the guide continued his rehearsed patter informing the tourists of the security measure employed by the President to protect him in flight and on take off and landing. Of course he didn't know the details, but the seed of a plan had begun to grow. In the next few days he researched the possible scenarios, weapons and what cover he could engage to execute the mission and escape after he had completed his mission. Roza, the Assassin, had chosen this river cruise because it was as if it was especially designed for his mission. The cruise he chose included several bus excursions visiting all the city highlights, including a stop at the Kremlin's Gardens. Roza couldn't believe his luck when he discovered that the specialist weapons supplier he had enlisted was actually one of the cruise highlights. However, few knew this craftsman lived a dual life making deadly items for a highly specialised group. That was how Roza now found himself on that same company's tour three weeks later. He had even ensured that Sasha was to be his guide. However, although he knew that this was the safest way to get within striking range of the Target the Assassin was conscious of wasting time on this river cruise. Travelling from St Petersburg to Moscow, the Volga had always bored him, and it was living up to his miserable view of the world. However, if not happy, it was understood that the required weapon was highly unique. The Target couldn't have been of a higher value. The risks couldn't have been greater, nor the fee. The method demanded creativity like no other method had before. Begrudgingly, he accepted those two factors dictated a lot more Security that just going to the Railway Station and opening a locker like usual. This was outside his usual SOP; hiding in clear sight among American and Australian tourists was pushing his limits. His Standard Operating Procedure was defined by one word 'smoke'. One minute, he would be there, just a hint, an aroma, or an irritant in your eye. Then, a moment later, as the Target was still falling to the ground, he would be gone like a puff of smoke. He left those present would be looking around bewildered, questioning their own senses. Did they really see someone? Did they hear something?

The tourist ship was once a Hospital ship supporting the Motherland's Baltic Submarine Fleet during the Cold War based at the mouth of this very river. The small cruise ship meandered from St Petersburg to Moscow and, once replenished, cruised back. The rooms, while a little small, were exceptionally well renovated and worthy of foreign tourists seeking a little adventure. While Roza sought his own company, drinking his favourite Belvedere Vodka alone. Occasionally, he would sit out on the narrow deck appearing to be engrossed in the book he held to discourage passers-by from trying to talk to him. The Assassin had toyed with hiding amongst a large group of Danes on board. Due to the ridiculously high price of anything alcoholic in Denmark, this happy bunch drank from sun up to midnight and sometimes even later. He had decided that although they had welcomed him several times, he would look like a zebra running with a herd of horses. He couldn't act that happy all the time. They seemed to accomplish that state without effort.

The dining format forced him to eat his meals while surrounded by his fellow travellers. However, he refused to be more than barely civil and excused himself as soon as he had finished eating. Throughout his career he had survived, no, flourished due to his ability to compartmentalise and focus. A lesser warrior may have been distracted by the holiday environment and several single women's availability in semi-luxurious settings around the ship. While he appreciated the fact that he wasn't belly down in two feet of snow waiting for an opportunity, he also knew himself well enough to know that being comfortable too long could dull his edge. He allowed himself the tiniest of smiles as he thought of his trainers at the State Security Service, the SSS, the Serbian equivalent to the CIA or F.S.B.

A national champion with the rifle, he was quickly recruited, attracted by the elite reputation and adventure of the SSS offering an escape from the monotony of civilian life in a cold, harsh, unforgiving country. He was then educated in the art of assassination, everything from employing knowledge of anatomy, chemistry and physics to the more obvious martial arts, small arms and knives and, of course, bombs.

As he dressed for dinner, he looked at his reflection and couldn't help but smile. His usual blond hair was gone, his head shaved clean, and he was wearing a bushy beard with the only hint of his original hair colour. He wore a body suit of Hollywood quality that added fifteen or twenty kilos to his super-fit torso. Placing the thick black-framed glasses high up on his nose completed his visual disguise. He then placed a thick moulded insert into his left shoe, which caused his image in the full-length mirror to immediately tilt. He hunched his shoulders slightly to lessen his six-foot frame and left the cabin. As he headed to dinner, anyone observing him would wonder how he had been injured so badly for him to have such a pronounced limp. If it hadn't been for the orthotic insert, he may have even had a spring in his step. He noticed he felt a little elated and then realised that his spirits were lifted as he thought about tomorrow when the ship would visit Kizhi Island.

The sign greeting the tourists on arrival told the story about of the island. Kizhi Island is about six kilometres long; all the buildings are made of wood, and even the two famous churches are unique. The structures have survived even though they were built in the seventeenth and eighteenth centuries, and nothing much has changed since then. The island has successfully catered to thousands of tourists since the opening of Russia to Western visitors in large numbers. Somehow, the inhabitants have maintained an authenticity that provides an authentic experience of village life, including numerous crafts and local foods. He wasn't interested in any of that, pushing his way through a group of passengers waiting to disembark. The man with the limp and the gruff attitude headed directly for the Glassblower. He still made sure he wasn't being followed by covertly checking his six by stopping to take photos he would never look at. The last one in the row was an old grey wooden house with herbs and flowers hanging from drying hooks along the walls. It looked just like those around it except for a large glass ball swinging gently at its gate.

Pushing aside a multi-coloured woven curtain screening the doorway, he was expecting an artist's studio only to find a small room with crowded shelves of handmade glass items. No surprise, the artisan cum weapon supplier still had to pay the bills and maintain a solid cover. Another doorway led into what could have been a family lounge centred around a huge fireplace. On entering the area, the heat struck him like a blow. There was a smallish man with an out-of-proportion chest. The Assassin thought that the craftsman's lungs must have developed from blowing thousands of glass items. He was dressed in farm clothes with a well-marked leather apron, and was in the process of rolling a glowing glass ball across small brightly coloured glass fragments. The Assassin couldn't remember why or how he knew these sand-sized pieces of glass were called frit. The craftsman didn't show any recognition that he had a visitor; he was totally focused on his creation and continued to work on the piece. Eventually, he was finished and looked up, appearing to be surprised that the man was there.

"Dobre Utra," smiling at the customer, the Glassblower switched to English, "Good morning, and welcome," the Glassblower said warmly.

"Good morning, Sir," the Assassin responded." Initiating the required password, he continued. "I was wondering if you had any swans?"

The Glassblower was not surprised by the password; the man before him may look overweight, and he had noted the limp as he entered the room. He had seen too much death, too many killers. This 'tourist' had eyes reminiscent of a shark, black and without the spark of life.

"Not as many as this time last year," the old craftsman replied with the correct response.

"Good, I am ahead of the boatload of tourists, so let's make this quick," the Assassin said, never one for pleasantries.

Having the customer in his home worried the weapon supplier. It was highly unusual as normally the ordered item would be delivered by a trusted courier to a locker or a safe drop. The Glassblower knew hitmen didn't like loose ends. A supplier of weapons knowing where they were or what they looked like, even in disguise was vulnerable. His gut was uneasy, and it wasn't just from too many Piroshkis, his favourite meat pastry. The weapon supplier's anonymity was as crucial as the Assassin's, but now it was blown. He could only hope that this mutual straying from procedure would protect both him and his limping killer. Deciding that, like the Assassin, the less time this shark was in his pool, the better his chance of survival the glassblower said.

"I will get your purchase from the back room," he disappeared through another heavy screen, moving deeper into the ancient wooden cottage.

The Assassin, always on alert, didn't like this man being out of sight; what if this was a set-up, an ambush? He made up his mind there and then. The old wooden floorboards creaked behind the screen, and the Glassblower pushed through the heavy curtain hanging across the doorway. He was carrying a gift-wrapped box about four hundred millimetres square. He placed the box on the table and turned towards the Roza. He had been paid in full, so there was nothing that would delay the customer's departure. No training or explanation was required as the Assassin had demanded the item and supplied all the technical specifications. The Glassblower started to breathe again, feeling a release thinking about the man leaving his shop and awaiting the flood of tourists from the cruise ship.

"It's all yours as ordered," the weapons supplier stated, knowing that men such as before him didn't need any flowery descriptions or sales talk.

"Thank you, your reputation promises quality," the Assassin stated in a friendly tone. The tenseness that he had noted in the Glassblower visibly left him. He took two limping steps towards the small man in the leather apron and offered his hand. The old craftsman responded in kind and even smiled. The sharp pain he felt in his palm caused him to retract his hand as though he had been bitten by a snake. In a way, he had. A miniature syringe loaded with the infamous Novichok that the Assassin had concealed in his palm had indeed bitten the Glassblower. Within seconds, the chemical caused the weapons maker's heart to fail, and he was dead before the Assassin had reached the front landing. Looking around, he made sure no one was nearby. Roza had ensured that he was alone by going straight to the Glassblower while his fellow passengers worked their way along a row of wooden houses filled with a variety of crafts and wares. By the time some tourists discovered the dead artisan, the Assassin would be back in his room onboard the ship.

"Welcome back, Sir," the young Sailor said as he stepped aside to allow the Assassin up the gangway. He was sensitive enough not to stare as the old man limped and struggled momentarily as he traversed over the gunwale onto the deck.

"Looks like you bought something nice, hey?" he offered in a friendly way.

"Yes, a beautiful handmade quilt for my mother," the Roza lied and calmly headed for his room. Like every Soldier who routinely checked his rifle, parachute or vehicle, he would thoroughly examine the item he had just received knowing that when you needed to use said weapon, it was too late if something was wrong. Back in his cabin, he planned to unwrap the box and check its contents.

By executing the Glassblower, he had created the situation that if anything was wrong or missing, it would be up to him to fix the problem. His peace of mind held no regrets.

FSB HQ

MOSCOW

Aleksey Maksimov, Director of Russia's Federal Security Service (FSB), looked up from the monitor before him. He was annoyed at the constant and urgent knocking on his thick wooden door. This door kept most things out of his office and protected him and his privacy. Without any insincerity, he had developed and nurtured a reputation of an angry ogre hold up in this majestic ornate cave.

Only his Second in Charge, Colonel Ivan Kolesneschenko, had direct access to him. This was strictly limited to Situation Reports and planned meetings. This knocking was not only annoying but also worrying. For his 2IC to need to see him this urgently, the sky must be falling.

"Vkhodit," "Enter, just stop that infernal knocking," he shouted angrily.

Saluting, the Colonel knew he had to be quick before the dragon burnt him to a puddle of uniform and melted brass. He reminded the Director of a timid schoolboy who was too scared to ask permission to go to the toilet. He took some pleasure in this as the man before him was a seasoned warrior of many years serving in Afghanistan and a quality Intelligence Officer to boot. But, in this wonderful country, ambition and treachery were close partners. A superior officer had to dominate all those below to maintain that Security. The Americans say: *'You treat them mean to keep them keen'.* He smiled at the thought. Ignoring Rank was another way to assert superiority, so he used his first name.

" Ivan, what can be this important?" the Director demanded.

"Sir, we have just received Intel that a foreign agent is in country and planning some form of attack," the Colonel spat the words like ridding himself of a bad taste in his mouth.

"OK, what are the details, and where did this intel come from?" the Director demanded.

Colonel Kolesneschenko pushed on.

"Sir, we have heard rumours about an operation named Poezd. Of course, that is what our beloved President will name the new High-Speed Train next week when he launches it. We don't know much else Sir. Our team is exploring any potential sabotage scenarios of the train; of course, we are checking for any HVTs planning to travel on it in the immediate future."

Sitting at his desk, he displayed no emotion. However, the Director was shocked to hear this intel. And more so, that his subordinate had linked this intel to the possibility of a plan to assassinate the Russian President. The Director had to be careful not to discount this intel or the Colonel's assumptions. If and, more correctly, when the President was assassinated, the last thing he wanted was a memory of such a huge oversight.

"Ivan, how certain are we that this foreign agent is already here?" he asked, more to maintain control of this discussion than actually needing the answer. He had several questions that he would typically ask. However, just in case this launching ceremony was, in reality, his Assassin's opportunity, he didn't want to pre-empt the plan. The last thing he wanted to do was to stimulate this line of thinking up and down the corridors of the Security H.Q. building where he now sat.

"Sir, the source is Andis; as you know, he has always been highly reliable, but at this time, the details are somewhat lacking. I knew you would want to be informed. I suppose knowing the code name for this is a bonus we don't usually get. Of course, I will inform you as soon as anything comes to hand," the Colonel's speech was rapid, as though he wanted this over. He was annoyed because he felt like a child expecting to be slapped by a disappointed father or teacher.

"Very well, Colonel, do that," the Director said, and the junior officer understood he had just been dismissed. However, he didn't realise that the shock of this intel becoming available cut the meeting even shorter than usual.

As the heavy black door closed, the Director reached for the Vodka and a glass in his desk drawer. Unusually, his hands were shaking.

CHAPTER 5

A pretty rose garden and a bird of prey.

RUSSIA

Finally, back in Moscow the last night had arrived, all the cruisers were bused to a Ukrainian restaurant in the city. Most of the fellow passengers had been waiting in the ship's bar for this excursion to disembark. As they alighted the bus, they were chatting away merrily. The Assassin ignored the bus protocol of alighting from the back first and stormed off the bus. He could hear the Danish contingent as they fell up the stone stairs, noisily knocking over a pot plant. The restaurant had two big windows at the front with horizontally striped curtains. The owner, dressed in traditional Ukrainian red pants and a long coat, welcomed them all as they shuffled through the carved wooden entry. The Assassin had seated himself to have a good view of the front door and near the back exit, just in case. Old habits never die. He was careful not to drink too much, but several Black Russians warmed him as did the excellent food that the restaurant served. He had developed a taste for the Black Russians in his previous life, the vodka taking the sweetness off the Tia Maria. The night was a huge success even for him; the Assassin sat with the tour guide, who was very good at his job and likeable even to the anti-social Roza.

MOSCOW
KREMLIN ROSE GARDEN
NEXT DAY

Today was the one the Assassin had been waiting for. The last day of the cruise included several bus tours of all the city highlights. The Assassin maintained his cover by going on excursions to the grand Tsaritsyno Palace of Catherine the Great and the Novodevichy Convent, including a stop at the Kremlin's Gardens. By the time the Assassin had finished his morning exercises and breakfast, it was time to board the buses for today's excursion. No one seemed to notice that for the first time, the man with the limp who had avoided making any friends on the cruise, was carrying a large box under his arm. He had carefully wrapped it and pasted on a fake address label. He had then slit the gap enabling the addressed lid to be removed and be able to be replaced without disrupting the wrapping. If an inquisitive fellow traveller or official asked, he would say he had plans to post it after the tour. It was so big that it stopped anyone sitting beside him, this suited him just fine. He was too professional to be anxious; however, he could feel the slow trickle of Adrenaline increase as the tour progressed. Red Square was impressive, bringing memories of massive communist rallies and military parades. They arrived at what he had been waiting for. There were no surprises; he had visited these gardens several times and he had studied and measured the buildings and surroundings in books, charts, and in person when he had visited Moscow by himself the month before.

His thorough reconnaissance and research had given him the idea for his final method of attack. This, in turn, had led to the master plan: the design idea of the specialised weapon he would use, and this cascaded into identifying the Glassblower cum weapon maker. Roza was pleasantly surprised to find a cruise that enabled him to pick up the weapon and eventually finishing where his Target resided; in the nation's capital Moscow.

He had to limp around with the other tourists, trying to look interested as though he was a first time visitor. The buses disgorged their bellies full of camera armed tourists at each stop. The Kremlin and Kremlin Corner, with their pink walls and cream trim, were the crowd's favourites. As Roza limped to the entrance of the gardens he had to quickly raise his camera to his face as three black F.S.B. sedans, a metre gap between them roared out of the Kremlin building, racing through the ornate entrance once used by horses and carriages. He was slightly concerned when the tour guide informed the bus that they were only allowed their cameras when they went to the Kremlin Armoury. This meant the Assassin must leave his large camera case that contained his Glock 19 handgun unattended on the bus. He had no choice.

The previous month, he had been in the garden independent of a tour; disguised differently and minus the limp. Roza had overheard the guide speak of a tour of the Kremlin Gardens. In fact, he had done the tour four times with as many different companies. During these tours, the guides showed the group of tourists several things that were adjacent to the gardens. This time the Assassin couldn't believe his luck.

The group beside him was listening attentively to their guide who was pointing down a slope to a concreted area. "Now, of course, we can't go down there, but those red patterns on the concrete are Landing Zones for the President's two helicopters. They...." The guide quickly masked his annoyance at the intrusion of his patter.

A small English boy interrupted him. "You said two helicopters; why does he need two?" The freckled lad asked.

"Well, just like the President of the United States of America. By the way, you know he has eleven helos. They are named Marine One, Two and Three and so on. Some of them are the famous Sikorsky VH-3D Sea King designed by a Russian, of course," the guide continued clearly proud of his statement, even if a little misinformed.

"Yes, but why does he need more than one?" The persistent boy asked.

The Assassin and the guide knew why, but he wasn't about to share a security factor with this midget tourist. He ignored him and continued his patter.

The little boy's mother knew her son would continue to nag the guide, so she attempted to help. "Mikey, he has two just in case one breaks down or something," she stated confidently and Mikey appeared satisfied, thankfully.

One of the other tourists elbowed his wife. "They travel in twos and threes, so if there is a missile attack, the shooter doesn't know which one contains the President." He whispered smugly.

The guide set off up the winding garden path surrounded by roses and other colourful blooms. He stopped and, after waiting for the stragglers, began to speak again.

"Now, here's another interesting thing related to the President's Helicopters. See that small black shed at the bottom of the garden." All the group focused on the little building reminiscent of a chicken coop or aviary.

He continued, "You would have noticed back at Red Square that it's infested with pigeons. Anyway, they like to roost on the Kremlin windowsills and swarm around these gardens. That is annoying to our President. They also fly across the Landing Zones we just talked about, which could be dangerous." He stated with a quick look at his freckled interrogator as though waiting for another question.

"Now, they have devised an ingenious method to deter the pigeons from coming here or at least staying here when the President is in his office. He paused for effect.

"You would never think of the solution to that problem. However, we have gone back to our roots, the old days when people would hunt birds, including pigeons. And does anyone know how they used to hunt?" He asked to keep the group involved.

At no surprise to anyone in the group, Mikey replied, "With a slingshot. Looking pleased with himself.

The guide was secretly happy that the English kid was wrong. "Nyet, No, with our beautiful Saspans as we call them in Russian, or what you would call the Peregrine Falcon. They live down there." He pointed once again to the little shed. "Six are released every afternoon after all the tour groups leave the gardens and each time the President is about to arrive." He said in a conspiratorial tone, sharing a secret as though the group was privileged.

When the Assassin first heard this on a previous tour it was a revelation. During the next few days, he kept going over the scenarios this created and the outcomes on offer. He had initially thought of a long-range hit on the President; however, the exfil was always dangerous. It was amazing how fast an area could be locked down, especially when someone had just killed their President. Lying in his hotel room that evening, he had his plan. He had considered hitting the President while he was in his chopper. Still, the multiple aircraft had the same effect as the American President's multiple Marine Helos.

The group had just arrived in the middle of the gardens. There was a pink granite water fountain round in shape with a large silver peacock at its centre. "Now everyone, have a good look around, and we will meet back here in ten minutes, please." The guide said.

The group went in every direction, and the Assassin sat on a bench in the dappled sunshine. The guide headed towards the road to grab a quick smoke away from his charges.

During the Assassin's recces the previous month, he had noted that there was a cordon around the whole precinct. Armoured vehicles with roof-mounted specialist antennas doted the boundary. Of course, the Assassin was very aware of the current anti-drone technology. SRC's Silent Archer counter-UAS (Unmanned Aircraft System) technology complete every task, detects, tracks, classifies, identifies and disrupts low, slow and small unmanned airborne threats. The technology is comprised of proven systems that deploy cameras and 3-D displays to defeat hostile drones, whether a lone target or a UAS swarm. However, the Assassin had evaluated this invisible force field as a deterrent to his plan. The actual weaponry linked and fired by the Anti-Drone System was an absolute blitz of cannon fire highly suitable for protecting a naval vessel, or camp. However, due to the area being populated by tourists and workers from the Kremlin it could not be housed or fired in such a location as the Kremlin surrounds and gardens.

Roza smiled when he contemplated the next stage of his mission and sat sunning himself less than two hundred metres from his Target. Now, finally, alone near the bubbling fountain, he hid his parcel under some thick rose bushes and waited for the rest of the group to return to the centre of the garden.

After a head count the guide said. "OK, that's everyone. Please follow me back to the bus," as he headed back towards the road and their waiting bus. The band of weary tourists walked toward the bus, merrily chatting away. The limping Assassin followed along behind. Stopping when he was alone, he called out causing the guide to jog back to him.

"Are you OK, Sir? Are you hurt?" He asked, his face showing concern.

"No, I'm fine, sort of. I've left that parcel I was going to post down near that fountain. I'm sorry. I'll just go and grab it, if you can wait," Roza said apologetically.

"As long as you're OK. Yeah, well, we'll wait while you get it. Please be as quick as you can, but go safely. These guards don't like us here after hours." The young man said realising telling a client with a limp to hurry was a bit insensitive.

Limping away as quickly as possible, Roza turned a corner and out of sight ran as fast as his orthotic shoe would allow. Once he got to the fountain, he reached under the bush and withdrew the box. He then carefully removed the prepared lid of the parcel. Removing a sheet of bubble wrap revealed a drone made by the late master craftsman glassblower to look like a Peregrine Falcon. Before removing the bird like drone from the box he looked around to ensure he was alone. Taking out a remote control from the box, he pressed the initiating button, turning the hawk-shaped drone on a small green light showed in the dull light of the late afternoon. There was a reassuring electrical whirring sound as the UAS warmed up. He touched a second button. The predator-shaped drone raised vertically from the box and then at his command returned to its cardboard nest. The drone was programmed to target the President's office window, so it didn't require manual guidance. Blind to the plump pigeons that its warm blooded peers were supposed to be scaring away this U.A.V. would not be distracted. Now the drone was switched on it's special programme had kicked in. The Assassin always kept things as simple as possible to minimise failure through complex equipment, however, he had taken an evaluated risk with the timer on this drone. The Glassblower had assured Roza that he had been able to design a noise activated timer into the drone. He had no idea what the drone was specifically built for. However, the Assassin had provided a decibel range that began where the Helo's engine noise started. This clock was started by the sound of the incoming helicopters. Then it would tick digitally off thirty minutes, allowing the Russian President ample time to be seated at his desk. It would then launch as the six real falcons were released to fly and swooped on pigeons that were unlucky enough to be caught near the pink Kremlin building. Roza figured that each Falcon would be diving in different directions, as they chased the terrified pigeons. Meanwhile, without this distraction, the drone would proceed towards its programmed Target.

Leaving the UAV in the rose garden Roza quickly re-wrapped the now empty parcel, and headed for the exit path out of the gardens. He got back onto the bus and was happy when they headed

along the road between the Kremlin buildings. Crossing the Red
Square the bus dropped everyone off outside Gum, a world-famous
Russian apartment store.

Roza even had one of their renowned ice-creams to celebrate
the end of the cruise and his mission. He had done all he could
to achieve the assassination of the Russian President. Roza finished
his ice-cream as he walked down to a line of restaurants and bars
crowded with a mix of locals and tourists.

He glanced at his watch and calculated that it had been nearly
an hour since he had prepped his drone. The Assassin was sitting at
a small table on the deck of one of the bars sited along the outer side
of the Red Square. Roza wondered if perhaps the President was not
returning to the Kremlin this afternoon. The sound activated drone
would work any time, however, the chances of it being discovered
increased with every minute it sat in the garden. Then the womp,
womp of two Helos bounced off the walls of the nearby buildings.
Roza had decided to stay in the bar waiting for the half hour that
should now be ticking away on the drone's timer.

President Adrik Orlov was exhausted as he collapsed into his
huge leather swivel chair. His meetings in St. Petersberg had not
gone well. And now being stuck behind his desk reading and signing
documents irritated him even more than usual. Like a hunting dog
chained to a verandah, he longed for action. As the President re-read
a report for the second time, his thoughts returned to those days
of action. He was ex-army, ex-KGB/F.S.B. and even though he was
heading towards seventy-three years old he missed the rush, the
adrenalin. Even his horse was missing him. He dreamed of rides
and hunting with the sun burning his bare muscular torso. It was
this romantic vision that the President had on his mind when the
hawk shaped drone's solid head smashed through the ancient glass
window. The drone packed with as much RDX explosive payload
as possible, detonated by the impact. The explosion vaporised

everything in the office, including President Adrik Orlov, who died instantly. His final thoughts had him shirt off, riding his favourite horse. The irony had crossed Roza's mind; that Orlov was Russian for Eagle and yet the more powerful bird would be destroyed by the smaller, yet more deadly imitation one.

He was taking a mouthful of his Black Russian when he heard the muffled explosion, all the tables rattled a little and a black cloud began to rise from the other side of the pink cream-trimmed building. All those around him stood up for a better view, many exclaiming surprise and wondering to each other what the noise and smoke could be. Without confirmation, Roza couldn't be sure of the mission's success, but unless Orlov had been out of his office when the UAV struck, the President was gone.

When a President dies, the news is usually held back for a while. People need to reorganise, circle the wagons, and prepare press releases for grieving politicians or Military Officers, you name it. The cruise was over, so the Assassin took a room at a hotel that was like going back in time but was safe and clean. He had thought about CCTVs around the gardens and figured the risk was minimal. They would show him arriving with a package and later leaving with that same box. His disguise was solid, and limping seemed to make people think he was offered no risk or danger. He now looked completely different to the person who took the cruise and whose passport he had used. The Assassin had used one of his other passports to check into the hotel and was, therefore, invisible. Forty-eight hours after the explosion, the TV and internet were overloaded with reports and eulogies for the now officially deceased President.

The entire country was in mourning, some sincerely, most to stay out of trouble. The power brokers were already pushing and shoving to get their favourite behind the President's new desk.

F.S.B. Director Maksimov was careful to display the right amount of shock followed by a convincing sadness befitting the loss of his old friend, the President. One of his closest supporters, he had been promised everything from a new Dacha summer residence to replacing him as leader of the nation, and everything in between. This was always couched in; "When I retire my old Tavarich Maksimov. We have been comrades a long time, who would have believed that we would both live this long, hey?" The now dead President would say to the FSB Director. He was confident but old enough to know you don't brag about winning a war when you're putting your armour on. You waited 'til you were taking it off. that usually means you have won the battle. He also knew that as well-planned and orchestrated as this entire project had been, power always corrupts. And the President of Russia was a load of power in some ways greater than his American counterpart. He had waited this long, and if Russian winters had taught him anything, it was that waiting a little while longer wouldn't be a hardship. He had become impatient eventually, betraying his friend and President. Such was Russia.

CHAPTER 6

A trip down under for POTUS, and a warriors reunion.

WEST WING
WASHINGTON DC

The Oval Office was always a pressure cooker; however, on this rainy Washington day, it seemed worse than usual suiting the mood of the group. The powerful men were seated facing each other across a coffee table that in times past had Napoleon Bonaparte's shiny boots resting on it. Henry Duke, better known as Trader Duke, who had been Director of the Secret Service under the last three Presidents, sat on one side. He was a U.S. Marine first and now only existed to protect POTUS. He was clearly uneasy. Sitting behind the inner circle, along the curved walls, Press Secretary Jerry Engel, frowned and jotted something down.

Until we know who is responsible for the Russian assassination, Mr President, I think you should stay safe within these walls, Sir," Duke said with feeling.

"Trader, from a protection viewpoint, you're right. I can't hide under the bed. What sort of message does that send? It would mean a lot to our boys serving down under and the Australian public to see that I think opening that new Marine Base near Darwin is so important. It's a big part of the trip. However, it gives me a chance to meet face-to-face with our closest allies, the British and Australian Prime Ministers, seeing that they will be there as well. I mean, wherever we stand up, Britain and Australia always stand beside us. I mean Australia is a small country with a tiny but well trained

Military, yet they punch above their weight every time. Now there seems to be a push from within the Opposition Party down under to ditch us and hold hands with China. Our ally Prime Minister may benefit from our presence. No, gentlemen, this trip is crucial in so many different ways," the President said calmly.

The other lounges and chairs within the Oval Office were full of senior bureaucrats, security experts and the Military. Although each of them was concerned with the implications of the President's speech, they had all heard that tone before. Once he had decided, you moved on and made it happen.

The President stood and slowly walked over to the full-length windows and sighed.

"Gentlemen, again, I know you have my safety in mind, but we are going to Australia. I am not being blasé or macho about the risks. I'll go along with every precaution you want. Don't forget we will be in the middle of nowhere and on a Base patrolled by a couple of thousand trained Marines plus air support. Only a fool would try anything there," the President stated as much to himself as the room full of advisers. "Now get together, make your plans and away we go, OK?" With that, the Leader of the free world stood, signifying the end of the matter.

"Mr President, you know you shouldn't stand near the windows like that," the Secret Service Director said softly.

"Yes, yes, and we all know it would take a missile to get through this bulletproof glass," the President said in an equally soft tone. However, every person in the oval office noticed that his face had drained of colour and wondered if the Russian President had thought the same thing immediately before he was vaporised by that drone.

Having this many Military, Security and Protective Services in one room was akin to having twenty hungry male lions sharing one small cage. The atmosphere was testosterone-charged, ego-driven.

Trust was a scarce commodity even though many of these Alpha Males had fought side by side and were long-term friends. The Secret Service considered it insulting and involving all these other agencies insinuated that they couldn't do their job. Having so many different agencies planning how they would protect the President while in Australia could descend into a bun fight. The USMC General was a muscular, tall, sad-eyed veteran with the standard buzz-cut that had now turned grey hair. He had served in every campaign or fracas the USA had been involved in over the last thirty-odd years. And more than a few that didn't make the files or the news.

"Gentlemen, please, let's try and put our egos and pride on hold for a while and focus on the Op. It goes without saying that the President's protection while on my Base will be my responsibility." The older man stated with heavy emphasis. His rich voice rumbled with the authority he wore as easily as his uniform. "That Aussie weapons company has learned some hard-won lessons on the battlefields, including Ukraine. Their radar-directed 30 mm cannon SLINGER System has more than responded to the worldwide demand for advanced counter-drone technologies. Those things work just fine; we'll be placing an order for them, that's for sure. The Russians didn't have that."

"Oh, come on, General, some new toys won't guarantee POTUS's safety," said the Director of the Secret Service.

"Trader, we all know there are no guarantees, but if Drones are the threat, then this Aussie gear reduces, if not eliminates it, at least to a range of eight hundred metres. That Russian egomaniac asked for it and had grown complacent because he's been in supreme power for so long," continued the General.

"General, that sounds logical, but high-tech gear doesn't change the fact that the Secret Service exists for this purpose. Sure, you'll have two and half thousand Marines on hand, but as well trained as they are, they are not trained to protect our President. We can't just let you take over while we hit the mess for some Bud Lights." Trader Duke, the Secret Service Director, asserted.

The General and Duke had been friends for over thirty years and respected each other. This wasn't the first time the President had put them on opposite sides of the table. They had always come to an understanding that they could live without compromising their roles. Smiling, the General responded.

"Sure Trader, I hear ya. You do your close cover; we will handle the air and the long to middle-distance threats. How's that sound?" the General asked in a conciliatory tone that few had ever heard him use before.

The National Security Advisor's role was usually outside this task. However, the President knew that these well meaning but territorial warriors may not play nice.

He appointed a fellow warrior in the lion's den with enough seniority to facilitate the countless future meetings and arguments he knew would follow. He had asserted his leadership like a mum over the dinner table.

The Nat/Sec/A smiled as he looked around the room. "That's encouraging and sensible. It's nice to hear you boys playing nice, and that even sounds like a good plan. Just to be perfectly clear, would it be true that anything outside the Tortilla Flats USMC Base falls under the normal Secret Service purview? Accordingly, POTUS has the protective cover he needs while he is in Australia and then even more cover once he's on the Base. It took some fur and feathers but guys, I think we can make this work. Of course, Delta Unit will be on standby within easy Helo infill and Casevac. Let's all hope and pray neither is needed." The old warrior stated calmly.

The Colonel representing Delta Force was more used to being the active force on an Op but could see the sense in this. He thought; *sure, we'll fly in and sort out the mess the Secret Service and Marines leave.* "Yes, Sir, that's a good copy. We will be there, he said confidently.

Smiling, the President stood and said, "Thank you, gentlemen, do your planning, keep the Nat/Sec/A...... not just informed, but involved. I say again involved. This has to go smoothly. We must send all the right messages we can at a time of potential turmoil such as the world appears to be currently experiencing." With that, the room emptied.

"Bill, can you please stay for a moment?" The President asked his old friend.

Bill Sadler was in his sixties and had kept his moustache from the same decade when every man civilian or Military wore a mo. He was definitely getting older but had kept fit and was a mile ahead of most of the ambitious young staff working within the West Wing. He returned to a chair facing the President's desk and waited for the room to empty before saying anything. "What can I do for you Mr President?" He asked.

"Thanks, Bill; it'll be like taming lions coordinating that group, but I needed someone with overarching authority and common sense." The President said, "I didn't want to emphasise the 'other' reason for my down-under. I know you get the updates, our Aussie mates are one step away from ordering a batch of Lockheed Martin M142 High Mobility Artillery Rocket System (HIMARS) under a US$385 million deal. Now, this is a huge win-win for us. It's a nice little cash injection for one of our largest manufacturers, plus it means one of our most trusted allies is tooled up in case of trouble in that region," the President stated as he picked up his specially emblemed coffee mug, a gift from the English Prime Minister.

POTUS continued, "As you know, the US Defence Security Cooperation Agency (DSCA) announced overnight that Australia had been granted Congressional approval of the system." Picking up the document marked TOP SECRET, the President handed it to the Nat/Sec/A, "This is the Aussie's Christmas letter to Santa," POTUS said.

Sadler quickly scanned the sheet of paper and exhaled through his teeth.

It listed:

20 M142 HIMARS, 30 M30A2 Guided Multiple Launch Rocket Systems (GMLRS),

30 Alternative Warhead (AW) pods with Insensitive Munitions Propulsion Systems (IMPS),

30 M31A2 GMLRS Unitary (GMLRS-U) High Explosive Pods with IMPS,

30 XN403 Extend Range GMLRS AW pods,

30 EM404 ER GMLRS Unitary Pods ad 10 M57 Army Tactical Missile Systems (ATACMS).

He looked up and paused briefly before continuing, "They got a look at that HIMARS launcher during that recent Talisman Sabre exercises, and as expected, it excelled. The Australians are getting pretty tech-savvy, and they can see the value that a launcher is capable of firing the Precision Strike Missile (PrSM) holds. Last August, Australia signed a Memorandum of Understanding (MoU) with the US Department of Defence for the development of the PrSM weapon. On top of that shopping list, the ADF is seeking to acquire a new, long-range rocket artillery system by the mid-2020s, as initially proposed in the 2016 White Paper and confirmed by the 2020 Defence Strategic Update (DSU 2020) and Force Structure Plan (FSP 2020). The initial work on the acquisition of such a capability is a $0.6 to 0.9 billion Long-Range Fires Program is being undertaken under Land 8113 Phase 1. Guys, you can see why I'm so keen. I mean, this is all a huge achievement, including the sales for our companies and the upgrading of one of our closest allies," he said.

"I see what you mean, Sir; your visit may be critical in helping them make that decision. And, of course, that's only the first order. I'm sure they'll add to that as budgets and politics allow," the Nat/Sec/A said.

"The money is important, but our friends down under have already stuck their necks out by letting us have a USMC base in the Northern Territory. That upset the Chinese and anyone else with a future strategic plan. We have to work with them, and I see how your visit is timely and crucial," Bill Sadler stated.

"Bill, I have one last meeting; you are welcome to stay," the President said lightly.

There was a soft knock on the Oval Office door, and, on hearing the President say come, the CIA Director and another man entered the inner sanctum.

"Close the door, thanks Jeff, and welcome. Bill has stayed to make sure he is over every aspect of this holiday to Oz," the President said warmly.

CIA Director Jeff Pidgeon, Pidge to his friends smiled and quietly shut the heavy curved door, making the room physically soundproof, especially when added to the modern electronic scrambling gear that eliminated any chance of internal or external bugging. The younger man who had followed through the doorway stood uncertainly behind the chair facing the Director. His name was Ben Winfrey, and he, too, had a nickname. Nearly everyone called him Oprah, except for a particular Australian Operative, Steve Wallace. But that's for later.

The President appeared more relaxed now the larger meeting was over.

"Thanks for dropping in Jeff, of course you and Bill are old friends."

"Jeff, you do the intros Bill and I haven't had the pleasure of meeting Agent Winfrey before." After the introductions the room fell silent, awaiting the President.

"I'm glad you brought Agent Winfrey with you. Son, your Boss here speaks very highly of you. It was your name that came to mind when I first asked him about this. Jeff, have you given this any thought since I mentioned it the other day? POTUS asked.

"Sure, Mr. President, the way I see this Aussie trip is that everyone will be there except the Boy Scouts. So, I figure the CIA should be there, too, but not in any numbers. It won't require any covert ops; it's not like it's Baghdad or even Moscow, right?" The CIA Director stated.

The four men nodded in agreement. Winfrey on the other hand realised he didn't know what the senior men were discussing so it was inappropriate for him to agree and stopped nodding.

"Anyway, Mr. President, as we discussed, I want Winfrey to go. Of course with your approval. You know, show the flag, be at the meetings, be seen by who counts, and report back as needed. He has worked with the Aussies before when they cracked that ISIS smuggling ring last year. My counterpart in Canberra informs me that the same Australian Officer, Steve Wallace, has been assigned a similar role for your trip." The CIA Director said casually.

The President smiled. Standing signifying the end of the meeting he said. "Winfrey, you'll enjoy Australia, cruise around with your colleague and come home with a tan and some good stories, hey?"

After returning to CIA HQs, CIA Director Jeff Pidgeon turned his back to Agent Winfrey and keyed in his office access code. Talking over his shoulder the Director asked, "Is that your first time with the Boss, Oprah?"

"Yes, Sir, I was glad you did the talking. I just sat there like an Elvis doll on the dash, nodding like a fool." Agent Winfrey said with a smile.

Director Pidgeon nodded. "In my experience, that's often the best strategy when you're in the Oval Office. He has you there for him to do the talking. Unless you get a question to answer, that is. Then, the secret is just to answer the question, no more, no less," he stated calmly.

"You're among the few people who know everything I've done and places I've been. I gotta tell you, I was more scared in there than most of the fights I've been in," the young agent said.

"We will have a few more detailed briefings before you go to Australia, but I just wanted to confirm what POTUS said to you. Now your...... what do Aussies call their friends? 'Mate', that's right. Your mate Steve Wallace was an absolute legend when he worked with us. The fact that he's been assigned to ghost his Prime Minister in a similar way to you and POTUS will open up an easy set-up for you. His people see it the same way we do. On this visit, there will be so much protection; your job will be more like a tourist than the close protection you've done overseas," the Director said.

"How do you see it working, Sir?" Oprah asked.

"Go over before the visit so you're ahead of the game. I'll fix it with all of our guys who might wonder why you're there. Just keep your head down. Sorry to treat you like a cutout but I wouldn't expect you will even have to say anything at meetings or briefings. You arrive Down Under, catch up with Wallace, go to the same briefings, and ride with him wherever he goes. You know your brief, and I am pretty sure Steve Wallace's would be the same. When POTUS is with the Aussie PM, you can even carpool," Director Pidgeon said, laughing at his own joke. Hearing the way his Boss was looking at this assignment, Agent Winfrey thought: *this is the first mission that has seemed to be tokenism; show the flag, they say, no action, all sounds too good to be true. It'll be great to catch up with Steve; we didn't have a lot of time together, but what we shared, has made us brothers.*

CHAPTER 7

Steve Wallace the Romantic Warrior.

I left cold Canberra behind, and a few hours later, my plane touched down at Roma airport; I had to get a taxi as Chris had a shift to work, thankfully the air conditioning was cranked up to combat the oppressive dry heat. Being a local cop on a Friday night she expected just about anything but an early finish. This suited me; I had missed her, but I needed a few quiet JDs on the patio stroking Jake's head to distance myself post-op and wash the sand off. In the last few days I had been in Afghanistan, Canberra and now here. I was tired to the bone and mentally exhausted. I think a deep recess in the back of my mind was part of the exhaustion. My recurring dream had always been the bomb making teacher beheading my informant. The guilt had scalded me for well over a year. It was biblical that I had been tasked to take the bomb maker out. I was unsure setting that suicide vest had been cathartic. I was interested to see if that dream would ever haunt me again. It was nice to be home. I always looked forward to seeing Chris, and it was good for all of us, for me, to have this transition from adrenalin, danger, and noise to my little sanctuary in peaceful rural Queensland.

Chris and I had been together ever since we had met during my run-in with the local terrorist training camp. Sure, like any relationship involving someone in the Military, there were always absences. I had come out of retirement with an offer that was too good to knock back. My set-up was pretty unique for an Army Officer, but my being on call as compared to having to front up every day to a post made it as good as it could possibly be. At least we knew that I wouldn't get transferred out every few years. A wife-to-be was always going to miss her man; at least I hoped so. Managing the worry about whether I would make it home was always there like a dark cloud on the horizon. A simple thing like Chris watching the news and wondering if I was making that news could put pressure on a long-distance relationship. Chris was slightly better in that, being a copper, she understood guns, danger and duty. It didn't make it disappear but maybe made it a little easier to manage.

I was sure no expert in all this stuff, but I was trying harder than ever to be mindful of these issues. All this Dr Phil stuff was based on previous mistakes and one divorce. I had been too gun-shy at first to even have a relationship, but I soon realised that with Chris I had no choice. I had never really had these thoughts before. Maybe, it was love at first sight for both of us. She was different; she was good for me in so many ways. That in itself gave me confidence in the way I felt about Chris. However, I also knew Chris was my anchor in a rough ocean of mistrust and actual threats. Before I met her, I had been a barely functioning alcoholic hiding out on my mate's cattle property with Jake, my dog, and Jack Daniels as my only companions. My discovery and eventual attack on the terrorist camp forced me kicking and screaming back into the Military that I had run from just a few years before. By linking up with the Australian National Security Centre, Australia's sort of CIA, but under Military Command, I had been given another chance.

I still liked my solitude and the odd whisky. Now I had a reason to keep mentally and physically sharp. Chris kept me grounded and emotionally stable. As I thought about all this for the thousandth time, I felt a bit selfish. I figured it was up to Chris to have the same sort of thoughts from her perspective, to decide where we went from here. Maybe, we would go no where. A lack of strong confidence about relationships and ever present trust issues were always eroding my thoughts. Could a wonderful woman like Chris really love and settle down with someone like me? Jake barked just once, telling me

Chris had just arrived home. I met the love of my life at the door. She looked tired, but her smile said it all. As always, when I returned, we just stood there and held each other, grateful for the opportunity, the gift of just being together again.

The next day, we were sitting out on the patio and it wasn't any cooler. Roma was always hot unless it was freezing. It's a wonder the Army didn't have a base here like they usually did with this sort of weather but it was still our favourite place. I topped up our wine glasses and popped a local olive into my mouth. Jake was asleep under the table. He was just happy to have us both there.

"Hon, we've been talking about this for a long time. I don't want to be like one of those old guys at the bowls club. You know. 'Hi, this is Chris, my fiancee.' Oh, how long have you guys been engaged? Oh, yeah, that's right, it's comin' up to forty-three years now," I said seriously. I was sure, but in a way, this whole deal scared me more than facing a Taliban machine gun.

Chris looked at Jake and put on a cartoon voice. "Jakey, Stevo's had too many wines, me thinks." She laughed. Then, seeing the look on my face, realised that joking wouldn't cut it. "I'm sorry, baby, I didn't mean to duck the idea," she said.

"Well, that wasn't quite the response I was looking for! I know it's hard being married to a Soldier. No, honestly, I was hard on my first wife, that's for sure. I know the divorce stats. It is much more likely than in the real world but, I was young, ambitious, selfish back then, and full-time."

"Now you're old, careful and a sensitive new-age guy, right?" she said as she smiled and lifted her wine glass to her lips.

"Man, why are you makin' this so hard? I thought it was what you wanted but one more joke, and you can just forget it," I said bitterly, my lack of confidence surfacing.

The look on Chris's face told me she realised this wasn't like our typical friendly banter. We were just two warriors with quick whits, iron sharpening iron and usually it was fun for both of us. I was so worried about this huge step. I also knew that Chris wasn't my ex, and I wasn't that young dumb Lieutenant anymore. My fears were robbing me of my humour, and Chris had been enjoying my apparent lack of comfort. I saw her do a double take when she finally realised how important this conversation was to me. How troubled I probably looked.

"I'm so sorry, baby. I was just doing what we always do. Just joking, I'm sorry," she said, taking hold of my arm. "Rubbish aside, I would love to get married. Now there. I've said it, and I couldn't mean it more." Her eyes began to water after seeing the relief on my face.

"You don't have to cry hon, I thought, I'd hoped you'd be happy," I said as for the thousandth time I attempted to understand women in general and especially the one in front of me.

Sobbing, Chris answered me," I am happy, you idiot. "Can't you see that?"Now, all we need to do is decide on the details. It's our day." She said, blowing her nose on a tissue.

I was relieved and happier than I'd been for a long, long time. I didn't know much about such things. However, I knew women love planning; a happy spouse is a happy house etc.

"I have a growing feeling I'm going to be busy for the next few months. Can I leave you to work out a date and the details? Just ask for anything you need from me. I want a military wedding, as in us guys in uniform. Otherwise, it's all yours, and I will be happy with whatever you want."

"Oh, sure, the uniforms are a great idea; you'll be so handsome, are you talking swords, medals and everything? The photos will be awesome." She said with a huge smile.

Chris had to work the next three days, so Jake and I headed out of town to chase a few wild pigs and maybe some deer. We had lived out there before I moved into town with Chris, so my camp was well set up and like a second home. The hunting was good; the rains had brought in the pigs from the drier Western plains. Later, sitting around the fire with Jake lying nearby, with a metal mug of JD in my hand, I began poking the fire with a stick. "Jakey how good is this?" I said to my dog. He agreed by wagging his tail.

I was awake well before dawn, and after a coffee, Jake and I hit the trail. The other bonus out here was that there was no phone signal, except up on a granite ridge east of camp. Like any hunting property you return to, memories abounded as I walked for miles. I came to a small dam where I had scored that big boar the year before. Just down from there was a stand of Brigalow where I had shot my first ever Red Deer buck years before. My heart rate increased as I remembered the thrill of that stalk. Then, I came to a boundary fence and looked over the narrow dirt road. It seemed a lifetime ago, but this memory wasn't hunting, and it wasn't good. I had accidentally discovered a terrorist training camp on the neighbouring property. An all-out battle had ended their plans, but not without a heavy cost. It was also how I ended up back in the green machine.

Present Day

I returned to my camp knowing Chris would finish her last shift in about three hours. Reluctantly, I packed up camp and headed home. Jake looked mournful as I sang along with Toby Keith. Who would believe a country dog that didn't like country music? As usual, when you're on the way home, you see a mob of pigs running across the road.

"I'll get them next time, mate." I said to Jake, who had got excited watching the black blobs run past.

I slung my pump action 308 over my shoulder as I opened the little wooden gate to our front path. With a good hour to spare before Chris would get home, I reluctantly rejoined civilisation. I cracked a beer and cleaned my rifle, waiting for Chris to finish work. Jake barked once his usual welcome home.

"Hey, hon, it's good to see you. How's Roma's top crime fighter going?" I asked, smiling. I grabbed her and, holding her close, I kissed her hard.

"I've missed your smiling face and your rapier wit," she said, breaking away for a breath. "You smell terrible. Did you and Jake roll on the dead pigs or something out there? Before I could answer, Chris asked "Have you seen the news since you got home?"

"No, you know how I avoid their lies, and besides there is no reception out there," I said as we walked, holding hands, into the kitchen.

"Well, you haven't been to Russia in the last three days, have you? She asked.

That was a weird question to ask. "No, I haven't even been to Brisbane. Why?" I asked as I opened the fridge.

She shook her head and continued, "With no signal out there, I suppose we could go to war, and you wouldn't know. Someone blew up half the Kremlin, including the Russian President. His horse riding and bear hunting days are over. All confirmed, and there's been nothing on the news except it. All the usual speculation from the news talking heads, desperate to look intelligent and failing. But no one really knows, or if they do, it's not public. No group has claimed it." She said.

"Wow, that's huge. My guess is it was an internal hit, someone close in, but I suppose the Chechens, even the Ukrainians, have plenty of reasons, but, I doubt anyone outside the country would see it as a good move. He was at least predictable." I said.

My thoughts flew to Canberra to the offices of the Australian National Security Centre; *I could only imagine how busy the backroom boys and girls would be trying to work that mess out. I also wondered if I would hear Colonel Goodrich.*

"Chris, I can't really be sure why, but we need to make those wedding plans sooner rather than later just in case I get the call." I said. My head hoped no, but my gut was already packing for the trip. I figured I had forty-eight hours max.

CHAPTER 8

The tourist takes in the sites.

ABU DHABI

He had taken three flights in the wrong direction before back-tracking on the Etihad jet to Abu Dhabi. After an uneventful flight and taxi ride from the airport, the Assassin approached the check-in desk at the luxurious Conrad Abu Dhabi Etihad Towers Hotel.

"Welcome, Mr Klinkenberg. Is this your first time in Abu Dhabi?" the young Asian woman asked politely. As there was response, she continued.

"Your room awaits you; please don't hesitate to call reception if there is anything you require once you settle in. The information regarding our wonderful services is in the red book on the coffee table and Channel 1 on your TV. The Spa has a special on massages today after your travel. If you require this, just call 333 to arrange it. The lifts to your tower are behind you to the right." The beautifully attired receptionist handed the Assassin his room card and signalled the Porter, who had been waiting with his trolley loaded with the Assassin's luggage.

"5th Floor it is, Sir," the Porter stated as he held the elevator door open.

With that, not another word was spoken by either man until the Porter swiped his master room card and opened the solid door. He stood aside, allowing Roza to enter his room, and returned with the Assassin's luggage.

"Where would you like these, Sir?" the Porter asked, playing the charade that every Porter in every hotel goes through, hoping these words prompted the guest to come forth with a tip.

Understanding the ritual, Roza's goal was to be remembered favourably and then forgotten rather than stay in the Hotel Porter's angry mind as someone who didn't talk and didn't tip his hard work, "That's fine, thanks; here is a little something for your help," he said, handing him a folded note.

Encouraged further, the Porter asked,"Sir, would you like me to show you around your room?"

Suddenly overwhelmed by a desire to be alone, Roza had to gain some control so that his response wouldn't be rude and aggressive. "NO! no, please I am fine, just very tired," he said, using his own body to move the Porter towards the door.

"Thank you, Sir, I hope you enjoy your stay," the Porter said as the solid door closed softly behind him.

Until he felt that pressure on him, the Assassin hadn't realised how fatigue had magnified his innate desire for solitude. He hated airport crowds and queues, sitting cramped up with two strangers for fifteen odd hours. His psyche had always needed solitude, peace and quiet, just comfortable in his own company. As a child, he had never felt the need for others to play with or to share some experience or event. He was the perfect Assassin or sniper.

He thought of some American who had said: 'The more people I meet, the more I like my dog.' He grimaced as he thought; *I don't even like dogs.* He prided himself on showing no emotion, not allowing his environment to control his thoughts or actions. Speaking aloud to the empty room, he said. "This was not right. I can't afford to feel that sort of pressure. I must be tired. I need to focus." He carefully unfolded the news clipping that read:

'*CANADIAN PRIME MINISTER TO VISIT ABU DHABI*'. The reason he was here. He lay down, clutching the newspaper page, and was asleep in seconds.

The Assassin hadn't stayed in the hotel before. However, he had carried out some thorough research on the hotel and its surrounds. The hotel's website was extremely helpful, especially due to the clever use of drone photography. He had confirmed this vision using Google Earth giving him the expanded view the surrounds of the hotel. He had the beginning of several plans. He couldn't believe how slack the security was around this VIP's itinerary in Abu Dhabi. The paper even itemised the daily events and schedule. He had chosen the hotel because it sat in just about the centre of a circle encompassing the Canadian Prime Minister's visit venues. He showered and dressed for lunch in a lightweight cotton suit, selecting a crisp white button-down shirt with no tie. As he walked to the elevator, he was thinking about several of these planned VIP venues; he had already discounted all but two.

One was on the Yellow Boat Abu Dhabi, a high-speed small boat tour of all the famous sites showing off the unique architecture and beautiful shorelines and bays. A well-placed bomb, or a RPG rocket launched from one of the many bridges the Yellow Boats would sail under. The Assassin gave it a lot of thought because he had done the boat tour twice on a previous reconnaissance visit. He had seen various opportunities to smuggle an explosive device onto the boat prior to the Canadian Prime Minister's embarking. Roza noted that there were four identical boats. Not knowing which boat would be deployed the following day eliminated the option of placing the bomb on an unattended boat the night before. Sneaking onboard in daylight once the boat was confirmed was out of the question due to the tourists that swarmed the wharf all day long. Security would be heightened some hours before the PM's visit, especially after the Russian President's recent demise while he was safely ensconced in his office. Roza had evaluated the method of detonation of such a bomb. He decided this was fraught with danger due to the nature of the boat trip and all the high rises that could block the Assassin's view. A Rocket Propelled Grenade was the better option. The Assassin put that at the top of his list. The opportunity for a shot would be limited, but it could still present as the best option.

After a light meal, Roza returned to his room and, after a cold shower, lay down and perused the itinerary again. His eye was caught by what was, at first glance, a benign event with no political or tactical importance. The Canadian Prime Minister was to meet the United Arab Emirates Minister for Presidential Affairs. In this planning stage, the venue was more interesting than the participants. They would meet in the Old Palace had been converted into a top-class hotel. It was literally across the road from where he was currently staying. A static target in a static location appealed to his basic strategy approach, always keeping his plans simple where possible. The Assassin phoned the Concierge and requested information regarding the Old Palace Hotel.

The phone was picked up on the first ring, the Concierge going through his answering mantra.

"Yes, Sir, it is a magnificent place to visit, especially when you can return to the modern, friendly sanctuary you are currently enjoying," the Concierge stated, probably thinking he was being subtle by his comments regarding the competition over the road.

Roza understood the man's motivations. "Certainly, this hotel is exceptional, and I am very happy here. However, I have heard that the Old Palace is worth a look around, surely?"

Sounding more relaxed about sending his customer to the opposition, the Porter dropped any concerns and became helpful.

"Sir, if I may suggest something, a way to enjoy a look around, as you say, is to partake in their famous High Tea. It has a worldwide reputation, many say surpassing that of the famous Raffles in Singapore."

"Wonderful suggestion..... I am sorry I didn't catch your name?" the Assassin flattered the Concierge a little more.

"Tanhum, Sir, can I be of further assistance?" the man asked as he thought hopefully, about being mentioned by name when this customer eventually wrote up his satisfaction survey.

"I'm wondering if you could book a High Tea for one at 10 tomorrow morning, please? I'll also need transport over and back, I realise it's close by, but there are flyovers and sub-roads to traverse, and it's too dammed hot in any case. Make it an hour earlier to give me time to walk around a bit, hey?" the Roza requested.

"Most certainly, Sir, consider it done. I will, however, message your room with a formal confirmation," the Concierge stated confidently.

"Thank you.... Tanhum," the Assassin remembered his name perfectly but stuttered to build on his image of a tourist struggling with the language. "I appreciate your suggestions," with that, Roza hung up the phone. He hid the copy of the Canadian Prime Minister's itinerary to avoid the room cleaner noticing or remembering its presence on the bedside table.

Next day about thirty minutes before his High Tea booking, the Concierge, phoned to inform the Assassin that his transport awaited him at the hotel entrance. He took the elevator to the foyer and exited the hotel to the undercover circular driveway. Assisted by several Valets, he entered the car. The Assassin cum tourist was rolling through the entrance to the Old Palace five minutes later. After traversing a palatial garden with statues and fountains, the car stopped outside the impressive entrance to the palace cum hotel. A valet opened the door, and it was not until Roza turned to thank him that he realised the man must be nearly eight feet tall. Dressed in royal colourful robes made him seem even larger.

The international Assassin walked into the luxurious hotel past some high-end shops and counters more akin to a jewellery store than those selling exquisite cakes and sweets. He looked up and saw an atrium with floor upon floor above him, each with gold railings. At five minutes to ten, he entered the area dotted with lounge chairs and coffee tables surrounding the floor below the atrium. He had photographed and noted every exit, service door and alley. His mind was full of possibilities, contingencies, and potential ambush-killing zones that the Canadian PM could access.

Roza assumed that the meeting with the Minister for Presidential Affairs would be set in private to avoid the tourists that at present swarmed over the dining area. For now, he, too, had to play the part of an awestruck tourist. After he could eat no more, he allowed himself the luxury of appreciating what he had just experienced. To him, the tiered serving trays full of little unique sandwiches, the mini-pies and the incredible cakes were even an amazing offering. The other distinctive feature was that the coffee had a real gold leaf on its surface instead of the more commonly used cinnamon. It was outlandishly expensive but a once-in-a-lifetime experience.

However, to the Assassin, this luxury was just part of his cover. To him, this was no different to standing in some rain-soaked jungle for days. Just a different part of any mission. He finished the coffee, scanning the entire ground floor over the rim of the fine-bone china cup. Mobile phones have made life so easy for anyone doing a Recce of a target zone or photographing a subject. He moved away from the coffee table and the chair he had been sitting in. Looking like every other star-struck tourist, he started taking photos using the zoom to capture the detail, every door, elevator service entry. As he exited the main ground floor, he continued to take more pictures. Often, he photographed something by appearing to take a subject in the foreground while, in reality, his zoom was capturing the item in the background. This continued as he moved through the covered driveway and into the heat of the ornate gardens and paths. His mind was open, approaching what he saw as collecting information, not the evaluation phase. Satisfied he had achieved all he could, he retraced his steps to the driveway. The giant valet he had seen earlier waved up a taxi for him and opened the door.

"Thank you for visiting the Old Palace Hotel. Sir, please come again," his deep voice rumbled as he shut the door softly.

Instead of returning the same way as when he arrived, the taxi headed in the opposite direction from where the Assassin had come into the palace entrance. He figured the guy was trying for some extra fare as his hotel was just across the way from the Old Palace. Roza never stopped observing and evaluating options and alternatives as they presented themselves. He had learned long ago that often, the unplanned or unexpected produced the solution to a problem. The road led past a soccer field that appeared to be no longer in use, its grass unkempt and weeds growing around every fence and goalpost. Noting this, but as of no apparent value to his Recce, he continued to look out the taxi window.

CHAPTER 9

Steve is set for a visit to the Northern Territory.

I had been called back to Canberra from our little cottage in Roma. As usual, Chris was disappointed that we didn't have more time together. She knew the system and, being a cop, understood duty and shifts and sacrifices. Colonel Goodrich's phone call was guarded as expected, but I could tell from his tone it was something important. He only phoned me when this was so. I was on the plane out of Roma Airport four hours later, back to beautiful Canberra, back in uniform. A Sergeant I hadn't met before escorted me to the Colonel's office.

"Thanks for coming back so soon. You going OK?" Mutual respect had grown between us, founded on trust and blood. We both knew I had no choice about coming when called, but I appreciated his manners by thanking me.

"Yeah, Sir, I'm good, what's up?" I asked.

As usual, getting to the point quickly, he continued, "Steve, you should be proud that you donated that Northern Territory cattle property to the ADF. Without it, things may be very different," Colonel Goodrich said with a smile.

"I don't get it, Sir. I didn't know I had a cattle property; what's all this got to do with me?" I asked as I stood to grab a coffee; I knew it would be terrible, but I needed the hit.

"Well, talk about six degrees of separation or whatever. The cattle property that your terrorist mates landed on after rafting from Indonesia was called Caerhays. We found out later that they were smuggled from there in a specially modified cattle truck all the way down to Roma. You know the rest. Thanks to your Intel, we cleaned out that rat nest on a permanent basis. I'm not sure how much you knew about the follow-up. But it turned out that the Jihadists, via several shelf companies, had bought that Northern Territory cattle station as a base for that Op and any future attacks on Australia. Anyway, Caerhays Station is a bit more than 10,500 square miles of cattle country, nearly as big as Jamaica. Its northern boundary consists of 77 miles of coastline looking out on the Arafura Sea. The cattle station is rumoured to lose over 10,000 acres when the tide comes in. The original property was established in the mid-1800s and has grown steadily ever since," the Colonel said.

"Sir, I still don't understand why I'm here," I asked.

"Well, after you led the assault on the Roma training camp, the Government seized all the real estate, including the cattle property outside Roma, of course. Not only that, but when they found out about the cattle station in the Northern Territory, they grabbed that, too. Anyway, they never got around to selling it off, and when the request from the Americans for land to set up an Australian Marine Base came through. It made the top of the list. It's perfect, huge, far enough away from Darwin to be private, but close enough for resupply. Tactically, great as well, not sticking out on a point open to multiple assaults, a broad ocean front and land that requires a slog to get near the boundaries," he finished.

Relaxing back in his chair, glad to see that I had at least understood that part of his story, he continued.

"The old Caerhays Station is now Tortilla Flats USMC Base in the Northern Territory. Steve, we need you to be part of the circus attached to the grand opening of the new Marine Corps Base," my old friend and Commander said.

"So what's my actual mission, Sir? With the President and two Prime Ministers involved, I figure they'll all have their own protection. Not to mention that the American President has his Secret Service, plus the main event is on a Marine Base crawling with two thousand five hundred odd Jarheads. The UK PM will probably have his usual Metro Police specialist and a handful of Brit SAS. Our bloke has got his Special Protection Group (SPG). You know what those guys are like. Any outsider is seen as a threat or so inept; all they want is for you to keep out of their way. I'll be like a third person on a honeymoon, Sir," I asked, surprised by the mission.

"Steve, I totally agree, but with the Russian President being taken out last month, everyone is gun-shy. I'm surprised this shindig is still a go," Colonel Goodrich said. He continued, "Anyway, the Brigadiers talked it through, so here we are. I said the same things about all the foreign protective services. This is your mission, and I really think, except for being back in the bush, you'll be bored. Phase One: you turn up at all the meetings, you'll be given the Top Secret Plans of the opening and the High Profile's itinerary. Phase Two: Ride shotgun on the travelling circus as an overwatch. Out of sight most of the time, the protective crews and the USMC overwatch will know you're there. Just ghost alongside them and react as needed. Like I said, it will probably be boring."

Something slithered up my spine as soon as he said it. More than once before, ops that had looked 'boring' had gone pear-shaped in minutes. I had a month before the VIPs arrived, and I could see from the meeting schedule I wasn't needed for a week or so.

"Sir, are you OK with me heading home for a week? Our wedding plans have been put on hold a few times now. I'd like to set a date, say yes to all her plans, you know the story," I asked, feeling a bit strange as I had always put the green machine first. I was trying not to make all the same mistakes I had made that destroyed my first marriage.

Thinking it through, the Colonel smiled. "Under the thumb already, hey? Yeah, that's a great idea; you know how this works. You never know when you'll get the call. The only way it's going to happen is plan and hope."

"Thanks, Sir, she's a keeper, but I'm starting to make her think I've got second thoughts about getting hitched. I have another request as well. Is that OK?"

"How you off for socks and jocks?" Goodrich joked, smiling broadly.

"Well, ah, no one else has agreed to be my best man," laughing, I continued.

"I'd be honoured if you would agree to do the job, Sir," I asked.

Looking a little surprised, the Colonel replied, "Steve, that would be my honour as well; you thinking full Military?

"Not full, but uniforms and swords would be good, Sir," I answered.

"I hope at least on the big day you'll call me Pete," he said, smiling again.

A few hours later, I climbed into my old Landcruiser, which this time I'd parked at the Roma Airport. The heat hitting my face so hard my eyes hurt reminded me for the hundredth time that I should put up that reflective screen to keep the interior cooler while parked up. Surprise wasn't an option with Jake, my Border Collie, patrolling the front yard, but returning so quickly served that purpose with Chris.

She was on a day off and leapt into my arms as I walked through the front door of our cottage, wrapping her legs around me with an excited scream.

"What are you doing home so early?" Chris asked.

"We have a few days to make our wedding plans. Let's set it all in concrete and just do it.?" I said confidently.

"I love you so much," she said, hugging me even harder.

Jake was getting dizzy from circling us, trying to figure out what all the excitement was about.

Planning a wedding was not listed on my skill set. So lubricated with the occasional Jack Daniels for medicinal purposes, I attempted to maintain a level of interest motivated mainly by my love for Chris. All I did know, and I couldn't remember how I knew it, was my understanding that a wedding day is all about the Bride. So it began. I think we had more meetings than the Dover UK team planning the 1943 D-Day invasion. There were cars to decide on and book, flowers, catering. I just nodded a lot.

"Chris, like we decided, I've asked Pete Goodrich to stand up with me. He's my Boss, but we have become sort of mates, watching each other's backs and sharing the load. I'd like it low-key Military, just dress uniforms and swords. You sure you're fine with that?" I asked, but even to me, it sounded pretty close to a statement of fact.

"That sounds great, Steve; you guys will look great in the photos, all dressed up and shiny," she laughed.

It went pretty well working on guest lists, the location for the reception, menu, blah, blah. It was a big deal, so we planned it like a Military op. It's always the Bride's big day, so Chris was in charge. Having been a local copper for six years now, a lot of the residents would come, and all her fellow coppers, of course. However, the previous year, both her parents had been murdered in Johannesburg, South Africa, where they had been Pastoring a church. Senior Sergeant John Townsend had taken Chris under his wing when she was first posted to Roma, and this father/daughter relationship had only strengthened over the years. The remainder of Chris's family were spread all over Australia.

Chris looked over at her Senior Sergeant, who had just finished sharing a roast dinner with Steve and her.

"Oh, Chris, that was the best meal I've had for a long, long time. Ever since Ava died, I just haven't been bothering with cooking like that," Senior Sergeant Townsend said, wiping his mouth with a napkin.

"Yeah, John, if I was home full time, I would pack on some weight, I reckon," I said. And we all laughed. "Mate, can I get you a beer?" I asked.

"No thanks Steve, I've had a few and it wouldn't do for the Boss of the local Cops to get caught for drink driving, now would it?" the older Policeman said with a smile.

"Boss, there is a spare bed for you if you want, no pressure, it's up to you," Chris replied warmly.

"No, thanks very much, but I'm on earlies tomorrow, so I'm better off at home. Cheers anyway, I probably should get going, I s'pose," he stated.

"Yeah, well, you could go, but then Steve and I would have to eat all that apple pie I have in the oven," Chris said mischievously.

"I've just had a sudden change of mind about going; maybe I could stay for some pie," he laughed.

"Cream, Ice-cream or just pie?" Chris asked.

"Whatever Steve's having, Chris, that would be great," the older man replied.

"That's easy; he has the works, all three, and plenty of them," Chris said as she stood to get the dessert.

"Well, I don't have dessert very often, so I always make the best of it if I do," I said sheepishly.

The Policeman leaned over the table and whispered. "Steve, is Chris OK? She seems a bit nervous or edgy?" he asked, concern showing on his weathered face.

I couldn't answer him without pre-empting Chris's request, which I knew was coming and was also the source of the concern she was showing.

The room was filled with the beautiful aromas of pastry, apple and cinnamon, and we both looked expectantly at the kitchen door.

"There you go, you two. Don't wait for me; eat it while it's hot," Chris said as she placed the pie on the table and returned to the kitchen to get steaming hot mugs of tea for the Senior Sergeant and me. One more trip to the kitchen, and Chris was back with her own apple pie and another mug of tea for herself. Before she started on her dessert, she took an audible deep breath.

"Boss, I'm unsure if protocol will allow it, but would you walk me down the aisle?" she asked," she rushed the words out and then giggled nervously.

"Chris, I would be honoured, I'd love to; that would be great," the big rough diamond responded, his voice betraying his emotion.

I laughed at the usually confident Chris being so edgy, and now we all laughed, happy to share this moment. Twenty minutes later, we saw him off, I shook his hand, and after a slightly uncomfortable pause, Chris kissed her Boss on the cheek. He turned quickly and headed for his Landcruiser.

"Steve, did you see him? One of the toughest coppers I've ever seen, and when I asked him to walk me down the aisle, I swear I saw a little tear in the corner of his eye," Chris said, smiling.

"Oh, Honey, I can't wait. It will be a wonderful day. I love you so much," I murmured as she wrapped her arms around my neck. "I've never loved anyone so much. Well, maybe Jakey," This drew a left jab to my gut, and we both laughed.

CHAPTER 10

A tourist visits the Hardware Store.

ABU DHABI

Roza sat at the small desk in his room while he sipped his mint tea, a favourite beverage while visiting Middle Eastern countries. The Assassin revisited every photo he had taken across the road at the Old Palace Hotel. He was too patient to ever get frustrated, but Roza sensed a growing annoyance at the lack of an acceptable plan for the Canadian PM's hit. He thought a break might help, so he absently picked up an English version of the local Newspaper. The Front Page caught his eye, but it was the second story that took him by surprise. It revealed that an urgent OPEC meeting had been called due to civil unrest in Iran. The United Arab Emirates Minister for Presidential Affairs, who was scheduled to meet the Canadian Prime Minister, was needed to attend this oil regulation group. The article went on to inform in detail, anyone who chose to read it that the Old Palace meeting with the Canadian Prime Minister would still go ahead. By shuffling some appointments, both parties could still make it. In addition to this the Canadian PM would arrive via the Royal helicopter. The lack of security surrounding the Canadian VIP's visit astounded him. The Assassin nearly choked in surprise when the story continued stating that the soccer field adjacent to the palace grounds would be prepared as a Landing Zone, the same neglected field that he just photographed. Roza smiled like a white pointer shark sniffing blood in the water, the smile not adding any life to his dead black eyes. The media were doing his work for him.

Roza left his room and once again descended to the ground floor. As he exited the hotel's front entrance, one of the Valets asked if he wanted his car brought around.

"Shukrun, Shukrun," he used the Arabic for thank you and gestured the negative to the willing hotel team, who asked if they could assist. The Assassin declined their offers, proceeding on foot to the right, and heading down the ramp. He crossed three different roads to get to the soccer field and started taking more photos as any tourist might do. He was looking for a hide site, somewhere he could safely fire on the Canadian PM and still escape during the ensuing chaos. There wasn't a decent position of concealment; not a tree, scoreboard, or any type of platform within the perimeter or surrounds of the field. Once again, he was thwarted. There must be a way here; the opportunity was too good not to pay off, to be employed. Walking around the field for the third time, he searched yet again in case he had missed something. It had to be here, there was definitely an opportunity with the open ground, and time required to exit the helo, moving down the stairs and entering the vehicle. *That meant no protection for a few seconds, which made the LZ a potential KZ, a Kill Zone. But how?* The Assassin thought to himself. Where can I hide and wait for those precious seconds.

He kept walking to the right and down the vehicular exit. Roza was sure how to get to the soccer field.

The heat was oppressive as he worked his way down the sloping footpath and across the road. He had no intention of ever walking on or near the field. However, he needed to Recce its location, exits and any barriers that might block a shot. Of course, once he had this intel, he needed to choose a workable hide from which to shoot. So far even a bad option had eluded him. He had yet to decide on the weapon. He considered a long shot on a sniper platform for a surgical hit or a Rocket Propelled Grenade to take out the chopper and all its passengers. The availability of a hide with a line of sight to the LZ would contribute to several decisions to a large degree. After zigzagging around several gardens, median strips and low walls, he was finally looking over the soccer field. He did not think anyone was watching, but, just in case, he acted the role of an adventurous tourist pulling out a map. He then made a big show of turning it around several times, looking confused. He was studying the soccer field and its surrounds the whole time he pantomimed this. He was pleased to observe that there were no gates or roads at the end of the field nearest his hotel and where he was standing looking across the busy road. This would slow the VIP vehicle's ability to exit and might add another few seconds to the time he had to shoot whatever weapon he eventually chose.

The Assassin quickly realised that his hide options were virtually nil. From where he stood, the manicured Old Palace gardens and driveways took up the left side while the right was taken up by several dual-carriageway roads feeding onto a short causeway. Frustration wasn't a regular visitor to the Assassin, but he had thought there would be several options around a soccer field. Turning, he headed back to the hotel. Looking forward to going through the photos he thought; *hopefully the images will reveal an option*. The Etihad Towers were one of Abu Dhabi's unique and breathtaking architectural buildings. Waiting for a pedestrian crossing light, he glanced up at the stunning hundred and seventy-seven-metre towers. The Eastern Tower, where his room was located, was not visible from the soccer field. Immediately, he realised that the reverse angle was the same: one could not see the soccer field from his current room. He had it. The Western Tower overlooked the soccer field on a slight angle. The monocular he raised to his right eye had an integrated range finder that enabled him to quickly calculate what floor and how far the ideal room was located along that floor to where he was standing. He would have to calculate in the distance between the middle of the soccer fields and where he now stood. Being an experienced sniper he worked out the angle from the ground up to the hotel. That would be a crucial factor if his seed of a plan bloomed into a full on hit. He counted from the ground up to the selected floor. Now he just had to choose the best room.

Grateful he had allowed extra time to Recce Abu Dhabi, he retraced his steps back to his hotel. The heat was crushing, and as Roza wiped the sweat from his brow, he looked up at the beautiful towers of Conrad Abu Dhabi Etihad Hotel. Finally, he had his assassination plan in his mind, now he would refine and tweak it to perfection. Alert, the uniformed doorman came to attention primed to open the tall glass entrance doors to the foyer, as soon as the Assassin was a stride away. By then Roza had solved the room problem, or at least he knew what he wanted to do. As though he was heading back to his room, instead, he took the Western Tower elevator to the fifth floor. He chose this level based on his knowledge of the view from his current room, an educated guess that he would confirm once he had access to a new room.

Training and practice gave him confidence in estimating what was known in the 'trade' as the Barrel Cosine Angle. Looking like he was searching for his own room, with an access card visible in his hand, he set off down the long hallway, heading around a corner halfway along. He stopped outside room five four twenty-two. Roza figured that this room or one either side would serve his purpose. He then returned to the elevator, taking it to the foyer.

As he approached the Reception Desk, he was pleased to note that the Asian girl who had checked him in was now beaming with another welcome smile that appeared warm and sincere.

"Mr Klinkenberg, what a pleasure to see you again. Are you enjoying your time with us? Is there anything I can do for you to make your stay even more enjoyable?" the Receptionist enquired in perfect English with a hint of an Asian flavour.

Smiling to match her, he replied, "Yes, so far, it seems to be an amazing place. I've never seen such architecture before. The hotel is wonderful, and the food is exceptional," Roza the Assassin said, emphasising a Dutch accent to accompany his new Passport and name.

"I would like a new room, please. In the Western Tower about halfway down the hall on the fifth floor," he asked, sounding more like a statement of fact than a request.

"Oh, Mr Klinkenberg, if something is not quite right with your room, I will make it my personal duty to rectify it," the Receptionist asked with genuine concern replacing her hundred-watt smile.

"No, No, my room is fine, but after the five days I've been here, I just feel like a change of view, that is all," he said.

"Mid hall fifth level would be around Room 5422. Is this room special to you? I seem to remember that this is your first visit with us. I ask because, normally, when a guest requests a specific room, they have had a pleasant stay in that room on a previous visit. Like an anniversary or honeymoon," she said smiling again, this time at half power to ensure her questions did not seem intrusive.

He ignored the subtle enquiry, deciding that his cover was still intact if he kept it simple.

"I figured I was happy with that floor and location in my current room, so 5422 made sense. So I am in 5422 or is there a problem?" Roza asked, adding just a little impatience to remove any uncertainty.

Tapping on her keyboard she looked up, with a broad smile again.

"Oh, good news, Mr Klinkenberg; that room is available now. Please let me know once you have packed your bags, and I will have the Porter move you over," the Receptionist said.

"That's great. I appreciate your help so much," the Assassin stated sincerely. He reached into his pocket and subtly slid over a crisp American hundred-dollar bill, mindful that CCTV covered the Reception Desk and unsure if this was appropriate.

"Thank you so much, sir. When you move over, I will ensure a chilled bottle of Moet is waiting for you. Is there anything else I can do for you today?" she asked.

"No, that is wonderful, thank you, I'll call you soon about the bags," Roza said, beaming with getting his own way as he knew a genuine tourist would do.

Half an hour later, he was once again sipping mint tea, this time in his new room overlooking the spaghetti of small roads and traffic islands that lay between his hotel and the soccer field cum LZ.

He had rested his cup on the wide window sill and was sitting on a slight angle to maximise the view of the potential Killing Zone. The workmen had already started mowing. They were even making it easier for him by marking a white circle where the Canadian Prime Minister's helicopter would be landing in just three days. He had considered a Rocket Propelled Grenade to demolish the helo and all those on board. This was the Assassin's favoured option. That was before he had discovered that there was no viable hide near the Landing Zone from where an RPG could be launched. RPGs were range rated at 1,000 feet to a moving target 1,600 feet to a stationary target. However, the Assassin had seen trained Soldiers miss at their more common range of 150 feet. He just couldn't be set up and concealed close enough to the LZ. Roza had even considered moving further away from the field and using a Man-portable Air Defence System (MAN-PADS). While these could be fired three to seven Kilometres away, once again their more normal deployment range was around twelve thousand feet. Always, in feet because they were nearly exclusively deployed against aircraft. However, the MAN-PAD'S guidance systems were infra-red, laser-beam and line of sight. Roza was not confident that the local security build up would allow him to sit on a roof somewhere with the weapon resting in his lap. The bigger issue was that there was no way of knowing the VIP's Helo's flight path so he could well be perched up, and hear it go by behind a building, and not be able to see the chopper in order to launch. After these eliminations, firing from his hotel jumped to number one option. This in turn eliminated any thought of firing on the helo in flight. Once that was confirmed, the choice of attack strategy changed and therefore dictated the weapon of choice.

Roza had worked his angles to where the men had unwittingly marked the Kill Zone. This informed him of the size of the hole that he would cut in the window, ensuring that it would provide the optimal sight picture covering the entire diameter of the marked LZ. This would ensure that Roza could hit the HVT a target on whichever side he exited from the chopper. Guessing the target area was a bit over six hundred and fifty yards, he lit up his Safran Vectronix laser rangefinder from his room to the far extremity of the LZ cum Kill Zone; the precise result was six hundred and forty-four yards. Roza had already discounted the super long-range sniper platforms such as the Barrett 50 Cal, or the one made famous by Chris Kyle, the McMillan TAC-338A Sniper Rifle, chambered in .338 Lapua Magnum calibre. He had successfully used both systems many times; however, with the target range under seven hundred yards, he had chosen the 7.62 millimetre M110 Semi-Automatic. The world-class Assassin had no intention of missing; he lived and breathed the sniper's age-old mantra. One Shot. One Kill. It was part of his psyche. However, on the angle, he had to work with the possibility of another of the helo passengers blocking his shot, which was a potential risk he had to resolve quickly. He knew he might have to drop the person blocking the Primary Target. As quick as he was at working the rifle bolt on a Barrett, more rapid follow-up shots were required to allow for this contingency. This time, the range to the Target allowed for a Semi-Automatic Sniper Rifle rather than a bolt action to be right for the job. The M110 having a suppressor was a bonus that should allow him time to escape from the hotel. A non-suppressed 7.62 in a hotel room's confines would be extremely loud. Even if guests and staff didn't identify the exact room, they would know that the shot or shots originated on that floor.

The rifle incorporated an upgraded 3.6-18x scope with an Army-design MIL-Grid 4 grid-style pattern reticle. He had some errands to run, so he headed out from his hotel again. He had dressed as a typical tourist, including the obligatory small backpack. After changing taxis three times, he entered a phone store, turning his head to the left and right like he was looking for some product. He walked straight through the crowded store, exiting onto a side street, and crossed over three more city blocks. A high-end clothing store was his next stop. Without even slowing, he chose and removed a red Versace button-down shirt from the rack and entered the change room. Ignoring the crimson shirt he swapped the clothes he had brought in the backpack with those he was wearing. A black long bill, unbranded cap completed his transformation. Exiting the store, he turned left, finding himself at the base of a steep escalator leading up to the Abu Dhabi Metro.

Avoiding CCTV cameras as best he could he kept his head down to maximise the cap. Instead of continuing on to the platforms, he headed for the temporary locker hire area. Roza then took a small key marked number ten from his pocket. Yet another feature the Assassin loved about the M110 Semi-Automatic Sniper Rifle he had chosen was its compactness for storage and transport. At just a shade over a metre long with the Buttstock fully compressed and the six-inch suppressor removed, it was easily disguised in a sports bag. This also enabled it to successfully fit into Locker ten. The Assassin figured he had been out of his lair long enough. Taking two taxis back to the hotel this time. To ensure the last Driver was unsure of his actual destination, he got out four blocks early, placing him in the vicinity of any of three different hotels, not including his own.

The next day, Roza left the hotel to make his final purchase. Unlike in the movies, a cool looking clamp tool that spun in a tight circle to cut the thick glass used in hotel windows did not exist. He had solved this problem many years ago with a simple tool one could buy at most hardware stores. Many trades and crafts, including lapidary, used the tool when polishing or carving to make jewellery or displays. It was called a Dremel, in essence, an electric drill with either a cutting clade or a polishing stone or brush attachment. Following the same basic evasive protocols, he dived in and out of taxis and shops until he was confident that he had not been surveilled. He had no reason to believe that his cover was blown or that anyone would be interested in a Dutch tourist doing some shopping. However, the world class Assassin had succeeded and survived in a career that was usually short-lived, ending either in a cell or on the wrong side of the turf.

Although the hardware store differed from Home Depot or Bunnings, he quickly found what he was looking for. Selecting a high-quality Dremel and six spare cutting blades. The Assassin then selected a twenty-foot extension lead to bring power from the bedside table to the hotel window and, therefore, would power his new cutting toy. Two more hardware items, and he would be done. He had learned long ago that the more complex or technical the equipment you used in a hit, the more likely some supplier would betray you if caught by the authorities. Also, being complicated often made that item more likely to let you down. Accordingly, he preferred where possible to set himself up at a local hardware store. He threw two rolls of super strength gaff tape into his trolley and set off to the kitchen department. Here, he chose a thin but firm dark coloured plastic cutting board.

Once he paid for his selections, he headed back to the sanctuary of his hotel room. There, he felt less vulnerable, less threatened, but still, he never relaxed, ever.

CHAPTER 11

Air travel can be dangerous.

0545 Hrs.

Room 5422

Conrad Abu Dhabi Etihad Towers Hotel

The day that the Canadian Prime Minister was to visit the Old Palace Hotel dawned with a strange orange light. Roza, the Assassin, was up early and, after an hour in the hotel gym, was enjoying the double-headed shower turned on hard enough to pummel the rolling muscles of his back and shoulders. He decided he would not have room service this morning and went down to the hotel dining room for breakfast. The Assassin felt good about the world, as he always did just before a hit. The Recce had been exhaustive, the plan finally falling into place, and now all preparations complete. As he entered the dining area, the hotel staff member welcomed him and requested his room number, and the assassin responded. As the man's eyes went down to put a line through his name, Roza casually reached over and took a black marker similar to the one being used to cross off guests as they came to breakfast, putting it into his pocket. He enjoyed his breakfast of chicken sausages, no pork here, pancakes and eggs overlooking the private hotel beach. The Assassin finished his third coffee with a satisfied sigh. Roza had never believed what many said: that caffeine made you shaky. He wiped his mouth with the expensive linen serviette and stood up, checking the room covertly. Roza headed up to his room, satisfied with his meal and security check. He still had a good two hours to spare before the Canadian PM was scheduled to land across the road.

He hadn't cut the hole in his room's window which could cause an air conditioning serviceman to attend. He had already put out the Do Not Disturb sign to discourage the maid from entering the room and noticing the damage to the glass, and then informing management. The Assassin was unhappy about leaving such an essential action until so close to the PM's arrival. He had made a tactical decision, and second-guessing led to failure. Sitting on the wide window sill, he confirmed the precise location where to cut the hole in the hotel room window. Roza had decided to make the hole low enough to allow him to sit comfortably with the folding rifle bi-pod legs resting on the windowsill. He had also figured that a square cut would enable him to traverse the weapon if this need arose rather than be restricted to a small round hole. The hole's location in the window also factored in the down angle of the shot. He turned on the television and cranked up the sound to cover the Dremel's motor and cutting noise. It wasn't great, but hotel guests were always noise-sensitive. Being the morning Roza believed that they would assume it was some maintenance repair. Roza again noticed the strange colour of the sky reminiscent of the threatening sky that proceeds a storm.

However, this time, it was a dull yellowy orange. He used the black marker he had stolen at breakfast to draw a square roughly twelve inches by twelve inches on the glass.

Roza assembled the Dremel with one of the diamond cutting blades he had purchased, attached the extension lead and drew a chair over to the windowsill. The one-inch toughened glass resisted the efforts of the Dremel's blades, and although the machine was made to work hard for hours, the Assassin had found he needed to change the blade four times. Finally, he had a one-foot square hole in the window, in precisely the correct position to maximise fields of fire laterally and vertically within reason. Roza had anticipated what would result from this compromise in the vast building's glass membrane. It was the opposite of what is portrayed when a window is shattered on a plane. Five floors up, the wind poured through the twelve-inch aperture, blowing the curtains and bedspread towards the opposite wall.

Before the Assassin had commenced cutting the hole through the window, he had measured off six two-foot strips of gaff tape. He then stuck about half each strip to the windowsill, leaving the remaining twelve inches free ready to use. As Roza finished the cutting, he was careful to manage the now free square of glass. Spreading his fingers he supported the loose piece before the wind could blow it into the room. Quickly, he then picked up the plastic cutting board he had purchased. He had to lean hard against the window, pushing the cutting board over the newly cut hole. Roza then placed all six gaff tapes over the board, covering the hole and stopping the howling wind that had been battering the room. Standing and arching his back, he drew the heavy curtains, turning his room into night and stopping the internal light from illuminating the hole in any way. He knew it was very difficult to see into hotel rooms, and improbable that someone flying past would notice the patch. However, taking anything for granted was against his training and experience, especially this close to Mission Execution. Satisfied with the success of all these actions, he collapsed into the chair, where he power napped for twenty minutes.

T minus 2.35 hrs.

Room 5422

Conrad Abu Dhabi Etihad Towers Hotel

On waking, he splashed cold water on his face and then, Roza checked the rifle for the eighth or ninth time. He had chosen the 3.6-18x scope with an Army-designed MIL-Grid 4 grid-style pattern reticle, as he liked the Mil-Grid system. In the event of having to take some rapid semi-auto shots, the ability to use the variable settings was great. He would normally set the magnification fairly high for long-range shots, making the target area clearer and larger. The target would appear as though they were close to the shooter, even at a ridiculous distance. This system was successful for one target a long way downrange. However, with the telescopic sight set on high magnification, the shooter could not orientate himself quickly enough for any rapid follow-up shots if the target had moved. For instance, if the shooter knew the shot would be a running target close by, the scope might be left on as low magnification as the 3.6 X, the fitted scope's lowest.

Accordingly, for this mission, Roza set the variable at eight magnification; this would be sufficient for what he considered a fairly close shot. More importantly, Roza would be able to acquire multiple targets quickly and employ the semi-auto function if the need arose.

Unloading and reloading the twenty-round magazine with his eyes closed, the professional was careful not to nick the projectile by doing so. Although at this range, a little mark on the bullet wasn't as crucial as his normal thousand-yard plus targets demanded, he left nothing to chance. After reassembling the weapon, he dry-fired the rifle several times, ensuring the function and getting used to the trigger pull, which was non-adjustable. The trigger was Match Grade, requiring far less pressure than most Military weapons making the rifle highly accurate and popular as a sniper platform. Roza inserted the loaded mag and placed the now loaded rifle on the bed with the bipod down, ready for action in the event that the Canadian PM arrived early. The PM's meeting time, as published in the newspaper, was 1400 Hrs. The Assassin's mind was automatically counting down to that publicised schedule so he knew he had plenty of time. However, he was on high alert, with everything in readiness, removing all distractions, the Do Not Disturb sign on the front door, and the phone silenced. He sat in the chair near the window, reading a novel set in Africa. If a doctor had monitored his vital signs, they would have read as if he was sleeping. Roza had long ago trained himself to be on high vigilance and alertness but to also be calm and steady. Hunters called it buck fever, heart rate increased, shortness of breath, and shaking with excitement, which didn't make for accurate long-range shots or life-saving decisions.

T minus 1.42 hrs.

Room 5422
Conrad Abu Dhabi Etihad Towers Hotel

Looking up from his novel, and although it was unnecessary, the Assassin checked his Citizen Pro-Master watch, chosen for its Military attributes but its civilian appearance. The last thing Roza wanted was someone noticing his watch and thinking Army. He smiled as he thought about all the cold, dirty, smelly, cramped and highly dangerous hides he had used over the years. Here, Roza was in a comfortable, clean, warm, and very secure setting. Roza wouldn't do it, but if he chose to he could call room service when he was hungry. He thought about all that as he sat in the chair, still in place near the window, even though the curtains were still drawn. He had been operational since he had sat down earlier, ready to react if needed but still calmly waiting as snipers have always done throughout history. However, now it was time to go on Full Alert. He stood drawing back the heavy curtains. What was happening? Instead of the bright clear day that had been shining when Roza had closed the heavy curtains the room was engulfed in a dull orange light casting a strange gloom over the hotel room. Looking across the city, he saw the source of the peculiar ambience. A dust storm filled the sky, obliterating the city's high rises with bellowing red and orange dust that blocked out the sun.

Roza immediately thought; *will they fly the helo in this storm? A dust storm won't stop me.* He had been infilled and exfilled in choppers in zero visibility and knew that the flyboys didn't like it, but they could do it in a pinch.

This was virtually a social visit; would they risk a VIP and a helo crew for that? The last time the Assassin had panicked he was seven years old, it wouldn't happen this afternoon. He looked again, his eyes searching the city, the horizon seeking respite from the dusty onslaught. The storm was still rolling directly towards his hotel and, therefore, the soccer field cum Landing Zone across the road.

Although many weather factors always come into play when planning a hit, snipers could never control the weather, only accommodate it. Over the last few days he had identified and measured the prevailing winds that scattered trash across the soccer fields around the time the Target was due to arrive. That was not today; the dust storm had increased pressure, and the winds had picked up, swirling, and gusting unpredictably. A sniper's nightmare had arrived from nowhere and threatened to derail so many planned and calculated factors.

He turned on the TV to see if there were any updates on the dust storm or the Canadian Prime Minister's visit. There was neither. The Assassin had no options, no contingencies. All he could do was watch and wait in his glass tower, immune to the noise and grit those hapless mortals on the ground must have been suffering. So, that's what he did; Roza watched and waited. Systematically, Roza worked through all the scenarios. *Would the Canadian PM's helo even arrive? If it did, would visibility from here in my hotel room allow a kill shot? Should I pack up and walk over to near the soccer fields/ Landing Zone?* Those and many more options and variables passed through his filters. These thoughts weren't second-guessing his plan; it was adjusting for anything that may change the fluid environment. He decided to hold the line, stay set up and see what this dust storm produced. No second-guessing, no wondering, no worrying as most people might do. Turning towards the city skyline, he noted that the overall vista seemed brighter. The sun was slowly overpowering this dust-laden onslaught. He had seen plenty of Middle Eastern dust storms, but not like this, the slight improvement in the little bit of sunlight fighting through looked hopeful.

1218 Hrs.

Emirates Palace Mandarin Oriental

Abu Dhabi

VIP Suite of the Canadian P.M.

At the same time the Assassin had gone on full alert over at his hotel, the Canadian Prime Minister was sitting in his high-end hotel. It was a basic room at two thousand dollars a night not that the Canadian Prime Minister had even considered the cost.

"Sir, we may not make that helo transfer to your next meeting; it's a pity the Minister couldn't come here to you," the PM's Personal Assistant stated.

"Well, yes, Jacques, that would have been more convenient, but he's trying to emphasise his position. We are the visitors, of course," the PM stated evenly.

Turning and walking three steps towards the huge picture windows, he took his phone from his pocket. "Robby, what's the latest?" he asked the helo Pilot.

"Sir, I'm not sure, but the word is this crazy dust storm will clear. No guarantees, but the locals reckon we'll be on," the Pilot said, hoping he sounded more confident than he really felt.

Turning back to the Prime Minister, the Personal Assistant took the chance.

"Sir, it's up to you; however, the word is we should be able to get to your meeting. The dust is clearing, or at least that's what I'm being told. If that becomes evident, I'll let them know whatever you decide. As you know, your meeting at the Old Palace is scheduled for two o'clock, and transit time is something like fifteen minutes max. So, worst case, we get on the helo at 1345 Hrs....... I mean a quarter to two. This dust storm is obviously out of our control, so no one will care even if we are a little late," he said.

"Jacques, you don't have to translate the time. I realise I haven't done any Military service, but I can understand their time system," the PM said, a little annoyance in his voice.

"Anyway, that is good news; I'll change and be ready whenever you come and get me. And Jacques, would you mind ordering one of those mint lemonades? They are so refreshing; I think I am getting addicted to them," the PM said laughing, the petty slight forgotten immediately

"Sorry, Sir, will do; I'll keep you posted."

T minus 42 minutes.

Room 5422

Conrad Abu Dhabi Etihad Towers Hotel

Grateful there was still plenty of time before the Canadian Prime Minister's meeting, Roza made himself a pod coffee, hoping everything would fall back into line. Taking his cup over to the window, Roza parted the heavy curtain and settled in to wait. Looking towards the dust-shrouded high rises of Abu Dhabi's central city, he was a little disappointed to see that it didn't appear to have cleared much at this stage. With the scheduled meeting at 1400 hrs, he figured due to the sand-storm the helo would have to adapt a flexible timetable. If the dust cleared he expected that it would land in the next thirty minutes or so. For now, it was unsure. He would remain vigilant until it was confirmed that the meeting had been cancelled, or was going ahead. Parting the curtains again what he saw this time encouraged him, that the meeting would proceed. The light had increased even more as the coffee ground cloud of dust swung away from where he sat.

Talking to himself: "This is going to happen; another half an hour and the dust will be gone. I'll have my shot." He laughed at how silly he sounded talking to himself. However, he realised it was a sign of the managed pressure that had been palpable within the hotel room ever since the dust storm began. As quickly as it had smothered the city skyline and nearby suburbs, the bellowing dust had diverted and diminished to a vague, nebulous brown mist-like cloud travelling away from the Assassin's hotel.

T minus 2 minutes.

Room 5422

Conrad Abu Dhabi Etihad Towers Hotel

Roza only thought about the Canadian Prime Minister as his High-Value Target or HVT because to the Assassin that is all he was. Never a person with dreams, a man with desires, a husband or father. An assassin had to look at his mission like a Delta Force Operative tasked with a kidnap rescue.

They must see the man, woman, or child they had been sent to rescue as nothing more than a package. Otherwise, you get sloppy; emotions might cause a fraction of a second of hesitation. He made minute adjustments to the rifle, careful not to allow the suppressed barrel to stick out and potentially betray his presence. He was sitting in the same chair that he had occupied so much in the last twenty-four hours. He had adjusted the chair to facilitate his sighting comfortably and accurately. Roza bent over the sniper rifle and, for the fiftieth time, imagined where the helo would land, where the door would open, where the bottom of the stairs would be.

Roof Helipad

Hotel of the Canadian P.M.

Emirates Palace Mandarin Oriental

Abu Dhabi

The Canadian Prime Minister and his Assistant were no strangers to helos flights. They climbed the stairs and settled in, routinely placing the green headphones on and buckling up. Not that this was a gutted, rattly Military chopper, no. This was a Sikorsky S-92 an American twin-engine luxury medium lift helo. Although the sleek machine could carry nineteen passengers from the factory set-up. They had reduced this helo to just nine seats, affording its VIPs all the room and amenities they desired. The flight lasted exactly twelve minutes; the two Canadian visitors were to be met and then chauffeured to the Old Palace entrance a few hundred yards away, and from there proceed to their meeting. The Canadian PM had been practising his greetings, thank you's and goodbyes in Arabic. Sitting in the kid leather lounge he rehearsed for the introduction with the United Arab Emirates Minister for Presidential Affairs. This meeting was the cherry on top of this trip's diplomatic and trade meetings. He had been busy attending meetings and functions since arriving in Dubai first and now in Abu Dhabi. He looked up as the helo's skids gently touched down on the dry grass of the soccer field. The Co-Pilot opened the door while the Pilot spooled down the two powerful engines. By the time the PM was at the door, the noise had reduced significantly, and the grass cuttings and dust raised by the huge blades had subsided.

Usually, the thick hotel glass would have muffled any helo's chop-chop noise, so a guest would not even be aware of its presence. However, the twelve-inch square hole Roza had cut allowed the sound to intrude into Room 5422, much to Roza's pleasure. He was too experienced to get excited. Buck Fever was something he had dealt with a long time ago. With some deep breaths, he relaxed all his muscles and waited.

He searched the sky for the helo, finding the dark blue twin-engine coming around a hotel from the North. The Pilot adjusted the Cyclic, pointing its nose towards the soccer field LZ. The helo passed in front of the sniper's hotel room hide before bleeding off some power. Roza had seen so many Military choppers land he could see this guy was giving the VIPs in the back a gentle ride. The Pilot applied an aft cyclic flaring, raising the nose so subtly that the passengers belted into their high-end kid leather armchairs would not have noticed it. Now that the dust storm was no longer pushing against his window, and the fact that the helo had just past the sniper's view, he was able to remove the Gaff tape. Exposing the hole he had cut in the hotel room window the hot external air rushed in hitting him in the face.

Immediately on landing, the Co-Pilot opened the rear door and lowered the stairs. Mindful of their tardiness, even with a valid excuse, the Canadian Prime Minister was in the doorway as soon as it opened. His Assistant Jacques could be partially seen waiting behind him. The Limousine, which had been waiting nearby, moved up and stopped at the bottom of the stairs, leaving enough distance for a narrow red carpet to be rolled out. The Driver held one end and let the roll go; then he knelt to smooth it as he walked towards the helo. As an experienced chauffeur in a furnace-like country, he had left all the doors shut in the limo, preserving the air-conditioned temperature. He stood at the luxury vehicle's rear door closest to the stairs, ready to open the door for the P.M. First out the door was Jacques, the PM's Personal Assistant carrying a silver briefcase in one hand, an elaborately wrapped gift destined for the Minister for Presidential Affairs wife, in the other. The Canadian Prime Minister followed his assistant down the helo steps, grimacing as the heat hit him in the face like a punch from hell.

The Assassin loved his targets penned up in some structure; it didn't have to be like a jail cell or a tunnel; the helo stairs would do nicely, with nowhere to run and virtually nothing to hide behind. Roza waited on his prey. He had studied his targets and had no confusion about who was descending the helo steps. He quickly identified the second man as the P.M., his Target whose head now filled his scope. With a gentle pressure applied to the trigger, that same head that the media loved to describe as boyish good looks exploded. The near headless body's downward momentum collapsed forward, hitting the Personal Assistant in the back of his legs. He, too, fell forward. Turning, he looked back at the P.M., thinking that his Boss had stumbled. Of course, the Assassin couldn't hear anything, but through the scope, it was clear that the survivor was screaming. The chauffeur had been looking up at the P.M. as he came down the steps, so he knew what had happened the instant the Prime Minister collapsed. He was ex-military and immediately threw himself onto the ground and wriggled under the Limousine.

The Assassin had only one Target; he would have killed twenty others to get to that HVT, but that wasn't necessary. His work was done. Roza stood and stripped off the full-body suit and gloves he had been wearing. By doing this, he effectively left all G.S.R. gunshot residue on the floor. He then walked into the bathroom, taking a tissue. He cleaned the inside of his ears as thoroughly as possible. This was an old trap that most murderers or ordinary people who murdered in passion or anger didn't consider. G.S.R. could enter a shooter's ears and lodge on the skin and ear wax. Once he was satisfied that he had done his best, he flushed these tissues down the toilet.

During his downtime, waiting for this day he had wiped down any area he may have touched while he occupied the room these past days. The Assassin had known this was a requirement, so he had been super mindful of what he touched to minimise the wipe-down. He had also bleached the toilet, sink and shower to destroy any DNA he may have inadvertently deposited. The room was clean. He was clean.

He had packed his wig, beard, and moustache, which he would dump at the airport. Discovering these items there was unlikely, but in any case no one would connect these items with an Assassination executed miles away.

Travelling on yet another passport three hours later he did up his seat buckle in preparation for take off. Roza closed his eyes and was asleep before the plane had fully loaded.

CHAPTER 12

Worrying news hits Washington D.C.

WEST WING
  WHITE HOUSE
  WASHINGTON DC

The Oval Office lighting was subdued due to the lateness of the hour. Holding a crystal tumbler of whiskey, the President asked his Director of the Secret Service if he would like a drink.

"Thank you, Mr President, I think I need one."

"Yeah, this time of day, I get it. Duke, how ya goin, keepin' out of trouble?" the President asked his old friend.

"Sir, I thought that this would become easier as I got older, but I was wrong," Duke responded.

"Well, I'm sorry, but I'm going to add to your troubles. I want to visit an Aussie company called DroneShield. I'm not sure you heard about it, but we just signed a thirty-three-million-dollar contract with them. I reckon it'll be good PR to show that the money and the tactical support flows both ways. You know, all the Presidents before me felt the same way as I do about the Aussies. I'm glad they are always on our side, they're also a clever bunch. I mean, even though they are a small population compared to us, and they operate with limited resources, they keep coming up with smart toys we can use."

The head of the Secret Service knew not to argue with the Boss, "Sure, Mr President, I'll get the details and organise the Recon of the route and venue. Hopefully, they're not outback somewhere," he stated.

"Great Duke, the rest of the plans going OK?" the President asked.

Knowing the Chief of Staff had kept the President informed on every aspect of the planned trip to Australia, Duke knew the President was really asking him if he had any worries about the security.

"Sir, everything seems squared away. I'm unsure why the CIA will be there, but we probably won't even know their guy is around. One man is not going to make much difference anyway," Duke said.

The President understood the concern and said that keeping things simple was always the best plan.

"Duke, I just thought they should be represented, and you wouldn't be aware of this young guy's O.M.P.F. (USA Military Service Record). But, his track records show he's ex Mil, Delta actually, and since he went over to the dark side he's had some hairy missions while operating off the grid. Like you said, and between you and me. I pretty well said the same thing to him. Probably, no one will even know he's there," the President said, attempting to dilute the situation while making it clear it wasn't up for debate.

Suddenly, there was a loud hammering on the curved door. An aide rushed into the Oval Office, looking around the room for the President. "Son, are we on fire or something?" the President, quickly rising from his chair, said with a hint of anger.

"Mr President, I'm................ Sir, sorry Sir, busting in like that, but the Canadian Prime Minister, well he has just been shot in Abu Dhabi," the young man said with emotion sounding in his voice.

"Trader get on the phone, I need to know if that's true. What on earth is going on?" The President demanded.

The Secret Service Director picked up his phone straight away barking at his assistant, demanding, "Confirm this Canadian business as of now, I want the details STAT.

Well, that settles it, Mr President; surely you can't go now?" Duke said.

"Well, let's not get too far ahead of ourselves. Wait for that confirmation, yes?" the President said calmly.

"In the meantime, we continue to evaluate and plan because I still believe I must go to Australia." Picking up the phone the President spoke to his Secretary, "Get 'em all in Marj," he said.

"Already made the call Mr President, they will be here in thirty," Marjorie responded.

Forty minutes later the Oval Office was once again full of some of the most powerful men in America. The room hummed with several discussions as the small groups surrounded the lounges and coffee tables. Having this many Military, Security and Protective Services in one room was akin to having twenty hungry male lions in one small cage. The atmosphere was testosterone-charged, trust was a scarce commodity even though many of these Alpha Males had fought side by side and were long-term friends. These were men of authority not used to being questioned or requiring a justification. The Secret Service took the other service's involvement as an insult and an insinuation that they couldn't do their job. To each group's representative having so many different agencies planning how they would protect the President while in Australia didn't sit well with any of them. The President stood and commanded attention.

"Thank you for coming in so quickly. This new development demands our discussion and response. Please be seated, there is coffee and some sandwiches," POTUS said calmly.

Trader Duke, the Secret Service Director, took the chance, "Sir, the Russian and now the Canadian, with all due respect, you don't have to be too bright to see that you might, or must be next on that hit list," he said calmly, tiredness and concern etched on his face.

"I can't really disagree with you, Duke, but I'm not much of a World Leader if I stay here hiding under my bed. We were going there before, and probably the security will need to be beefed up even more, but it's doable, right?" the President stated, leaving no room for discussion. This brought a surge of heated comments and disagreements from around the inner circle of the various security experts.

"Gentlemen, please, let's try to put our egos and account abilities on hold for a while and focus on what we do know. Trader can you confirm any details, tell us anymore information?" POTUS asked.

"Sir, it's all confirmed by multiple sources. First reports had told us that the Canadian P.M. and his Secretary were shot and killed as they descended the Helo stairs on their way to a meeting in Abu Dhabi. It turns out only the P.M. was D.O.A. at Burjeel Medical City.

Apparently the Assistant was knocked down by the Prime Ministers body falling down the stairs after he was shot. The Chauffeur is one of ours, we had lent him to the Canadians, and he reports that the Assistant is shaken up but uninjured," the Director of the Secret Service stated confidently.

The President had a goal, and was still convinced that his planned trip to Australia was achievable.

"Right, well, that is terrible news of course. We will pass on our Nation's condolences as soon as we get out of here. At the risk of seeming unfeeling gentlemen, moving forward from here is important," the President stated quietly.

The USMC General was a muscular, tall, sad-eyed veteran with the standard buzz-cut grey hair. He had served in every campaign or fracas in which the USA had been involved over the last thirty-odd years. And more than a few that didn't make the files or the news. The tension was now multiplied by the confirmed news, but the General was resolute. It goes without saying that the President's protection while on my Base will be my responsibility," the older man stated, emphasising both uses of 'my'. His rich voice rumbled with the authority he wore as easily as his uniform.

"Considering the Russian hit, we will definitely deploy that Aussie company's weapons. They are real-world tested and have we learned some hard-won lessons from the battlefields of the Ukraine. Their radar-directed 30 mm cannon SLINGER System has more than responded to the worldwide demand for advanced counter-drone technologies. Those things work just fine; we'll be placing an order for them, that's for sure. The Russians didn't have that," the General stated.

"Oh, come on, General, some new toys won't guarantee POTUS's safety," said the Secret Service Director, immediately regretting saying it.

"Trader, we all know there are no guarantees, but if Drones are the threat, then this Aussie gear reduces, if not eliminates it, at least to a range of eight hundred metres. That Russian egomaniac asked for it and had grown complacent because he'd been in dominant power so long," claimed the General.

"General, that sounds logical, but a few high-tech toys don't change the fact that the Secret Service exists for this purpose. Sure, you'll have two and half thousand Marines on hand, but as well trained as they are, they are not specialist trained to protect our President. We can't just let you take over while we hit the mess for some Bud Lights," Trader Duke, the Secret Service Director, asserted.

The general and Duke had been friends for over thirty years and respected each other. This wasn't the first time the President's will had put them on opposite sides of the table. They had always come to an understanding that they could live without compromising their roles. Smiling, the General responded.

"Sure Trader, I hear ya. You do your close cover; we will handle the air and the long to middle-distance threats. How's that sound?" the General said in a conciliatory tone that few had ever heard him use.

CHAPTER 13

Australia is his next tourist destination.

Roza had decided to enter Australia as a photojournalist travelling on a Hungarian Passport here to cover the American President's visit. He was sure his accent would satisfy any super efficient Australian Border Security Officer he might meet. More used to colder climates, he recoiled as the Northern Territory humidity hit him and seemed to drain his energy the moment he exited the plane. Not for the first time, the international Assassin thought how correct he had been when he had forecast that this contract would be the most demanding and complex Op he had ever planned and executed. It was a given that anything involving HVTs, such as this shopping list, would demand every skill and experience he possessed, and, in proportion the same High Value Targets were why he was receiving a fee comparable to a small country's GNP. He had gained this contract through a hard-won reputation of being one of the best, if not the best Assassin on the planet. The Warrior within told him that the coming weeks would require all his skills, both in logistics and in execution. He was also very mindful that thirty-five million dollars was valueless if you were dead.

He had prearranged the weapons and gear he needed through a contact from the old days who operated on the Dark Web but, fortunately, was based in Australia. He didn't trust anyone, but at least this contact wasn't a complete stranger. Roza considered this semi-lack of his usual anonymity a threat but an acceptable one. By wearing a plain black cap with a long bill he ensured that the airport CCTVs failed to collect any clear facial shots. Casually, Roza avoided looking towards the cameras mounted high on walls and ceilings as he made his way to collect his baggage. Of course, he had meticulously packed his bag, ensuring there was nothing to motivate a closer inspection. Thankfully, the bag went through the X-ray check without comment. Dreading the heat that must be waiting to pounce on him outside the terminal, he headed for the taxi rank.

Two taxi changes later, the Assassin asked to stop at a corner three blocks from the car rental station. It would have been simpler to pick up the car at the airport. However, it would be the first place the authorities would check once his plans had come to fruition and every law enforcement officer in Australia was looking for the Assassin. The other benefit was that returning the vehicle away from the airport on his way out of Australia minimised the chances of being held up or triggering a red flag alert and avoiding the airport's bristling security.

He had hired a white Toyota Landcruiser wagon with a lockable, watertight, private storage compartment for his mobile Base. The other benefit of the Landcruiser was that every second 4WD in the Territory was the same colour and model. Roza was careful to hand over his other licence, this time an English version in the name of Clive Banks. Like most warriors, the Assassin adapted quickly to a fluid environment and was immediately comfortable driving on the left-hand side of the road. Roza had purchased a street map to ensure his movements were not recorded on the vehicle's Satnav. These devices were a diary that could hang a person in the hands of Law Enforcement.

Careful not to create any traffic infringements that might attract attention or leave a trace on a speed camera, he proceeded to the prearranged storage facility.

On his way to his next stop, he stopped in a remote area and changed into local uniform of jeans, tee shirt and work boots. Once again, hiding under the long bill cap, he used the code he had been given to enter the Kennards Self Storage Facility. He backed the nondescript white 4WD to within two metres of the roller door of his storage unit number 107. He was happy to see the surf motif bags containing his weapons of choice on opening the large door. He appreciated that the supplier had thought to avoid camouflage and military colours on the cases. In the unlikely event that a member of the public saw the cases being carried around or sitting in the vehicle they wouldn't be encouraged to think of guns. The Assassin assumed that several steel carry boxes he could see at the back of the storage unit held the required ammunition and explosives. A black hard plastic case that, by its moulded shape, told him it was a set of NVGs (Night Vision Goggles). These would enable him to see at night if this mission required it. Roza had most of his plan formed and set about collecting the needed resources. Several American USMC Officers' uniforms were hanging from the wire cage wall. They appeared brand new and were wrapped in dry cleaner plastic bags. Several pairs of boots sat on the floor under the uniforms. Pulling the roller door down from the inside, Roza systematically checked every item in the storage unit.

Years of training and experience demanded that you never assume anything is right; you can only really depend on yourself. Out there getting chased by some hotshot trying to kill you and get a promotion via your scalp wasn't the time to discover you had the wrong ammo for what you were carrying or not enough detonators for the bang you had in your bag. He smiled as he removed the specialist sniper rifles he had ordered and field-striped each weapon. He ensured that the firing pins were fitted, the guns were clean and weren't worn, or over greased as was common if they had been stored for a long period. Of course, he would clean them daily, but this was to ensure there was no pitting in the barrel or rust that would negatively affect the weapons his life and the mission's success would depend on. He even checked the Night Vision Goggles to ensure their full operation would be available when he needed them. Roza looked over the storage unit, ensuring the weapons and equipment were secure and covered. This would ensure nothing was visible from the lane way as he entered or exited the storage unit. More than one criminal had been caught by the curious eyes of someone casually seeing something incriminating, prompting a call to the Police. Once satisfied with the locker contents, he rolled up the storage unit door from the inside, ensuring that the driveway was clear and headed to his accommodation.

Two days later, the Assassin checked into another motel; he was breaking up his trail by changing motels every two or three days. Not happy with the idea of having to involve a stranger, his plan dictated that Roza needed some local knowledge and Intel. He would gain this by recruiting a local volunteer to assist him. As a chameleon changes colour, the Assassin dressed like the men he had seen around the shops and hotels. Escaping the incessant tropical heat he enjoyed the coolness that confronted him as he walked into the dimly lit bar. After buying a beer, he surveyed the drinkers sitting around the bar seeing them as prey like a lion evaluates a herd of wildebeest.

Roza was looking for just the right one, the weak one. The guy he had settled on had been carefully selected. He was sitting by himself, taking a week to finish his beer, suggesting he wasn't flush with funds. He was dressed like a welder or maybe a mechanic. Roza thought he might even work on a cattle property but doubted it after a bit more assessment. Finally, the man finished the drink he had been nursing so long. Roza, who always thought ahead, considering every little subtlety and refinement to his plans. Accordingly, he had placed himself beside the quick service area. He expected his chosen prey to come straight to him like a crocodile awaiting a thirsty zebra to come down to his waterhole. Unwittingly, the Australian fell into the invisible trap as he walked over to the quick service area. The Assassin knew how to blend in quickly and pick up a Mark. It was easy for Roza, who had studied the NT News sports section of the creatively named Northern Territory News Paper.

"So those Nightcliff boys got any chance in the final this year?" he asked, sounding a little English but not overly so.

"Only if that Full Forward gets a new friggin Seeing Eye Dog to help him see the goals," The young Australian responded sarcastically, and laughed.

"Michael Thompson," Roza said, offering his hand.

"Luke Edwards, pleased to meet ya mate," the Aussie said warmly.

"Good pub, hey?" Roza shouted over the live pub music and noise.

Looking a bit sad, "Yeah, I liked it better when it was Lilly's. They changed the name to Hotel Darwin, and they've tarted her up a bit, and everything's a bit touristy. Dark and a bit noisy, but the beers cold," the young Australian said clearly missing his lost haven.

And that's how it started, with Roza slowly cultivating a relationship with the local he hoped would satisfy the plan's requirements. He remembered how, over the following two weeks, he had dreaded his daily sessions drinking with Luke. Here, he would milk the dumb Aussie for intel and ideas slowly so as not to appear like an interrogation. These times were worth it. The Assassin couldn't believe his luck when he learned that Luke had worked on the new Marine Base, from clearing the first trees to the fencing.

"Anyway, the place used to be named somethin' else, but the Yanks had to change everything, it's called Tortilla Flats now, like they were in Mexico or some place," Luke said bitterly.

Roza as Mick Thompson, said he was new to town and looking for gold and gems. He was amazed at how easy it had been; buying the guy a few beers had him singing like a canary. Roza looked at his new Aussie friend and thought; *I'm glad I factored in the time needed to gather the Intel, formulate a workable plan, and recruit a local.* Thankfully, the patsy named Luke liked a drink on a hot day, or any other day for that matter, and was clearly he was willing to do anything to make a buck. Like most locals, the tradesman had no idea of the importance of security, especially on something as full of tech secrets and gear as a USMC Base. The fact was that talking about the Base was a potential threat to the area by attracting terrorists or even a full-blown military assault in the time of war. The old adage still applied; 'Loose lips sink ships'.

Darwin the Capital of the Northern Territory had more bombs fall on it by the Japanese than Pearl Harbour and had experienced sabotage in the early days of WW2, but those who were there were either dead, had moved South or were too old to remember.

Roza smiled as he recalled one conversation he had with Luke the tradie. The younger Territorians resented the American presence, not appreciating what it brought. Jobs, money, and safety in many ways. Even Luke, who had benefited directly by working on the Base, didn't really get it.

"Anyway, me and my mates were talking about all these Yank heroes. They come in and take all the girls with their flashy uniforms and haircuts. Well, they can't be that brave, these Marines. I mean they drive around Darwin wearin bullet proof vests and big helmets like they are in Iraq or somewhere," the Aussie tradesman said with a boozy slur.

Not in any way caring to defend the Marines, Roza thought to himself; *well, if you had ever operated in Iraq or Afghanistan where an IED was at every turn, you'd wear a helmet to bed, you idiot.*

"Yes, they've seen too many war movies, mate," he said embracing the Aussie terms easily, building rapport by joining in with the silliness of their attitude. To develop this relationship Roza had been enduring this banality for close on two weeks now. The Assassin found Luke Edwards uneducated, boring and monotonous. However, over many beers and many days, he had harvested enough intel to answer nearly all his questions without risking exposing himself by doing several physical Recces out at Tortilla Flats USMC Base. Instead, his Recces were more to confirm what Luke the tradie had described. Being so isolated and barren meant that satellites, drones, Helos and any form of ground patrols had plenty of time to catch you out in the middle of no man's land. From Luke, he learnt that there had been many discussions about the boundary fence. Luke had reported that the Yanks wanted it electrified, but it couldn't be done due to its incredible length.

"Then the Yanks wanted to try friggin pressure plates buried all over the place; we told 'em they wouldn't work, but they pushed it. My Boss saw the bucks, and we gave in and did a trial. The friggin roos, wild cattle, buffalo and every other critter, set the test plates off so often the Marines were out there more than they were in."

They had both laughed over their beers about that. The Aussie tradesman enjoyed getting paid for his work on the base, but saw the Americans as pretty stupid. The biggest laugh came about most of the tracks on the place.

"Anyway, of course, the main road into the camp is cleared to maybe a hundred metres on either side, but any track that goes through the sandstone country meanders around rocky outcrops and stuff like a drunk goanna. Anyway, guess what?" he said as he wiped the beer foam from his top lip with a smile. The Assassin realised he didn't need to reply.

"Humvees mate, frigging Hummers. Might have been great in Iraq or somewhere. Can't fit through the gaps on most of the tracks in about fifty percent of the Base. See us Aussies; we have always had Landrovers and then later Hiluxes and Landcruisers, all skinny 4WDs compared to Hummers," Luke said, enjoying the fact that he thought he was entertaining Roza. He wondered why he seemed not to have to shout his round anymore, but not often.

Roza had plans for Luke that didn't include him growing old. He was very annoying. While invaluable to the mission, his willingness to share information was not an endearing quality to a man like Roza whose very survival depended on security and confidentiality. The old adage still stands; Loose Lips Sink Ships. That's why Roza had planned the Aussie's future.

The Assassin figured even beer-loving Luke might figure out that his new best mate was involved once something big happened out at the place called Tortilla Flats. It was never really in the plan for Aussie Luke to make it out alive from the Marine Base once his use-by had expired. If by some miracle Luke actually escaped the Marines, Roza would end him as soon as they met up again.

Luke's criticism of the Hummers had given Roza a seed of an idea. The Assassin started the ball rolling by testing the Aussie's willingness to step over the line to make a few bucks. "Luke, I was talking to a guy the other day who said he'd pay big time for two Hummers. He was pretty careful, but I think he's goin to take 'em South and sell them. Any ideas? I was thinking maybe grab them when the Jarheads were in town," he said, setting the trap.

Adopting his impression of a Chinese accent the Aussie said with a grin,

"Grasshopper wisdom is chasing you, but you are always a little faster,"

Roza laughed and thought; *I'm surprised Luke gets that joke, and then maybe, he's just repeating because people laughed when someone said before.* Roza had no friends, even when he was a child, no relatives, no one he loved, or loved him. Luke had somehow got as close as anyone ever had over the last few weeks with his humour and humility. He carried no threat. The young Aussie had no agenda except maybe milking a few free drinks from his new friend who seemed to have plenty of money. Luke didn't have a clue that he was being suckered by this generosity. Roza laughed and thought; *He still has to die, but I'll make sure it's quick.*

Luke had 'Australianised' the Assassin's adopted name, Michael, within an hour of meeting.

"Mick, I gotta a much better plan, unless you wanna get your butt shot off by some Marine with his gat in one hand and a Big Mac in the other. Stealing a Humvee outside a McDonald's has its problems. I mean, I might make fun of 'em, but they are Soldiers, not soccer mums. You know what they say; 'Never insult seven men when you only have a six-shooter'," Luke said seriously. He looked very satisfied with this wisdom, which was unusual for him to either have or demonstrate.

Thinking there was more to this Luke than his appearance suggested, Roza was surprised by the Aussie's seriousness and focused response.

"You're very deep today, full of wisdom, even wise sayings. Who are you, and what have you done with my mate Luke?" Roza asked with fake seriousness.

"Very funny, but I want to help, and I'm not as dumb as I look," Luke responded, laughing.

"OK, I can see what you mean. It's not about looking dumb but about not taking chances unnecessarily. What's your idea?" Roza asked trying not to seem too interested.

"I was talking to a mate of a mate who's a panel beater spray painter. Anyway, these Yanks are forever hitting trees and rocks and plenty of roos as well; one of the silly buggers knocked a friggin camel over the other day. Like I keep tellin' ya the Hummer's width doesn't help 'em any. He reckons they have a couple in the shop nearly every week," Luke said as he finished his beer.

"I think I can see your idea, great. We take 'em from the panel shop, no protection, no weapons," the Assassin said, trying to embed admiration as he spoke.

A new idea had just come to Roza's quick mind; he would revisit it later. Roza had another question for Luke, the gold mine of information.

"Luke mate, can you get in there, you know, into the Yank base?"
the Assassin asked as if he was asking the Aussie if he wanted some
lunch.

"Oh, oh, no, that's not a good idea, mate," Luke stuttered.

Roza could tell there was something behind this, instant
palpable fear his drinking mate hadn't shown before, so he took a
chance.

"Mate, you've done it; I can tell that you've been back there since
you finished working on the Base. Tell us what happened, hey?" Roza
said, complimenting himself mentally for sounding so careless and
Aussie.

Looking sheepish, Luke answered hesitantly, "Yeah, you're right.
Me and a mate snuck in there one night. The plan was to knock off
some gear. We weren't even sure what it might be, but all that Yank
stuff is brand new and Mickey Mouse."

"Well, seeing you're sitting here, you must have made it, what
happened?" Roza asked casually.

"Well, we were havin' a great time goin through this guard hut
thing, it was pitch black. We were havin' a few beers as we worked,
you know. These Marines are like Christmas Lights; they hang
around together, only a few work and most of 'em aren't too bright,"
he looked pleased with himself, probably repeating something he'd
heard and thought was clever," anyway, maybe we had set off an
alarm or something," Luke said, trying to sound confident and brave,
"Anyway, we're goin like a train, and then suddenly we see a vehicle
heading our way. So we packed it in and took off. We only got a cool
camo flack jacket and a couple of Marine water bottles," he stopped
and went to grab his beer, which he found empty. The Assassin didn't
want to pause this flow of Intel to go to the bar.

The Aussie, used to his new friend keeping a steady flow of drinks looked slightly bewildered by this lack of lubrication but continued in the hope that his new mate would shout him a drink soon enough.

"Anyway, me mate and me we drive off like scalded cats and parked up around this rocky outcrop until the Hummer went past. The Marines didn't even slow at the guard hut, so we figured we were OK. But mate, enough is enough, we headed home. There's is nothin that would get me back there I'm tellin you right now," Luke said.

"Well, mate, that's a big pity because I heard there were some interesting deposits in the there. I want to look at some rocks, and you wouldn't believe where they are. They are sitting inside that very boundary fence you put up," Roza said as he stood up.

"Mate, I feel like something a bit stronger. Do you want a rum or maybe a JD?" He asked, chumming the water in preparation for when he came back from the bar.

"Sure, a Bundy rum would be great; thanks, mate. None of that Yankee rot gut," the young Aussie replied.

The Assassin would not normally be so obvious, but poor old Luke liked a drink. It didn't have to be a hot day, and Roza needed to speed up this next stage of his plan. Being subtle was wasted on Luke, so, when Roza showed up with a tray carrying eight glasses rum and Coke, Luke's eyes lit up like a kid's on Christmas morning. Luke had never learned that most free things have a hidden cost.

CANBERRA

I picked Ben Winfrey up from the airport, we hugged as brothers and I helped him with his bags as we walked to my truck. On a previous operation involving ISIS smugglers Ben had actually brought me back from being clinically dead thanks to a nearby defibrillator after a guy the size of Shrek had crushed my throat with a weights bar when we were on an operation aboard a cruise ship.

I planned to catch up over dinner and drinks at Canberra's famous Trident Seafood on Cooyong St, Braddon.

"Mate, it's my shout tonight. I don't want you putting your hand in your pocket for anything, OK?" I said, smiling.

"Steve, why would you do that when Uncle Sam's covering the check, let me?" my American counterpart said after taking a sip of his whiskey.

"Ben, I owe you my life. It was all too busy to catch up on that op. Then that ISIS smuggler shot you. It's so good you're here and OK; for a while there we weren't sure that you would make it or even walk again. Let alone go operational."

The American CIA operative smiled. "Yeah, well, it all worked out. We did the baddies a lot of harm and hopefully saved more than a few Aussie and American Soldier's lives by doing it. Buddy enough serious talk. I'm starving, and I want to try all your Australian seafood. I've heard about Balmain Bugs, are they insects or fish?"

"Alright, I'm starving too, no, bugs are like weird looking little lobsters. I won't argue about who's paying; it won't be our last feed together anyway. Now, I'll order what I think you'll like: oysters, mussels, crab, hot and cold, and I won't forget the bugs. And of course prawns, you Yanks call 'em shrimps, don't you?" I said, laughing. We had a great night swapping yarns, interspersed with incredible amounts of seafood and plenty of Jack Daniels.

AUSTRALIAN NATIONAL SECURITY CENTRE
CANBERRA
AUSTRALIA
NEXT MORNING

Brigadier William Watson 'humphed' for the third or fourth time. He wasn't needed at this briefing but had in his usual leadership style, made an appearance. Next to the Brig was Colonel Goodrich, my direct link with H.Q. Trader Duke had sent his Deputy Director Secret Service, Sal Marcello, a New York Italian who had been a Police Officer before applying to the Secret Service. At fifty-something, his big round head was devoid of hair. Standing at around five foot eight with broad shoulders he always looked a bit overweight, even though he still ran five miles every day. Opposite him, looking impressive in his dress uniform and a chest full of medals, was the US Marine Lieutenant Colonel from the Northern Territory base. His name was Randy Norris, but predictably, he was better known as Chuck Norris. He was representing the Base Commander Colonel Patton who had stayed on base to ensure preparations for the big visit were on schedule. Ben Winfrey, the CIA Operative, sat beside me.

"Steve, this will probably be boring compared to your usual ops. You and Mr Winfrey can probably try some Northern Territory seafood for a change while you're up there," Goodrich said with a big smile.

How he knew where we had been last night remains a mystery, but it confirms why he is such a good contact. His Intel network operates here and abroad. The representatives around the table made lovely speeches and promises that we had all heard before. Just the names and locations varied. My gut was telling me again that it didn't like it when I was told something would be easy or boring. The old thought kicked in: *Hope for the best, prepare for the worst.* The Secret Service Assistant Director had made it clear that the CIA's presence was surplus to needs, but Winfrey and I had already discussed that fact. Our superiors had told both of us to ghost the other services and just nod at meetings like this. So, as obedient little pawns, we nodded like a dash ornament on a rocky road. I saw

Colonel Goodrich try to hide a smile. He knew I had the same brief, and we all hoped it would work out that way. Two hours later, all the Americans were on their way home, and so was I. I slept all the way to Roma, dreaming of Chris, my fiancee, and Jake, my dog, not necessarily in that order, but keep that to yourself.

CHAPTER 14

Chemistry comes in handy for the Assassin.

US MARINE CORPS BASE
OUTSIDE DARWIN
NORTHERN TERRITORY

Using the young Australian Luke as a guide to sneak into Marine Base and make his Recce caused the Assassin to feel vulnerable. He had survived and earned his reputation by never trusting or depending on anyone else. However, after a few sessions at the pub with this Aussie, he knew that Luke had been all over the Base and that it was worth the risk. The Australian was easily fooled by the Assassin's explanation of why he wanted to get a look inside the razor wire. Roza, the Assassin, thought; *how gullible the Australian had been after several rum and cokes.*

"Mate, I've done a heap of research, and I believe there is gold to be found inside that Base. I just need someone to get me inside." Roza said convincingly.

And, here they were, looking like ninjas all dressed in black, their faces striped with grease paint. The Australian was like an excited child playing a war game, dressed up and doing something that was an adventure. The Assassin, in keeping with his character, acted the same way, "Luke, this is a bit scary. Are you sure they don't patrol this area?"

"Like I told ya, me and my mate came in here a few times to knock off Yanky gear. We'll be right; where do you want to go?" the Australian responded.

It was 0200 Hours on a moonless night as the Toyota Hilux rumbled along a well-used track. Roza knew where the track led, and that his Targets would use the same route on their way to observe a battle demonstration. The Australian laughed as they approached a rocky outcrop that stuck out into the track.

"You know how I was tellin' you about them Hummers being too wide for our dirt roads. It's a bit hard to see, but that rock there has paint all over it. I s'pose it's to stop those Yankees scratching their shiny Humvees if they don't swing wide enough," he laughed.

Roza sensed that a flicker of an idea had entered his mind. However, for that part of a plan to amount to anything he also needed another feature well away from the track. Roza stopped the Hilux next to the track and walked closer to the rocky outcrop to inspect it more thoroughly.

Although the Assassin was listening to Luke, he gaze was drawn to a rock formation about three hundred yards from where they stood. There were two large rocks that sat side by side, creating a sort of roofless garage. He needed to measure the gap between these rocks.

"Luke, I think that rock feature might be an old river bed. Can we head over there, please? And mate, can you turn off Toby Kieth for a while so we can hear each other?"

"Sure, no prob," the Aussie said as he turned the wheel and went off-road towards the rocks.

The terrain was clear and flat in that direction, and the Hilux soon drew alongside the twin rocks. The Assassin climbed out of the 4WD and immediately turned to face the outcrop they had just left. In the dark, the Aussie couldn't see Roza raising a Range Finder to his eye. The Assassin smiled as he read Two Hundred and Eighty-Three Metres. The smile came because he knew the weapon he had chosen, and unlike other platforms such as the Barrett, it had a limited range. Those others stretched out to as much as two kilometres, but that didn't concern him. Roza realised that being so close to the Targets was a risk; however, with potentially three High-Value Targets, he had to have a way to shoot all three in rapid succession and without giving away his position. One rifle would do it. He had chosen the V.S.S. Vintorez silenced sniper rifle favoured by Spetsnaz (Russian Special Forces) operators for several reasons. Disassembled, it could easily be smuggled into a suitcase. Chambered in the 9×39 mm calibre, the 9 mm eliminates the sonic crack and is more controllable should you need full auto.

With no sound and no visible flash, he could keep firing after his first shot. This weapon enabled him to engage multiple Targets, in this case, the President of the United States, followed by the British and Australian Prime Ministers. The Assassin wanted quiet Subsonic rounds that did not 'whizz' as they flew by. The commonly used cartridge was the armour-piercing SP-6 cartridge (9×39 mm), capable of penetrating body armour that stops the standard Kalashnikov rounds. The potent round only had a range of four hundred metres and closer to three hundred metres if required to penetrate body armour or bulletproof glass. But the range finder had just confirmed that he could stick with his choice of weapon. One more thing needed to be right for these two rocks to become his hide.

"Luke, come here and grab this will you be mate?" he asked the Aussie who had stayed in the 4WD.

The young Aussie climbed out, joining Roza, who was standing at the entrance to the space between the two rock features. He handed Luke the Dill end of a tape measure and walked over to the other rock, reeling out the tape. It read eight feet or just over two and a half metres. The Assassin was having a great night; he smiled again because the space between the rocks would be perfect. A Hummer is seven foot one inch or just over two metres wide, so it would fit perfectly. Now that the hide had been established the Assassin surveyed the various fields of fire that the target vehicles would enter. Once again, he was happy with his options. However, he always sought perfection when he set up his kill zones. That outcrop that the USMC Drivers had been scraping on gave him an idea that would force the convoy to slow, possible stop and swing side on to his hide. Everything was good without this refinement, but he would continue to think about it to see if he could push it all into perfect. For the Australian's benefit Roza looked at the rock profiles and pocketed a few rock samples imitating a prospector. He wondered if Luke had bought it.

"Luke, I'm pretty right, thanks. Let's get out of here; we've been lucky so far; let's not push it, hey?" Roza said calmly. An hour later, they were at Luke's place, enjoying their second beer.

"OK, I'm just a dumb ass, but you weren't lookin' for gold back there. What's the game? What are you really doing?" the Aussie asked.

Roza, a little surprised by this comment, but was still prepared for this.

Before they entered the Marine Base, he had decided he wouldn't waste time with any complicated play-acting by swinging a metal detector or digging holes. He figured that Luke would do nearly anything for money, so that's the card he played.

"You're right, I've got some plans, and I needed to see how you performed under a bit of pressure or at risk of getting caught. You did really well. Now, I always work alone, but I need the help of someone who can drive a four-wheel drive and keep his nerve. Luke, I can't tell you everything right now, but when we get a bit closer to the time I'll explain it all. One thing I can tell you, is you will make a heap of dollars helping me," the Assassin said, baiting the hook. He had already figured Luke into his plans in any case.

On his way back from the Marine Base, he was happy with the outcome of the Recce. There was a problem to solve, but he was sure a solution existed. His mind buzzed with the plan that had fallen into place. There was only that one refinement. Could the convoy be forced closer to his proposed hide and turned on a slightly better angle? This was akin to a dear hunter, whether using a bow or a rifle, waiting for that buck to turn sideways, offering a perfect heart shot. Roza had an idea if he could just blow that jagged outcrop that the Hummers had been caught on. The Marines should have done this months ago. For the Assassin's purpose, two critical components came into play. First, the rock must fall on the track, blocking it. If the rock was shattered by an explosion, the debris would be scattered widely. It would fail to block the well-worn path. The bonus of dropping the rock on the path was that it would force every vehicle to swing wider and turn towards the rocky feature and bring them closer to the Assassin's chosen hide. Second, an explosion would likely alert the whole Base, and the shattered rock would be easily assessed as a demolition spoil. Roza had to find a way to move a few tons of rock and make it look like a natural occurrence.

The Assassin was always amazed at the info you could find on Google, you could perform surgery, build a bomb or fix a tap. Well, he had an idea and wondered if it would be there. Sitting in his hotel room, he did a Google search. The result leapt from the screen.

Cracking agent for rock & concrete breaking solution.

EXPANDO is an **expansive mortar chemical** that cracks rocks and concrete **without using explosives**. It is a concrete cutting, granite breaking and general demolition solution. This non-explosive demolition agent is easy to use, cost-effective and a safer option for silently breaking up hard materials like rock or concrete. Simply drill, mix and pour.

As Roza read the product website, he thought, *I can't believe this stuff answers my every need, no dust, no noise.*

EXPANDO is the ideal alternative to noisy, risky concrete and rock-breaking solutions like explosive blasting, jack hammering, concrete saws and stone cutters.

He read on immediately, calculating and solving the little problems as his mind imagined how this miracle chemical had just overcome a major hurdle, that of forcing the convoy into the Kill Zone.

EXPANDO is a **cracking agent** that comes in powder form and expands when mixed with water.

When poured into pre-drilled blast holes, it produces an extreme pressure of 18,000 Pounds per Square Inch. After a few hours, the tensile strength of the rock or concrete is overcome by the cracking agent. The rock or concrete then breaks following the pre-drilled hole pattern.

OK, I need to buy or hire some drilling equipment and a few buckets of this chemical, and by the next morning, the rock face will have collapsed onto the track. He didn't rely on luck, but he did know how the Military thought and operated. Visualising how things would proceed the Assassin figured that; *The Marines were sure to send out a last-minute Reconnaissance Patrol a few hours before POTUS and the English and Australian Prime Ministers were due along that dirt road.*

OK, this means:

1. I can only drill and insert the Expando the night before the VIP visit.

2. When they discover the rock slide and attempt to report it, I need them to be forced to move away from the site.

3. Right, I have to set a phone and radio comms jammer to minimise the time that Recce Patrol is standing near the rocky collapse. I don't want them to notice any drill holes that may be obvious once the rocks fall across the track.

4. The dead comms should, without their knowledge, move them away to an area where their radios will kick back in. By the time they are describing the damage, they will be fifty metres away from the rock slide.

Roza was further rewarded by the fact that EXPANDO had an Agent right here in Darwin. By the time he arrived at the store, two hours before they closed, he had a believable cover story.

"How ya goin?" the grey-haired man standing behind the Formica counter had a dark complexion and deep crow's feet pinching his eyes.

"Hi there, we are heading out to a bit of prospecting, and a fella at the pub said I should have some of your rock cracker," the Assassin said easily with just a hint of an Australian accent he had picked up over the last few weeks.

Half an hour later, the two men were loading two twenty-kilo boxes of EXPANDO chemicals into Roza's 4WD.

Before them were several buckets and bags that resembled how cement or sand was purchased by any handymen. There were several things that he still had to buy, however, these could be obtained from any hardware store.

"I'm happy to sell it, mate, but are you sure you need this much?" the grey-haired salesman asked.

Roza had prepared for this question and replied, "You're probably right, but I'd hate to have to come all the way back to town if I needed more."

With that, he closed the vehicle's back door and headed back to the hotel. When he had parked, he brought a spare set of number plates out and screwed them on. It wasn't the same as buying explosives, where I.D. and lots of paperwork were mandatory. He didn't think the salesman would have taken note of his plates, but you never knew.

CHAPTER 15

Everyone is busy getting ready.

THE NIGHT BEFORE
THE ATTACK.
TORTILLA FLATS USMC BASE
NORTHERN TERRITORY

On the way out to the Marine Base the Assassin had pulled his Hummer off the sealed road with Luke his young assistant following close behind in his own Humvee. Five hundred meters down the track they stopped. The Assassin took two Marine uniforms from his vehicle.

"Luke get into this while I set up some beer cans as targets."

While the Australian was getting into the USMC uniform Roza lifted a tarp from the rear of the vehicle and removed two rifles being careful not to let Luke see what other equipment lay under the tarp. It was easy to get Luke to participate in what might become another nail in his coffin. Luke was so excited about dressing up he didn't notice that Roza was changing clothes, staying in his jeans and camo shirt.

"Mate, I have never worn a tie in my life." Luke said looking bewildered as he held up the Marine neck tie.

Roza laughed and said," do you want me to tie your shoe laces as well?"

The Assassin stood back in fake admiration as he surveyed the young Australian dressed in a USMC Major's uniform.

"Come on mate come and try these rifles and have some fun." Roza said.

The 'pfft' noise of the ten shots fired from each of the Russian made V.S.S. Vintorez silenced sniper rifles wouldn't travel far but, even if heard the sound would not cause any concern. This was the Northern Territory where hunting water buffalo and huge feral pigs was a common pursuit.

This was just a further stage in the plan. It accomplished two things simultaneously. As usual, Roza had planned every facet ahead of today's operation. He was sure that the rifle would be forensically tested once the Australian was captured and the rifle seized. By firing off the ten rounds, the Australian's weapon when tested would prove to have been shot recently. Secondly, and by no means of any lesser importance Luke's hands and uniform would test positive for G.S.R, or Gun Shot Residual.

"Mate we better get a move on, you all good?" Roza asked.

"Wow, Mick, I'd love to use this gun on a buff or a camel," Luke the young Australian said excitedly.

"Well, mate after all this is over it's yours," Roza the Assassin said generously.

"There is something else I want to tell you, I had to wait until now to be sure how this would all go. First, I am going to pay you $25,000 for all your help. Now, listen carefully to what you need to do in the next twelve hours or so. Follow all my directions and the money is yours," Roza said in a serious tone.

The Assassin went on to explain to Luke how to set up his hide once he had backed his Hummer in. He also described what would happen the next morning, how he was to take off fast when he saw a Marine vehicle approach the hide.

"And keep running until they catch up and see your USMC Major's uniform.

"Oh, that why I'm all dressed up like this, now I understand." Luke interrupted.

Roza continued, "Now, that should be enough, but if they still seem unsure I want you to show them your rifle. When they see that they will know your one of them and keep going. Got all that Luke?"

"I knew it, I knew it. You got somethin' else goin' on. Yeah sure, lookin for gold and rocks my hat." Luke said looking very pleased with himself.

"I can't tell you what's going on, just do what I've asked and you get to enjoy all those dollars, what do you say?" Roza said in a tone that did not encourage discussion.

"Your right, I talk too much sometimes." Luke said as though he sensed that he had no choice but to obey Mike or whoever he really was.

Talk over. They climbed into their respective Humvees and headed back to the road to continue towards the American Base.

Roza had timed the trip to get to the Base at least two hours after dark. The two Hummer convoy travelled without lights. The terrain was flat and without any dangerous tree stumps or washouts. They had removed the bulbs from both vehicles' rear lights, especially the reversing lights. When the two vehicles arrived at the boundary fence they cut a bolt hole out of the fence and Roza pinned it to his Sat. Nav. Once inside the Base they re-hung the wire using black zippy ties to secure it. Roza figured that if in the unlikely case that he was being chased he could bust his way through the fence without even slowing down. From there they headed to the rock features they had identified on their earlier Recce.

The two rock vehicle parks were nearly identical, but close to five hundred metres apart to reduce creating dust trails and visibility from above through coming and going. The rock formations they were heading for were akin to small ridges of harder rock that had not eroded away like the rest of the giant prehistoric floodplain. Roza and his Aussie accomplice had moved into their separate hides before the small slice of moon came up. Roza stopped just past the second rock feature and watched the Australian come up to it. The Assassin guided the Australian as he backed his Hummer into the slot between the rocks. Luke quickly got out and spread the cam net to create a roof over the vehicle as he had been instructed. He secured its edges randomly with small stones, a camouflaged car park to avoid the rectangular shape being seen from above. Credit where credit was due, his Australian helper, dumb, untrained and naive as he was had followed his plan so far. He had even remembered to make sure the rocks were flattish to minimise the satellite's 3D image.

Once happy with Luke's set up Roza drove over to his own hide. He then backed his identical Humvee between two similar but still natural rock features. And like his naive apprentice, he proceeded to spread a cam net between his two rocky ridges.

Resting in this camouflaged parking spot the Assassin waited for an hour to ensure there was no patrol around attracted by a satellite photo or a patrolling drone spying their arrival.

Meanwhile the Australian was settled back into the Hummer thinking about how his luck had changed for the better when he met Mick. Ever since meeting his new wealthy friend, he had been drinking more and eating better. Now, he had this easy gig.

All he had to do was sit tight and when he saw the Marines coming, drive out and head for the main gate. He didn't know what was really going on, and for all that money, he didn't care. It was cold but roomy sleeping in the big American Mil 4WD. Mick, who was in charge and paying the bills, would freak out if he knew that the Aussie had snuck a flask in, but, the Bundy Rum had worked well in warming him up a little. Not for the first time, he surveyed his appearance. Dressed in a the Military uniform, he felt pretty good about himself. Imagine if those guys at the pub who always treated him like he was a loser could see him now. Mick, his new mate, had said the vehicle and the uniform would get him through the Main Gate, no worries. This made sense to him; he still didn't know why he was needed, but that twenty-five grand kept answering any question he asked.

Luke was surprised when Roza informed him there were to be no radios and there would be no communication between them once they backed into their respective hides. The Assassin had decided this for at least two significant reasons. One was to ensure that no

SIGS unit monitoring random frequencies would be alerted. The other was that when the Australian was caught, he would be, if he had comms, the Marines would know he had not worked alone. Roza had greatly benefited from the talkative Aussie, but his relationship was only one of using the younger man. An identical weapon to the one the Assassin would later use to kill the U.S. President was sitting on the passenger seat of the Australian's Humvee. Luke had fired it just a few hours before and would make all the little Marines feel like they had caught the Assassin before he got off the USMC Base.

Meanwhile, with every eye focused on the fleeing Australian, Roza would sit tight and later make his escape. Exfil one was through his well-used bolt-hole through the fence. Plan B he would approach a minor gate leading off the Base if that was cut off. Dressed in an identical stolen USMC Major's uniform, he was confident he could bully his way through. If, by then, the gate guards had heard that their cohorts had already captured the Assassin they would be relaxed, not expecting any threat to come to their side gate, and wave him through.

Roza could not discover the precise time the President's convoy would pass his hide. This didn't concern him; waiting for a world-class sniper time wasn't a factor. Hidden in his rocky hide the Assassin had a great field of fire to the track the President's vehicle would use in just a few hours. However, he had no way of directly seeing the Australian; his last sighting was when Luke secured the front corner of the cam net. He was happy, though; the Humvee was invisible from ground level and was only visible to Roza because he knew the hide was there.

Roza surveyed the surrounding desert in every direction and found it clear. Slowly leaving the hide he drove over to the track meeting it about half a Klick away from the rock outcrop. Once there he followed along the track to ensure there were no tyre prints leading out to his hide.

Once adjacent to the outcrop he unloaded the Hummer and set up to carry out the required work right in the bullseye of tomorrow's Kill Zone. The day before he had hired the industrial-type drill and bits without concern of raising anyone's interest; tradies and amateur miners would have rented the machine regularly.

The Assassin felt he was breaking his standard rules by leaving such a key preparation to tonight just hours before the planned hit. However, there was no choice.

This work could not be done any earlier. If it had been carried out before tonight it would have been discovered and cleared by the Marine Engineers.

After visiting the USMC Base on the two recces guided by the young Australian Roza was feeling extremely vulnerable and exposed when tonight they entered the Base once again. Especially now, as he had been working on the rock outcrop for nearly three long hours. Half an hour into the work he regretted his decision to come alone, preferring not to have to explain to the Australian why he was breaking the nose off the small cliff next to the track he worked on. Roza stayed hyper-vigilant, searching the flat desert for a glow of lights on the horizon or any movements that would betray a USMC Patrol or a Drone. Soaking wet from the exertion of drilling ten holes in a line across the rock he wiped his forehead with his sleeve again. The machine had a forty-millimetre drill bit with a one point-five metres long reach. Even carrying the drill with the bit locked in was heavy hard work. The sense of relief was palpable when he reached the cliff face's far edge, completing hole number ten.

The Assassin celebrated this achievement with a minute break as he swallowed the contents of a sweating bottle of blue Gatorade to replenish his overworked body.

It was time to mix the chemicals and pour the creamy liquid into each hole. The instructions talked about the effect of temperature on the product. Roza had figured that because he was using it at night and it was winter, he would have plenty of time before the chemical started expanding. Of course, this being his first experience with the splitting agent, all this was supposition. Roza hoped he had gotten the mix right. According to the product description, the rock should be split apart and fall across the track within a few hours. He had done all he could.

The shot would now be closer to the optimum range for the silenced rifle, but only if this fake landslide succeeded in forcing the President's vehicle to swing out towards his hide. This was especially important because this was to be a multiple hit. Knowing that POTUS and the two Prime Ministers would share the same vehicle Roza was planning to kill all the passengers in the HVT Hummer. All the Assassin could do now, was to go back to the hide and wait, glad the physical work was done, hold up and see whether all this creativity and muscle work would have the desired outcome. Whatever happened, Roza would take the shots as the High Value Targets presented and passed by.

Part of Roza's strategy in bringing the cliff down the night before the HVT visit was not to give them time to bulldoze the rock slide out of the way. At first light Roza surveyed the piece of track where under a slither of moon a few hours earlier he had imitated a thousand years of erosion by drilling and inserting chemicals to split the nose from the outcrop. He was relieved and happy to see he had successfully split the outcrop. Large jagged boulders had fallen perfectly and now lay strewn across the track.

CHAPTER 16

The Circus comes to town.

0400 Hrs.
TORTILLA FLATS
USMC BASE HQ
COLONEL PATTON'S OFFICE

USMC Colonel Larry Patton, who would have loved to have been related to the famous General George Patton of WW2, but wasn't looked up from some papers on his desk he'd been shuffling around, waiting for the first stirrings of daylight.

"Morning, Lieutenant Walker. You've won this morning's prize. You get to take your patrol out again and check every inch of the road the VIPs will use. I can't believe anyone could sneak into the Base, but look for any signs of incursion. Gil, you've done two tours in the sand box so you've been there and done that. Same story look for IEDs. It's doubtful, but who knows? And, of course, anything that is out of place. Anything son. Big deal today, I don't have to tell you," the Colonel said to the young Marine Officer standing before him.

"On our way, Sir. For what it's worth, I'll be glad when our Commander in Chief and all these Pollies go back to where they belong," the young Officer said.

The Colonel made to return to his paperwork to camouflage his smile at the Lieutenant's comment and then looked up.

"You, me and every Jarhead on Base agree on that one. I know the likelihood of any attack is slim, but still, with the Russian and now the Canadian Assassinations, it is a crazy new world. Off the record, POTUS is either extremely brave or just plain stupid to leave the Whitehouse at the moment. But, who am I to ask such things?" the Colonel said quietly.

He knew the Lieutenant was a squared away Marine, but everything about today's visit was above everyone's pay grade. The Colonel silently prayed that the Australian Company, Silent Archer, that had developed the two-vehicle Anti-Unmanned Aerial System he had deployed along the VIP's convoy route would operate as promised. It had been adopted by the U.S. and Australian Military and had performed incredibly well in demonstrations. One of the main features was it was vehicle-mounted and therefore mobile. Most importantly, the system did the whole job; detect, assess, and destroy. It threw up a screen of protection against Drone Attacks, whether single or in a swarm. The Colonel had deployed three of the two vehicle sets. A set consisted of a Radar Vehicle to detect threats, the other to electronically disrupt any non-American Drones. In addition, a third set of two identical vehicles would ghost the convoy. Other vehicles were deployed out of sight to avoid causing concern to the VIPs but still within range to throw up a protective shield. The track had been recon'd several times over the last three days. This final check which Lieutenant Walker was about to go off Base to carry out was just a last tick of that box. 'Plan for the Worst but Hope for the Best' was always going to be the Colonel's fallback strategy. A few minutes later, the Reconnaissance Patrol approached the Main Gate of the Tortilla Flats USMC Base. As per Standard Operating Procedures, SOPs, the patrol notified the base Radio Room.

"Base, this is Papa Lima Patrol leaving camp, Main Gate. Over," the Patrol Radio Operator called.

"Copy that, Papa Lima. Take care. Over. And have fun. Out," the Base Radio Operator responded.

THE ROCK SLIDE
VIP ROUTE TO USMC DEMONSTRATION AREA.
TORTILLA FLATS USMC BASE
NORTHERN TERRITORY

The Reconnaissance Patrol was switched on even though this was their third go-around, complacency and US Marines had never been partners. "Heads on a swivel, you guys. This is the real one, OK?" The Lieutenant warned his Patrol.

They were the real deal, too well trained to slack off when the Commander in Chief was visiting. They were about halfway through their Recce patrol along the VIP's route when sitting forward, suddenly on alert Lieutenant Walker asked the Driver.

"What's that up ahead, Sergeant?"

"Looks like a cave-in, I mean a landslide, Sir," the Sergeant said, accelerating a little in anticipating what they would find at the scene of the rock slide.

"Pull up beside it, and I'll let Base know," the young Patrol Commander said calmly.

Gee, I would never have thought of that, no wonder you're an Officer. The Sergeant thought to himself. He stopped the Hummer next to the rock slide.

"Ham Bone, Get Base, ASAP." He said to his Radio Operator, who was sitting behind him.

"Roger that, Sir." The Radio Operator squeezed the Press to Talk button or P.T.T., "Papa Lima to Base. Over." The Marine Corporal called into the Mike. No answer.

"Papa Lima to Base, over," the Marine Corporal radio operator tried again.

"No answer, Sir. That hill there is probably full of iron ore. That's why it didn't wear away a squillion years ago like the rest of this flat, empty country," the Corporal said to the Lieutenant.

"We have to get some comms somewhere. Take us up about fifty, just around that next bend." Lt. Walker instructed his Driver. The Marine Hummer idled forward about fifty yards and stopped. Now, if the radio had worked when they had stopped the first time beside the rock-slide they may have gotten out and carefully inspected the damage they had found. An alert marine might have noticed the cylindrical drill-holes in a line across the rock debris.

IN THE SNIPER HIDE
ON THE VIP ROUTE
TORTILLA FLATS USMC BASE
NORTHERN TERRITORY

Roza had deployed technology to ensure that the MarinePatrol had to move away to report the rock slide's existence. He had correctly anticipated a last-minute patrol and was encouraged when the Marines stopped at the damage. As per SOPs when any Patrol stopped some focused at the item of interest, while other Marines scoped the surrounding area. Roza could tell from their body language that they had not discovered his nor the Australian's sniper hides.

He had anticipated correctly that the rock cave-in across the track would distract the searchers in any case. Just as he had choreographed, they had stopped near it, staying in their vehicle while they tried their radio for a couple minutes. Then he observed the Patrol move away about fifty metres or so. He noted the dust being blown around by the Humvee's exhaust settled, suggesting that they had turned off the motor. He let a breath through his teeth that he had been holding as he waited for them to follow his plan.

"OK, Jimbo, this is far enough. We will see if our buddy here has discovered iron after all," The Lieutenant said calmly to his Driver.

"Try again, Ham Bone; they are probably outside having a smoke," the Marine Officer stated.

Close on five minutes later, static broke the silence of the Radio Office.

"Papa Lima to Base. Over," the Marine Corporal Patrol Radio Operator called into the Mike.

This time, an instant response. "Copy Papa Lima this Base, over," a distinctly Southern drawl replied.

Sir, I got 'em on the line for ya," Corporal Ham, the Patrol Radio Operator, called to his Lieutenant, who was standing off the track looking through his Tactical Binoculars at the rocks covering the track. The Officer quickly walked back to the vehicle, resting his foot on the rock guard step as he took the mike.

"Base, this is Papa Lima 1, I need direct comms with Mr George. Over," the Patrol Officer's Call Sign was Papa Lima 1. Mr George, the standing Call Sign for the Base Commander, Colonel Patton. Lt. Walker knew that the Base Commander would want to question him on this new intel. Especially, with only a few hours to go before the VIPs would be on the track.

"Base to Papa Lima, copy that, wait one, over," the on-duty Base Radio Op said, as he put the mike down and picked up the phone to get the Colonel.

While concerned that he was needed in the radio room, Colonel Patton was secretly happy to have something to do to stop the ongoing videos of things going wrong that had been playing in his mind's eye since he woke.

Corporal Jones, the Base Radio operator, stood as Colonel Patton entered his small office. Saluting, he immediately set about re-establishing the link with the patrol.

"Base to Papa Lima, over," he said clearly into the hand mike.

"Base, this is Papa Lima 1. Is Mr George there. Over?" Lieutenant Walker asked.

Taking the Mike from the Sigs Corporal, Colonel Patton responded.

"Papa Lima 1, this is Mr George SITREP. Over," the Colonel demanded a Situation Report.

"Sir, Dalmatian has significant damage. Over," Dalmatian was the assigned Code Name for the track that the VIPs would later traverse.

"Copy that Papa Lima 1, full report over," the Colonel demanded.

Lieutenant Walker reported using the formal USMC Reconnaissance Report Format, employing only the relevant sections.

"Mr George, Recon report as follows.

ALPHA: eleven mikes from your loc.

BRAVO: fiver-three-three, two-four-one, I say again. BRAVO fiver-three-three, two-four- one, over," providing the exact location as a grid reference.

"CHARLIE: Type X. I say again, Type X," describing the track as an all-weather route.

"FOXTROT, Code 2 is CRITICAL," Code 2 referred to the width constriction.

"Mr George, this Papa Lima 1 description of damage and impact follows. A rocky outcrop at this location has collapsed and covered the track. In the vehicles assigned, this will cause the slightest diversion without any identifiable risk. End of Report Over," the Lieutenant released the call button on his Mike.

After a few moments, the Colonel responded. "Papa Lima 1, are there signs that this slide was man made, use of Bang or machinery? Over," the Colonel asked.

"Mr George, Negative, the rocks have just collapsed under the outcrop, no dispersion or spread. Over," Lt Walker answered.

"Copy that. Complete Recon. Great work Papa Lima 1, finish Recon and R.T.B. Over," the Colonel ordered.

"Copy that. I will see you on my return. Over," Lieutenant Walker concluded the transmission.

OUR BARRACKS
TORTILLA FLATS USMC BASE
NORTHERN TERRITORY

Dawn was threatening as a yellow glow broke through the trees that seemed to fence the horizon. I bent to shake Ben's shoulder.

"Come on, Ben, you look good enough; you don't need any more beauty sleep." The room filled with the tantalising aroma of strong black coffee as I poured two mugs.

"Yeah, well, Steve, you should have slept in by the looks of you," the American CIA Operative said as he yawned and climbed out of bed.

"Today's the big day. We get to ride around in that beach buggy on steroids, and then you go home. Are you excited or what?" I asked as I handed him his coffee.

"*Or what, probably.* Did we drink a bottle of J.D. last night?" he asked, feigning a headache.

"We did, but we were solving the problems of a troubled world, so it had no effect," I stated sounding serious, but smiling.

We both laughed and started to get ready to meet up with the circus when it arrived.

ORDERS GROUP
TORTILLA FLATS USMC BASE
NORTHERN TERRITORY

Minutes later, the Colonel called an Orders Group earlier than scheduled, demanding that anyone involved in protecting the President of the United States and the British and Australian Prime Ministers must attend. The room was abuzz with energy that this number of warriors carried with them like a distinctive odour. Especially with everyone wondering why the O Group was called early.

Colonel Patton stood and addressed the high-powered group.

"Gentlemen, thank you for coming so quickly. As you'd expect, I sent out a final Recon this morning before dawn. The Patrol Commander has reported some damage adjacent to the route the President will take later today," the Colonel stated calmly.

The room exploded with nearly every attendee asking all the same questions.

The Colonel, just like them, had asked the same questions, but he also possessed the answers.

"Gentlemen. Please hold fire on the obvious questions. I will brief you thoroughly. Hopefully, this will answer your questions," Colonel Patton said with authority. Supported by a quickly prepared PowerPoint display. He went on to show the group photos of the rock slide the Patrol Commander had taken of the scene. The Colonel went on to evaluate each image, addressing whether the rock slide had closed the Top Secret route. He emphasised that the fallen rock had not been dispersed and appeared to have simply fallen away from its original setting.

This he stated confidently, confirming that the damage was not caused by an explosion of any sort. Therefore, it did not appear to be man made. Lastly, he showed a very clear photo of the track blocked by the rock fall from above, a Drone photo. This showed that a vehicle could easily sidestep the rocks with a slight turn of the wheel. The convoy could then proceed, probably without the VIPs even noticing the slight chicane as part of the winding dirt track.

"Now, are there any last-minute concerns or questions?" he asked the room full of security and protective services representing the U.S.A., U.K. and Australia.

He had spent many hours with this group, briefing them and listening to their concerns and suggestions. Mutual respect and empathy had developed organically, and Military men always eventually found ways to work together, being goal-oriented and following orders that drove this. Everything had been covered, and all parties knew their roles and responsibilities. This is what they did. The room murmured assent and a buzz of 'Let's get this done'. The Secret Service representatives stood and shook hands with their counterparts from the Royal and Specialist Protecting. RaSP, as it is better known, is part of Protection Command and looks after the Royal family and the British Prime Minister. You would have thought they were about to leave the locker room to start a football game. Winfrey and I were like poor relatives invited to a party for the rich uncle. We stood, anxious to get out of there. Everyone knew we were 'OK' but not mainstream. They all knew I wasn't A.S.E.O., our equivalent to the CIA, while Winfrey was CIA. Not being part of the official party, we were seen as token tourists. That is, if seen at all.

The Colonel spoke again, "Convoy ETD is zero eight hundred hours. Please note we are dealing with VIPs, and as you already know, that is like herding cats. With all due respect." Laughter spread across the room as Colonel Patton continued, "OK, gentlemen, Godspeed, and see you all back here for a celebratory drink, my shout as our Aussie mates say, in approx five hours." The briefing was over.

Every briefing or Orders Group we had attended was the same. We weren't there, never mentioned, never included in discussions or direct orders of procedure or plans. We were Ghosts; that was our job and our designation. Within the group, it was as if we were invisible. We returned to our barracks, where we changed into our bush gear. We hydrated in prep and rechecked our weapons yet again. I went outside at zero-seven-four-five hours and kicked over the L.S.V.

"Come on, Winfrey, stop brushing your hair. That dog is gonna bark any minute, and the circus wagons will move on. I don't want to miss that parade," I said from the door of our hut.

I had started the Marine Buggy a few minutes earlier; in this heat, it probably wasn't vital, but, old habits, I liked to warm up any convoy vehicle. I felt weird because I was dressed in A.M.C.,

Australian Multicam. However, to be on net with the convoy and all other support troops, I was wearing a Helmet with fully integrated coms in the style of the O.C.P. Occupational Camouflage Pattern favoured by the USMC. Winfrey, being a Yank and no longer Delta Force, was kitted out one hundred per cent Jarhead. The Military had learned a lot about desert vehicles during the Gulf War in 1991. Desert Patrol Vehicles (D.P.V.s), formerly Fast Attack Vehicles (F.A.V.s), were deployed extensively during Operation Desert Storm. Eventually, these were replaced by Humvees in general Military use.

However, the gunned-up beach buggies still had a role to play, mainly with Special Forces and the Marines.

To become accustomed to the Buggy, we had driven it since we arrived on Base three days before. These things could carry a fifty cal, even TOW Missiles. However, before signing for the Light Strike Vehicle, assisted by the motor-pool team, we stripped it down to pretty close to a bare shell. Winfrey and I still had our personal weapons, but it was only a four-hour operation. We would be OK with minimal fuel and water, virtually no recovery gear, and definitely no fifty. We would have plenty of Marines to help if we got bogged, and this wasn't Iraq or Afghanistan. This was good old oz and we were surrounded by thousands of well-trained Marines, and it was remote. If this Base wasn't the middle of nowhere, I was sure you could see it from here.

Finally, Winfrey graced me with his presence and we mounted up.

"Glad you could make it, mate," I laughed.

"Just like Nam, you Aussies always want to get everywhere first," The CIA Agent laughed as well.

"We are both too young for Nam, so did you read that somewhere, or have you been studying Chuck Norris movies?" I asked with a smile.

He laughed. "OK, let's head over to where you and I identified a good position to join the convoy," he said, putting on his game face.

"Sounds like a plan. Have you turned on your radio link?" I asked.

"No, but let's do that. Hopefully, these Marines will keep the chatter to a min, but it'll be good to have Control over-watching the whole deal," Winfrey said, clicking the On button on his helmet.

I did the same and headed for the main gate. Credit where credit is due, SOPs that apply immediately before a VIP convoy is about to pass through their checkpoint would be that no one but that convoy moves. However, we had informed Major Patton of our plan to tag onto the convoy en route. Clearly, he had briefed the gate sentries as they raised the boom and waved us through as we approached. I enjoyed driving the L.S.V. as my first car had been a Manx Beach Buggy, one of those fibreglass Volkswagen conversions. Many a happy hour had been spent roaring up and down South East Queensland beaches. The girls loved it until it rained or started to get a bit cold. My mind drifted back to those days many lifetimes ago as I flicked the Mil Buggy through a few bends in the track. We arrived at the loc where we would park and wait for the VIPs to come alongside, and then we would simply tag along.

CHAPTER 17

Time for the grand parade.

IN THE SNIPER HIDE
ON THE VIP ROUTE
TORTILLA FLATS USMC BASE
NORTHERN TERRITORY

The Assassin was buzzing with anticipation; doing Recces, researching, and planning were only stepping stones to the hit. Today, they all came together. The fact that he hadn't been wakened through the night by a Marine Patrol poking their M16A2s into his ribs meant a couple of things. It confirmed that neither he nor his Australian helper had been discovered, and it meant that his plan was on track. 0515 Hrs Roza reached for his rifle as he observed the Marine Patrol in case they were here for him. Instead they discovered his handiwork with the rockfall. It had all gone to plan as though he was directing their steps with a remote control. As always Roza left nothing to chance, thinking through every scenario every twist and turn. As well as splitting the huge rock last night, the Assassin had deployed two hi-tech eight-band jammers in preparation for the hit. One was to disable the USMC radio the patrol was carrying. The other jammer would close down any cell phone traffic accessing the nearby Phone Tower. He had hidden an Electronic Warfare or E.W. jammer adjacent to the rock slide. This was why the Patrol radio wouldn't work when the Humvee was parked beside the rocks.

To disable any cell phone use Roza, although exhausted from the rock drilling had driven slowly across the plain under the moon's soft glow making his way towards the phone tower. He was had enjoyed the cool desert air as the breeze dried his sweat-soaked clothes. Before he could return to his hide he had one more detour to make. Roza appreciated the irony that an Australian Scientist had invented a cell phone jammer he was about to deploy. Fitting the device to the Base of the telephone tower, he had set the timer for four hours before the VIP visit. In the morning, the Assassin knew the jammers he had planted were functioning perfectly when he saw the Patrol Commander unsuccessfully try to use the radio and then his phone.

Roza had thought it through his plan depending on this communication black out causing a quick look by the patrol who would then failing to discover the drill holes that would be visible now the rock had fallen away. This was a crucial factor, but his risk evaluation was acceptable and proved correct. He had planned the radio jammer to force them away from the rock slide when the Patrol Commander needed to find somewhere his radio or phone would work so he could report the damage.

The Assassin hadn't been able to find out when the President's convoy would leave the Base and pass his hide. He had assumed that good security would mean that the Final O Group would see the E.T.D. time released. This didn't concern him; to a world-class sniper, waiting was like breathing, so automatic that the time wasn't even registered. Hidden in his rocky hide Roza had a great field of fire over to the track the President's vehicle would use.

However, he had no way of checking his Australian assistant cum decoy; his last sighting was as he secured the front corner of the cam net. He was happy, though; the Humvee was only visible to the Assassin because he knew the hide was there. Roza surveyed the track and was relieved to see that the Marines hadn't repaired or cleared the rock slide.

ZERO HOUR.
TORTILLA FLATS USMC BASE HQ.
NORTHERN TERRITORY

Colonel Patton had handed command of the base to his Adjutant, Lieutenant Colonel Norris, while Patton accompanied his Commander in Chief in his specially prepared Humvee. The motor pool had modified the seating in the rear to four, two up and two down, they had tinted the windows and beefed up the A/C. The President, while still comfortable, was clearly enjoying this departure from his usual Limo that came with a minibar and kidskin upholstery. The convoy consisted of a forward Scout Hummer two hundred yards ahead of the main body, it carried the front mounted M240 Machine Gun. Well back from the Scout two more Humvees crammed full of Marines in full battle rattle rolled just in front of the VIP vehicle. The next Humvee in the convoy carried two Secret Service (more to satisfy their needs more than operational reasons) plus any spare Marine Officers. The armament, deployment and the perceived threat seemed to be in correct balance. It was, after all, a Restricted Area, a USMC Base in an isolated part of the world. The Sweeper or the last Humvee in the convoy carried a few leftover Officers heading out to the demonstration area.

Col. Patton was sitting beside the Driver a crusty old Marine E-9, Master Gunnery Sergeant, named Eli Jennings. They had served together in Iraq and Afghanistan and enjoyed each others company. The Australian Prime Minister and the English Prime Minister sat facing backwards so they could converse freely with the President who faced forward. The convoy's wheels began to roll at zero-eight-ten hours. Col. Patton thought to himself that alone was a miracle. The planned spacing was in place by the time they reached the main gate. Col. Patton had delegated the Base Command to Lt. Col. Norris, whose radio Call Sign was BRAVO 5 . He had also appointed Major Bates as Convoy Commander, deciding that he had to focus on being a tour guide for POTUS.

"All Call signs, this is BRAVO 5." Norris didn't wait for a reply as inside the Base all radios would have a strong signal. "OK, everyone, heads on a swivel; don't relax until you're back behind the wire," he stated calmly from the Base Radio Office.

"Convoy Commander, you have control. BRAVO 5 Out," Col. Norris said over the convoy's assigned frequency.

"Copy that, BRAVO 5. Out." Major Bates said as the forward scout vehicle passed through the gates. The Sentries, forming up in a straight, line saluted their Commander in Chief.

As planned, Winfrey and I were parked up about a mile down the route, and when we heard the Command handover messages, we knew it was on.

"Here we go, mate. Time we earned those big American dollars they pay you," I said to Winfrey as I put the L.S.V. into gear.

The C.I.A. Agent sat up a little straighter as we awaited the convoy. We had parked at right angles to the track to see its approach clearly. However, due to our role, we were hanging out about a hundred and fifty yards East of the track they would use. Once the V.I.P. Humvee containing POTUS and the two Prime Ministers, passed our loc, we would keep the distance from the track but staying up parallel with the HVTs Hummer. We could see the dust cloud the convoy was throwing up before we saw the forward vehicle.

I edged the L.S.V. forward with a throaty rev as the main body of the convoy came around the corner, pacing ourselves to maintain the gap between us and the President's and the Prime Ministers' Hummer. After a while, I turned to Winfrey to see if he was still awake. He gave me the thumbs up and a smile.

"Yeah, I'm still awake, the way you hit every pothole sees to that." He said.

The convoy had been travelling along as though it was riding on rails. Due to it traversing a dirt track and not a Washington three-lane, the speeds were down, but the vehicles maintained a steady pace and demonstrated spacing. I knew the Marines had been practising for weeks, and it showed.

One way to the demonstration area was eighteen miles; I turned to Winfrey as we passed about the halfway.

"My Boss was right; this is a bit boring. But, don't get me wrong, I'm happy with that," I yelled above the Buggy's engine.

"We've both been around long enough to know that can be a worry in itself." Operative shouted back.

"That rock slide should be coming up soon if that Patrol Commander can read a SatNav screen. Hopefully, we will hardly notice the convoy go around it if it's as described," I said, checking my SatNav as I took a suck of water from my camel-back.

Right on schedule, I spotted the untidy spill of rocks that had covered the track. Something in my gut pinged, but I let it go, not mentioning it to Winfrey. The Lead Hummer veered around the rock slide. All seemed well so far.

The Humvee carrying POTUS, the British PM and the Australian Prime Minister was still on our left. We were maintaining the hundred-metre ribbon away from the track. All good, the President's Humvee smoothly skirted the pile.

Roza checked his monitor one last time to be sure the Australian Mick was obeying his instructions. The Assassin knew he couldn't have done anything about it if the young Aussie had been stupid and moved around, potentially compromising the whole deception.

It was good to have a complete picture; a warning of a few seconds could prevent his capture. He was glad he had installed this to remotely control the Australian's action or at least be aware of it. He wasn't smart enough to know he couldn't be punished from that distance. However, the young Aussie knew he was being observed, and this encouraged his close obedience to his orders.

Well, except for his flask of rum which was unknown to Roza. The Assassin recalled his conversation with his Australian helper as they had made their final preparations before heading out to the Marine Base.

"Why are you screwing that camera to my window sill, mate?" Mick, the Aussie, had asked.

Roza was trying to sound more local, "Well, mate, it's for two purposes; first, for me to be able to look around at what's going on. Second, I can keep an eye on you, so you don't get tempted to walk around the hide when you get bored. Between Satellites, Drones and Helos we can not exit our hides. Not for any reason, OK. I'll know if you do. Just follow your orders, and everything will be fine," Roza had said menacingly. Luke noticed the change in tone, but wrote it off as stress.

As the first signs of the VIP convoy came into view, the Assassin's heart rate showing no change, appearing as calm as though he was lying in bed reading a boring novel. He had remained hidden under the cam-net but could still observe the track from the entrance. He, too, saw the dust plume alerting him to the convoy's imminent arrival to his Kill Zone. The timing here was absolutely critical. He wanted to shoot from his vehicle while being seated in the driver's seat and using the padded windowsill as a rest, this way he would still be able to drive away if the need arose. He didn't expect it would, but the time to climb back into the Hummer might be the difference between him escaping or not. The plan was to immediately remount the Hummer when he witnessed the Forward Scout vehicle pass the rock slide. He would then edge the Humvee forward just enough to give himself a field of fire but the bulk of his vehicle to stay under the net behind the rocky ridge. Once he had executed the V.H.T.s he would quietly reverse the vehicle back into the hide and wait. Unusually, his actual escape wasn't to be immediately after he shot. It would take nerves of steel, but he would wait until the coast was clear, while the Marines were distracted by his decoy. That was the plan.

He was pleased with his choice of weapons. Roza the Assassin had assessed early in his planning phase that a long shot on a well-guarded moving target was, even for a world-class marksman like himself, a low-chance shot at best. He had also planned to take out his next three Targets together. After looking at weapons, distances and other options he eventually chose a Russian-built V.S.S. 'Vintorez', originally developed to take out terrorists in urban settings. Chambered with subsonic 9 X 39 mm rounds, coupled with an integrated suppressor, Roza was sure his position would not be betrayed by either muzzle flash or noise. These same rounds could effectively penetrate 2nd-grade body armour plates at two hundred metres. This was vital to penetrate the bullet proof windows. He was also sure that the U.S. Secret Service would require the American President to always wore a bullet proof vest. This was the driving force that had required the Assassin to creatively and covertly bring the target closer to his hide. So, by his orchestrating a little rock slide, he had closed the distance to a workable figure. The weapon could put shots in a ten-centimetre circle at a hundred metres.

However, Roza's usual surgical precision was not an option with this hit. He flicked the rifle to auto. This was all against a quality Assassin's one-shot one kill maxim that he had lived by, but flexibility was always just as important as rigid rules. The thirty-round magazine would be empty by the time the Assassin was quietly returning the Humvee back into its hide.

"BRAVO 5, this is Charlie One 1, you copy. Over?" The co-Driver of the Lead Humvee said and released the send button on his mike.

"Charlie One, this is BRAVO 5. Over," the Convoy Commander's responded.

Winfrey and I heard the positive report regarding the rock slide and the ease of going around it.

"Charlie One, this is BRAVO 5, Roger that. OUT," the Convoy Commander stated calmly, knowing that all call signs had heard the coms and that as reported earlier the convoy could proceed around the rock pile without concern.

What was that? Something had caught my eye, the slightest flicker of sunlight off a reflective surface, maybe from a telescopic sight lens. Without thought that would slow me down. Instinctively, I pulled down hard right on the small diameter sports wheel of the Buggy and buried my foot on the gas pedal. The acceleration threw the Buggy sideways and kicked up a solid wall of dust and gravel. I had created a natural smoke screen. Quickly figuring angles and distances from the target to the shooter I attempted to place our vehicle between the reflection and the VIPs. I screamed the L.S.V. towards where I had thought I'd seen the reflection. I'd had no time to brief Winfrey or radio the convoy.

Winfrey screamed, "What are you doing?"

As he did so, the Buggy slew sideways and he saw the windows of the President's Humvee shatter. Neither of us had seen any muzzle flash or heard any sound of shooting. It was clear that whatever weapon had been deployed was an auto and quiet. An automatic weapon usually makes lots of noise compared to the one chance you have of hearing a single shot. However, in a split second, I assessed the situation. In a close protection scenario, we would have, of course, covered the Principal. Typically, we would have headed in as fast as we could but we were already too far away from the President to cover him. I had decided that the current status of the V.H.T.s wouldn't change with our rushing into the convoy loc and that they already had enough people around them, even if it was only for first aid. We were going to hunt down whoever was shooting.

Reefing on the wheel to fly right had caused the Buggy to fishtail, and the rear wheels seeking purchase in the soft dirt raised a thick red cloud. As I powered through the dense cloud of dirt and gravel, we saw a Marine Humvee lurch from behind a small rocky ridge straight ahead of our loc.

I pushed the accelerator through the floor, and the engine screamed in complaint, but it responded beautifully, just the same. Although the Humvee in front of us was identical to all the Marine Hummers on base, it simply couldn't be legit. We were the outer wheeled cordon; anything past us was airborne, whether a Helo or one of the many MQ-9A Reaper U.A.V.s Marine Drones.

This Hummer had to be the Assassin; in any case, he was running. The bigger 4WD had a massive engine compared to our overgrown Beach Buggy. However, we had better acceleration and could fit in places the Humvee had to lose time avoiding. After a couple of miles, these little pieces of gained time added together, and we were nearly alongside the fleeing vehicle. We confirmed that there was only one occupant; this was another tell-tale as the Marines always travelled in pairs as a minimum.

Fifty metres further, Winfrey had a clear profile view of our Assassin. Tempting as it was, I couldn't risk a glance over as one of the L.S.V.'s small front tyres would roll us for sure if it hit a log or rock.

Winfrey knew better than to use the radio; he yelled above the screaming motor.

"Steve, we got him, what now?" he asked because as he knew the standard two-car shuffle wouldn't work. We both knew our vehicle would live up to its name, an L.S.V., with the emphasis on Light. Us trying to hit the rear panel and push the Hummer into a spin was akin to a Cheetah trying to roll a Rhino.

Unbeknown to Winfrey and I, the Assassin had conned dumb Luke one last time. The gullible Australian had one more action that Roza had commanded him to follow:

"Now, Mick, it won't happen, but if any Marines get close, have your rifle on the seat beside you. Now, really slowly, just rest the barrel on the window sill. Then they will know you're legit and probably drive on past. Do it when the gate sentries stop you, and they'll let you through," the Assassin had said sincerely.

Winfrey yelled that the Driver of the Humvee was a Marine Major, or at least he looked that way. I was about to reply when Winfrey interrupted me.

"Gun, Gun."

Smiling, the Hummer Driver slowly raised a weapon above the door sill.

The CIA Operative reacted as anyone in the same position should. Winfrey opened up with his weapon, sending a burst of ten rounds into the USMC Hummer running beside us. The bullets stitched a neat diagonal line across the Driver's door, neck and face, and the last few shattered the windscreen. Without the Driver's foot pushing the gas pedal, the Humvee slowed and then stalled. I drove over to the immobile 4WD, and we got out. We couldn't be sure there wasn't someone hiding below the windows so I cautiously went in first; Winfrey covered me from the Buggy. Once I had come around the nose of the L.S.V. and had a full view of the Humvee. I cautiously edged along the side of the Hummer and reaching through the shattered window checked for a pulse. Confirming that the driver was dead, I called,

"Clear, all clear."

Winfrey climbed out of the roll cage, dismounting our vehicle, and came to the same side as me to avoid any danger of a crossfire situation if something happened.

We both had to shout over the Buggies noise as I hadn't turned it off.

Sarcastically, I said, "Well, it seems he was alone, and you ruined our chances of questioning him."

"Yeah, I figured I wouldn't act like in the movies where they always let the enemy shoot first," Winfrey replied.

As I walked further around the Hummer, I said, " Well, a few answers might have been helpful, but I'm glad you reacted faster than he did. But I tell you one thing, he may have been in USMC Major's uniform, but he wasn't what he seemed."

Winfrey radioed in, and we waited for all the players to arrive. Neither of us knew whether the hit had been successful or not. Whether our Principals had been assassinated on our watch. That was the end of our private conversations.

Two Helos landed nearby kicking up a storm of dust, and several Hummers skidded to a halt blocking our path. The Marines poured out like meat ants stirred out of a mound. As per their training, they looked outwards and formed a perimeter around the Assassins and our vehicles.

NCOs yelled commands and we stood awaiting all the questions we knew must come. What wasn't noticed was the small camera that was mounted on the Driver's door sill.

CHAPTER 18

Things are seldom what they appear.

The attack had been meticulously planned, innovative and audacious, and after the Russian President and Canadian Prime Minister's assassination, it had shaken every Political Leader worldwide to their foundations. That the President of the United States could be attacked at all, was amazing in itself. For it to happen in the middle of a United States Marine Corps Base on full alert only emphasised the enormity of the action and the quality of the Assassin. For once all the usually competitive alphabet services and law enforcement agencies throughout the world believed these hits had to be from one Assassin. They were all too intricately planned and executed for anyone to think it was coincidental or even a copy cat situation. By us immediately turning towards the reflection that had caught my eye, Winfrey and I had placed enough pressure on the shooter to disturb him. Thankfully, the thirty-round burst that was supposed to rake the back window and rear seats, killing the President and the two Prime Ministers had failed.

Sadly, the same burst the Assassin had to fire blindly due to the dust created by our L.S.V. had struck and killed the Driver Master Gunnery Sergeant Eli Jennings who had taken the full brunt of the attack. Col Patton had been hit in the shoulder, fortunately the bullet had deflected out and not into his chest cavity. Clearly, if the shooter had fired unimpeded, the President and the pair of Prime Ministers would have been slaughtered as well.

In progressive stages, the entire scene had been taken charge of and passed from one group to another, claiming jurisdiction and or expertise for investigation. By the time POTUS was safely back on Airforce One, the President's bullet riddled Humvee had been cordoned off, as was that of the shooter's vehicle. We had been commended for our quick action in catching the shooter. However, our intervention that had possibly saved the President's life only came out during the investigation and was always going to be a theory. The Assassin's plans were found to be intricate and creative. Looking into the dead shooter's history in and around Darwin, they discovered that he was an unlikely Assassin and that even a tiny part of the planning was above him. He was a local, had a rep as someone who didn't have steady work and spent any money he did earn on booze. Nothing about him, his skills, intelligence, experience, funding, and especially motivation, suggested that he was a world-class Assassin capable of this sophisticated assassination attempt.

Initial investigations confirmed that his Hummer had been stolen a few weeks before, along with the USMC Major's uniform he was wearing at the time of his apprehension and death. The investigators had brought in a Geologist and a Mining Expert to assess the rock slide as, on closer inspection of the debris, the cylindrical drill holes had finally been noticed. Later, the expert's report stated that a rock-splitting chemical called EXPANDO had been used. Who could believe this stuff? It wasn't difficult to trace the purchase. Our super-intelligent Assassin had used the name he had been throwing around locally. When the dead Australian was researched, it came to light that he had worked as a contractor on Base. CCTV confirmed this showing his ute coming and going. This would have explained his knowledge of the entry points and topographical features.

They were sure he was a patsy to the real Assassin. But where was this man? How had he escaped the Base when it was on High Alert.

Unbeknown to any of us, the real Assassin had demonstrated his confidence, courage and commitment to staying on plan. He had sat quietly in his own Hummer parked back in the rocky hide that was closer to the track where the attack had occurred. The Assassin watched us fly by with ice water flowing in his veins. His diversion had worked, the Australian taking off in a Humvee as he had been instructed. This magician's redirection worked perfectly because the second Hummer had flown out of the hide. With seconds to assess the correct angle for the shooting and probable distance for a sniper, it had drawn the attention of every Marine in proximity. These actions were enough for all concerned, including us, to be sure that he was the Assassin attempting to bug out in the aftermath of the attack. The Assassin had watched the lightweight Buggy pass by and chase the decoy Humvee. The Assassin had watched the finer details of his escape plan play out until every vehicle drew out of sight.

As he sat in the hidden Hummer, his thoughts ran through the mental checklist he had created for this escape phase of this op. He did not know whether his decoy Assassin had made it, stranger things happen when this type of chaos hits. Roza's end plan for Mick, his Australian helper, crossed his mind; *If by some miracle he made it through the boundary gate by impersonating a USMC Major, I'll have to end his life. It would be disastrous if he was caught later or just bragged about knowing me after a few rums. There is no way I can leave him to tell the authorities how, when and most importantly, who.* Roza had waited until twenty hundred hours the following night; now, he was sure he was alone in the desert. He deducted that the decoy must have got a good distance from his hide before being apprehended. He believed this because he knew that every second Marine on Base would swarm around the Australian's Hummer and Roza had not seen any traffic. He had observed the attacked convoy recover quickly and return towards Base. Since then all had been quiet. Once again without lights, he headed for the disguised break in the boundary fence, exited and was on the highway back to Darwin before midnight.

Five miles from the Base Roza turned off the unfenced and deserted highway. He stopped beside a Landcruiser ute he had stolen two days before. He put down the Landcruiser's windows and enjoyed the cool desert air. His disciplined mind worked through every aspect of the operation. Why had it failed? Every part of his plan had rolled out like a red carpet. The Lieutenant doing the Recce had missed the drill holes, then manipulated by both the coms jammers the Assassin had deployed worked a treat. Like clockwork, the Recce Patrol had moved away from the rock slide, so they had coms. Of course, Roza couldn't be certain. However, the body language showed a lack of any urgency. It suggested that the Lieutenant was reporting that he was sure the collapse was natural. And that although the debris covered the track, it did not cause any significant danger to the VIP's route as it was east to side step.

The actual attack phase had also been on script. Seeing the dust cloud raised by the VIP carrying Military Hummers, the Assassin had edged his vehicle forward in his hide. The nose was still under the cam net, but to put his window sill in line for the field of fire, he was in front of the rock that had successfully shielded his Hummer. He knew this was the weakest and most vulnerable part of this op. All the benefits made this risk worthwhile. On cue, the predictable convoy configuration of a Scout Vehicle leading the way came around the rocky corner. The Assassin's trigger finger twitched as he remembered what happened next. Allowing for the forward movement, the he had sighted on the President's Humvee. Taking up the pressure on the trigger, he loosed the contents of the thirty-round magazine. There that was it. On a usual sniper-type hit, Roza had trained himself not to be distracted by any external stimuli. Literally, a bomb could explode beside him without affecting his aim. And yet.

Roza thought it through; he rewound the mental video of his attack on the convoy. Then he had it in his memory. Without any apparent reason a Marine Buggy had slewed sideways, clearly heading in his direction. The fishtailing Buggy had raised a dust cloud temporarily blocking his view of the Target vehicle. The Assassin had kept the pressure on the trigger until the weapon went silent after the hammer hit an empty chamber. With no hesitation, his cat-like reactions had the motor running and the vehicle in reverse, gently returning to the darkness in the rear of the rocky hide. He was banking on the Buggy's crew reacting without really being sure what they had seen or what had worried them. He knew the decoy Hummer hide was in a straight line directly behind his location. He was putting everything on the table. It now depended on the young Luke Edwards. Roza remembered what he had told him before they had left their garage.

"Now Luke this vitally important, so please focus. You can see the track from your hidy-hole. Now, mate, as soon as you see the convoy stop, this is what I need you to do. I want you to take off like a bat out of hell and head away from the track as fast you can go," Roza had paused to emphasise the seriousness of this order.

"In fact, I just had a thought, if you get this right I will give you a Twenty-Thousand- Dollar bonus. How does that sound mate?" the Assassin said convincingly, knowing whatever happened the promise would never be kept. Roza knew how Military personnel were trained and would react. The Marines, disorientated by the convoy stalling unexpectedly would look outwards to all points of the compass. They would see the other Hummer take off and the chase would be on.

Roza hoped they would fly past his hide in pursuit of the only vehicle they could see from the track. The crew of that Buggy had ruined his shot; their vehicle and dust were just enough to fire where he had last seen his Target. At over eight hundred rounds a minute, this distraction was a millisecond, but it was sufficient to cause the bulk of the projectiles to miss their Target, the VIPs in the rear of the Hummer. The Assassin knew for certain that he had still hit the President's Hummer. However, the outcome was yet to be confirmed.

Anger and revenge were not usual emotions or actions experienced by Roza, as an international Assassin. However, this felt different. His red-hot fury dripped like fat onto a fire; it crackled and sparked. That Marine Buggy's action, even though random in the long run, had cost him. His reputation of never failing to fulfil his kill contracts had been destroyed. In addition to this, his progressive payment would never be banked now.

He was relatively wealthy already from the Russian and Canadian ops plus his lifetime savings. However, due to the importance and number of High-Value Targets, this contract represented his retirement fund. In dollars, they had cost him millions.

Roza decided right there as he headed for Darwin that whoever they were, they would pay for their intervention, their intrusion into Roza's life.

Australian National Security Centre
Canberra Australia

Two months later, the report, redactions included being a C.I.A. document, was provided to the Australian National Security Centre. Colonel Goodrich allowed me to read through the over nine hundred pages. A pleasant way to spend another wet day in Canberra. I was interested in all of it, especially the weapon used and the ballistic forensic results surrounding the actual shooting. The weapon found in the shooter's Hummer explained the lack of noise. It also explained why the shooter had set up in close compared to where most snipers or hitmen would have. Ballistic testing confirmed the weapon was the same calibre as used in the assassination and that it had been fired recently.

Due to projectile distortion, there was a lack of absolute confirmation regarding matching the actual bullet to barrel rifling grooves. While this was unusual, it was not unheard of. The fact that G.S.R. Gun Shot Residue had been found on the shooter's hands and arms assured everyone that they had the right man. All the VIPs were safe and uninjured, and the assassination attempt had been thwarted. The last paragraph stated that it was unfortunate that no trace of who hired the Assassin was discovered. The motivation behind the attack was impossible to confirm. However, due to the Targets, political reasons could be assumed.

After studying the report, I was back sitting in Colonel Goodrich's office waiting for my Boss to get off the phone.

"You sure of that? That changes everything. I'll get back to you; yeah, he's sitting in front of me right now," he said into the phone.

Taking a mouthful of coffee, I wondered who he was talking to. I didn't have to wait too long to find out. He hung up and looked at the receiver thoughtfully. I gave him time to re-group his thoughts before talking to him.

"Steve, welcome back; well, we couldn't have been more wrong when we all thought your mission would be boring," the Colonel said as he picked up his coffee cup.

"That's for sure, Sir, we still don't know any firm details. They quarantined each segment of the whole op. So Winfrey and I only know what we saw and did at the time," I stated.

"Speaking of Winfrey, is he here? Did he end up staying on for a while like you planned? Is he going back to Roma with you after we debrief?" the Colonel asked.

"No, after what happened, you can imagine what Washington was like. They recalled him as soon as we were dismissed from Darwin. We are both still wondering how an Assassin could get so close to the President and our Prime Minister in the middle of a Marine Base," I said.

"I can't help but feel a bit sorry for Colonel Patton. It looks like he'll be OK, that is after a few more shoulder operations. He has a good reputation, and they wouldn't have him as Base Commander if he was a turkey," the Colonel said sincerely.

"Sir, I agree. Everything we saw of him was spot on, with no fuss or anything, and his O Groups were thorough and smart. He's not an ego tripper. We saw him listen and adjust as different stakeholders chipped in. We both thought he did a great job.

Of course, that won't save him; he'll probably be commanding a base in the Arctic or somewhere within three months give or take his shoulder," I said.

"Steve, you did a great job up there, and until a few minutes ago, everyone in the know believed that you and Winfrey's quick reactions had killed the Assassin."

I resisted the temptation to interrupt. What did he mean by suggesting we hadn't chased and stopped the shooter?

"Anyway, Steve, it's all turned upside down. They have only had a few days to investigate the entire attack. They were a bit concerned by some of their early background checks. The guy you dropped was a local yokel with no job, no political profile or friends, and pretty well no education. Definitely no Mil service of any kind. Bluntly, the bloke was a yobo who drank whatever he earned," the Colonel said.

"I know it's all TOP SECRET as you would expect and we only have a few details, but that Aussie doesn't sound like a mastermind international Assassin to me. You know, I don't believe in coincidences. Do you really think this local bloke hit the Russian President in his Kremlin office and the Canadian Prime Minister in

Abu Dhabi?" I said, thinking of the rumours circulating on the Base. There were scraps of Intel about the rock slide and even someone jamming coms in that AO, Area of Operation," but you know Mil Bases, Sir, rumours are what they run on," I said.

"Well, I was just talking to the Officer in Charge of the investigation. And the opinion of many of the investigators lines up with the Aussie not being the real Assassin. That there was actually another shooter. Sorry, Steve, they are beginning to think you and Winfrey got a decoy," the Colonel said.

"Of course, that doesn't take anything away from the fact that your quick action spoiled the aim of the real shooter, even if you didn't actually know his location," the Colonel said in a friendly manner.

I had been through too much for the Colonel's statement to upset or offend me, but he had undoubtedly raised a concern.

"Sir, why would they say that?" I asked respectfully.

"Well, in the full light of the next day, a team of investigators followed your Buggy tracks from the VIP route to where you apprehended the alleged shooter. As they slowly travelled toward the known hide, one of them saw a cam net hanging on a rock feature closer to the track. Apparently, it was about halfway between where the President's Hummer was hit and where you saw the shooter escaping from. Further investigation revealed a sort of ad-hoc vehicle park between small rock ridges about three metres wide and maybe seven metres deep. They discovered that the net that had alerted them to the hide was the length of the vehicle park, a roof that camouflaged the entire set up," the Colonel said.

I was in a type of shock at these revelations.

"Sir, I s'pose it couldn't be a leftover from Exercise Talisman Sabre last year? There were Marines and most of the Aussie Army crawling all over that Base for that exercise," I said hopefully.

"They actually thought of that but were able to dismiss that possibility quickly. Steve, there's more. They proceeded towards where you intersected with the dead shooter's tracks. Guess what, the second cam net they found turned out to be another vehicle hide, virtually identical. They said the best way to you envisage the hide would be to imagine backing a Humvee into the mouth of a sea container shape. Two parallel rock walls, deep enough to secrete a Hummer and both with a cam net roof," he said.

I stood up, feeling uneasy with this news. I grabbed my coffee mug and filled it up, gesturing to the Colonel to see if he wanted more. He waved my offer away and continued.

"The other startling news, or, more accurately, evidence, was found when the Forensic Team ran a check on that Russian rifle you took off the guy you stitched. Now, it had definitely been fired recently and he tested positive for G.S.R. But here's the kicker, Steve; the projectiles they recovered from that unlucky Gunnery Sergeant driving the President's Hummer don't match the rifle you found in his hands. Therefore no murder weapon on hand," the Colonel said with a shrug.

"That's impossible, Sir; it all happened in under three minutes. Shots are fired at the VIP vehicle, Hummer takes off, and we catch up and shoot him in preemptive defence. He has to be the Assassin, Sir," I said feeling shocked, hoping I sounded more confident than I was starting to feel.

"Steve, no one doubts anything you just described, but with time, some forensic investigation and good old-fashioned observation have brought new information forward. I think that's about all from my side Steve. I realise this has unsettled you, but I don't think there is anything more for you to do. Mate, you may as well head home to your beautiful bride to be. Of course, I'll let you know if I hear anything else," Colonel Goodrich said.

Half an hour later, I was on my way back to the Canberra Airport, my head still spinning with these revelations. I was looking forward to seeing Chris and my dog, Jake.

CHAPTER 19

The best day of our lives arrives.

THREE MONTHS LATER.
ROMA.
QUEENSLAND.

"I don't know what I'd do without you girls," Chris said to the three best friends cum bridesmaids.

"Have a little more bubbly; it'll calm those nerves. Your hair is amazing," Cheryl her Chief Bridesmaid said.

They had all spent close to three hours at the local hairdresser. She and all the girls had gone to school together, played sports together, and even starting to go out with the local farmer's sons at the same time. The other two girls were chirping like a pair of grass parrots interspersed by giggles that suggested that there may have been a few empty bottles of bubbly in the bin. Cheryl had done a great job organising, moving them along, and even staying off the plonk so she could drive.

"Couldn't have our favourite local copper Chrissy getting done for drink driving on her wedding day now, could we?" she had said as they piled in the car to head off to the hairdressers. All the their nails had been done the day before, she thought; all items ticked off the list, *so far, so good; when we get home, time to get all dressed up.*

Arriving home from the hairdressers later that day Chris asked, "Cheryl, did Jake get a bath, and did you lock him on the patio to dry. That dog will always find something disgusting to roll in otherwise?"

"That's the third time you've asked me about Jake; yeah, he's fine. He's probably happy to be outside and away from the noise all of us girls are making," The Head Bridesmaid said gently.

"OK, Chrissy, time to make you the most beautiful bride in all of Queensland. No, make that Australia. Let's gown you up, girl, you first and then all of us," Cheryl said, thinking not for the first time that; *maybe she should have limited the bridesmaid's intake of bubbly. I hope they'll be right. We still have about three hours, it should be OK.*

"I sure do love that dress we chose, I can't wait to see the look on Steve's face. At least being cold today, we won't all be melting, especially the boys in their dress uniforms," Chris said excitedly.

Time seemed to fly by as the bride and the bridesmaids donned their gowns. Filled with the joy that the day was bringing the girls laughed and chatted as they helped each other to complete the finishing touches to be perfect for the big occasion. Finally the big moment arrived as Cheryl placed the veil on Chris's head. The girls all stood in silence blown away by how stunning Chris looked.

The wedding was now less than an hour away.

"OK, I think we all look amazing so let's get this show on the road. Girls you head off in Judy's car, I'll follow you once Chris gets picked up. I'll see you girls down at the church.

Chris, the Limo will be here in about half an hour to take you to your loving hero," Cheryl said with a huge smile. She noticed Chris had a little tear in her eye, understandable, but a call to duty for the Head Bridesmaid. They all hugged one another, with lots of giggling, at the same time being very careful not to smudge makeup or mess up their hair-dos.

In the calm that followed Chris carefully sat adjusting her beautiful white lacy wedding dress so as not to crush any part of it, resting only on the edge of the lounge. She sat soaking up the first peace and quiet the house had experienced that day, or in fact several days. Somehow understanding that the three girls had left his home,

Jake came in from where he had been sleeping in the sun. He sidled up to Chris, presenting his two ears, letting her know that they really needed scratching. Steve was his master, his hunting buddy, but Steve was MIA, and Chris was here most of the time.

Looking out of the motel window into the car park full of white 4WD utes belonging to gas pipeline fly in fly outs. I smiled as I thought, *I'm sure Chris's management planning of the weather ordered a cool sunny day.* The morning of our wedding had turned out cold, and the westerly wind blew, making it even colder. Because Chris and I had lived together for just over two years now, it was decided that I would move into a motel on the other side of town for the wedding day. Roma isn't huge, so we figured that at least either end of town would minimise the chance of us running into each other. We knew it was supposed to be bad luck to see each other on the day of the wedding, so we joked about not doing Face Time. I think the truth was that it was Chris's way to keep me out the way of the girl's wedding day preparations. Neither of us could sleep the night before, so Chris and I talked on the phone until the early hours on the big day. Chris was excited about all the plans and was looking forward to all the different stages the day held. Me, I was just wanted us to be married and everything return to normal. I have been in the sandbox a few times, jungles all over the world and big cities plying my trade, usually ending the life of some well deserving enemy of our country. I had been outnumbered by hard men with knives or guns, and sometimes just one mean monster twice my size. I had seen death and felt the bite of hot metal. But today, I was more doubt than I could remember ever having. I wasn't second guessing myself I was way past doing it twice. My mind invaded by random thoughts; *Chris is too good for me in so many ways, she always made me want to be a better man.* I loved her and wanted to marry her more than I could explain but I was scared of wrecking what we had, after stuffing it up last time. All night and all through that hour or so before dawn, when it somehow gets even colder. I shivered not from this morning mist but feelings of dread. Chris could read me like a book if we were face to face, but I could hide it on the phone. I got away *with it*. But I didn't get away *from* it.

If I had been downrange and felt this way, I would have known what it was. A highly developed gut feeling that had saved me and others many a time. If I had been in some war zone in harm's way and my gut was sending me messages I would know that the enemy was here, close, not in sight, but still here just the same. I shook myself as I thought; *Well, it can't be that I'm in Roma in rural Queensland and it's my wedding day.*

In the Best Western Bungil Creek Motel Colonel Goodrich (today I could call him Pete) and I were ready to drive to the church. Well, nearly ready, one more job before we go. Unbeknown to us, just like the Bridesmaids, we too were doing our own pre-parade inspection.

"Pete, do you know where these little flowers go?" I asked sheepishly.

"Yeah, I vaguely remember my wedding and these little things, can't remember what they're called," he said, laughing.

"OK, prom date, I'll do yours now, then we've got time for a celebratory drink and off we go for you to re-up for life," he said as he took my 'posy' from me and pinned it on.

"Since when have posies been approved as part of our ceremonial dress uniform?" Colonel Pete asked.

"Yeah, I know, Sir, I mean Pete, but Chris wanted this little romantic touch. Seeing that I hadn't made a decision for about two months now, it was a given. Anyway, hopefully, when the Brigadiers see the wedding photos, they won't notice or care," I said, laughing.

"Anyway, stop talking; I can always tell you talk more than usual when you're nervous. I don't know what you have to be nervous about; you're just walking the plank. I think we both need that drink, and it's your shout," he said, getting two tumblers from the cupboard. I got the ice and the square bottle that had been full the night before. Knowing what I had to go through in the next few hours I poured us a generous drink and laughed.

"You know, it's funny. I must admit it's kinda nice to be wearing this formal gear without having to go to a funeral or an ANZAC Service. Today should be a lot of fun," the Colonel said as he toasted us with his Jack Daniels.

"Pete, that was a very wise suggestion, having my buck's night two days ago. I'm getting too old for big nights these days. We all did it when we were younger, rolling up, and acting fine on parade at 0500 Hrs. The thought of having a buck's do the night before and ending up chained naked to the local cop shop's fence just isn't me. Especially seeing the Senior Sergeant was our designated Driver on the big night," I said as I swilled the last of my JD around the ice cubes.

"Yeah, Steve, it was a bit tame, just 'mature' fun, but let's face it, Roma isn't exactly Kings Cross Sydney. Nothing like a huge feed of ribs at the Club Hotel with a lot of drinks there, and then visiting several other watering holes after, to make a good night," Goodrich stated, enjoying my grimace at the memory of my sore head that resulted from our 'mature' outing.

"I'm not sure if it was a good idea to spend all afternoon at the RSL (Returned Serviceman's League). I don't think we paid for a single drink because although none of those old diggers know what I really did, they obviously know I am current. And with your haircut and look even for a desk Officer, it's not hard to work out that you don't sell cars for a living," I said, knowing the Colonel was every bit a warrior Soldier.

"I do remember the drinks. It was a bit embarrassing, but I couldn't say no, and they were enjoying it too much. Of course, it didn't hurt that they all knew and loved Chris too," the Colonel said as I grabbed my keys and threw them to him.

"As an Officer who is a meticulous Ops planner, this question is probably insulting. But, you remembered to give the rings to the stand-in father of the bride so he could put them in Jake's special collar?" I asked more from nervousness than really doubting him or even needing a reply.

"I knew I'd forgotten something," he said laughing.

The trip to the church was uneventful, with Pete Goodrich taking his time and making sure nothing happened to the bridegroom in the home straight. We could have walked in any case. Just up the road from our Motel the Bungil St Saint Paul's Anglican Church seemed to loom in front of us. It is a beautiful church, built before the Second World War an old-style church with stone arches and pillars. Chris was convinced that the photos would be 'Amazing', quote, unquote. After Pete and I adjusted our swords and caps, we entered the cool of the old stone church which seemed quite gloomy after the bright Western Queensland sunshine that we had been praying for.

I was hoping my face didn't show how nervous I was. I knew I had no doubts about marrying Chris; it couldn't happen soon enough for both of us. This was a nervousness I remembered, that had once plagued me as a young Second Lieutenant just before a big parade or ceremony. I wasn't sure what it meant or where it came from. Probably, that I didn't want to muck it up, I suppose. Later, but definitely in a different way, adrenalin just before a jump or the beginning of an assault had always masked any fears I carried. We sat silently and waited for all the invited friends and family and of course the blushing bride to arrive.

The pew was starting to feel hard on my butt as we sat in the shady church. It wasn't the hard wooden seating that was making me feel uncomfortable.

"Pete, you know waiting, holding is a given when you're in a hide. Once, I had to wait nearly thirty-two hours for my Target to arrive into the KZ. I gotta tell you, the last quarter of an hour is the longest fifteen minutes I can remember," I whispered.

My Colonel, now my best man smiled, clearly enjoying my discomfort.

"Sorry mate, but it's pretty funny to see one of the calmest operators I've known to squirm in this type of deal. Steve, I've seen you two together. Mate, a blind man could tell that she obviously loves you. I could see within ten minutes of arriving the other day she is so excited about getting married. She'll be here mate. Relax, OK?" This warrior friend said. "And Steve, don't you ever tell anyone I said all that soppy stuff," he laughed and slapped my shoulder.

CHAPTER 20

How white can quickly turn to black.

"Babe, do you want me to help you with that?" Cheryl the Chief Bridesmaid asked seeing her friend trying to sit down, and struggling with the hooped underskirt of her dress.

"No thanks, I'll be right. Chaz I'm a bit worried about Jakey. He's so smart and there has been enough changes going on for him. " Chris said as she continued to arrange her dress on the lounge.

Jake the Border Collie knew something was on, something was out of the norm. His soft master Chris had just called him off the patio. Chris's hooped wedding dress surrounded her making it hard for him to reach him. Jake couldn't understand why he couldn't nuzzle her legs like usual. She brought him to the side of the lounge instead of in front of her and scratching his ear took off his collar. The dog wondered what was coming next. Chris brought out that strange collar, the one with a little red box attached to it. Steve and Chris had been putting it on Jake two or three times a day for the last couple of weeks, letting him walk around with it, getting used to the feel. Of course, Jake didn't know it, but the two wedding rings would eventually be placed inside the velvet box for him to walk down the aisle to the front of the church.

"Chaz, I couldn't have got all this done without you. Thanks so much," tears welling up in Chris's eyes.

"My absolute pleasure, and honour to be asked," Cheryl said tears forming again in her eyes.

"Goodness, I'm glad Steve isn't here to see all these tears. He'd think I was having second thoughts," Chris said trying to laugh and fanning her eyes to protect her make up.

Cheryl looked at her phone to check the time.

"That wedding car should be here any minute mate. Do we know where our favourite Senior Sergeant might be. He's cutting it a bit fine," she said looking at her friend and smiling, before turning from her to wipe away a small tear of joy."

As she went to put her phone down it vibrated in her palm, surprised she answered. "Hey, were your ears burning? You should be here, it's nearly time that you guys were on your way to the church," the Chief Bridesmaid said trying not to sound too Bossy to her friend's Boss.

"I know, I know, that's why I'm calling. I've been held up at the Station, Plan B, I'll meet you guys outside the church, OK?" Senior Sergeant Townsend stated unhappily. The connection ended.

Just as Cheryl was explaining to Chris that the Sarge would be late there was a polite knock at the front door.

Cheryl restricted by her gown shuffled up the hall towards the front door opening it to discover a good looking man in a chauffeur's uniform waiting at attention, his cap ceremonially tucked under his arm.

"Good afternoon Mam, I am here for the Beautiful Bride, Ms Jackson if the lovely lady is available?" he said in a deep voice with the slightest tinge of a foreign accent, linked with the use of 'Mam'. Cheryl thought; *Maybe American, I don't care, he is a hunk, wherever he is from.*

Cheryl's excitement level escalated as she walked back into the lounge.

"Chrissy, the Limo is here, you right to go babe? Actually, he's so good looking I might swap cars with you," she whispered giggling.

A minute later Chris, with Cheryl holding her elbow for support, made her way up the hall towards the front door. Jake followed the girls, his paws making a pleasant tapping sound on the polished wooden floor. The Chauffeur did not move until he saw the Bride approaching the front door. He straightened up even more if that was possible.

"Good afternoon, Mam, my name is Andrew and it is my absolute honour and pleasure to escort you and the dog to meet your future husband at the church," he said with a huge smile.

"Good day, Andrew, lovely to meet you. Thanks for coming," Chris responded in her friendly country town manner.

"Oh Mam I wouldn't miss today for a truck load of money," the Chauffeur said sincerely.

Seeking visual permission for Cheryl to relinquish her support of the Bride's arm. He offered Chris his elbow, assisting her down the porch steps to the garden path heading towards the gate and the waiting Limo. Jake didn't really quite growl, but Chris heard him make a sound that meant that he wasn't happy about something. Jake was staring at the Chauffeur, legs stiff, his back fur standing up.

"Jakey behave, he's OK. He's allowed to take my arm," Chris said thinking it was unusual for Jake to dislike someone like that and instantly.

Cheryl faithfully followed behind, catching up and lifting the hoops of Chris's dress. They got through the narrow gate framed by magnificent rose bushes that sighed under the weight of their dark red blooms. She continued to carry the dress hoops as they crossed the footpath to the waiting Limousine.

Looking around, the Chauffeur turned to Cheryl, flashing a thousand watt smile, "Thank you for your assistance Mam."

He then opened the rear door. Being a professional he hid his disdain when Jake the dog was told to jump in first. Just before Chris climbed into the Limo she looked around the street where she had lived for over a decade. She gave a wave and a smile to her neighbours who had come out of their houses to see her leave, wanting to share in the Chris's special day. Most of the street's residents had come onto the footpath to see their local girl all grown up, dressed up and WOW, look at that Limo. Cheryl, ever alert to Chris's needs assisted her again to settle into the Limo. Then she stood back and offered some last words of encouragement.

"See you there Chrissy, you look fabulous girl," Cheryl said as she stood back.

The Chauffeur moved forward to close the door. He then went around and got in behind the wheel.

As they drove away Cheryl wondered; *Why is the Limousine heading away from the church,* rationalising the observation by thinking; *He's probably taking the long way there to ensure the bride doesn't get to the church too early.*

Jake was sitting up alert and looking out of the tinted window as if he was used to always travelling first class in a Limo. Chris starting to feel tired from the emotional stress sank into the plush upholstery and closed her eyes for a moment's rest. She felt the car make a turn and opened her eyes taking in all the polish and chrome, it even had a little bar with crystal decanters and an ice bucket.

Chris began to wonder why the Chauffeur had turned left instead of right at the end of her street, however, she too rationalised this; *Well, he is not a local so he wouldn't know the quickest way to the church.* She was patting Jake and checking the ring bearing collar for the third time when she started to feel a little discomfort about the detour.

She hesitated again thinking; *Maybe, he's ensuring that the Bride keeps the Groom waiting for the accepted* time. *I won't try and direct him yet. Oh, hang on, he's definitely lost. One more turn and we will be heading out on the Mitchell Road.*

"Hey Andrew, mate, I figure you're new to town, but this is definitely the wrong direction," Chris said, trying to sound much calmer than she was feeling.

Chris was immediately concerned when Andrew didn't respond in either word or actions.

She knocked loudly on the glass screen separating the front seat and the rear compartment of the Limousine.

Still no reaction from the Chauffeur. Chris was an experienced Police Sergeant and was well known to be unflappable on the job. However, the shock of this happening, whatever was going on, when it should have been an exciting happy experience had thrown her completely. She tried to calm herself so she could think this through. Ensuring the Chauffeur could not see her movement she tried to open a door. It was centrally locked, she was a prisoner. Now she lost it.

This time she grabbed the ice tongs to bang on the divider and started screaming, however, the Chauffeur acted as if he had not heard anything. He didn't even turn his head to look at what was making the noise.

They drove on for about twenty minutes on a road that Chris had driven and patrolled dozens of times. But this familiarity did nothing to ease her fears. They had grown from wondering about his navigation to strong concerns, and now her fears were fully blown into unknown monsters. Was this someone who she had upset in her Police work? She was an experienced cop who didn't forget faces. Chris was certain that she had never met this man calling himself Andrew before. Maybe, he was seeking some sort of revenge for an unhappy relative or something. She thought; *Come on girl. This is Roma rural Queensland not New York or something out of a movie. This sort of thing just doesn't happen not here and not to a local general duty Police Sergeant like me who isn't even a Detective. What could all this be about?* Chris knew she needed to be strong, and was annoyed with herself when she had to wipe yet another tear away. Sadness hit her like a punch to the stomach as she remembered that only an hour ago her tears were of expectation and joy, shared with her best friend Cheryl.

Abruptly, the Limo slowed and left the highway shuddering its way across a cattle grid as they entered a fifth generation cattle property with the name Waterloo displayed over the main gate. Ten minutes into the station a well used side track took them over to a shady billabong. Chris knew the waterhole well because unbeknown to the Chauffeur it was a favourite fishing spot for some of the Roma locals including her and Steve.

Over a hundred years of cattle coming in to drink the mud and dirt around the water hole had been ground to fine dust by thousands of hooves. The Chauffeur sat patiently behind the wheel, waiting as this dust cloud raised by the Limousine's own tyres settled or blew away assisted by a light breeze. Finally the Chauffeur opened his door and with a remote control he was holding opened the rear doors. As quickly as her gown would allow Chris slid over to the side away from where Andrew the Chauffeur was standing. But, he was too quick for her. As she exited the Limo he seized her wrist squeezing it tightly, which caused her to scream in agony. Chris thought and hoped that he had forgotten about Jake. She knew that the loyal dog would tear the Driver to pieces where he stood, especially when the dog heard her scream. However, the Chauffeur was never to be underestimated, he always thought ahead, every opportunity, any contingencies were considered and his plans would incorporate these to guarantee success. Still held in a vice type grip by the wrist, Chris stepped aside to allow Jake to launch from the Limo's back seat.

In the days before when thinking about the way today would go the Chauffeur had been unsure if the Border Collie would attack.

However the dog's subtle reaction back at the woman's house when tested by a stranger touching his master had predicted that the Border collie would indeed attempt to defend the woman.

Fascinating, as he had never had a pet, but now he believed what he had heard that dogs could sense a man's character or even intentions. The dog's owner should have trusted the animal's character perception, oh well, 'too bad so sad'.

There was no warning growl, no scratching of claws on the back seat's upholstery as the dog launched from the Limo's rear seat. The Chauffeur's battle sense warned him as it had in so many places and times before. As the dog leaped from the Limousine the Chauffeur smoothly pirouetted as if he had expected this exact scenario. And, this was the case because he not only expected it, he had attempted to prompt the dog's attack purposely by making the woman scream.

Unseen by the woman or the dog the Chauffeur's other hand held a razor sharp three-hundred and five millimetre green handled knife. His lifelong success was founded on making sure the smallest details were known and integrated in every plan he developed. He had taken his time selecting this knife. It was for a single purpose, one use only; to quickly dispatch an attacking dog the size of a male Border Collie. He had observed the Target's dog in its yard the week before, and had noted that it possessed unusually long legs for that breed. In addition to this dog's physical make up Border Collies were famous for their agility and speed. He anticipated that this extra height when combined with the fact that the dog would be launching from the back seat dictated a very specific knife. The Chauffeur had decided that he needed a long, strong and wide blade to slice into the dog quickly, instantly inflicting the maximum damage as it penetrated the dog's chest cavity. He also assessed that the whole weight of the dog would land on him and even wounded would have the potential to dislodge the knife when pinned under twenty kilos of snapping angry dog. Especially if a flood of blood lubricated the knife causing it to slip from his hand. To overcome these factors the LSK-01 OD Green Large Survival Knife was highly suitable with its palm and finger grip sculptured handle. He had even further roughened the surface of the curved grip to help him keep hold just for the required second or two. He was confident that he had been one-hundred percent correct with his selection. Now, he was about to find out.

Jake flew at him like an arrow, capitalising on the Chauffeur being momentarily distracted. Chris shook free from the Chauffeur's grip and fell backwards to the ground, cursing how cumbersome her bridal gown made her. The Driver took a classic Karate stance. His front foot facing forward, back foot a shoulder's width behind and at right angles to his front, knees bent a little. A stance of strength to counter an attack from the front. Jake enraged by the troubled screams of the master he loved attacked without fear or hesitation. The Chauffeur tightened his grip on the knife ready to receive the dog's attack. Between the lightning speed of Jake's attack and the Chauffeurs counter attack the knife entered the beloved brave dog unseen, the razor sharp blade masked by his flowing black and white coat. Jake's scream betrayed the dreadful reality that he was fatally wounded and was dead before his body thudded to the ground.

Chris, was horrified by what she had just witnessed. Then the Tsunami of shock hit her. As though to torture her beyond her remaining sanity the Chauffeur bent over the beloved Jake's corpse. Chris frozen in grief and fear could only sit in the dust and watch what followed. Grinning mercilessly the Chauffeur roughly grabbed Jake's head by both ears causing his tongue to loll sideways from his mouth. Making sure that Chris was watching he bent Jake's lifeless head back, and once again using his knife he drew the blade across the dead dog's throat. Seemingly motivated by Chris's cry of anguish he sawed through the animal's neck until the weight of the dog's lifeless body pulled itself free from the now decapitated head dripping with blood.

"OK, Chris, can I call you Chris? Of course I can, in fact I can call you anything I want and do anything I want," he said leering at her. "Now, that was necessary, I don't like dogs anyway, and especially ones that attack me. That last part was for a couple of reasons. Firstly, to take away any doubt or hope you might have been holding onto, in case you were thinking that this was some mistake, mistaken identity or something. Secondly, that you have any chance at all of escaping. Forget it. There is nothing I haven't thought of and prepared for," the previously friendly Andrew the Chauffeur said harshly with a smirk.

Chris hated to show weakness at any time, and she knew that she shouldn't let this mongrel have that pleasure or encouragement. However, the emotional roller coaster she had been on today was beating her into submission. On the day that should have been the best in her life, the Limo ride to the church had thrown her wedding day off track on a hairpin turn. And she had landed hard. She could already tell the man before her was a master of psychological torture and manipulation. However, she had learnt by hard experience from this nightmare that he was clearly skilled at intricate planning and the execution of it as well. Although she didn't realise it at the time, shock building on shock was crushing her spirit. Sitting in the bull dust she looked down her once beautiful white wedding dress, now filthy and ruined. Feeling useless at reacting to such a stupid thing under these circumstances, Chris burst into heart wrenching sobs. She thought about the last time she had cried this hard and how Jake had tried to console her by licking her tears away. Thinking of the Border Collie she squeezed her eyes shut. As much as she tried not to look at the mutilated body of the dog that she and Steve loved so much, she failed. Jake who was so smart, so loyal and had shared so much of their lives. Now gone forever. It was all too much for anyone to comprehend or to cope with in just a short time. She rolled onto her side just in time to vomit into the dirt that she lay in, rather than on her dress.

Because he had not introduced himself properly when he had sarcastically asked if he could call her Chris she could only think of him as the Chauffeur. Whoever he was, he had walked out of sight behind the Limo. She hated him for so many reasons. The fact that he had kidnapped her for starters, then killing her beloved Jakey, and now she could actually hear him laughing as he saw her retching into the dirt. This man could not possess a heart. She believed in God, in Heaven and Hell. Maybe, he was a Demon.

The Chauffeur returned dragging something heavy. At first whatever he carried was hidden behind his body. Chris could see that whatever it was must be heavy as he struggled with it. She shrank back in horror as the murderer threw a man's body on the ground next to poor Jakey. Chris realised that the man was only dressed in his underwear.

The Chauffeur smiled like he was Chris's best friend.

"Chris, may I introduce you to Andrew, the real Andrew that is. He's your Chauffeur, the one who was to take you to your wonderful fiancee Steve baby," he said with venom.

That made Chris think; *how could this animal know Steve? All this was more than any nightmare could contain. Being kidnapped, Jakey and now this innocent man, murdered as he was just trying to make a living driving her to her wedding. How could all this be? How did it all fit? Who was this psycho who stood in front of her next to the dead Chauffeur? Who was he? Why was this happening, what did he want?* She felt another tsunami of fear and shock roll over her.

The Chauffeur then took a jerrycan of fuel and soaked the Limo and the two bodies.

Chris was terrified that as he clearly hated her so much, he would burn her alive by tossing her on top of the bodies of Jake and the real Andrew. The fake Chauffeur took off his uniform and threw it on the fire.

Chris couldn't help but notice that his body was like Steve's; ropy muscles, a flat stomach and jagged scar tissue here and there all over him.

She shrank back as he approached her thinking he was about to cut her head off or simply soak her once beautiful dress before he set her alight.

Instead, he picked her up by the shoulders and dragged her away from the funeral pyre. She was terrified in any case.

He carried her some distance from the Limo and bodies, and she was surprised to see a white Toyota Landcruiser she had failed to notice before. Unceremoniously, he dumped her on the ground, she didn't feel it as shock had numbed her for now. Through a haze nearing unconsciousness she saw the man get dressed into jeans and flannel check shirt. She had decided that at least for now that she was in no shape to escape. Chris had never felt so tired in all her life. In any case she knew she wasn't dressed to walk fast let alone run anywhere, the hooped wedding dress was akin to having her ankles tied together.

All of a sudden Chris realised the man had disappeared. Fear filled her again, she was terrified by the unknown after what she had seen this man do so far. A loud WHOMP coming from behind the Landcruiser accompanied by a wave of hot air from under the 4WD hit Chris. He had now torched the Limo, the dead Chauffeur and poor Jake. She sobbed and starting shaking. When he returned he roughly dragged her to her feet. Turning to face away from him she felt him undo the top button of her wedding dress and slide the zipper down to her butt. Just when Chris was sure her day could not possibly get any worse, she realised that she had been so wrong.

"Are you going to rape me now, what have I ever done to you?" Chris asked with a tremble in her voice.

"Don't flatter yourself, this is purely professional and the only hint I'm giving you is it's virtually got nothing to do with you. You're of no more value to me than your little furry friend barbecuing over there. You are just bait for the real Target. So get out of that stupid dress, we have to get a move on," the man said without any emotion. He then threw her some jeans and a tee-shirt.

"Put these on, and hurry up. We have wasted enough time already." Roza said.

CHAPTER 21

A Bride, a Man, a Dog and a Limousine disappear, but the Black Dog returns.
ROMA POLICE STATION
THE NIGHT OF THE WEDDING

As soon as everyone had realised that Chris and the Limo were missing Senior Sergeant Townsend sent out the usual Missing Persons Geo-Targeted SMS to every cop in Queensland and neighbouring New South Wales emphasising that Chris was one of their own. That had been nearly six hours ago. And nothing, not a sighting even a false one, just nothing. The Senior Sergeant was exhausted in every possible way. His thoughts drifted to a similar day when that terrorist business had shaken his quiet country town, a year or so before. That was the fateful day that Steve Wallace had saved Chris's life and with lots of help destroyed the Taliban Training Camp. Just like on that terrible day everything appeared good, normal, even quiet but again Roma's tranquillity and reputation as a safe place to live had been shattered. Things had changed, one minute he had been in his best uniform, annoyed at not making the Limo ride with Chris to accompany her to the church and then down the aisle. Next minute she had disappeared. He had manned the Station all night while the Police Vehicles never stopped searching up every dirt road and track looking for a glimpse of the missing Limousine. As the sun was peeking through his office blinds exhaustion won and he had just closed his eyes, hoping that when he opened them again that he would find the whole disaster turned out to be a sick nightmare. He woke with a start as Police Constable Wes

Faulkner rushed into his office. "Boss, Boss, they've found the Limo. It's out at the billabong just inside Waterloo Station," the young Constable nearly shouted.

Looking up with red rimmed eyes Senior Sergeant Townsend jumped to his feet.

"They find anything else Wes?" he asked quickly. Both he and Faulkner knew he was really asking if they had found Chris's body.

"No firm details at this stage Boss. Gus Hough phoned it in, I told Gus, you know him he's the manager out at Waterloo. He said that he and Judy were having a cuppa out on the verandah and saw smoke rising. They figured that it was down at the billabong, but they hadn't given anyone permission to fish or camp down there this weekend, so Gus headed down there and discovered the mess. He phoned straight away, the fire was still burning, and he said he could smell flesh burning but couldn't see what it was. I figure from that we can't be too far behind them. I asked him to leave everything alone until we get there." Constable Faulkner said excitedly, as his Boss quickly changed out of his dress uniform into his field service kit.

"OK, Wes call the Hospital and warn them that sadly the new morgue will be needed in the very near future and get onto FSG, (Forensic Services Group), we'll need everything they can send. Find any of our boys we can spare out there to cordon the crime scene. Call State Emergency Services (SES), ask them to be on site at first light. We will need them to search the surrounding area, and direct some traffic," the Senior Sergeant demanded.

"Sure Boss, already called all them except SES, I'll do that right away and then we'll head out there, yes?" Wes said, looking pleased with himself that he had predicted what was needed.

As the Police Landcruiser pulled up short of the burnt out wreck Senior Sergeant Townsend's heart sank as he saw the twisted blackened corpse.

"OK, Wes, whatever we find we keep to ourselves as long as we can. I don't want this to become public gossip all over town. Set up all those lights we brought and get a cordon out. Start from the highway to the gate, then to here. I know that's a lot but we might jag a tyre tread we can mold and match." he said as calmly as he could. Hearing an engine slowing nearby he looked up to see the two forensic wagons arrive.

As with all murder scenes processing it would take days to complete. The team members poured out of their vehicles and immediately put on their crime scene protective outfits. Each knew their jobs and set about taking photos and specimens that would be studied and analysed back at their lab.

Senior Sergeant Townsend drove up to Gus and Judy's place to see if they had any more to add to what they had reported by phone. He could have sent a Constable, but waiting around for Forensics to finish was driving him crazy. He got out of his Landcruiser and stepping around a barking Blue Healer dog stood at the bottom of the front steps.

"You home Gus or Judy?" he called out.

Both Gus and his wife came outside the screen door slamming behind them.

" Hi John, how's it goin down there?" the farmer asked.

"Hi Gus, sorry for all this trouble on your doorstep. I was just wondering if you had thought of anything else." Townsend asked.

"I'll put the kettle on Sergeant." Judy said heading back into the house.

Looking back at the Police Sergeant Gus shook his head. "No mate, I think I covered pretty well everything when I was talking to young Wes after I found the fire." He said thoughtfully.

The Senior Sergeant casually asked a few more questions but nothing new came to mind. Thanking Judy for the cuppa he bid his farewells and headed back towards the crime scene hoping the lab rats had finished.

He still had another hour to wait and was sitting in the Land Cruiser enjoying the air conditioning when Constable Faulkner and a red headed Constable interrupted his peace saying. "Boss, Forensics have released the bodies, and they are packing up and getting ready to head back to town. They said at this point it looks like one human, and one dog. Both are terribly incinerated, they can't even tell the gender of the human remains. It looks like the creep cut the dog's head off, the sicko," Constable Faulkner stated gently.

"Thanks Wes, you escort the ambulance into town. Do we know where Steve is?" Townsend asked.

"Not sure, after I finish at the hospital I'll call around and see if he's at the cottage. What do you want me to do if he's there?" Constable Faulkner asked.

The older cop shook his head.

"I'm not really sure, he will be racing around trying to find out what happened to Chris and his dog. Hopefully, he won't have heard any rumours about the Limo and the bodies. I'd sure love to have the ID of those remains before we tell him about that mess out there. Between you and me, you don't have to be Sherlock Holmes to figure out that the poor old dog they found in the ashes missing it's head has gotta be Jake. Phone me when you know where he is, and I'll make a decision, OK," he said.

ROMA POLICE STATION
2 HOURS LATER

The Senior Sergeant's ring tone sounded. "Hey Wes, what's happening?" he asked.

"Boss, everything went as well as could be expected with the Hospital. The FSG boys have arrived and are starting on the Postmortem straight away. I've been round to Sergeant Chris's place, there were lights on and Steve's old Landcruiser was parked in the driveway. "Boss, it looks like he's home but for how long I couldn't guess."

"OK, Wes we will stall telling him anything, until we know for sure. If that's Chris's remains it will be confirmed by morning, then I'll slip around then and tell him, one way or another.

Once we were positive that Chris was missing along with Jake and the Limo, Pete Goodrich and I had raced home. We quickly got into jeans and Tee shirts and hit the road searching during the rest of day light and well into the night. We didn't have any idea where to look, only what Cheryl had told us, that the Limo had turned in the opposite direction to the church. That was all we had to go on, so systematically we began searching every street and alley across Roma. After I had gone through another tank of diesel driving around town, we filled up again and headed along the road to Mitchell hoping to see something. Discouraged and exhausted we arrived in Mitchell, had a cup of coffee at the roadhouse and headed back to Roma. Colonel Goodrich had to fly back to Canberra the next day so we grabbed a few hours of rest. I had no sleep. My mind was racing with random thoughts about what might have happened. After dropping Goodrich at the airport I headed along the Injune Road feeling like I was wasting my time but I could not rest, driven on to keep trying, doing something, doing anything in the absence of any leads.

Unbeknown to the local Police I had left my ute at the cottage and walked around towards the church. I was looking for anything that was out of place, something of Chris's, just something. It was unlikely that I would find anything but I had driven around without any plan or direction all the previous afternoon and night and had found nothing. I had hit the road at first light returning later for some food and exhausted managed some sleep until mid afternoon. Based on Cheryl's report I had thought searching on foot the surrounding blocks where the Limo may have gone might I might find something. Knowing Chris's as well as I did I was praying that she may have left me some clue.

ROMA POLICE STATION

Senior Sergeant Townsend's phone chirped with a message. It was from the Forensic techs, they had attached the Postmortem Report. Normally, in a murder investigation Time of Death TOD was crucial, impacting surveillance, alibis and flow charts. When the victim has been burnt beyond recognition it is extremely difficult to establish a TOD except when they actually died due to the fire itself. Instead, the M.E. looked for two things initially, the Sex of the remains and COD, the Cause of Death. The Medical Examiner knew who was missing and knew that it would be good news that the remains were that of a Male aged between mid to late twenties. Cause of Death had been confirmed by locating a uniform entry wound to the back of the skull, and the resultant recovery of a nine millimetre projectile inside the cranial cavity. The bullet was distorted and partially melted by the fire however the weight and what remaining shape confirmed the calibre.

As soon as the Limo had vanished three separate but linked 'Look Out To Be Kept For' (LOTBKF), (in America the Police call this an APB) had been issued for Chris Jackson, the Chauffeur and the Limousine itself.

Initially, the Chauffeur was the main person of interest. They didn't have anything better to go on and Cheryl had reported that the last time she saw Chris was as she was getting into the Limo and this was the time Chris had been said by anyone.

Townsend thought; *OK, so unless there were two Offenders, and somehow one was shot, I am pretty sure we have found the real but very unlucky, very dead original Chauffeur.*

The State Emergency Services volunteers had searched the area until near dark.

The Forensic team had discovered what may have been a fresh set of tracks not far from the burnt area. However, due to camping and fishing traffic, just how fresh they were was difficult to know, and may well be useless unless some damage to a tyre tread was identified, and could therefore be used as evidence to place the offender at the scene.

I had known the Roma Senior Sergeant since the whole terrorist camp thing some two years before; we had learned to trust each other through facing a common enemy. After the dust settled and I started dating Chris who was his Sergeant, we began sharing enough BBQs and beers to be mates. I had never seen him so shaken so stressed.

From talking with Chris I knew he would have delivered bad news to so many parents that he fall into that role automatically. I knew as soon as I saw him walk up the path, no hurry in his stride. I thought; *There is no hurry when news about the dead are involved.* My heart seemed to stop beating as I held my breath and waited for the terrible news I had been dreading.

We moved into the lounge, each finding a seat, both uncomfortable and edgy. The old cop did his best to be professional, probably in an attempt to ensure he passed on all the information he had planned to say. He started speaking, and it took all my self control to really hear what he was saying, my senses reeling.

"Steve we have found the Limo now....."

No longer being able to sit still, I jumped up from my chair interrupting him. "Was she there John, is she dea......?" I couldn't finish the word.

Holding up his huge hands he raised his voice above mine. "Steve, Steve, settle down mate, and listen. Now take it easy. OK. The Limo was found out on the Mitchell Road near Hough's place beside the billabong. Everything was burnt."

Something stabbed my heart as I realised that only yesterday we had driven past the front gate not a kilometre from that waterhole. Now there *was* a body incinerated but it wasn't a female. We aren't sure until the DNA comes back but the male remains are probably the real Chauffeur," he said.

Relief flooded my body for a millisecond, but Chris was still missing. The relief was replaced by guilt when I realised that I was happy it was this stranger and not Chris.

"What else did you find, were there any leads, any clues as to explain why this is happening?" I asked, my words coming out like a machine gun's bullets.

I tried to listen, but I couldn't concentrate. I wanted to get out there to examine the scene for myself. His next words penetrated my tortured mind.

"I'm very sorry, Steve. I know how much he meant to you and Chris. It looks like they killed Jake, his beheaded body was on the fire along side the chauffeur's remains. I 'm sorry for being so graphic but in a town this size you would have heard about the mutilation in any case." The senior Police Sergeant said sincerely.

I had cradled mates as they passed on a battlefield more times than I wanted to remember. Grief and loss are a Soldier's lot but Jake, well, he was family. Murdering the soft loving dog I'd raised from a rescue puppy was bad enough but butchering him. This was personal. Many would not understand the crushing impact this had, maybe it was magnified by the stress and emotion of Chris having been taken. I sat there in front of this leathery old copper wanting to scream, to cry, to lash out at something, anything.

Instead, I sat there motionless, my poker face hiding all. I had always made jokes about loving Chris and Jake and of course there was no loving one more than the other. It was a different thing, a dart of guilt flew at me, how could I care so much about a dog when my fiancee was missing? Guilt is a strong force in my life, even without death to evoke it. I realised that the Senior Sergeant was still talking.

To this day I would like to believe he hadn't planned the next part of this conversation. He too was impacted by fatigue, worry and guilt.

"Steve, you know that girl is like a daughter to me. Damn it, I was going to walk her down the aisle and hand her over to you just like her real dad would have if he was alive," the hard Senior Sergeant John Townsend said with a trembling bottom lip.

"John, I hear you, and you know how much I loved her too. I mean, love her," realising I had spoken in the past tense, more guilt flowed in like sewerage. Speaking louder than I had intended, my heart crushed under the thought that she might be gone.

"Love her, love her," his voice was nearly a scream, "The moment you got into her life, she was dead; your whole life is nothing but lies and trouble and death. It hangs around you like a cloud of bush flies," he spat.

More black filth poured into my thoughts: *Yet man is born to trouble as surely as sparks fly upwards. I think that's an old ZULU saying. Am I born to trouble? Do I bring trouble to those around me? Is God punishing me for all the harm I've done?*

"I'm amazed you haven't crawled back into that Jack Daniels bottle you're so fond of," he spat this at me. His Queensland Police Service uniform, all of a sudden hanging loosely on his huge frame, seemed to deflate like a party balloon.

I felt sorry for him, but his words had stung like 7.62, nicking my bicep.

"Blame me later, mate, I feel enough guilt for all of us, but that won't find Chris or the mongrels who have her. Now's not the time for this crap" I said much softer than I really felt.

His tone dropped in volume but not the passion. He turned to go. Looking over his shoulder, his big weathered face red with emotion he said, "I s'pose you're right; I know we need to work together, Steve; I'm sorry about the cheap shot about the JD.

I just can't believe this is happening to one of mine, and here in sleepy hollow Roma," he stated, sounding exhausted.

"For what it's worth, I'm real glad you weren't in that wedding car when it was hit," I said, trying to get a little closer to a man who had been my friend until this threatened to tear us apart.

"Yeah, I missed it because of a late work call. But, you know Steve, you haven't got an exclusive on the guilt. There's not an hour goes by that I don't wonder if I had only been there, could I have stopped it? If I had been, where I shoulda been. I was supposed to be where her dad would have sat, right there beside her" the Senior Sergeant said quietly.

He had vented his emotion the only way he knew through anger, but I could see and hear he needed some support.

"Unless you were carrying underneath that wedding suit, all that would have happened is you would be dead along with that poor chauffeur your boys found on the side of that waterhole on the road to Mitchell. For some reason, mate, your time just wasn't up," I said sincerely, attempting to suggest that I was grateful for that.

Standing, he headed toward the door. Looking back over his shoulder and without sounding overconfident he said.

"Looks like the grubs headed through Mitchell to parts unknown, maybe branched off North or pushed East to the coast."

"Yeah, and by now, they could be down on the Gold Coast sipping Margaritas. There are no leads, are there? We haven't got a clue," I said, feeling so helpless, wondering if he agreed because I hoped my words were untrue. He left without answering.

Happy he had gone, I was sorry he had ever come. I was alone again. For the thousandth time, I imagined Chris kidnapped. I thought about her all alone, terrified, cold and hungry. Chris dead. Not knowing the truth was eating me alive from the inside. I was glad that no one was around. I needed to be alone, like I needed my next breath. I had never needed other people's company. I think it was an American President who said; 'The more people I meet the more I like my dog'.

I love my solitude. That was until about a year or so. Now, I still didn't need company; I only needed one person. Only one, the woman I loved, Chris. Everything within me shouted Chris, barked Jake, but they were both gone. The silence was deafening. I looked up from where I was sitting and there she was, proudly smiling in her Police uniform. I placed my head in my hands and wept. Eventually, I ran out of tears, at least for now. I stood up with my coffee and walked out onto the patio, where Chris and I had spent so much time enjoying the peace at the end of the day. Jake's food bowl was on the deck. When I saw it, my eyes filled with more tears and then became red with anger. I kicked the dish so hard it bent out of shape as it flew towards Chris's sad little veggie garden. I couldn't remember the last time I'd cried. But unashamedly, I sobbed until again I had no tears left and no breath.

THE BLACK PAST
BEFORE I MET CHRIS

Even in the hazy days after I got out of the Army, I didn't cry. I was falling apart then. The Black Dog of depression chewed on me. I was falling apart now. I knew I was, but I couldn't afford to. I had to be sharp for Chris.

Back then, I would head bush.

I was all anger and drinking and killing wild pigs. Nothing worked, but I sure kept trying the same old things. Trying to forget. I knew what I had to do; I wanted to move on like my dwindling number of friends kept telling me to do. Move on, meet new people, get a job, start a hobby. All the different DVA Counsellors I had seen encouraged me to pursue all these strategies. They were well-meaning and well-trained, but it was not for me. My other 'counsellor', Professor Jack Daniels, they didn't know about, seemed to work better, so right or wrong, I spent more time under his care.

I pretty well lived on my mate's cattle property outside town. Jake didn't tell me when to get out of my swag or when to stop drinking and have something to eat. He just loved being in the bush with me. I was too well-trained and careful not to be stupid to chase pigs or deer after a lot of drinks. Jake and I walked for miles every day checking game trails, water holes and thicker scrub. I had everything I needed to be happy. The only problem was I was miserable, which led back to too much thinking and then a few whiskies to dull the aches. I was hiding in the scrub but the recurring dream found me there in my camp, nearly every night.

Of course, that all changed the day I stumbled onto a Taliban Training Camp on the cattle property next door to where I was camped. It's a long story, but that's when Chris came into my life, and I scored a dream set up with the Australian National Security Centre. In the most positive sense, my life had never been better secured between those two anchors. The dreams still visited me, but my days were better.

THE BLACK DOG RETURNS AGAIN

My thoughts were hazy, not from booze but grief, and yet, at times, I could recollect conversations Chris and I had verbatim. Guilt, as usual, raised its ugly head; *every time I was with Chris, I should have been more patient and more interested in what was being said. Could I have come home from the RSL just a little earlier to be with her?*

Willy Nelson or Garth Brooks should sing a song about it, yeah? *Did I tell her I loved her enough?* A few days after our aborted wedding day, I stumbled into the kitchen to make my morning coffee. As I'd done a thousand times, I got two cups from the cupboard, one for Chris and my own. I thought; *You fool, you only need yours, not hers. She's not here, you idiot.* I threw her favourite cup against the wall as though it had leapt from its shelf to taunt me and bitten me like a scorpion. Immediately, I was crushed with guilt and loss; I had just destroyed a symbol of Chris's very existence, of living with me here in our home. Of something she would need when she returned home. Hang on, she wasn't dead. What was I doing? I was acting like she had gone; we didn't know that. It couldn't be true; there was no evidence to even suggest it. My crushing imaginings were interrupted.

The phone was ringing. I could hear it, but it wasn't mine. It was way off, like in a dream. No way, I was answering that. The coffee was half gone; I topped it up with smokey whiskey and headed out onto the deck. Maybe our resident Senior Sergeant was right all along; I was just a drunk. No peace here, no Jake's ear to scratch, no wagging tail. Not anymore. Nothing here anymore but sad, guilt-ridden memories everywhere I looked. What sort of man am I? Am I grieving for my dog more than Chris? Idiot. Chris was missing, not dead. Poor old Jake, on the other hand, was found decapitated lying beside the chauffeur's burnt body. The black and white Border Collie

with the long legs and loving eyes had been a big part of our family.
He didn't have a mean bone in his body and he'd kept me sane when
I was alone. I always believed that God had sent him to take care of
me. Then He had sent Chris. Jake had loved Chris like I had. He had
a role in the wedding ceremony that had cost the poor dog his life.

That was why he was in the wedding Limousine with Chris.
Chris and I laughed so much as we practised getting Jake ready to
bring the rings down the aisle.

The Kidnappers had taken Chris, but not before they had cut
Jake's head off. I sobbed a rapid intake of breath as I thought of poor
Jake, I prayed that he was dead before.........

The lowlifes that had hijacked the wedding car, killed the
chauffeur, and Jake, and took my Chris. Whoever had done all these
terrible things would pay for it in ways they couldn't imagine. No
words, or big threats just cold retribution. Whatever happened I
would do what I do best. Hunt them down and end them.

They must have made a mistake; all crims make them. They leave
something at the scene, a print or some DNA, they brag at the pub,
or in bed; someone always slips up. With that Statewide alert surely
someone will see them when they stopped for fuel or something else.

I was hiding in our home. I had learned the hard way not to
venture outside. I was ambushed by our next door neighbours as
I put the bin out. They didn't realise how their words pricked my
heart.

Well-meaning though she was, one neighbour had said, "You
should have seen your Chris leave for the church oh, she was like a
Princess off to the ball. Steve, don't you worry she'll be back soon."

The one on the other tried as well. She had seen all the TV shows
and kept saying, "Surely, they'll phone with some demand. They will
contact you soon enough."

Sitting alone in the dark I had thought that through; *But, why would they? Everyone knows we aren't rich; what would they want?* I had never believed in coincidences, and I wasn't starting now. I took a generous pull at my large JD and thought some more. Not just from my truckload of guilt, but from common sense I thought; *All this happened on my wedding day six plus hours west of Brisbane. The grubs had to have planned it and come all the way out here to execute their plan. Hijacking a wedding Limo, killing the Driver and kidnapping the bride wasn't a spur-of-the-moment crime. Not unless you needed a vehicle, but they'd left the Limo behind at the waterhole.* Senior Sergeant Townsend was right; this was about me. This was my fault. Chris was gone because of my work. I kept questioning myself over and over again, and asking God was He punishing me for all the people I had hurt or killed? I had often wondered whether He could really forgive me. I knew the scripture promising forgiveness if I confessed. But was that for everyone else, not me.

There were always 'bad guys', but these Tangoes (Targets) were still men, just as much someone's father, husband, brother or even son. I was following orders, but that doesn't cut it when it comes to facing your actions or your Maker. Was this my punishment?

I promised myself that I would soon find out why this had all happened, but no one knew anything for now. All that could be done had been done. Forensics, CCTVs on some local businesses around Roma had not shown any sign of the Limo. Once the Limousine had been discovered Senior Sergeant Townsend changed the original Missing Persons Geo-Targeted SMS to a 'Look Out To Be Kept For' (LOTBKF). Every cop in Queensland and neighbouring New South Wales now had a photo of Chris, who was identified as one of their own. For now, all we could do was wait.

I looked at my coffee mug, half caffeine, half JD, and threw it away. I had to get out, away from all these memories. I'd had a gutful of everyone and everything. I was heading bush again.

Sergeant of Police Jock McKee was about as far from his birthplace of Glasgow as he could be. He had learned his trade as a Scottish cop on the hard streets of one of the toughest cities in the world. How he had ended up in sleepy Roma, in South Western Rural Queensland, was to his way of thinking just how Police Forces all over the world operated.

You were a stock item, a number to be sent wherever that particular spare part was needed to keep the Big Blue Machine running. He had moved to Australia with the future in mind away from the cold, the crims he had locked horns with and an unhappy marriage that had finally issued its last gasp. Some wee lassie had been kidnapped on her wedding day, a sad story, but he had seen worse. She had been the local Sergeant here in Western Queensland, and with her gone, Brisbane HQ had sent him out to fill the posting until they knew what was happening.

He had been around long enough to know what that meant; he was probably here for the duration. Not being involved, not knowing her, he had already decided she was long dead. The murders and kidnapping on the big day didn't suggest that she would have lasted the three weeks since she had disappeared. He had to be a bit careful with his language around the Station. Clearly, this was a close-knit team, and the Senior Sergeant was more emotional about it than the hard Scotsman would have expected.

Getting to know his new patch McKee was walking along the main street, looking around at shop windows that allowed him to watch across the street, a skill learned on the beat of Glasgow lanes and alleys. He was about to walk across the drive-through of the Commonwealth Hotel when an old Landcruiser ute screamed in, the 4WD nearly collecting the huge Sergeant who had to jump back, cursing as he began to fall backwards. The Driver ignored the near accident and continued into the drive-through, stopping near the bottle shop counter.

My mind was so intent on restocking my supply of Jack Daniels in preparation for heading bush that I didn't notice the angry Police Sergeant stalking towards my vehicle now parked in the Drive Through.

Someone grabbed my arm, and I reacted automatically, spinning low and launching at my attacker.

Stepping to the side, a Police Sergeant I hadn't seen before stated calmly in a harsh Scottish accent, "Listen, laddie, if you want to add to your problems, just keep fighting."

I finally noticed the uniform and backed off.

"Sorry, Sergeant, I don't react well to being grabbed," I said.

"Och lad, you don't notice pedestrians walking on a footpath either. Now, get me your licence and be quick about it," the Sergeant demanded.

I retrieved my licence from the ute and handed it to the tall, redheaded Officer.

"Och, Mr Wallace, do you know how close you got to sending me flying with that wee old bus oh yours? You roared in here like something was chasing ye, and all for a wee dram," the Scottish words aside his anger and meaning were not in any doubt."

"I'm sorry, Sergeant. It was a stupid mistake. I've been a bit distracted, and I am sorry," I said, meaning it.

"Mr Wallace, it's not lunchtime yet, and you smell like a whiskey bottle. If I had a breathalyser on me, I'd be putting you on the bag, and that's nae mistake for sure. Now, I think it would be best if we head down to the Station. I might be new, but between your driving, your reaction and your American-style mouthwash, There's more to ye laddie," the Sergeant stated.

"Sergeant, if you would like to phone your Senior Sergeant, he'll vouch for me," I said more confidentially than I really felt.

"Och nae, that's not what I'd be doin'. I can tell how ya has been wearing out that Sergeant business; you're probably Army, and maybe used to givin orders. Well, Mr Wallace, you'd do well to never try to make my decisions or give me an order ever again. I'll drive us both down to the Station, that's it," he stated, leaving me no doubt that it wasn't up for debate.

Surprise, surprise, I wasn't allowed to buy any grog. With my new Scottish 'friend', we headed off with him behind the wheel. My mate at the Drive Through who had come out to serve me stood stunned, not sure whether to laugh or look worried. I knew how he felt.

"This is a heap a junk, Wallace, I've gotta mind to put it over the pits, that'll slow ye doon. How ye get a famous Scottish name like Wallace anyhow?" the Sergeant said, smiling for the first time.

"Don't know, never looked into it, but if liking whiskey and being stubborn are Scottish traits, we might well be related hey?" I asked trying for my most charming smile. I needed to calm this situation down a notch or two. The Sergeant was too experienced to be swung by my colonial charm and ignored my attempts.

Arriving at the Station, we turned off Mcdowall St, the Sergeant using the official entrance on the right of the Police Station.

"We'll park out the back, laddie, in case ye end up staying over-nicht; it's up to the Senior Sergeant," he said as he stopped under a stand of Bottle Brush.

Being an Australian Army Officer, I was more used to being on disciplinary boards judging soldiers who had stepped outside Military Law. Being brought into a Police Station through the side door gave me a bad feeling, knowing that was where all the drunks and even worse offenders that were under arrest were brought.

"Now, Laddie, you're not under arrest, well not just yet. But, I wouldn't want ye to wander around and hurt ye self. I'll be puttin' ye in this holding cell for a wee while, and I'll be catching up with my Boss. We'll soon find out if he knows ye, won't we?" the big Scot said, not leaving any doubt I had absolutely no choice.

Sergeant McKee thought as he opened his Boss's door that Townsend looked even more tired than he had an hour ago.

"Boss, I just pulled in a Steve Wallace, he nearly ran me over in town. He claims that you know him, is it true?"

"Yeah, Jock, I know him; he's a hard case; something special in the Army, all Top Secret, usually lives in town. His wife-to-be was our girl that got kidnapped on their wedding day. Of course you know you are filling her post here." Pointing towards the holding cells Senior Sergeant Townsend continued, "Now old mate there, he's moved out to a cattle property on the Injune road. Well, he and his best mate Jack Daniels. He's takin' her disappearance hard like you'd expect. He believes it's tied up with his Army work and is feeling pretty guilty, and so he should," Senior Sergeant Townsend stated, attempting to leave the emotion he felt out of his voice, and only succeeding to a degree.

"OK, Boss, it's your call. Do I bag him or let him go. I'm not carin' so much, but if that had been an old lady or a mother with weans instead of me, he would have cleaned 'em up," the Scottish Sergeant said sincerely.

"Of course you're right, Jock, what a weans? They're kids, I guess, but if he was driving in a dangerous manner, he needs a kick up the rear. If he's over the limit, book him by all means." Townsend said.

"Och, I'll put him on the breath analyser and check his reading. He smells like he should be over, but we'll see. He seems pretty calm, but from what you say, he could be numb, not caring rather than cocky," Sergeant McKee stated as he stood to leave his superior's office.

"Jock, don't get me wrong, he and I were friends, but I blame him for bringing these murders and Chris's disappearance to our quiet town. So do whatever is right with him, and you won't hear any complaints from me," Townsend said firmly. "And Jock, try to speak Australian at least some of the time, hey Laddie," he said with a smile.

The Scottish cop laughed at his Boss's attempt at bonding, it was vital especially, in a small Station. He was also was pleased with this statement about Wallace. The last thing he wanted was a town that protected citizens, putting them beyond the law because of friendship or being related somehow.

"Boss, I'll get 'im," Sergeant McKee said as he closed the door behind him.

He took me into a small white walled office where an operator put me on the Breath Analysing Machine. I think I was as surprised as the Cops that I was under the limit. With my mind focused on buy some more booze, I hadn't given a thought about leaving my camp and driving into town and whether I was over the limit. Driving more carefully this time, I returned to the Commonwealth Hotel much to the surprise of Dougie, the Drive- Through attendant who had witnessed my 'arrest'. With a box full of Jack Daniel's bottles rattling on the front floor, I headed towards to the solitude of my camp. I didn't even have a dog anymore since Jake had been killed by whoever kidnapped Chris. Although I still ached with missing her I had become able to think things through without dissolving into a pool of tears. I held out as much hope as I could muster, because whoever had taken her had murdered the chauffeur and Jake next to the Limo. So if their plan was to murder Chris, you would think her remains would have been there as well. That was my logic; I had to cling to something. If I'd known what was going to happen the following day, I would have stayed in town, but stuff like this is seldom convenient.

ROMA POLICE STATION

Carol had been the civilian admin girl for the Roma Police Station for about nine months. She had moved from Toowoomba after a messy breakup with her boyfriend. He was the mayor's son and wasn't going to move away from his income and his family's power base. So far, Carol loved Roma. It was friendly and peaceful, surrounded by cattle properties and full of country boys whose fathers owned these vast tracts of Queensland. Carol was no gold digger, but these boys loved life, and the future was looking good whatever happened. She had never seen herself as beautiful but was an OK country girl in every way, especially wearing tight Wrangler jeans and her Akubra hat. Carol wasn't blind to the fact that as a new girl in town, the local girls didn't like her because of that. The local boys were interested in her because they had known her competition since kindy.

One girl who had been friendly because she wasn't in the cattle boy markets, was one of the local coppers, Sergeant Chris Jackson. She, like Carol, wasn't a three-plus-generation local girl like the rest. Still, Chris was popular and seemed accepted by everyone. Carol couldn't remember a sadder scene than when she and the other cop/ friends from the Station had been waiting in the church for Chris and their Boss Senior Sergeant Townsend to come down the aisle. She had been so excited and happy just to be invited.

As she sat at her Admin desk near the front counter of the Police Station her daydream about that sad day was interrupted by the deep buzz of the Station telephone.

"Roma Police, how can I direct your call, please?" Carol answered as she had a thousand times before.

"Put that fat old excuse for a Senior Sergeant on, do it now," a deep, metallic distorted voice demanded. She froze; the voice was non-human, and the disrespect to the Senior Police Officer threw her.

"What's the problem? Townsend is so old the Dead Sea was only sick when he was born. Get him on the line," the same robotic voice demanded.

Carol ran from her desk, her headset still plugged into the machine jerked it from her head because, in her haste, she had forgotten to unplug it. Carol crashed into the Senior Sergeant's office door and banged on the glass top half.

Smiling, the Senior Sergeant asked, "Carol, I nearly drew my weapon when I heard something crash into my door. Where's the fire, my girl?"

"Sir, Siiiiir, I," Carol clearly distressed stuttered, "there's a call, yes, a call for you. He was rude, and he didn't sound, well, like a normal person. Carol said, a little more calm now she was in the older Police Officer's presence.

"Well, put it through like usual, Carol, I'll be OK. You got the recorder on, yes?"

"Sorry, Boss, I wasn't sure; he sounds so weird. I'll put it on straight away," Carol said quietly, obviously shaken by the harsh voice of the caller.

Roza the Assassin had waited three weeks. He had been busy during this period. Although Roza was incapable of grieving for another human, he understood the Psychology of the process. By waiting, he wanted to provide Steve Wallace time to slide off balance, with no sleep, stewing in guilt and incapable of thinking straight. That was Roza's hopes and plans. From observation Roza knew Wallace liked a drink on a 'hot day', as the sarcastic comment goes. Roza was confident that Wallace would have remained alert in the period immediately after the kidnapping. However, he was just as sure that after three weeks of mental torture Wallace would be hitting the bottle. The Assassin was preparing his prey by lessening his ability to think and act as he had been trained to do.

Annoyed at his staff being spoken to rudely, Senior Sergeant Townsend didn't attempt to conceal his anger, "Senior Sergeant Townsend, who am I speaking to?" he demanded.

The metallic voice responded without emotion, "Listen, my fat pig, I have that sow you have been missing......"

"What do you want? Where are you?" Townsend asked trying to remain calm and control the conversation. Relief dripping through him, at least Chris was alive.

"Well, the first thing I want is for you to never interrupt me again. I'll cut a pinky off for each interruption if you do. You got that; you're not in charge this time. We understand?" the distorted voice echoed.

Not being used to anyone speaking to him like that, the Senior Sergeant bit his tongue and waited.

"The old abattoir just out of town. Now I can see for miles in every direction, so don't try any tricky local cop stuff. I don't want Wallace there. If I see him, I'll cut more off his sweetheart here than just a finger. You hear me? You do what you're told, and I'll bring the blushing bride. You arrive at exactly 1800 hours and wait. Like I said, I'll know if you set an ambush, and I won't hesitate to make her so ugly no one will want her. At that time of day, I don't expect to see a Council truck or a Telstra van out that way. If I do, I'm gone, and so is she," the menacing metallic voice demanded. The phone went dead as the Senior Sergeant started to speak.

Did you get all that, Carol?" he yelled to his Admin Clerk.

"Yes, Boss, all recorded," Carol stated triumphantly, then her duty done she began to shake terribly.

"OK, get onto Telstra and get them to run a track on that call. It's probably a waste of time, but everything is worth a try.

Ten minutes later, Carol knocked on the Senior Officer's door, "Boss, the telcos were quick on that one, but you won't like the answer. I checked my list, and it was Chris's phone. Whoever it was had her phone. They did say the call used the tower on the other side of the Sale Yards, but that's all they could tell me," the Admin Clerk said.

"Thanks, Carol; I s'pose that at least confirms that they have Chris if they have her phone; it's not a prank or anything," he stated.

As she returned to her counter, the Senior Sergeant called out "Do you know where Sergeant McKee is?"

"Yes, Boss, he's out at Coey's place; they had about fifty yearlings stolen last night. He headed out there early, he hoped to be back before lunch," Carol said, happy she had a quick answer.

"Great, can you please call him and tell him I need him back here ASAP. And Carol, if you can't raise him on the phone, try the Coley's landline, often there's no service that far out a town," he demanded.

An hour later, Jock McKee was sitting in the Senior Sergeant's office nursing a mug of coffee. "Boss, I thought I was coming to a sleepy wee village, and the last thing I expected was a kidnapping and now this mystery phone call. It's like some crazy Hollywood movie, Sarg."

"I hear you. And it's not going to get any simpler. We have to go tell your new best friend, Steve Wallace. I know he doesn't look anything right now, but the guy is a fair dinkum hero to those who know what he's done," the Senior Sergeant said wearily.

"Och Sarg, I was following pretty well until that fair somethin' popped up," the Scotsman said as he took a deep draught from his mug.

"Sorry Jock," the Senior Sergeant said. " 'Fair dinkum' is Aussie for authentic, the real deal. Now, I know that experienced Police gut of yours wouldn't want him involved, and I'd like to agree. However, he would be out of control if we tried to rescue Chris without him. If something goes pear-shaped, we need him on our side. And Jock, the real reason is I've seen him in battle, and we can do with that kind of help."

"You want me to collect my new mate then?" the Scot said in a terrible Aussie accent.

"No, he might shoot you if you went out by yourself. He and I aren't really on talking terms either because he knows I blame him for bringing all this violence to our door. I'll come with you; then, if he shoots you, one of us might get away," the Senior Officer said, attempting a little humour.

"It'll be good to spend some time driving out there. Ye can give me the guided tour on the way." The Scotsman said appreciating the Cop joke.

The Senior Sergeant nodded as he wondered what state Steve Wallace might be in and what sort of a welcome they might receive. Even though the mystery caller had said not to tell Wallace about the meeting, one thing he was sure of was that he had to get Steve Wallace involved. Wallace would be unpredictable, to say the least. The most important thing was Steve Wallace's skill set, especially being a top Sniper, and that may prove invaluable. The Senior Sergeant knew he needed him on their side to go up against this new enemy it was unlike anything he had faced in twenty-eight years of Policing.

Roza smiled as he hung up the phone. He knew that those country coppers would do anything to rescue his hostage. Much more important to him, the Assassin was sure that these local clods would be rushing to tell Wallace about the meeting at the abandoned abattoirs. That meant that although he had expressly demanded that Wallace not come, the Assassin had, in reality, invited his adversary. Wallace and Roza were like a reflection of each other. It was as certain as taking the next breath that both killers would see the same things and think in the same ways. Roza had spent time researching his quarry. He knew that Wallace was well trained and in the way he would think. He would use this to finally kill the Australian who had cost him so much. Wallace would want to Recce the place and find a hide from where he could cover the meet. Of course, having chosen the place, Roza had carried out his own assessment at his leisure over the last few days. He had decided on the best hide and a few secondary alternatives. Roza was looking forward to seeing the man who had thwarted his brilliant Assassination plan on the Northern Territory Marine Base. Wallace would pay dearly. This afternoon was his time to die. For the third time Roza checked his weapons and chest rig. He was ready. You could never be too careful or too prepared.

CHAPTER 22

Steve goes hunting, but he's not the only one.

So much for winter in Roma, Western Queensland, freezing at night and still stinking hot all day. After another sleepless night I rolled out of my swag and was hit by that cold hour before each dawn. Putting on my Ghillie suit brought back memories of when I had bought it from a US Marine in a Hawaiian bar. We had gotten to know each other and had spent some good times out on the town in Honolulu. Their Sniper Suits were better made than the one I had been issued back home. The Ghillie came in two pieces which was much better especially in the heat of an Australian summer, so I had grabbed it. Today, I needed meat and was sick of wild pork, and I refused to eat kangaroo meat. I had never seen so many worms as in 'roo meat. I always laughed when I saw it as a delicacy on some flash restaurant's menu in Canberra. In reality, I didn't care; I don't think I'd tasted my food since I had gone bush. There was just a dry acid in my mouth, like my life. I ate simply as fuel to keep going. I had walked about two clicks from camp, and I was overlooking a well-used trail that led up to a turkey nest dam, named that because of its circular shape. There were deer sign all along it, fresh droppings and trees where bucks had scraped their antlers. I was banking on a buck or a few does coming down, looking for a drink. Not long after the sun came over the ridge, the sweat started pouring down my back, and again, I wondered why I had bothered wearing the Ghillie. In the hide, I hadn't moved for nearly two hours. Although I had done all the right things I had been trained to do to alleviate numbness in my arms and legs, they were feeling the inactivity. Was I getting old, or was it all these healthy life choices I had been making? Wild Pig meat was starting to look a lot easier than this.

The realisation that this had been about the longest period that I hadn't thought about Chris since she was taken hit me, and I felt a pain in my heart followed by more guilt. I was big on guilt. Was that a flicker of an ear or a tail? A rooky mistake would have been to quickly moving my head one eighty degrees to confirm whether it was a deer or some other critter. But I wasn't going to waste all this time and sweat like that. I knew I was invisible if I held fast, I had the wind in my face so everything was right. All I could do was wait. The buck sent the doe down alone to check the water hole. I could have dropped her; my Remington 308 pump was loaded and cocked. I wasn't interested in taking a trophy, but any hunter wants to see a buck when given the chance. The remainder of his heard came down to drink he arrived, and I was glad I had waited. I couldn't believe my eyes. This was an old boy I'd only glimpsed a few times in the past. His majesty had got this big by being smart. I think the experts who score deer trophies would call him an Imperial Stag as he carried an impressive balanced fourteen-point rack. Today, his luck was still good. I wasn't looking for a trophy; I just wanted some meat. I took the smallest doe as I only needed enough for myself. After all, I was alone, wasn't I? Painfully, I remembered how much Chris loved her venison steak. Even though the doe turned side-on to look at her leader, offering a classic heart shot to minimise any meat damage, I head shot her where she stood. The world-class buck was already out of sight before she hit the ground.

The report of the 308 was so unexpected and close, it motivated him and his little harem of ladies to seek shelter, disappearing like wisps of steam.

In the background I could hear a vehicle coming up the road to my camp. As though I'm not angry enough all the time. Whose that heading my way? I'm usually alone on this property; if the owner has to work the cattle, I either help or stay out of the way. So, it can't be him. About two klicks away, I could hear the intruder's 4WD labouring across the creek and up the steep bank heading towards my camp. I was upset at the intrusion. Who were they? The possibility of wasting my deer was annoying. A life I had taken shouldn't be wasted. I wondered if I would get back to the body to harvest the meat before the pigs and flies carried it away. The other deeper concern was the threat to me, that they could be enemies. At least I had a weapon with me, and I knew the place like the back of my hand, whatever that means.

I made several rapid decisions that saw me jogging back to camp; I needed to get there before they did. The Ghillie suit wasn't made for running, and now, jogging, I was really cooking, but I didn't notice any of it. I was more focused than I'd been since Chris's disappearance. I stopped and looked around. I wanted to settled far enough off the track not to get run over by my visitors but close enough to welcome them with my knife. I spotted the place, just there will be perfect. Usually, I'd take a lot more time to identify a hide, but this time I only had wait a few minutes before the white 4WD crested the rise and pushed toward my camp. When the big Toyota came alongside me, I saw the Police sticker on the door. My mind flew back to when I was a teenager working nights, pumping gas on the Gold Coast. My best mates were coppers. They came in for a coffee this night, they always visited me. Someone had ripped the PO from their car sticker, leaving the word LICE. I remember laughed, and they had acted like they were annoyed, but eventually, they joined me in laughing as well.

My memories were interrupted when the 4WD door nearest me opened.

The redheaded Sergeant's Scottish accent rang out, "I canno' see him, Boss. He's probably asleep under a log nursing a bottle of that Yanky whiskey he seems to like."

"Maybe, but you don't know him, Jock, he likes a drink, but he could be right beside you before you knew he was within a mile of ya," Senior Sergeant Townsend said as he came around the front of the vehicle.

"If the streets of Glasgow taught me anything, it was how to make sure no one could sneak up on me," the Scottish cop said as he laughed. There's one thing worrying me, Boss. Do you think the Laddie is up to this fight? He added.

"Seeing we are so close, can I call you Jock too? And it's not me; you should be worrying about Laddie," I said sarcastically as I stood up, both of us knowing I could reach him without taking a step.

"Och! Where did you come from?" he asked as he backed away from me. "Attempting to regain his Copper's position of power, he angrily demanded, "And, no, you can't call me Jock."

Shaking out the leaves and sticks from my sniper suit, I laughed at his surprise.

Senior Sergeant Townsend came around the 4WD and couldn't help but laugh at the scene before him. "OK, Jock, I warned you about him. Why are you all cammed up, Steve?" he asked.

"I was hunting some deer, looking to harvest some venison. I nailed one just before you drove in. Whatever you want, make it quick so I can get back to butchering and hanging that doe before it gets any hotter," I said, making it clear they weren't welcome.

"Steve, we've got news about Chris; stop mucking around." The no-nonsense Senior Sergeant said not wanting to waste any more time.

The mention of Chris hit me like a physical blow. I had gone bush because there were no leads to her whereabouts and I had to get away from the memories our cottage held. Although I had worked hard not to believe it, the idea that she had been murdered and I would never see her again was constantly slithering into my thoughts.

"OK, sorry about the attitude; what's happened? What have you got?" I said, desperation sounding in my voice.

"We got a phone call, and please don't interrupt with all the obvious questions like we had never thought of, like tracing the call. Just listen, and then we can cook up a plan between us, OK?" The Senior Sergeant continue to relay the rest of the kidnapper's phone call. "The whole thing stinks of an ambush, but we've got no choice; we have to do what he demanded." He waited for my nod of agreement.

The Senior Sergeant continued speaking as we walked towards camp, "Now, it's legit; the call came through on Chris's phone. The voice was electronically modified, so I couldn't pick up on an accent or anything. I couldn't even be positive if it was a male or female. One thing I am sure of is that they mean business."

I led the two Cops into my camp, and after stirring up my fire, I put the billy on to make us some tea. Once we all had a mug of tea, we sat around staring into the fire to avoid eye contact with each other. Townsend continued to fill me in on the sinister phone call; at least we were somewhat encouraged knowing that Chris appeared to be still alive. We still didn't know what this Kidnapper wanted, but we had no other option but to follow the instructions.

"Steve, he demanded that we meet him at the old Meatworks just out of town. Jock and I are to come alone. One big demand was that you're not to come anywhere near the place. The Assassin also warned that the area should have no work trucks or vans hanging around. If he sees you or any other vehicles, he's threatened to kill Chris," the Senior Sergeant stated calmly. He decided to leave out the specific details of the threats of removing her fingers.

"And yet the first thing you did was come out here. I'm glad you did, that's for sure," I stated sincerely.

"No way was I going to try to handle this without you, so what are your thoughts?" he asked.

"He's made a mistake already. His big advantage is having chosen the location of the meet. By doing that, he's given us a window of a little over four hours before the meet to Recce it for ourselves. I will head out there, look around and choose the best place to overwatch you guys," I said, trying to sound happier about it than I really did.

"I know you are good at this stuff, Steve, but don't forget if he sees you, he will hurt Chris." The Senior Sergeant stated.

"Come off it, Townsend, I know all this is my fault, but do you think I'd ever do anything to endanger her?" I growled.

"What are those charts you got there? Let's have a look."

Using the building plans for the old Meatworks, we identified the entries and exits and decided which one the two Cops would use.

Senior Sergeant Townsend was clearly frustrated by the lack of intel and control.

"OK, we'll go in as he instructed, and you'll be there somewhere but not visible. I'll leave you to decide where you work from, but I want you on overwatch covering us. I don't like being told what and how to do something so important and dangerous and I sure don't want any surprises. That's where you come in. You are my surprise for him," the Senior Sergeant stated.

Signals and electronic comms, such as throat mikes and earbuds were too complicated and likely to fail, and, if the Kidnapper searched the two Police Officers and discovered some comms gear he would know others were close by, which could seriously cause everyone some grief. They would move in and secure package as I would still be at a distance. I shuddered at how I could ever think of Chris as just a package.

"Laddie, we may have gotten off on the wrong foot. After what I saw when we arrived at your camp and, what the Boss here says about you, I'm glad you're on our side. I'll look after the Senior Sergeant as much as I can. But like he said, we don't trust anything about this," the Scottish cop said in a much more friendly tone.

Ignoring him, I ended the meeting. "I'm going to head out there now, and have a look around, and choose a hide to overwatch the meeting place. Hang up the road until just before the meeting time and then move to that open area we identified on that old plan of the Meatworks. After a while go through that door. He or they'll expect you to stop in the middle, so stick to the plan and make them happy," I said, sounding more confident than I was feeling. So little intel, we were not even sure if we were up against an individual or a platoon, and so many things we didn't know made all this far from ideal by a long shot.

"It sounds like the best we can do, Steve. I just hope you still shoot as good as you used to," the Senior Sergeant said with a smile as he would have when we were friends. But even though we had been friends before Chris' kidnapping, that had all changed. Too many harsh words had been spoken between us.

"With no Intel, this is a blind op. We all have to play it by ear. You know fluid doesn't start to cover what might happen out there. But what choice have we got?" I said. I said, as I turned my back to them, and began to prepare my gear for the job. Behind me, Senior Sergeant Townsend held up his hand to silence his partner's response.

A few minutes later, the two Cops drove back to Roma. Obviously, my priority was getting Chris back. However, I was still angry at wasting that doe's life, she would be nothing but a blood stain on the dirt by the time I got back here. I climbed into my old pickup and headed towards the abattoir on the other side of town.

The mind is a funny thing at times. As I rolled past the local KFC, a thought exploded in my mind; *AMERICAN........ POTUS........ Yeah, this is all about me. This Kidnapper is the Assassin from the US Marine Base attempt on the President and Prime Ministers. Somehow he has found out it was me who wrecked his day.* I didn't have any proof but it all made total sense.

As always, guilt flooded in to drown me, this time even worse than during the last few weeks which I had spent wondering why this was happening to us. The guilt was rock solid; my part in this had now been confirmed. Driving out of town, I wondered if I would ever get Chris back, or if any of us would still be alive by nightfall. I focused on the Op and threw these thoughts out the window.

Only a fool would assume that the Kidnapper cum Assassin didn't anticipate my being there.

He may have made out that he didn't want me there, but it was just another ploy of his wider game. I was sure that my being there was the main game on this afternoon's timetable, even though he had stated otherwise. I had noted a few high points on the Meatworks building plans, such as water towers and cranes. As I drove through Roma, I thought about this. Visualising the plans we had looked at, trying to decide which would provide the best angle for the shot I would be taking, and which would provide me the best field of fire. I evaluated each platform, running through the criteria that had been drilled into me so long ago. One stood out as best, especially considering the sun at that specific time of day. Then I thought about the Kidnapper and what I'd seen on the US Marine Base when he had attacked the US President and our Prime Minister. I was confident he was a highly trained, experienced, creative, and intelligent sniper. One of the basic Counter-Sniper strategies is to think like your enemy. The obvious problem this time was that I knew we were both trained and experienced. What would either of us do? Both of us knowing that as well. OK, so he would have chosen the same platform and would be waiting for me or expecting me to be heading there. With this in mind, I thought in reverse and chose another platform I would typically have rejected. I prayed that this sort of reverse psychology would work. It had to.

My ute shuddered as I drove over the second cattle grid after entering the cattle property next door to the Meatworks holding yards. Quietly closing my door I left the Hilux parked out of sight under a gum tree. All the things I would typically do were still against me. I would have preferred to move into the stand under the cover of darkness. No choice, I didn't have all day to get into place, so I moved as quickly as I could from cover to cover. When I reached the end of the neighbouring paddock beside the pens, I ditched the Ghillie suit; it was no good in an industrial setting. Crawling under the bottom rail of the disused cattle yard I stayed on my belly to reduce my profile. The smell of the thick layer of decayed droppings left by thousands of long-gone cattle and sheep lingered on. I had figured that the Kidnapper would be on high alert in the hours before the meeting time. I would have liked a longer Recce, but the more time I was there, the more likely I would be discovered.

With this in mind, I decided to stay put until the coppers arrived. I was counting on their noise and movement to distract the Kidnapper long enough for me to get into my hide. Using a water trough as cover, I waited just off the edge of the hard standing. I heard the familiar sound of the Police 4WD entering the main entrance. I had even loaded some empty jerry cans in the back and told Senior Sergeant Townsend to drive over the speed bump without slowing to maximise the clatter, while revving of the big Japanese motor. I had to gamble these ploys would give me at least a few seconds. I went to an old loading platform where I believed the Assassin cum Kidnapper would have crossed off as a possible place I would head to.

I made it. Well, at least this far. I settled in. Looking through my scope I was not surprised that my sight picture was blocked on the right by a brick wall. This was one of the reasons a good sniper would not have chosen this hide. But I was happy with making it so far without drawing fire. I traversed the scope slightly to the left, away from the wall's profile.

The Meatworks had the typical deign, a concrete floor with offices above and a huge open area similar in looks to a shopping centre car park lay before me. Much of this ground floor would have been enclosed in the factory's heyday. I could see what appeared to be the back of a high-back office chair, my mind registering that it was unusual for that type of chair to be located on the vast concrete killing floor. I figured it probably came from one of the abandoned offices. Kids had probably been playing with it.

My high-quality scope changed my sight from patches of glaring sunlight to a workable green shade. My scope swept over the chair, searching like a hungry shark, hovering momentarily while still covering the entire floor. With both eyes open, one on the scope, I was seeking out a target, a human shape, a flicker of an uncovered shiny surface, or any movement. Nothing. It wasn't beyond possibility that he had placed the chair to be a distraction. That's what I'd do.

The Police 4WD had come to a halt adjacent to the entry gate, a faded sign with the words 'Staff Entrance' hanging lopsidedly above it. As arranged, after plenty of unnecessary revving and with the jerry cans rattling noisily they turned the vehicle to face the entrance through which they had just come. Good practice. You never knew when you might want to leave a party in a hurry. All the noise and the extra manoeuvring of the Police Landcruiser seemed to have given me the time I needed. So far, so good; I was still alive. Although we had agreed coms were dangerous because we expected the Kidnapper to scan for them, we hadn't gone entirely low-tech.

Both the Cops were wearing their tactical vests and Senior Sergeant Townsend had activated his body cam as he exited the vehicle to record everything that occurred. I had propped up an Ipad with a direct link from his chest camera.

On the second sweep, a movement, no, just some rubbish blowing around the office chair caught my eye. In the scope, it looked like white rags or paper flapping in the breeze. I turned up the magnification on the scope, and my heart stopped. It wasn't paper, it wasn't rags, it was lace. My heart was bouncing off my rib cage. The white fabric billowing now must have been anchored to the chair. I could see it might be a veil or part of a wedding dress. But not just any wedding dress. OH, Chris, are you really there? Baby, why aren't you standing, running why, why? My eyes filled with tears; I was hit by the shame of being so unprofessional. I was trained to be unattached and unemotional, but this was no stranger, no assigned package. Shaking myself I reset my mind back into the game. This was the love of my life, the one person on this planet I trusted and could rely on whatever happened. A human who had brought me back from a would-be drunk hermit to a new Military career and a sort of normal everyday life.

By now, I had broken every rule of my sniper training. My mind was everywhere but on the job. Through teary eyes, I hadn't moved my scope for several minutes, my focus on the chair and its dancing lace.

The two Police Sergeants had made their way to the person-door, opened it with some difficulty, and disappeared into the lower floor of the building. They were temporarily hidden behind the same brick wall that had blocked my view for a third of the ground floor. I desperately searched the Ipad video, but only gloomy grubby concrete walls were visible. Townsend turned to his left and I was looking at the reverse side of the brick wall that was hiding the two Sergeants from my direct sight. Surely, they must have seen the chair by now. On the right edge of the circumference of my scope, their forms appeared and then filled it with their black ninja cop suit uniforms. Townsend stepped to the right, clearing his companion. The chair was immediately visible sent from the body cam video to my little screen. Nothing about this setup was good.

Surely, after all the murders and keeping Chris since our proposed wedding day, it couldn't be this easy. This guy had proven himself skilful, resourceful and creative and ruthlessly murderous. No, this was wrong. Everything in my heart wanted it so easy. Everything in my gut and mind knew it couldn't be.

I was spending too much time watching the body cam images; I was failing to keep my scope moving, looking for any sign of the Kidnapper/ Assassin.

The wind must have gusted again; the lace had blown around this time, like the flapping wings of a swan. NO! As the wings parted I could see blond hair wrapping around the back of the chair. The two Police had stopped and were looking around; I couldn't tell what had caused them to baulk. The last thing I wanted was to stop looking at that scene, to miss Chris moving away or the two Cops grabbing her and carrying her injured or drugged body to their vehicle, to safety.

I tore myself and my scope from them and began to check every loading platform or window on the next floor up. Where this dramatic scene was unfolding was the same place the cattle would have met their fate and been butchered. The irony wasn't lost on me. There was a corridor of offices at the front of the building, the floor finishing and creating a walkway where supervisors could observe the killing floor below. I scoped along about half the building without a signs, when a slight movement in an office caught my other eye. I returned my scope to the office on the far end. Someone exited the room. None of us were wired for coms, but I sure wished we had them now.

By now, the two Police Sergeants were walking under those offices on the first floor. Unbeknown to them, someone was on that floor just above them. As they passed under the floor's edge, they didn't realise that their backs had become easy targets from above.

I could shoot in front of them to warn them, but without explanation, they couldn't be guaranteed to understand the warning. All I could do was watch them walk into whatever awaited them. It was crushing for me to be this close and not be able to rush in and do what was needed. I had the skills. I'd done hostage or prisoner rescue all over the world. Chris was my fiancee. And I couldn't help. I just had to stick to the plan and provide overwatch. I focused on the first floor, seeking any movement or any part of a target to show. I decided that I would take him out before he could open fire on the two Police Officers below him. A quick glance at the body cam monitor confirmed their location, heading towards the chair. Again, my scope showed movement in the office.

I stilled my breathing and my heartbeat in readiness for taking a shot. I snatched another glimpse at the body cam image. There! That was so quick, another shadow of a movement in the office. Alarm bells rang. The movement was too uniform, too regular. This was yet another misdirection from the Assassin; somehow, he had rigged the movement. WW 2 snipers used to use string attached to a dead ally, pulling the string to make it look like the soldier was still alive. This, in turn, attracted others who came to help their fellow soldier. The sniper would sometimes milk this to score multiple targets from the one bait. In this case, I doubted he was there pulling a string, but it further confirmed his skill and craftiness.

I had to make the hard decision, listen to my gut feeling and ignore the movement or keep sharing my concentration between both views. I backed myself and gave the two Cops my undivided attention. *What if I was wrong?????* The body cam showed them taking two more steps, and as they came into view through my scope, I saw them prop.

As still as statues, what could they see? I swung my scope ahead of the two Cops, trying to glimpse what had worried them. Nothing, I could not see anything that might worry them.

The office chair that Chris was sitting in, filled my scope, her blonde hair waving to me to come and get her. It would be so easy, but that was the whole point; nothing that easy was safe. As I watched, my anger at being played with and made to feel so impotent sent bile to the back of my throat. The Police hadn't moved forward as I would have expected.

BOOM... WHOMP.... A massive ball of yellow and orange flames blanketed the scene. Years of deposited dust and debris were blown out, hiding everything under the concrete killing floor. I got a glimpse of the black chair hitting the concrete ceiling above it. A scream, more akin to a wounded animal or startled bird, left my lips and was muffled by the sound of the explosion reaching my stand. Abandoning my hide, I raced to the ladder, sliding down the rails and ignoring the rungs. My knees buckled as I jumped the last few metres, and my boots ploughed into the concrete. I ran towards the building, my eyes filling with tears as deep in my gut, I knew no one could have survived that explosion. As I headed under the building, my lungs filled with acrid smoke, and I couldn't see anything. I tripped over something; looking down, I was horrified to see a blood-soaked arm dressed in a black sleeve. Selfishly, I was relieved that it wasn't Chris's. I kept moving.

I reached the point where the office chair had once stood. There was nothing left, not even fragments of the chair. I looked up at the concrete ceiling, and my heart broke as I saw a familiar crimson stain I had seen on so many battlefields. I fell to my knees and wept. I understood how important any brother-in-arms would always be. Because this was Chris, I was shaken beyond my training. However, drawing on reserves instilled in me, I stood and turned towards the fallen Police Officers. The redheaded Sergeant must have owned the severed arm. I found the rest of him and was sure he was long gone. The smoke and fumes had started to clear, and I could now see the Senior Sergeant. It looked like his companion had taken the brunt of the explosion, and although he was not moving, he appeared untouched. This too I had seen on the battlefield and knew the lack of blood or obvious wounds did not necessary mean he had escaped unscathed. I knelt beside his prone body. I gently rolled him onto his back. His face, tactical uniform, and vest were covered in blood and reeked of explosives and smoke. I checked his neck for a pulse and was surprised to find one. It was weak but still there. I quickly checked him for wounds and was amazed that all I could find were a few lacerations but no actual gashes or shrapnel damage as I had expected with so much blood. He would need to be thoroughly stripped and checked at the hospital to be sure of this. I wondered if all that blood might be the dead Sergeant's.

I took my mobile phone from my vest pocket to phone for an ambulance; turning it on, I was relieved to see some bars. My call went through, and after the operator went through her Standard Operating Procedures and I was confident that the Ambulance and Police were on their way, I went to hang up. As my fingers moved to end the call, I nearly dropped it because it began to vibrate in my hand. The shock was not just to get a call but the fact that it was coming from Chris's number. My heart leapt. Had the Assassin faked her death to torture me?

Was Chris phoning me to say where to pick her up and take her home, safe and sound? I answered, my ears filled with the sound of metallic laughter. Even as he spoke, I could still hear his taunting laugh.

"Hey, Steve, that was fun. Well it was for me anyway. Now you know what it's like to lose everything. You're nearly as good as me at this. Pity about the bride. By the way, I enjoyed your honeymoon in your absence. I'd like to say Chris enjoyed it as much. But I think, as brothers, we should be honest; what do you think?" The metallic voice questioned.

I answered, attempting to hide the shakiness in my voice, "Firstly, we could never be brothers. Secondly, you're a dead man walking. I was committed to your death before, but now it's all I breathe for," I spat with unbridled venom.

"Too bad, so sad. This is all your fault; you cost me millions, and more importantly, you ruined my reputation of never failing a job. That was to be my retirement contract. I was going to retire undefeated and buy an island. You know the story," the robotic voice droned on.

"I'm starting to think you bore your targets to death. If you see us as peers, let's do this. Meet me now and see who is best. You won't, though, I know because you're a coward who murders women," I goaded.

"Seriously, it must be the shock or maybe it's just crushing grief; I could understand that," the Assassin's distorted voice replied.

"Even on that machine, I think I heard you getting a little excited. Did I push a button?" I asked. You couldn't say I was enjoying the banter, but for now, it was all I had, and every interaction might give me a little clue about this unknown Assassin.

"I'm getting bored with your childish attempts. I've got to go, I left a shovel nearby for you to take Chris home with you," the Assassin said, followed by a metallic laugh, as he cut the connection.

I fell to my knees and was still sobbing when I heard the siren as the ambulance turned into the driveway.

Senior Sergeant Townsend had been rushed from the old Meatworks to Roma Hospital Emergency. He had arrived unconscious and covered in so much blood that they hadn't thought his chances were good. However, when they checked his vital signs and cleaned him up they were amazed to find him to be in pretty good condition for someone who had survived a bomb explosion. He had a few lacerations that needed stitches and suspected concussion.

Forty-eight hours later he was back at work, sad and sorry for himself, but even more so for his Scottish Sergeant who had paid the price. He was sitting at his desk when Carol, the Police Station's civilian Admin, came in.

"Boss, the tests are all back from the bombing. They must have rushed them through all considering what happened," she said quietly, thinking of their lost team member.

"Thanks Carol, I suppose I should go around and tell Wallace the news." The old cop said sounding like the idea was a burden. He opened the envelope containing the test reports and quickly looked up.

"Yes, he'll want to know this sooner rather than later. I am going straight over there, Carol. Call me if you need me, yes?" he said.

I must have driven home after the disaster at the Meatworks, but I can't remember anything of the journey. I had witnessed Chris being blown to pieces, imagining her beautiful body being slammed into the concrete ceiling. I saw it again every time I shut my eyes. My mind was crowded with guilty condemnation; *I'd let her down again, there must have been a better way I could have tried. I had failed again.*

Now she was gone forever. That Scottish Sergeant was dead as well. Thank God that Townsend was OK. He sure looked in a bad way when the Ambos were working on him.

Two hours after I got home I felt no pain and passed out. The trouble was I woke up, I sobered up and I was still here. A few days later and I was into my second bottle of JD that day. I was in a stupor of whiskey and grief so deep I had thought about doing myself in on an hourly basis. A thought I hadn't had since I had started going out with Chris. But she was gone, Jake was gone! Everything I loved was gone forever!

CHAPTER 23

I fail yet again & Roza finds help at a Roadhouse.

BANG, BANG, BANG. What's that banging in my head? Stop, please stop that noise, my muddled brain screamed.

"Open the door Steve, or I'll kick it in," someone shouted. I sort of knew the voice but couldn't place it.

More knocking and banging started. 'There's someone at the door.' I said to myself; "Can't you just go away, leave me alone, won't you," I whispered, or thought I whispered.

"No, Steve I'm not leaving until I see you," the harsh voice responded.

I stumbled to the front door brushing against two coats hanging on pegs, Chris's coats, one for work, one for whatever. *Chris won't be needing them anymore,* I thought as an aside as I struggled with the lock and finally jerked the door open.

"I shoulda known, look at you, what a mess you are," Senior Sergeant Townsend, the man I'd once considered to be my friend, stood before me.

"Oh, Hiya Sarge, what da ya want?" I slurred.

Shaking his head, he took off his Police cap. "This is important. Well, the DNA results from the Meatworks have came back. Steve, that wasn't Chris. Mate, it wasn't her. I know that this may be hard for you to take in at the moment, but this is great news." he said with a happiness in his voice I hadn't heard since Chris had been kidnapped.

Through the smoky whiskey induced haze I wasn't sure what he had said. I probably looked confused. I lent on the door frame for support.

"What did you say?" I asked trying not to slur my words, but failing.

"Listen you weak minded...... drunk. That poor girl that was blown up at the Meatworks wasn't Chris. Sadly, it turns out that a blonde girl who strongly resembled Chris was kidnapped from outside the Bunnings in Dalby the day before we went to the Meatworks. Innocent parents lost their precious daughter but it definitely wasn't Chris."

Guilt slammed me from another direction. Was it wrong to be glad it wasn't Chris?

The door post failed me and I slid to the floor. I was unsure what to do, laugh or cry. I had no choice, no control so I did both. If I had been sober, I would have had empathy for the murdered girl and her family. However, in my state of numbness I could only feel relief.

"Oh, Sarge, she's alive, Chris is alive," I slurred happily from where I sat on the floor.

"Yeah, we certainly hope she is, and if we are going to find her you need to quit drinking that stuff long enough to get the job done," he said angrily.

"I know, I know, you blame me for all this, and you know what? You know what? You probably know what, yeah? You're one hundred percent right. No, one hundred and ten percent right. It's all my fault," I slurred with tears in my eyes.

He and I had enjoyed many a beer or whiskey when we were friends, but he had suffered a career of putting up with drunks. He had no time for them, especially when he knew the man. Looking down, he said. "You're disgusting Wallace. I know somewhere deep in there is a smart, brave, tough and resourceful bloke, Steve. You dig deep and find him by tomorrow morning. I'll come by and pick you up. But if you're still looking at the world through the bottom of that bottle I'll leave you where you fall," the hard Senior Sergeant said angrily, and walked back to the Police 4WD he had parked on the road.

As he opened the cabin door he turned, "Son, we all love her, and we miss her, and we would both die for her. Pull your head out of your butt and get on board."

I didn't answer, I just sat on the floor in the front doorway and wept.

About the same time Senior Sergeant Townsend was nagging me, unbeknown to us Roza the Assassin was having breakfast at a roadhouse. He wasn't enjoying the food. The breakfast wasn't to his taste, but it was more about what he was thinking. He was sitting in the garish vinyl booth pondering a man he had never met, but a man who had single handedly destroyed his career, Steve Wallace.

Roza was a disciplined assassin, a skilled sniper and his profession was always founded upon the ability to wait and then to wait some more. However, while he could be still for hours in torrential rain or insect infested jungle this was different.

But this was different, this pause had extended beyond the normal hit. He was still a hardened warrior but had now grown more accustomed to top class hotels, international resorts and luxury yachts in between contracts. Living in an RV even a very nice modern one like he was currently using, had it's limitations. Operationally he was outside his comfort zone and everything in him knew that his ability to adapt and blend in was why he had been so successful. He was usually comfortable just about anywhere. Seeing revenge had knocked him off his rails, he was doing things that he would never have contemplated at any point during his career. The Roma Meatworks Op was sound. The world class Assassin was sure when he planned the Operation that he would have succeeded in settling the account, but this Steve Wallace, an unknown Australian Soldier kept acting out of the norm. Wrecking

Roza's ingenious attack on the American President and the other Prime Ministers was not a counter genius. In this instance he had not been ahead of Roza, but, it was the other requisites for any Assassin, that of observation, reaction and resolve that Wallace had undone even with weeks of planning. The boring hours spent grooming the young Australian decoy Luke. The wrecking of Roza's creative actions and creative solutions he had devised to mould the environment to suit the attack. It didn't matter how Roza looked at it, Wallace had beaten him. Then back to the Meatworks, he did it again. Roza had set it all up, he would either shoot Wallace, or blow him up. Roza had set the bait, so that Wallace's guilt and grief should have caused him to rush in. Again, the Australian out played Roza, avoiding any of the fire lanes Roza had established, and then letting those two country Coppers spring the bomb. Wallace was more than annoying.

Roza decided to do something that he very rarely did and that was contract out the job.

Now in a way he realised that revenge was supposed to be personal, one on one. But, he knew he couldn't go into Roma and do it himself, and Wallace seemed to be wallowing around in a pity party about his blushing bride. The international Assassin had decided his taste of the revenge was hearing the anguished sobs over the phone.

He congratulated himself on the touch of using his missing bride's phone. Roza had also learned to respect Wallace, credit where credit is due. He was, for a local boy, a very good operator. To see him fall apart and not do everything he could to find his fiancee's Kidnapper was another sweet revenge from Roza's viewpoint, he needed everything to be taken away from Wallace and then he would take whatever he had left. The Australian had to pay with his life, and everything he loved. The Bikies had been easy to arrange and had been a spur of the moment decision.

Roza had been in a roadhouse between Roma and Carnarvon Gorge eating some unidentifiable Australian food.

Not that he would know what road-kill kangaroo would taste like, but it wouldn't surprise him if that's what he was chewing on. The Bikies had stormed into the Aussie diner like they always did, like they owned the place.

Intimidation was their stock in trade. No one noticed the covert scrutiny that Roza had put the outlaw Bikies under. In under ten minutes he knew who led the group, who was second in command and who were drones.

Roza was a master in appraising a situation and manipulating the variables to provide himself with the outcomes he desired. He waited for the Leader to separate from the group. Roza was aware that the Leader

would be careful of a blunt approach. However, time was tight, they would only be in the roadhouse for half an hour max. He knew that he would have to make his move quickly.

The international Assassin was already outside his comfort zone but he had learned over many years to trust his instincts. He was also very sure that if he tried his newly acquired Australian accent the Bikie would be put off by it's falsehood.

"My friend I have no time, but I do have a lot of money. I also have a need for a group such as yours, I believe you may have the skills and the motivation for a job I need done." Roza said quietly.

"You know that is strange, because I didn't realise we were friends. I have no idea what you are talking about, mate. Do you make a habit of walking up to strangers and talking in riddles?" The Bikie Leader said sarcastically, with an undercurrent of implied threat.

The Assassin was a little surprised at how well spoken the Bikie Leader was.

"No offence Sir, I must have been wrong, I thought you might be a man who could make quick decisions about making quick money. I assume your response was to guard against Under Cover Police entrapping you in some scheme. You strike me as an intelligent man. Do you really believe that the Police would place a man such as me in the middle of nowhere, hoping you or someone similar might happen along?" Roza asked, being careful not to sound like he was making fun of the Bikie Leader.

"OK, point taken. Come over to that booth and you can tell me when you want your wife's boyfriend scared outta town," the Bikie said sarcastically.

Ignoring the sarcasm Roza went onto explain that the job was more serious than such a menial domestic problem, and that the Target lived in the old Police Station in Roma and that he was ex-military.

The Bikie Leader was ex-army so he wasn't phased by that. They had negotiated back and forth a little, but only so the Bikie thought he had won the first fight. The other reason was that Roza wanted the hit to seem low level. He didn't want to appear to be some international high flyer, which of course he was. Finally, the deal was struck, half now in cash, the other half in cash if the Bikies wanted to come back and pick it up, or bank transfer if they trusted the stranger to complete the transaction. The Bikie Leader had returned to his gang, bragging about the deal he had just done.

"Guys how good is this, we are heading up to Roma and now we get an all expenses paid job on the way. Waste this guy who lives there and we are on the road before the gun smoke clears. The guy paying us said the target is ex- Army, but most of them are as dumb as a bag full of hammers and, besides there are six of us, one of him, and he doesn't know we are about to visit him." The Bikie Leader didn't share how much the deal was really worth to all the gang, he always kept a little aside for the rainy day that would eventually come.

"OK, guys, we are flush with cash, so order whatever you want." The Leader continued with a smile. As he said it, he looked around the room for the stranger but he was nowhere to be seen. He thought nothing of it.

CHAPTER 24

Some friends drop into Steve's.

Senior Sergeant Townsend was right.

A stronger man would have listened. A better man would have sobered up. But I was neither. Instead, I was wallowing in self-pity and guilt, grieving the loss of the love of my pathetic life. I should have sworn: "That's *my last drink until I get Chris back.*"

But I didn't. Mr Jack Daniels and I had a special long term relationship.

Even I know that's weak and doesn't make any sense. BUT! There are always buts, excuses, reasons.

I didn't make the Senior Sergeant's threatened deadline. I don't even know if he checked on me because I was probably in a stupor and wouldn't have noticed him anyway.

He never mentioned whether he had dropped into check on me. In fact, he never mentioned anything to me again. He never spoke to me again. Well, until not until later on when he finally ran me out of town like some cowboy movie Sheriff. I figured that I was on borrowed time.

The beautiful country town of Roma had a quiet couple of weeks, and so did I, and that meant the local Senior Sergeant and all his crew were as happy as they could ever get. But it couldn't last; the old cop was right. I attracted trouble like flies on roadkill. I was so down I couldn't even be bothered to go bush. Everything out there reminded me of Chris and Jake, the border collie the Kidnapper had beheaded on what was supposed to be my wedding day. And..... And it was a big AND. I could easily walk to the bottle shop and drink my way home.

A noise startled me as I stumbled along humming a Toby Keith favourite 'Beer for My Horses'. Ten or so Harleys were rolling through town, and every head was turning because city Bikies seldom made it this far West. The teenage girls giggled and pointed, and their mums frowned. I turned off McDowall St and never gave the gang another thought.

The Leader of the Bikies, who everyone called Wolf, saw the KFC and headed for it, turning into Bowen St and then into their driveway. He figured they hadn't eaten since the Roadhouse near Canary gorge and maybe they could find out some info on the Target when they went inside for food. The gang rolled into the parking lot, attracting the same stares and the attention they drew everywhere they went. The noise was so oppressive it rattled the big restaurant windows. The thunder of the combined Harleys seemed to put pressure on everyone as it reverberated off every surface and then, as one, it stopped, leaving a vacuum of silence. The Bikies all took off their helmets. Stiff-legged after so many miles the one wearing the Sergeant of Arms Patch walked over to where Wolf still sat astride his Fatboy Harley.

"You'll be livin' up to your bike's name if we keep visiting every KFC you see," he laughed. He was one of the few people in the world that could stir his Leader like that.

"You know, Warthog, my motto is everything in moderation. Even moderation. Besides, some junior in here might tell us what we need to know," Wolf said evenly.

"OK, I guess we want to keep it calm in there? So they aren't overpowered by all these smelly apes, you and I alone, yes?" Warthog suggested.

"See, you got it. It's already working, with moderation; good work. Find out what all those vegetarians want. We'll pull over somewhere down the road and rest up a bit," the Leader stated. He like all good Leaders was already thinking ahead.

Pushing through the doors the aroma of fuel, leather and unwashed bodies followed them to the counter. The two Bikies strolled through the restaurant and up to the counter. The three KFC crew looked like they expected to be robbed, the pimply young male taking the smallest of steps backwards. Like the animal he was named after, Wolf smelt fear in that one. Most people acted this way when confronted by him and his gang. Reading his name tag, he smiled,

"Brett, how you doin' today? Can we get two Giant Feasts, all original recipes, please?" he said.

"Oh, and throw in a twenty-one-piece pack as well in case the boys get hungry." Wolf added politely, smiling. Even though Wolf had addressed his order to Brett, the two girls jumped to action. The boy pretended he was a statue screwed to the floor, and this suited the Bikie's plan to ask some questions.

"So Brett, you always lived here? Before he could answer, the Leader continued, "It's a nice lookin town. Come over here, son, we aren't goin to bite."

The boy obeyed like his feet were in molasses, hardly moving his legs but still ending up in front of Wolf and Warthog.

"That's better, mate. I can understand you being a bit careful, what with all that trouble I hear you guys had. There was some Driver or someone killed and then..... Where was it? at an old Meatworks or something? Wolf had Googled Roma for a quick digital Recce. He had read a story about some Chauffeur being shot and then a bombing. However, he had no definite reason to believe it was in any way related to this job, although he was bright enough to work out it could have been because the Target seemed to be involved somehow in everything that had rocked the country town.

The boy behind the counter seemed to relax a little, perhaps mentioning something familiar, a thing away from here was not quite as scary.

"Yes, Sir, that sure was a lot of action for around here. This new Scottish Cop got all blown up; they said there was nothin left but his cap," the boy said, warming to the idea that he was the centre of attention as he knew something that this scary dude was interested in.

Wolf figured the kid was just repeating what he had heard from the tenth teenager who would have also repeated the story.

"Now, Brett, what was it all about?" Warthog asked in a friendly tone.

"Well, it's a long story, but it's gotta do with one of the local Coppers. She's hot as, for her age I mean," the boy said with adolescent appreciation.

"Anyway, she was s'posed to marry this guy. Everyone is still trying to work him out. Most of us reckon he's gotta be Army or somethin secret because he's always disappearing for a week or two. He looks like somethin' out of a Rambo movie."

Wolf was being patient, but Warthog was struggling. "Yeah, yeah, sure, kid, what happened?" he spat the question at Brett a little too forcefully.

Wolf stepped towards the counter, edging Warthog away from the boy. "Brett, it's been a bit exciting around here. I hear there was a some drama at a wedding, or something?" he gently asked glaring at his Sergeant at Arms.

The timid boy was trying to keep his audience, he wasn't used to people listening to him. "Well, no one knows, but the papers and the TV said that the Limo Driver was murdered. Chris, that's the chick Copper I told ya about, has just disappeared. Anyway, we are pretty sure the bombing out at the Meatworks had something to do with that," the KFC boy said.

Wolf had been keeping an eye on the girls assembling their order and had kept the conversation low to avoid alerting them of his interest in the local history. He knew he was pushing his luck.

"Did that Army dude stay around?" he now whispered as the girls approached the counter with the Bikie's order.

"He did, but I hear he just stays in his little house at the old Police Station down on Queens St. and hasn't been sober since that crazy wedding day," the boy said, not realising the value of those few words.

Few people would have noticed the subtle nod that passed between the two Bikies, of agreed success and the end of business. Having paid when they ordered the two Bikies grabbed the KFC bags and headed for the door. Brett looked sad because the only adults who had valued his conversation for a long time had just walked out without even a goodbye. The girls stared out the windows at the leather-clad men with their tattoos and dirty, long hair. None of the local farm boys looked that good. Bad boys always seemed a better alternative to boring cowboys.

The Bikies mounted up, and a convoy of Softails, Fatboys, Cruisers and a few Choppers roared out of town.

When they had got back to their bikes, the Leader said to Warthog, "You guys head back to that little park we saw comin into town. I'll be there in a little while."

They didn't know why he wasn't staying with them, but he was the Boss. He always knew what was going on. The Bikie Leader knew the value of good intel and had decided he needed to Recce this guy's place. The last thing he wanted was a heap of noisy bikes driving up and down some quiet street attracting attention. Some old granny might even phone the Cops. He wanted to have a look, do the hit and be gone before anyone noticed his gang was in town. By the time he had finished looking around, he knew the house and yard layout. He had also decided to park the bikes around the corner, away from the Target house. This should ensure that no one would remember them being in the neighbourhood at the time of the imminent attack. His plan was to be two hundred kilometres from Roma by the time anything could be organised. Satisfied, he headed for the park.

He was hungry, and now he hoped the boys had left him some KFC. Knowing them, probably not. Respect was big, but they were like a big family when it came to food. Stepping over the low treated pine log barriers surrounding the park, he joined his gang. Surprised, he found that they had left him some chicken.

He ate as he explained the layout, and his plan. The guys struggled a bit with their

Leader's way, none of them were ex-military. He went all formal and detailed at times like this, but everyone liked knowing their jobs and how things would work. They had all gone into situations with no plan and had seen how things worked out. Making it up as you go usually meant getting bashed or being caught by the pigs.

"OK, you all good?" The Leader asked, after a pause he stood shaking off the chicken crumbs. "Great, let's hit the road. Don't forget, no revving your nags, low key, yes?" He said as they all headed back to their bikes.

Even though we were hundreds of kilometres from the ocean, in my drunken misery, I had become an avid fan of the YouTube channel, Roger Osborne Fishing. I left it on pretty much twenty-four-seven. This may be what saved my life. Unbeknown to me, the Bikie gang had silently arrived on foot. However, instead of being in front of the TV, I was sitting in total darkness with a JD in my hand. Roger Osborne was explaining some fishing techniques. Half asleep I hadn't heard or seen anything at this point. Suddenly, I was on full alert. Something or some one had just walked past my window.

The two outlaw gang members assigned to breach the back door had walked down the side path and then they had returned to the front yard. By doing so they confirmed to their presence to me.

"What's wrong? I need you clowns to be where we planned," the frustration evident in the

Leader's voice.

"Boss, Boss, he's watching TV; you see that flickering light about halfway down the path," the bigger of the two said quickly, not wanting to give Wolf an opportunity to get angry. Even though his training demanded staying with the plan, the Boss quickly realised the value of this up-to-date intel.

"OK, boys, good work. The plan is still good now we know he's in the lounge. Let's get you round the back, and when you hear us breach the front door, come flying through the back entry point," the Leader stated, replacing the initial frustration with an encouraging tone and slap on the big Bikie's shoulder.

I had only been home from the bottle shop a little while and had already made sure what I had bought was in good condition. I was hungry, so I went into the kitchen. However, as I had done so many times before, by the time I stood in front of the fridge, I had lost my appetite. Instead, I opened the freezer door, scooped a handful of ice into a tumbler, and had my first 'formal' drink for the day. Being ARMY and working twenty-four-seven, I had no hangups about all this rubbish about waiting for a civilised time of day to start drinking. Now, I was back in the lounge watching yet another fishing video. Even in this haze, I still had two people's share of paranoia. Maybe not on full alert, but it was always present like a slithering reptile on a subconscious level. It's what makes veterans sit in restaurants facing the entrance, identifying exits and potential threats. It's also what has kept me alive all this time, a gut warning of an unseen ambush or boobie trap.

This is the same feeling that I get when I meet someone and that feeling warns me that they will become a threat, perhaps not immediately, but one day.

Two silhouettes moved behind the vine-covered trellis; two men were heading towards the backyard. *If there's two, there's gotta be more.* I thought. I had two advantages. First, I knew the house, and they didn't; second, I already knew they were coming, any surprise as mine. I had seen two shapes pass by my darkened window. I silently moved into my bedroom, quietly pulling my gun case from under the bed. I had no idea how many I was up against or who they were, but their intentions were clear. I would probably end up running through the house either from or towards the intruders. I planted three handguns around the house, guessing possible firing positions or fallbacks.

Next, I went to an old 7.62 Ball Ammo box I had under the bed. I withdrew a green curved plastic item.

Most people would not have known what it was, and even the words moulded on convex side only provided a small hint. FACE TOWARDS ENEMY. I had handled hundreds of these and I never failed to smile when I read this instruction, always finding it amusing. I quickly took the M18 A1 Claymore Mine out. I had already set it up for just such an occasion as this, so the boobie trap was all rigged. All I had to do was set it on the floor and hook the cable to the front door. Anyone opening the door would be blasted by seven hundred thirty-two calibre steel balls travelling at just under four thousand feet a second. I also grabbed my Remington 870 short, with a pistol grip and a sling, perfect for close fighting inside a building. OK, I was as ready as I would ever be, all that had taken less than a minute. However, I figured my assailants had also had enough time to get just as ready.

Now all I could do is wait. I knew I wouldn't have to wait long, these guys should be ready by now. If it was me I would breach the front and back doors together and sweep the house, being careful to only fire left or right. This way the two teams wouldn't shoot each other. I sat down in the hall facing the front door, a Glock 19 in my hand, and the shotgun slung over my shoulder. I heard the crunch of the gravel on the front path going past the roses that Chris loved so much. Seconds later two sets of boots quietly trod on the bottom step, it always squeaked. The front door flew open and set off the Claymore shattering the silence along with my front door and surrounds. I was always in awe of the destructive power such a small device delivered. This time was no exception.

The two Bikies coming through the front door were now smouldering, bleeding lumps of flesh. The one in the middle who had booted the door open had been vaporised; little bits of him littered the stone path all the way to the letterbox. A few moments later, the smell of burnt flesh was carried down the hallway on the breeze that usually brought the sweet scent of roses.

The entry was filled with smoke and through it, light now flooded in uninhibited by doors, curtains or windows. I knew that I didn't have time to survey the damage. Confirm my suspicions the back door shattered inwards as two Bikies entered the cottage.

The hall went from the front door straight to the back which meant they were looking along the straight hallway, now illuminated by the huge opening created by the blast. I was silhouetted in the light encouraging the Bikies to open up with their twelve gauge shotgun and big slug cut off 30/30. I had only time to think; *It must be an auto because the shots are coming so fast.* All I could do was drop to the floor. Thankfully, they weren't bright enough to aim low, which is common when people use shotties. They rely on the spread of the pellets to hit the target by pray and spray rather than actually aiming.

After their initial burst the two moved from the back door running down the hall and opening up again. Bikies are sort of street tough, but they aren't well-trained or military-equipped. I rolled left into the kitchen putting all my money on them thinking I would keep running away from them. Instead, I unslung the Mossberg and turned back into the hall. They were so sure they had me in the kitchen that I could see the surprise on their faces as they slid to a halt just three metres from me. The 12 Gauge loaded with SGs mostly hit the Bikie on the left, removing his head from his bottom jaw.

The Glock barked twice. The 30/30 Bikie fell clutching his throat as he died, collapsing to the floor.

Another guy, (I would read later from his jacket that his name was Warthog, the gang Sergeant at Arms) snuck in through the patio door.

He got a barrel full of SGs, the 32-calibre balls peppering across his chest and right shoulder, spinning him backwards through the hallway entrance where he had appeared. He would have died without further assistance but I couldn't wait. I drew my Glock and nailed him between the eyes as he turned back towards me. I had no way of knowing how many invaders I was up against, but it had gone very quiet. Had I got them all? Had others run? What I really suspected was that the remainder, the smart ones were playing possum waiting for me to relax.

Once again, my gut was true. The smoke and dust from the Claymore explosion still filled the entrance. As I slowly walked down the hall, it was difficult to see. The smell of the various weapons that were now silent filled my nostrils. I was as nervous as a cat in a retirement home full of rocking chairs. Maybe they were all gone.

I looked into my bedroom.

BANG. BANG. Even though I had half expected more assailants, it was awful close. I had one play, and I made it; I had a stun grenade in my jacket. Pulling the pin in one action, I threw the cylinder over my shoulder and crunched into the fetal position, plugging my ears with my fingers. I felt the Magnesium burn over me, singing my hair. I rolled over and stood up. I was a little stunned, even though I knew it was coming. With nothing left but strength of will, I drove myself towards the bedroom. There before me was a Bikie on his back, bleeding ears, and crying. His sight must have recovered enough to try a shot; he raised a Glock of his own. I was ready, my pump-action shotty barked and a hole the size of a soup bowl appeared on his chest.

How many were there? They must have hired a bus.

I sensed more than saw another one. He was quick, but he still left half his Bikie boot showing around the wooden trim of the entry to the lounge. He had snuck in the back door when i busy ending his mates. I could only see the leather straps holding a silver ring at the side of his ankle. It provided me a nice target. Taking careful aim, my shot entered his left ankle cutting the metal ring and adding shrapnel to the projectile's devastation. He screamed and sort of staggered/fell back into the hall. My next shot gave him an extra eye between his others.

I could hear sirens, and in Roma, it doesn't take the Cops or the ambulances long to get to a job inside the town limits. I knew I had no time to even think of a plan, so all I could do was buy myself a little space and time. I quickly packed bag, I knew I couldn't run, but I was hoping I could talk my way out of this battle field. I carried my bag out to the Hilux through the demolished front entry.

CHAPTER 25

The Cops cut me a break & I take a visitor to my hunting camp.

All Chris's roses were like little Christmas trees decorated with random bits of leather, flesh and blood. Bile rose in my throat, not from the gore, but from the desecration of something beautiful that she loved. Anger rose up again as I missed her for the millionth time. As I surveyed the bloody scene I saw a slight movement, my mind telling me it must have been a small bird attracted by the colour or smell. I carefully wound my way through the carnage. Lying in a flower bed was a leather clad body.

"HELP ME." The bearded face cried.

"Well, well, look what we have got here," I said.

My mind wrapped around this unexpected gift. I already figured that as my 4WD was parked out front the cops would assume it had no part in the attack. I picked up the semi-conscious Bikie, well, sort of, because he was huge and dragged him to the Ute. I let gravity and a push from me get him onto the tailgate. Climbing into the tray I pulled him in, I zippy tying his hands and feet, like a rodeo champ, and putting a gag over his mouth to keep him quiet. I threw an old tarp over everything and jumping down slammed the tailgate shut. As I hit the ground I could hear sirens coming around my corner. I hoped that it wasn't my ex-friend, the Senior Sergeant. However, apparently, I had used up all my luck for the night. I braced myself for the tsunami I knew would engulf me when the Senior Sergeant arrived. Starsky and Hutch arrived, pumped up with adrenaline, looking disappointed that the excitement was over. Neither of them had ever fired their weapons in anger.

They weren't going to today. I knew the two Constables that arrived first, like something from a movie, they entered my shattered home, all stiff armed holding out their Police Glocks, shouting 'clear' as they made their way from room to room. They found me sitting in the lounge facing the hallway, this time with all the lights on. They both came in looking around in amazement at my damaged home.

"OK, OK, take it easy. It's all good, I'll explain when your Boss gets here.

Where is he, guarding the bakery like normal? I said cheekily, knowing it would settle them down. We all turned towards the doorway at the sound of a vehicle hard breaking hard sliding on the loose gravel on the street and of a car door slamming shut.

"What are you two standing around here for?" Senior Sergeant Townsend yelled. Everyone knew it was a command requiring action, not a real question.

"I know it's rare to have a crime scene but let's switch on. Scotty, get the tape out, cordon off what you can, until we can get some help. Jones, get on the phone and get

everybody in. I don't care if it's their day off, or they're nearing death. Huey and Dewey are out catching speedies on the Injune road. Get 'em back here ASAP. Get them all here now" he said as he surveyed the scene.

"I think the only thing that is for sure about you Wallace is that you attract trouble and death like roadkill and flies. Do you hate our town so much that you want to bring war to the streets that made you feel welcomed?

"As soon as I heard we had a shooting, I knew it had to be you. I should have known," the Senior Police Officer continued angrily.

"This isn't my fault, I didn't invite them. Would you rather it was me on the floor instead of them? Because, that's what you sound like." I said sounding as angry as I felt, at the same time disappointed in myself that I was showing it. I could nearly hear the senior cop's mind working through the mess.

"You don't move, don't talk, just sit there and hope that I think this is all a bad dream." The Senior Sergeant spat.

I wasn't used to being spoken to that way, but I wanted this to play out, hopefully allowing me to eventually spend some quality time with my mate friend trussed up in the back of my Ute. My ex-friend Senior Sergeant Townsend was no fool. I had to cooperate but with a degree of unwillingness so as not to set off any alarm bells in his cop hardened mind. I could hear him walking around the house, taking in all the details, knowing that he would not be touching anything. I knew that the others would be would be doing standard cop stuff. I had bet all my money on my Hilux not being included in the crime scene by the Coppers. If it was, and they looked in the tray, I was in for a long free stay down in a Brisbane jail. The old Senior Sergeant turned back to me. "You are the biggest trouble magnet this town has ever been unlucky enough to see. This can't happen, not in Roma. Roma is a sleepy, safe place to enjoy working, full of families, schools, and churches. What have you brought here, Wallace?" he spat again. I could tell he had come to a decision.

"I want you out of here NOW!" the Senior Sergeant shouted as he stepped towards me.

"OK, don't get all excited. I figured I might have to move out of the house until your guys were finished," I said calmly.

"No, you're not hearing me. I want you out and out for good. As he returned from the front entrance, he said incredulously, "Seriously, a Claymore in this quiet street that was home to you and Chris. Do you ever stop to think? All around you are lovely old ladies seeing out their twilight in a sleepy country town. Not a war zone, not even a busy road." His anger confirmed by his reddened face. Go and don't come back. We don't want your type of trouble. It's a deadset miracle that your neighbours living both sides of you didn't cop a wild shot. I'm surprised that frigging whizzbang thing didn't give 'em a heart attack. We've got children walking and riding past. Don't you get it? This is not Afghanistan or somewhere." The whole time he was making this speech, his voice had been rising, bubbling like molten lava, like a warning of an imminent eruption.

"I get it, but I didn't ask these scum to come here and try to kill me," I said allowing a little amount of pleading to be heard in my statement.

"OK, OK, this is what we are going to do. I have had enough of you. Chris is gone, so you have nothing here. You will go to the Station and make a formal statement. Then I want you out of town, never to come back. You hear me. NEVER, EVER!" the

Senior Sergeant shouted.

"Now just wait a second. This isn't the Wild Wild West, and you aren't the

Sheriff," I said to appearing to be unhappy with the outcome, even though it fitted my developing plan perfectly.

He cut me off as though I hadn't spoken.

"Now, for old times sake I'll do you a favour. Just in case I hear something about Chris, you need to keep your phone on. I don't owe you anything, but for Chris's sake I will call you. Now, listen very carefully. I want you gone, out of town as soon as we have that statement. No discussion, no conditions. You hear me?" He demanded.

I understood. He had seen me come into Chris's life, and just as it looked like we were settling down with each other even the proverbial white picket fence, it all went pear-shaped. Starting with the death of the Chauffeur and the kidnapping of the bride, who he loved as a daughter, and then, in a sick ambush, his Scottish Sergeant had been killed, and he was wounded. Yeah, he was right. I'd turned a beautiful cattle town into a war zone. I decided that he was right. I had to go.

"Sergeant, is that really fair? Like he keeps saying, he's the victim here," the young Constable asked.

"First of all, you know I hate it when you try to sound like some Yankee TV show. Sure he might be the 'victim,'" the senior man emphasised, making exclamation points with his fingers. "But, he has cost us several lives and much drama. The point is none of this would be happening, or at least not here if he wasn't here too. You see, I don't care about fair, I care about peace. I care about the old ladies that could well have been killed today. Doesn't matter if it was an accidental stray shot, they would still be just as dead," the Senior Sergeant said convincingly.

"Thanks Jonesie, but he is sorta right," I said. I'd had enough.

"OK, sorry, I see that you're right. I'll move out of town. Can you give me a few hours to pack?" I asked humbly.

"We still don't know about Chris, so can you please let me know if you hear anything? I know it's hard; you want me gone, but I must know and try to get her back if we can," I pleaded.

Irritated the Senior Sergeant snarled, "Like I said before, you keep that phone on and I'll keep my side of the bargain. I'm very sure that's the first time, in a long time, that you begged anyone for something. I know you love her, but this is all too crazy for anywhere, especially here. You pack and don't take all day, then come up the station, and make the statement. Then get."

"Sergeant, if I go, I need to be armed, this isn't over," I said, bluffing that I hadn't already emptied my gun safe.

"I thought I was being over generous as it was. Would you like me to make you a nice little dinner before you go?" He responded sarcastically.

"Yeah, OK, I can't expect you, of all people, to travel without a weapon, so I'll cut you a massive piece of slack. Constable Jones, seeing his well being is so important to you, this is what I want you to do. You walk through this battleground and he can have any weapon that he didn't use, hasn't been fired. You understand, Jonesie?" He asked as though talking to a slow pupil. Get the rest bagged and tagged as evidence."

"Got it Sarge, then what?" the Constable asked.

"You stick with him like a Siamese twin. Sure, let him grab some personal stuff. Whatever gets him out of my town," he growled.

And, if you are needed at a Coroner's Inquest, you better show up," the Senior Sergeant said, in the quietest tone he'd used on me since the kidnapping. It was still as real a threat as I'd ever heard.

"You have my word on everything that we have said. Thank you, Sir," I said.

"Jonesie, he packs, then you escort him to the Station to make a formal statement. No detours. Got it mate?" he growled.

With that the Senior Sergeant walked out of the house. His Landcruiser Wagon was heard to start up, it's tyres spinning in the loose gravel as he sped away.

Like any normal workplace, when the Boss leaves, the pressure in the atmosphere seemed to drop like a switch had been flicked. I stood to start packing, thinking to myself this has worked out better than I had ever expected. As ordered the Police Officer followed me around like a shadow.

Jonesie walked around, stopping at each weapon and deciding whether it was evidence, or if I could take it. Constable Jones was wearing blue latex gloves to preserve fingerprints. He carefully pick up each gun to smell the muzzle to confirm if it had been fired.

With the Constable busy checking the weapons and recording details, I was able to load all the things I had previously left when interrupted by the sirens getting closer by the second. The hardest part was that the other young copper wanted to help me.

I held my breath every time we carried armfuls of gear to my 4WD. I hoped that the gag would keep working if the Bikie woke up at just the wrong moment. Finally, I had everything. There were lots of memories I could have taken but I knew they equalled heart break as well. I left them fooling myself I was actually moving on.

I turned to the two young Cops."Thanks guys, I know this is hard for everyone, even old grumpy, deep down doesn't want it this way. But, I can see where he's coming from. I'm heading down the Station. He wants you to escort me to make sure I get there. So let's hit the road, hey?" I said as though we were heading for the pub, and not to the first step to my exile.

POLICE STATION
44 QUEENS ST
ROMA

Two hours later I quickly signed two copies of my statement, standing immediately, ready to take my second step in exile. I was very mindful of my guest trussed up like a turkey, resting in the back of my Hilux outside the Police Station.

"OK, Wallace, I know you loved Chris, and that is why I've stuck my neck out for you on this. You should be locked up until we confirm all this. However, we have already started tracking the Bikie gangs movements since they hit town. They got a heap of Intel from a kid over at the KFC. Just a dumb kid talking to much. Apparently, they milked him for info about you. That, in my mind confirms that they came here for one reason and that was to pay you a visit," the Senior Sergeant stated.

"Now, if I need you to come back to answer any more questions about today, I want you back here before I put the phone down. You hear me? NOT NEGOTIABLE! Do I have your word on it? As long as you stay away from Roma I will happy every which way. You got that?" The Senior Sergeant said wearily.

That was my farewell from the beautiful country town of Roma that had been my sanctuary and my home with Chris for nearly two years. I was escorted out of the station all the way to my pick up.

A kitchen chair was one of the last things I had loaded into my ute, it was tied on top.

The young Constable that had been assigned as my shadow smiled.

"Tell me to mind my own business if you want, but what's the one chair for Steve?" he asked.

"No, I don't mind you asking, that chair is for me. When I go bush, I'm sick of sitting on an old stump or my tailgate; a bit of luxury is what that chair is," I answered.

"I'm sort a sorry for what the Boss said, and you gettin' kicked out a town. You know he's just upset. He loves this town, and the Senior sees the people sorta like his family. I can remember him bein' so happy that Sergeant Chris had finally met a real bloke. Then the wedding. The Boss was over the moon at being asked to walk her down the aisle. Ya shoulda seen him light up about it. He's like an ol' grizzly bear, alright, but I know a lot of the anger is because he likes you and he's got incredible respect for you. He's just scared, that's all. Worried like we all are about Chris, I mean Sergeant Chris," the young Constable said.

I shook his hand and thanked him for those kind words. "I believe what you said about him, and you're right; he's like an old grizzly, alright," I said as I climbed into the truck.

I headed out to where I had always gone, I turned onto the road to my mate's cattle property on the way to Injune.

This used to be my 'other' sanctuary with a bit of hunting, a lot of drinking and only my dog Jake for company. I never brought anyone that I had to talk to, Jake never demanded much of me. But, now all it did was make me sad, no, angry, maybe both.

"What's going on? Where am I?" the Bikie Leader slurred, blinking like an owl, his questions breaking into my memories. For a Bikie he was super-fit. I had checked his tatts when I had stripped him out of his colours, dirty tee shirt and jeans. Unless he was a poser, he was ex-Second Commando Regiment. Whoever he had been, or now was, he was a very unhappy camper. He sat naked as he had been born taped to the chair I'd brought from home. It looked a bit strange, certainly out of place sitting in my hunting camp.

For the first time I spoke, "OK, so here it is. You're all that's left of that rag-tag gang you brought to my home. I'm the one you were sent to kill. And, now, that's all you're getting because I've got a few questions of my own," I said, evil intent sounding in my voice.

I slapped him hard across the face, so hard that the chair threatened to tumble sideways.

"Now, who ya workin' for?" I demanded.

Spitting some blood, the Bikie continued calmly. "I don't talk to pig Coppers, and I certainly don't talk to my targets,"

"You don't get it, do ya? And, you're way out of luck mate. I'm no cop. Do you think you're in Queens Street having a latte`. This isn't some movie where you, the big Bikie hangs tough. We are in the middle of nowhere; there aren't even bars on my phone. You're mine," I said sarcastically.

"Yeah, yeah, big man, but I'm not that stupid. I'm dead either way. I tell you, you shoot me. Why should I tell you diddly squat?" the Bikie said confidently.

I had to give him some credit, even if it was an act, he was good and tough.

"OK, that was me being gentle to a fellow Soldier. I get it, you've been there. You're obviously a hard case, but even if you are. Well, right about now, your immediate future is all about whether you want to go quietly or painfully slowly," I said with icicles hanging off every word.

"You're startin' to bore me, and I've been in a bad mood for nearly a year now. Who sent you to kill me?" I continued as I drew my one-hander folder, a beautiful useful blade made by an Aussie knife maker called Alister Phillips. I flicked it open with plenty of flair to make sure the Bikie heard and saw me. I was done talking. I stabbed the Damascus Blade into the top of his leg and twisted the knife, so he'd notice. He was tough and stubborn; he fought showing pain by not screaming, but he couldn't control himself enough to not squirm.

"OK. So, mate, I knew you weren't goin to be easy, but I saw your toes curled a bit. Well, mate, that's just the start, I said with absolutely no malice, just certainty.

"Now, I'm no doctor, but I do know where your femoral artery is hiding, and if I remember right, it's just about here," I said as I pushed my knife into his leg. A dark crimson stained his jeans and pooled in the dirt under the chair.

"Your choice, old mate, die with some peace and dignity or die in pain and lying in your own blood and bodily fluids," I said in a deadly serious tone.

He was no coward, but he was no idiot either. Having said that, he wasn't convinced; he still needed a little encouragement.

I pushed a little harder and once again twisted the beautifully made blade further into his flesh. The blood started pulsing out where the slight trickle had once been. This time he screamed an obscenity.

"OK, OK. What difference does it really make anyway?" he said as his tan gave way to a pallor that confirmed his life was leaking into the dirt.

Because of the way the Bikies had been hired at the Roadhouse, there wasn't much he could really tell me. I started to realise grabbing him from that battle zone back at our cottage was a huge risk, especially with the amount of intel he could actually provide. I had a description that would fit about five percent of the population of Australia. This anonymity lined up with this guy's operation in every interaction we had. He was a professional, and seemed to anticipate every thought or move we ever made.

CHAPTER 26

I finally get smart, and old friends lend a hand.

Since our ruined and tragic wedding day, I had been crushed with guilt and by grief taking turns attacking my mind, body and soul. My grief for the woman I loved and to whom I owed so much, maybe even my life, certainly my sanity. The secondary pain was from losing a special dog who was more like a friend. Only some people would understand how much his murder had hurt, the hole in my life it had left. Losing Chris and Jake in one day, I returned to what I knew. I had gone back to my old ways, hiding in the bush like a sniper, but without a mission or even a direction to move towards, hiding in a bottle without a care. But by putting those Bikies onto me, the Assassin had just pushed me too far. I had come to a decision that only I could make. Senior Sergeant Townsend couldn't bully me into waking up; nothing and no one could. All the crushing guilt and grief couldn't, hadn't. But at the precise moment that I pulled the trigger on the Bikie Leader, I decided to wake up to myself.

Sadly, grief and guilt hadn't been enough, now anger, no, rage filled me. The Kidnapper had finally made a mistake, not in the way that he had betrayed his identity or whereabouts, but he had pushed me too far. He had driven me to the lowest point I'd been since meeting Chris. But, now, without realising it he had broken me through my whiskey-induced stupor. I was filled with a rage so hot it was like fat dripping onto a fire. If there had been any doubt, the rant the Bikie had repeated confirmed who was behind the attack. I'd had enough. I was Battle-Centric; I was back in the game, and the game was battle. I was focused on nothing else.

I had about one hundred and eighty-eight kilometres to cover as I headed to Chinchilla East of Roma. I had booked into The Great Western Motor Inn. I had stayed there before and found it a top place to stay. However, the main reason for this choice was that the owner was ex-SAS and an old mate, Tiger Thompson. When I had contacted him, I had told him enough of what had been going on so that he would be happy to take the booking under a fake name. He had seen his share of trouble and knew me well enough not to need to ask any questions. As I drove, I turned off Toby Keith and phoned the Senior Sergeant, wondering whether he would even take my call.

"What's happened? You run outta money for booze?" he barked as he answered my call.

"Yeah, OK, I deserve that," I said.

"My deductive powers know there is no phone reception out at your camp, so you must be in town. Are you? I said I never wanted you back in Roma," the Copper snarled.

I had never called him by his last name, but this wasn't two friends catching up.

"Relax, Townsend, I've obeyed your orders to leave Roma; you were right again; you're always right. And I like Roma too much to do it any more harm. I'm basing myself at the Great Western in Chinchilla. Please just give me a minute," I said.

"OK, that's all you got, one minute! That is, a minute after you answer some questions," the Senior Sergeant demanded.

Thinking that if I could cooperate or clear up something for him, it couldn't hurt our struggling relationship, I agreed immediately.

"How many Bikies attacked you? Do you think you saw them all?" he demanded.

Knowing straight away where this question had come, from I answered as calmly as I could,"I never really had time to count them. Two came through the back door, and two or maybe three came through the front. How many did your guys come up with?" I asked. Usually, I would have made some disparaging remark about how you'd need two Coppers to count anything right because one would have to take his boots off. We were not on that level anymore.

"By the way, I know words are cheap, but I'm off the sauce and ready to find this mongrel Kidnapper. If you hear anything, get me on the same mobile phone as before," I said as positively and confidently as I could. I wanted him to believe me, but I also wanted to move the conversation away from the number of Bikies, because I knew where one was stashed and wasn't about to confess it. He was an experienced Cop, and I hoped he hadn't noticed.

"Yeah, well, that's interesting, and yeah, words are cheap. The one on the front verandah, we had to count bits, but your maths are pretty right on a body count. But, have you ever known a Bikie to ride two bikes at a time? You see Wallace, they parked around the corner from your place. And, guess what we found; there was an extra Harley. I s'pose one might have run away on foot. What do you think?" the Senior Sergeant stated, his question mostly rhetorical.

"No idea, I had my hands full at the time and was just concentrating what was in front of me," I said convincingly while thinking of the Bikie Leader's body that I had left out on the cattle property, counting on the local wild pigs and dogs to dispose of his remains. I'd look after any leftovers next time I was out there, just in case a scull or something was lying around.

"Your minute's blown. If you're straight, I'll wait and see what happens," Townsend said and, without ceremony, hung up.

I drove on, wondering why I had even bothered. But I had to be fair; I'd let him down before, and deserved no better. I didn't know where to start; I had always been a loner. My Psych Eval' had identified this, and SAS had immediately matched this need to operate alone with being a Sniper. You often had a Spotter with you, but sometimes you were totally by yourself. From a Military point of view, this was especially critical as a solitary type flourishes alone or in small groups.

Conversely, that same Soldier looks inept and uncomfortable in a usual Platoon Company unit. That was fine; I didn't need anyone to hold my hand or motivate me, at least now.

But I was an Operative, not a Detective. I had no backup, no resources or databases to search. I sat in my hotel room, drinking coffee and wondering where I was going to go from here.

AUSTRALIAN NATIONAL SECURITY CENTRE
CANBERRA
AUSTRALIA
Canberra.

"Thanks for taking my call, Senior Sergeant Townsend; we met at Steve's Buck Night, and later in the church of course," Colonel Goodrich said.

"Sure, I remember you, a terrible next day, and it hasn't improved since," the weary Police Sergeant said."

"I just wanted to check on Steve; how's he going? He's been on sick and then compassionate leave since then, so I've had little or no contact with him. I always figure he is out at his mate's cattle property when there is no answer." Goodrich stated in a caring tone.

"Well, you're right about where he's been. He headed out there after the last war zone he brought to Roma. A small gang of Bikies attacked him at home. He sorted them, but this little town can't handle the shooting and the explosions that seem to be Steve's constant companions. You will probably think I was a bit rough on him, but I kicked him outta town the next day. That's when, as usual, he probably headed bush with a ute full of whiskey." Senior Sergeant Townsend said in a firm voice that didn't betray the conflict he held between anger and care for Steve.

"So he's not going too well by the sound of it. Handling the Bikies would be like breathing to Steve, all training and reactions, even if half-tanked. Do you know who they were, why they attacked him?" the Colonel asked.

"No, not a clue. This is Roma, not the Gold Coast, so we only have limited CCTV coverage. I've looked at all the videos. I have vision of the Bikies coming into town, then they went to the local KFC and then had stopped in one of our parks to eat. You can see them come back into town and turn off in Steve and Chris's house direction," the hard Cop's voice almost broke at the mention of

Chris. He continued, "But that's it, nothing more until the clean-up of what looked like something out of an Arnold Schwarzenegger movie. At first I thought there might have been a TA, a Traffic Accident or at least an incident, or maybe a run-in at the KFC or the pub between one them and Wallace. Nothin'. I have no evidence to suggest Steve even knew of the Bikie gang's existence until they attacked his house.

"You said they attacked his home? I don't believe in coincidences, but could they have had the wrong address? Was it the cliche 'burglary gone bad'?" the Colonel asked, already knowing the response would be.

"No, after the event we put it all together. The Bikies quizzed a kid at the KFC and then attacked," the Senior Sergeant stated.

"Now, I'm sure they only came here for him. I'm thinking the same; things don't just happen to people like Steve.

This was planned and executed; they parked around the corner so as not to alert him with the Harley's trademark exhaust noise. They used the old two-pronged attack, with two crews, front and back, the same as we would employ, for that matter.

The other thing is, we aren't talking about baseball bats and bike chains; these guys were tooled up," Townsend continued calmly.

"So Steve was uninjured, did what he needed to do and then you kicked him out of town," Goodrich said, anger starting to sound in his voice.

"Now come on, Colonel, I don't need you down in your Canberra ivory tower second guessing me up here in country Roma. Everything that has happened has rattled this town, I mean the murder of the Chauffeur, kidnapping of my Sergeant someone we all cared for, I mean care about, it's all been too much." Townsend corrected his use of the past tense, realising he had inferred Chris was dead. He then continued, "Then you know what?

This unknown Kidnapper or whatever he is, phones me, bold as brass here at my Police Station. He invites us, no he drags us into Wallace's war, to what turns out to be an ambush. No surprise. We knew it would be. Steve knew it too. But we had no choice, Chris was still missing. This was our first lead in weeks, if you want to call it that. We waltzed into a bombing at the old Meatworks, like it was Afghanistan.

A Scottish Police Sergeant they had sent out to replace Chris until we got her back, who was a good bloke and Copper was killed. He came all the way from Glasgow and there wasn't enough of him left to post home. Gone, all because of your good man, Wallace," the Senior Sergeant vented. He continued, "The Bikie attack was the final straw, Colonel. You might think I turned my back on him, but after so many 'last' chances, the guy's just a drunk. Colonel, this town can't handle any more violence. It's only lucky that the poor old Chauffeur has been the only civvy killed in the turmoil that surrounds your boy," the Policeman spat angrily.

Continuing as if the Senior Sergeant hadn't spoken, Colonel Goodrich asked.

"Yeah, yeah, OK, so how is he at the moment?" Goodrich hadn't been listening much since the phone call comment from the Senior Sergeant.

"It's funny you rang today out of the blue. He phoned me only this morning; he's moved to Chinchilla and swears that he's off the grog. I hope that's the truth. We may never know where Chris is. But staggering drunk, there's one thing for sure. For all his training and skills, Steve will never find her, and he'd be useless in trying to rescue her," the tired Police Sergeant said.

The Colonel had an idea, suddenly he needed to get off the phone.

"Thanks for your time; it's hard for me not to defend Steve. It's the way the Army rolls, but more than that, I know what he's done for this country. But I get where you're coming from after everything that's happened. I better go; you take care, Senior Sergeant," the Colonel said terminating the call.

He immediately put in a call to his contact in the CIA, Special Agent Munroe. They had worked together, shutting down an ISIS funding scheme involving the sale of antiquities. The Australian Operative who had done all the undercover work was none other than Steve Wallace. Colonel Goodrich was banking on this to get his requested favour approved. There was another card the Colonel held, the Trump card; Steve had recently saved the life of the President of the United States.

"How're you going, Munroe? You're working late, or is it early," the Aussie Colonel asked, accounting for the sixteen hour time difference.

"Colonel Goodrich, my old mate, what can I do for you," the CIA Agent asked attempting a terrible Australian accent.

"I'll come straight to the point. Of course, you remember Steve Wallace, ISIS smugglers, and, of course, that bit of help he gave POTUS when he was over here," the Colonel said casually as though he was talking about someone he had met in a pub.

"Steve, the man's a hero amongst those who know what he did; Top Secret, of course. But a hero just the same. I'd steal him from you guys, given half a chance," Munroe stated.

Encouraged by the CIA Agent's praise for Steve, Goodrich continued. "He's in trouble. It can't be confirmed, but as you know, the real Assassin who attempted to take out POTUS got away somehow. We all thought he would be on a beach somewhere nearer you than me. But, no such luck. He's here. We are sure of it and, he's hunting Steve Wallace. He's kidnapped Steve's fiancee and, since then, has had two goes at killing Steve, obviously motivated by revenge for Steve Wallace thwarting his OP on that USMC Base." Colonel Goodrich had set the trap to prepare to ask the favour that this call was all about.

"OK, OK, I'm interested; what do ya want? How can the CIA help?" Munroe asked.

He knew his Nation owed Major Steve Wallace a debt of gratitude that was near to immeasurable. He was pretty sure that if he sent that request up the food chain, POTUS would dispatch a Company of Marines to help the guy who had stopped the assassination attempt.

Goodrich had thought it through."Now, I need two things that should be easy for a smart guy like you. I know I don't need to say this, but I will anyway. Back when you needed an Australian Operative to go UC and gather Intel on that ISIS smuggling and banking ring, you got our best man. It all worked out, maybe beyond what you had dreamed. I need your Agent who Steve has worked with twice now. He was there in the Northern Territory right along side him. They make a good team, and Steve will trust him. You know what these door-kickers are like; they gotta know their six is never left hanging out."

"I'll need to bounce it off the Boss, but I'm sure that's all doable. What's the second thing?" CIA, Special Agent Munroe asked.

"The Assassin has made some calls, I want you to trace him. Get a loc on his base and Steve and Winfrey can end this," Colonel Goodrich stated confidently.

"The phone stuff might not work; this Assassin is world-class by all accounts. He went awful close to success over in the land of the bouncing kangaroo. Surely, he will now be three burners past the one he made those calls on," Agent Munroe said.

"That would be true in the States, mate, but here, we have a different system; you can't buy burner phones. You have to show heaps of ID to get a new phone, so it might work for us. It's the only lead we have to work with, OK," the Colonel paused and then continued.

"Munroe, I've had an idea; that young Aussie bloke Luke Edwards that helped him all the way through. The investigators have dissected his life from High School in Darwin until Winfrey ended his run. They have tracked him all the way from when the Assassin first picked him up at a local pub. The local Cops found their garage and worked out how they stole the two Hummers. They have even found out where he bought that stuff that cracked the rock. You're right about the Assassin being high-tech. The Marines discovered phone and radio blockers that he had deployed to disrupt comms near the ambush site." The Colonel said; there was a short gap as the words leapt the Pacific.

"As I just told you, Goodrich, chasing this guy's phone will be a waste of time." Munroe said, sounding a mix of satisfied and frustrated.

"Yeah, but guess what? He's been forced to use the only safe phones he had access to. The first calls were made on Steve's fiancee's phone and then he started using his Aussie offsider's phone. The Aussie probably told him it was stolen anyway and any trouble would come back to the real owner if it was traced. We've established that. But we haven't got the kind of gear you have to trace this rat down. I'll send you the data, call numbers, dates and times," Goodrich said leaning back in his chair.

"OK, give me twenty-four hours, I'll get it all approved, and I'll ask some friends over at the NSA. Talk to ya soon," Special Agent Munroe replied, and finished the call.

The Colonel had hoped for this outcome. He understood the set up of both American Intelligence Agencies. CIA is a civilian agency that specialises in Human intelligence, and the NSA is a Military Intelligence Agency specialising in Signals Intelligence. The NSA currently tracks millions of people's movements using cell phones' metadata.

After Colonel Goodrich had talked to Senior Sergeant Townsend, he had thought through this idea. Formulating his plan, he requested that the Queensland Copper send through the timings and details of the Assassin's phone calls. The Colonel knew that Police Stations logged every call, every visitor or incident. He figured the Assassin would have turned off the caller identification.

However, the time was enough, but only if you had the tech support. The call to Steve's phone on the day of the Meatworks bombing was from Chris's phone. And, once again, Police SOPs meant that the timings for that call were available from the Senior Sergeant's notebook. His email was pinged two hours after his call to CIA Special Agent Munroe. He was happy to see that it carried the Queensland Police banner. Senior Sergeant Townsend had come through with the required phone call info. The Colonel forwarded the email to Munroe, wondering if the CIA Agent would be in his Langley office due to the time difference. One way or another, Munroe would forward the call intel to the NSA. Goodrich headed home for the day satisfied that he had got the ball rolling.

CHAPTER 27

The Cavalry arrives in Chinchilla.

Colonel Goodrich's mobile vibrated loudly on the bedside table. Grabbing it he leapt out of bed more in surprise than purpose. He was still too slow; his wife, Bronwyn, was still complaining that he had woken her as he closed the en suite door. Sitting on the closed toilet, he answered the call.

Munroe had checked the time gap and decided the best way to get it done was to ignore it. "Wakey, Wakey, sleep is overrated, I reckon," Munroe said in a tone that was far too awake and way too happy for what was zero-two-hundred-hours Australian time.

"Yeah, you could be right. I sure hope this call is all good news, Munroe; I need my beauty sleep." The Colonel said in a sleepy, croaky voice.

"It sure is. No surprise 'whatever you Aussies want', that's what was the answer was. Like we both figured, Wallace has a solid CV of helping the United States when we needed it. But, I think that possibly saving POTUS's life gives him the keys to the kingdom," the C.I.A. Agent said.

"That's great news. In any case, none of us want an international Assassin who is clearly at the top of his trade running around. Not to mention, I think we all agree that this guy is the same as the Assassin who got the Russian Premier and the Canadian Prime Minister. He's gotta be on the top of the Most Wanted list for those countries and ours as well," the Australian Colonel said.

"Well, the operative you requested is on the next plane out of Hawaii, and the N.S.A. is running those phone times as we speak. I spoke to their expert nerd, and he reckons it's doable. You guys have so many dead areas that he is pretty confident they will be able to pinpoint this phone even better than they can here. The tower's locations force the caller into certain areas that might help you find him rather than a larger diameter circle," Special Agent Munroe stated.

Goodrich appreciated the positive response from the C.I.A. However, he also knew that the Americans wanted this Assassin just as much as the Australians did. This was for one reason and one reason only; this Assassin had tried to kill their Commander in Chief, and that could not be forgotten or allowed. He doubted that Steve's fiancee being kidnapped had much to do with their decision to help. If the Op. was successful, the Yanks would probably claim all the glory. None of that worried him as long as Chris got home safe and a world-class Assassin couldn't hide within Australia. Goodrich had requested Winfrey because he had established his creds on two shared missions as well as having a positive relationship with Steve Wallace. Unmentioned, but just as valuable, was the fact that the Colonel believed that Winfrey was still more Soldier than C.I.A. Agent. The Colonel also believed that, without any doubt, Winfrey would do all he could to apprehend or kill the Assassin. Also, due to his friendship with Steve Wallace, he would make sure that Chris's rescue would be a priority. Goodrich knew that this was the only way she would return alive. A perfect scenario, would be the Assassin taken out, and at the same time freeing Chris. The Colonel couldn't care less who took the shot as long as it was taken.

GREAT WESTERN MOTOR INN
CHINCHILLA QUEENSLAND

I had stayed in my motel room a few days before the bin, and the table were overflowing with empty bottles. Takeaway boxes from several places had replaced the square bottles I had relied on for so long. I've got to confess that I was struggling, especially after my not-so-motivational call with Senior Sergeant Townsend, but with everything I had lived through, I had learned long ago that I didn't need others. The only person I could depend on was me. It's a cliche, but the old adage "If it's meant to be, it's up to me" has always proven true. I was missing the J.D. but I reminded myself that I missed Chris even more, and this animal that had her was going to pay.

Months of wallowing in an alcohol bath of misery had dulled my usual rock-hard nerves. My room phone chirped, causing me to jump. This annoyed me no end; I had never been jumpy.

"Steve, you gotta visitor. Will I send him up?" asked my Army mate Tiger in reception.

He knew I was incognito; no one but he and Senior Sergeant Townsend knew I was there and what name I was using. My mate wouldn't drop me in it, not for any amount of cash. I didn't think the senior Roma Copper would either, except by accident. I figured my mate was savvy enough not to be standing in front of my 'visitor', so I asked, "What's your take on him?"

"Fit, a bit younger than us, blonde hair, a Yank, gotta be Military of some brand," he answered.

Well, that described about thirty per cent of America's population.

"Alright, mate, send him up; I'll handle him, one way or another." I said confidently.

"Roger that, mate, he's on his way," my mate hung up.

Two minutes later, there was a knock on my door. In all the movies, the guy inside looks through the peephole to see who is knocking, but this is how that all works in my world. If you're there to execute the person inside, or he has a bodyguard, you stand as far to the side of that door as you can. That way, the sucker on other side can't shoot you through the door. You then wait until the peephole goes black because someone on the other side of the door has put their eye on it to check you out. Phat! You shoot through the peephole, their eye and into the brain. The bodyguard or the Target is down; either way, it's a great start. So, here I was inside and all that had flown through my mind. I have done all those things many times in many different countries. So, I knew the antidote to the scenario. On the inside, I stood to one side behind the wall and reached over; then, I put a spoon I had picked up over the peephole. In my other hand was my Glock.

Anyone in the killing game knew this routine. There was another knock, a little louder and a little more insistent on a response. I leaned over and placed the spoon on the eyepiece. If the fella on the outside wanted to harm me, now was when he would shoot.

"Honestly, Steve, that is so old school, even for a pensioner like you," a voice said from outside my room.

"Don't move a muscle, young fella. Now, the last thing I want to have to do is clean your guts off that wall. But it's your choice," I heard my mate Tiger say threateningly.

"No way! Is that you, Winfrey?" I shouted excitedly as I opened the door.

It was Winfrey; he was leaning on the wall, his hands extended above his head. He was laughing. My motel owner mate had a sawn-off twelve gauge pointed at his back. Well-trained, he wasn't close enough for Winfrey to spin around and disarm him.

"Steve, it's me. Tell Bruce Willis here to tone it down a little, will ya?" he went to drop his arms and turn, which caused Tiger to make a quick step forward with the twin barrels of the shotty jabbing into his back. "Hey man, take it easy," Winfrey had lost his smile by now. I was enjoying myself, but these guys were my mates, and I didn't want either to lose it and drop the other.

"OK, children, play nice; Ben Winfrey meet Tiger Thompson. I don't actually know your real name, Tiger. It doesn't look like it, but you two should be good friends. Two grunts I'd trust anywhere, anytime," I said, laughing.

"I picked you as Military; I'm surprised you got behind me like that. You move as quiet as a shadow for a...." Winfrey said, trying to bridge the gap that was precisely the length of those shotgun barrels.

This young puppy didn't convince Tiger. "At least you didn't finish your shadow compliment with; 'for an old guy'. Listen, young fella, I don't trust anybody; I still look both ways on a roundabout," Tiger said, but we could both tell he was coming around.

"Hey, it's dinner time; how about we hit the Commercial for a steak and find out why this Yank is here, hey Tiger?" I said, laughing.

Like any trained Soldier, Tiger stood down as quickly as he had stood to. Sounds good I could do with a night off, Tiger said as he reached out to shake hands with Winfrey.

It didn't take long before the three of us were halfway through our steaks, Tiger and Ben on their second beer, and me nursing a Coke.

"I wasn't going to ask you to back me up when you said I had a visitor, but I was less surprised than Winfrey was when you turned up with that cannon." I said.

We finished our meals, and the others ordered another beer. It was great being out with a couple of mates and relaxing, at least for a little while. Not knowing whether Tiger was aware of the events of the kidnapping and the Assassin's involvement, Winfrey waited until we got back to the motor inn to discuss it.

Emptying his glass, Winfrey explained what he had been doing since I had last seen him. "Anyway, I was sitting in an office in Langley, thinking for the thousandth time I was missing getting dirty; out into the boonies, jungle, and desert. I didn't care where. Then I brainstormed. Freezing where I was, I thought how warm it would be where my little Aussie mate was down under," he said as smoothly as water flowing over ice.

Fifteen minutes later, we were in my room. It was a two-room set-up, and Winfrey would bunk in the spare.

"OK, Ben, why are you really here?" I asked as I sat on the end of my bed.

"If you had sent up a flare, I would have grabbed some leave and flown down. But, I didn't know that Chris had been kidnapped, and none of us in the States knew the Assassin was still in Australia. I mean, how many international hitmen would still be hanging around? We all thought he would have been on a plane or a boat out of Darwin within an hour of leaving that Marine base," Winfrey apologised.

I explained to Winfrey what had happened leading up to and during the Meatworks attack. "Mate, until the Meatworks bombing, we didn't know anything either. Then he phoned me on Chris's mobile; he's a mongrel, torturing me, enjoying watching me suffer," I said as Winfrey made us both a coffee.

"I was not supposed to be there, but the Assassin knew the Coppers would call me in. When that unfortunate Police Sergeant was killed, naturally, it was treated more like a Police matter. The Bikie attack went the same way: local Coppers, local incident. Between you and me, I kept one of the Bikies alive long enough to tell me that the Assassin had paid them to take me out for keeps. Although I've been on leave since the wedding day, I told Colonel Goodrich to keep Senior Sergeant Townsend informed. He's been great as expected, but it has been left to me or the local Coppers," I said without any hint of criticism or complaint. "Honestly, I've never been hit so hard; I've been out of control, but when the Bikie raid occurred it finally woke me up," I said honestly, humbly.

"Yeah, well, your Colonel must have figured all that out. I was told to get here on the double. It is now an official CIA OP. before you get excited, we will not be taking over. Simply put, because I know down here I gotta talk a bit slower, I am only here to help, sorta under your command," Winfrey said, smiling.

"Cheers, mate. We have been through too much, and I still owe you more than I can ever repay. So we will do this as partners. I can do with the help especially from a grunt with your skill set," I said.

"Thanks, Steve, you ain't gonna hug me or something?" Winfrey said with his unique laugh.

"No, but I'm grateful they sent you and not some stranger," I said.

"The other thing we bring to this B.B.Q. is some Intel support. Munroe has got the N.S.A. on board. It was the early in the piece when I was leaving Langley, but the word is they might be able to track this Target. As you know he's made a few calls on Chris's phone, and thanks to you Aussies having pretty tight phone laws here, we may have a lead. Anyway, we'll know in the next twenty-four," Winfrey said encouragingly.

I was trained and experienced in the art of waiting, in the rain, the snow, tropical heat or dry desert heat, waiting for orders or transport. But sitting sober in an air-conditioned motel room, I was finding a heap harder gig. Winfrey did his best to keep me busy talking about stuff that only people like us could or would understand. He wasn't trying to be some backyard counsellor, just a mate.

"It's taking a while, but between time differences, N.S.A. reporting to Munroe and then him getting back yo me, well, it could take a while. I hope it works, but there's always the possibility of it not working at all. It should; I've seen those N.S.A. boys come up with some amazingly accurate target locs," Ben Winfrey said.

"Thanks, mate; I'm not sure if that was meant to cheer me up or prepare me for the letdown. Let's talk it through so if or when the Intel arrives, we have some sort of plan in mind, hey?" I said calmly, hoping some planning would fill in the wait. There was a pre-arranged knock on the door. Tiger knew what it was like to wait on Intelligence.

The wait is like a hunting dog, all a quiver after its owner has taken a shot, waiting for the command to go and do what it loves and has been trained to do.

I let in the motel owner, who was carrying a tray of plates covered with stainless steel warmers.

"You guys must be hungry by now. Some B.L.T.s and decent coffee will help with the wait," Tiger said.

"Awesome mate, you joining us?" I asked.

"No, I wish I could; gotta a busload of fishermen comin' in from Brissy any minute. Not complaining, gotta pay the bills somehow, now most of the gas workers are gone," he said with a grin.

Wiping some B.B.Q. Sauce off his chin, Winfrey joined the conversation, "By the way, I've been meaning to ask you why this town is called Chinchilla. Do you guys have a lot of Chinchillas around here?"

I laughed at the reference to the small rodent whose skin is used to make the unique-looking and very expensive fur coats.

"No, never been any of those expensive rats here. I have been told Chinchilla comes from the aboriginal word "tintinchillla", which is what the cypress pine that are found around here are called. A guy called Ludwig Leichhardt named the tree; he was an explorer back in the eighteen-forties. I'm not sure who named the town, though," I said.

My phone rang. I jumped at it like a Murray Cod attacking a lure.

"Steve, Colonel Goodrich here, how's it going?" my Control down in Australia's Capital, Canberra, asked. Without waiting for my reply he got right to the point.

"I know Winfrey is already with you. I just got off the phone to Munroe. Finally, mate, I think we've got some good news or at least something to act on. Of course, the Yanks had never heard of the locs the N.S.A. have given me. But Steve. We believe that your Target is just down the road from where you are," the Colonel stated excitedly.

"Where? Sir, do you have got some G.P.S. co-ords?" I asked like an excited kid. I couldn't help myself; this was my first solid lead since Chris's kidnapping. My excitement was immediately extinguished by a wave of the guilt that had crushed me for the last three months. I thought; *Is Chris still alive? Is she locked up somewhere, living in a filthy makeshift cell someplace? Had this revenge-motivated Kidnapper tortured or sexually abused.....?* Still listening to Goodrich, I turned towards to Winfrey, my face revealing the torment of the questions he knew would be rattling around in my head.

"Sir, send 'em through; once we've looked at where they point, we'll come up with an Op. Plan and get back to you so you know what's going on in case we don't make it back," I said. There was no point in sugarcoating anything.

Sure, Winfrey and I were a well-trained team. But, this guy had demonstrated that he was creative, resourceful and just as well trained and equipped. He had also shown that he was absolutely fearless, holding his nerve back at the U.S.M.C. Base until he could escape. Even though revenge was out of character for a world-class Assassin, he had stayed in Australia. The cheeky Bugger, had even set up his base less than eight hours from where we were sitting in Chinchilla. My thoughts were going off like popcorn in a pan. That meant he must have driven only two-hundred-and-forty-five odd Kilometres to set up the Meatworks ambush. I couldn't believe his courage or lack of respect for me and Australian Law Enforcement to base himself within striking distance. All these thoughts had come and were gone in seconds as I focused.

"OK, Steve, I'll send you the exact co-ords and wait to hear back. To play the game both ways, I better keep Agent Munroe up to speed. Tell Winfrey I'll do that, and not to worry about doing it. Now, for the record you're back on duty as of now. If your plan needs any back up, maybe a quick helo support or something let us know. Anything else you need while we are talking?" Colonel Goodrich asked.

"Nothing at the moment, Sir. Thank you for getting Munroe and the N.S.A. involved. I might have thought of that earlier if I wasn't so busy feeling sorry for myself," I said, realising guilt had become too strong a force, clouding my thinking. I couldn't afford all this distraction and self-doubt when things got noisy. One thing I did not doubt was that things were definitely going to get loud.

CHAPTER 28

We look for a Carnarvon Gorge Camping Ground.

Ben, Tiger and I looked at the Intel we had. By basing himself near the Carnarvon Gorge, we already knew a lot about his Area of Operation or A.O., as it was a world-renowned tourist venue. This meant that there were unlimited maps, photos and descriptions of the whole place. N.S.A. had pinned the Kidnapper's loc to an area. It wasn't like the movies where they could tell you what room in what house. But we had an advantage. We were preparing for an Op., at least on a functional level; Chris had become like any kidnap victim. She had become the Principal. We automatically removed any emotion or any sensitivity in our language.

"We know he's in that zone, but let's think about it. He's got a prisoner, so straight away, that means he can't stay at some of the accommodation options in that zone. The Wilderness Lodge resort-style set-up is out of the question. There are too many tourists and staff servicing the rooms, and any sounds can easily be heard from the next-door room. The Wallaroo Outback Retreat Luxury Glamping has pretty well the same issues for our Kidnapper. Trying to keep his head down, daily servicing, lots of people walking past your luxury tent, it doesn't work. That leaves us with two options: the BIG4 Breeze Holiday Parks has self-contained studios, cottages and cabins to glamping safari tents. However, they also have standard caravan and camping sites."

My gut said no; even though this was getting closer to a possibility, there were still too many options, which meant too many people to notice something strange or hear a muffled scream.

"Then other accommodation option wins the race in two different ways. Sandstone Park. This sounded like a place where a person could set up a caravan or tent away from the crowd and not be noticed. This is more of a low-key camping area that is still close to the Gorge, or in our Target's case, perhaps a sanctuary to return to after his attack on me."

I was working my way through the search.

The website description made Sandstone Point stand out among the Carnarvon accommodation options.

"Ben, what do you think about this? **'It reads slightly outside the park (5 km); you can set up camp, caravan or RV. There's no risk of seeing neighbours on this campsite, which doubles as a cattle station with 41 unpowered sites spread over 50 acres,"** I read.

Standing up, Winfrey became more animated than usual. "If our Target has hired, bought or even stolen a caravan or motorhome, I reckon that's the one," the C.I.A. Agent said.

Our three man Planning Group could only progress further once we confirmed a more precise loc of the Target. Now that we had worked out our best guess of where the Kidnapper might be held up, we could move the plan up a notch, and we could start to explore the 'How'. We had all done enough Helo inserts to know a switched-on enemy would hear the chopper's approach in plenty of time to prepare a welcome or bug-out. Once again, though, Sandstone Point Camp Ground provided a solution.

"OK. OK, now flying in from here has gotta be the best way to go.

We get a chopper to pick us up, and we arrive unnoticed because, like the Website says, 'If you'd prefer not to go it alone, there are guided tours and even helicopter rides available from Sandstone Park,' I said quoting from their advertisement.

It was Tiger's turn to get excited now, "That's a deadset gift. It would be no good getting an Apache up here for that job. Even if helos run out of that park all day, an Apache will still alert a pro like this guy," the ex-SAS Operator stated.

We all agreed with this assessment. "Do we know what sort of helo your friends use at the Gorge?" Winfrey asked.

"Not exactly, but I have seen it when I was up there earlier this year. It's not that big, looks comfortable, and maybe three or four across the back seat," Tiger contributed.

"I just looked it up, something like a Robinson Raven 44. They seem the helo of choice for the small chopper tours. OK, how do we get that one to pick us up and bring us into the park?" I said.

"Well, maybe you don't need to. There is a farmer near town who has one that looks a bit like that one. He gets me out to his place for some pest control when needed. He takes the side doors off and flies me around, I've been out culling pigs and dogs for him a couple of times. It feels funny because it's so flashy with leather seats and stuff, but we get the job done," Tiger said.

"Mate, do you think he will fly us up to Carnarvon?" I asked.

"I reckon he will. We don't need to tell him the real mission; maybe say we are doin some pig culling for Parks & Wildlife. Those grunters plough up the soft stuff all over the park," Tiger said.

"That works for me; it explains the way we are dressed and why we are bringing the weapons. Sounds good," Winfrey said with his usual smile.

"We're gettin' there guys, but the park is......... What does that Website say? Forty-one caravan sites spread across fifty acres. We really need to I.D. the one site we are looking for," I said, trying to keep the negativity out of my voice.

"We need the camp Satellite surveilled, not just current, but past as well. I know it's a long shot, but we need to see everyone coming and going. The happy camper who doesn't appear to be leaving the van or RV is probably the Target. I'm planning that he won't stay happy," Winfrey said.

I had been doing some rough calculating myself.

"Tiger, assuming your farmer mate will fly us in, I'll cover all the expenses. I know we aren't exactly sure of the helo model, but I looked at the Robinson Raven's data. It should handle under three hours at cruising speed as the 'crow' flies. As we haven't got a definite loc to head to, we may need to refuel in Roma. These birds have a range of five-hundred-and-sixty Klicks, which should be heaps because it's about five-hundred-and-eighty by road. You know what Pilots are like, though, so he can work that out," I said.

We spent the rest of the morning working through all the bits and pieces, making lists and notes about things we needed to do. The first was getting that Satellite Data. I contacted Colonel Goodrich. He sent through our own Intel and asked Munroe for more help by continually checking the American Satellites orbiting the globe. Of course, the C.I.A. Special Agent would splutter that the Americans don't monitor allies.

Later, he would send an encrypted report of what we had requested. Tiger figured talking to the chopper owner over a cup of tea would be better.

So he and Winfrey headed out to the Pilot's cattle property on Burnt Bridge Road. The cover scenario was solid. This is my mate out from the States; we've got a chance to knock down some pigs up near the Gorge. Can we get a lift because we are pushed for time? When they came back, they brought dinner and the good news that the farmer had agreed without a moment's hesitation.

"I feel bad lying to the guy, but if this all goes the way we hope and there's some lead flying around some caravan or RV, I don't want him to be a party to it at all," Tiger said wisely.

I had waited for so long. We had waited long enough. Now we were waiting again, this time for the Intel. The Operator in me knew that this was vital. However, no one trusted Intel fully. It nearly always contributed towards a mission's success or team security. The man who loved and worried wanted to be there now. It was unspoken, but we all knew that if the Sat photos didn't eventuate in time, we would have to go in blind. The mission would move from a surgical Hostage Rescue Op to a two-phase mission of a search first. Then our three-man Hostage Rescue Team, H.R.T. would rescue Chris. I told myself this. We had all done it before, not together, but that was OK. Training and Trust would get us through that door.

My Laptop chirped, an email arriving from the Colonel. I opened the Encrypted attachment. The Colonel and Munroe had delivered the goods. Here before me were two weeks of focused S.A.T. passes over Sandstone Park. The detail was good enough for our purposes. We all crowded around the small motel desk.

"Let's rule any vans or RVs we can see leaving. We'll have to work on the basis that OK, that's not our target. I know that might be wrong, but we have to have a starting point. Now, we are looking for the aloof camper, the one who has placed himself as far away from any other holidaymakers as possible," I said impatiently.

We poured over the files for the next three hours, taking turns, offering theories, offering theories and throwing ideas (scenarios). By the time we realised how late in the day it was, we had identified four potential Target vans. All met the basic criteria; all appeared to be current, but two stood out. This was due to a lack of any traffic, either foot or vehicular, over the last two-week window.

"OK, let's hit the sack; it'll do us no good to be exhausted when we get to the Target Zone," I said, sounding like my mother. I could still hear my own words as I lay there counting fly marks on the motel room ceiling, in the dim light coming through the curtain. My mind was going like a blender at top speed, with all the guilt, regrets, shame, proper Op planning, and a million other thoughts flying around. Sleep wasn't coming anytime soon. I could hear my two friends snoring away, peacefully asleep, preparing for battle. I had always been like them, able to switch off and grab any available sleep, whether in a noisy helo or a rattling truck; none of that had mattered but two things had changed. My love for Chris meant I was emotionally invested, whereas emotions never came into play before. The second reason was that even though I had always liked a drink, this time, what had happened to Chris and Jake had somehow pushed me over an edge that I had always avoided before. The shame, guilt, and even embarrassment crushed me. It did my head in. I knew I had overcome the bottle, but if I was going to be as good as usual on this Op., I only had a few hours to make sure my head was screwed on properly, whatever that meant. I was still slowly falling apart, but that wasn't an option I could take now we were this close.

CHAPTER 29

I get by with a LOT of help from my friends

All the weeks of not knowing whether Chris was alive. And, if she was, where she was being held, had drained my emotions to zero. Not drinking was not helping me being fun to be around either. I kept trying to use my usual professional, cold and calculating approach on this. Still, I had never had so many distracting thoughts. This caused impatience to build along with frustration which was off the scale. With my experience and thinking it through I knew that this was a sure way to sabotage the success of this raid. Of course, this was the last thing I wanted. I had done more harm than good so far, and I knew I was snapping at the only two people willing to risk everything to help me. It wasn't good enough. A regular Hostage Rescue Team wouldn't have tolerated it for this long. I knew that without my history and relationship with Colonel Goodrich, as my Control, he would have replaced me on the team by now.

Chris was too important; enough thinking with my heart, instead of my head, I had to focus. I had to recalibrate back to the weapon the Army had moulded me into. As the saying goes: Weak men make decisions based on their feelings. Disciplined men do hard things regardless of how they feel. In the past, my loyalty had kept me in situations that common sense should have taken me out of. I wasn't going to let my mindset abuse these two brothers.

Winfrey and Tiger had handled my shortness so far; their friendship was covering me, but it had to stop here.

"Ben, Tiger, I've been a bit hard to live with, I know that. And I wanted to apologise for it. If I keep going the way I have been, I would have turned this Op., into a soup sandwich, one that I was forcing you both to eat," I said sincerely.

Like the good friends and warrior brothers they were, they moved on. "Yeah, you have definitely been a PITA," the American said, trying to look serious.

Tiger had to ask, "Ben, what's a PITA?"

"A Pain In The Ass," He replied, laughing.

"OK, I'll wear that, no argument from me," I said. "Now I'm back in the game. We can decide whether we are a go and, if so, when."

"Tiger and I were waiting on you," Winfrey replied.

"Well, Ben, the road is paved with dead rabbits that couldn't make a decision about going left or right. We go tomorrow. I was thinking it makes no sense to imitate the tourist helo and then wake everyone up by entering the park in the dark," I said.

"That's good thinking, Steve; I'll tell the helo pilot we leave at zero-eight-hundred- hours. That will get us there at a civilised hour that will be assumed to be the tour helo," Tiger commented.

Weapon-wise, we were tooled up. Winfrey, travelling on a Diplomatic Passport, had brought enough toys for all of us. Of course, Tiger, like most ex-SAS, had his own crowd-pleaser. I was fine as well. I had made sure these guys understood that the Assassin cum Kidnapper was extremely dangerous, being skilful and willing to do anything to get it done. It was still hard to figure that one guy against us three door kickers would come out on top. I had a few things on my mind that couldn't wait.

"Guys, I have a couple of things I need to bounce off of you," I said.

Winfrey and Tiger were packing gear and joking with each other, but stopped to listen to what I had to share, "Now, firstly, I want to thank you for everything you've both done so far, and you know there are no other Grunts on the planet that I'd trust my six to more than you two," I continued.

"Yeah, yeah, I guess every circus needs some clowns. No, but seriously guys, thank you. Now, what I really want to say is that this is my fiancée, my fight; I am the one this scumbag has tried to nail twice now. I'd understand if you boys bailed, no offence. The amount of help, support and advice you've already chipped in means neither of you owes me anything. Especially you, Ben; I would be dead if you hadn't saved my life on that cruise ship," I said sincerely. I was talking about when a giant Assassin had actually killed me in a terrible fight in the cruise ship's gym. Winfrey had not only taken out the giant but jump-started my heart using a Defib machine to bring me back from the brink.

Both men appeared hurt; I saw it as a flash of genuine emotion, and then their poker faces returned.

Ben Winfrey went first. "That was a mighty fine speech, Steve, but there are a few things you missed out. The first is that we are brothers after all the crap we have been through. I would have been here weeks ago if I had known what was happening here. Secondly, you forget this scumbag isn't your exclusive target. He tried to shoot my Nation's Commander in Chief. Mate, I have some chips in this game, and by the way, this party was organised through my chain of command. POTUS has ordered me to be involved. So lovely speech, but I'm in," the C.I.A. Operative said, about as serious as I had ever seen him.

Tiger responded next, "I wonder how anything ever gets done around here; you guys sound like politicians or WOKE Folks. No big speech from me; I'm G.T.G. If you think running a motel gets my juices flowing, think again. I haven't had as much fun as I'm havin hangin' out with you two marshmallows since I pulled my papers from the Regiment," he said, turning back to the gear bag he had been packing.

"OK, I figured that would be how it rolls, cheers. Let's finish storing the weapons and kit and get some shut-eye. By the way, how did you pick up a modern Grunt saying, G.T.G. Tiger?" I asked sarcastically, referring to his use of the acronym for Good to Go. Winfrey, being considerably younger than us, laughed at this.

"Don't you be too cocky, young fella; I'm really going because someone needs to look after you puppies when the bangs start," Tiger said in mock offence.

We arrived at the cattle property out on Burnt Bridge Road with an hour to spare. Tiger drove us over to a small hangar. The helo was sitting in front, and a bloke was fussing around it.

"That's Vince there. He's even older than me, but he's a good bloke and a crack pilot," Tiger said as we pulled up just short of the chopper.

We introduced ourselves all around and loaded our kit on board. I couldn't help thinking that although the cover story Tiger had spun seemed to explain the weapons cases and even our dress, we still looked exactly what we were: a three-man Hostage Rescue Team or at least some type of Patrol. Vince watched every move and item as we loaded it. He had a way about him that seemed to fit with the three of us, older, dressed in his RM William's cattle cocky slacks, shirt and boots. I could see his eyes were deep and calculating, he was appraising everything we did and said.

"OK, men, as everyone loves to say these days, this isn't my first rodeo. I look this way because I've travelled a long way, and some of those roads had potholes. Now, what are you guys really up to? As long as it's not criminal, I don't really care. But, if we are flying into something, I like to know what sort of storm to expect," the cattle man cum pilot asked.

Tiger looked at me, and I nodded my permission. "Well, Vince, I shoulda known better, and I am sorry we had to lie to you. It was more to protect you than anything else. I suppose, after three tours with Nine Squadron flying out of the Vung Tau airbase, you've seen plenty of patrols like us. Guys, he was fly-boy, so speak a bit slower to him," Tiger attempted the humour we all used in inter-service rivalry to smooth the embarrassment of misleading his friend.

"Tiger, are you kidding me? You thought an ex-Nam chopper pilot wouldn't pick us for what we are?" I said, realising I needed to give them an out, as this was my problem after all.

"Guys, gather round for a minute. Now I know that we have talked all this through, but I want to re-hash it one more time. Number one, this Tango is as good, maybe even better than anyone you've ever met. Everything he does is meticulously planned and executed.

Two, this is not the Army. It's off the books, but sanctioned. Winfrey and I are official.

Three, this guy has made it personal, so of course, I would go it alone if I had to because of Chris. I don't want Tiger and Vince to come along and get hurt or worse," I said sincerely. I searched each of their faces as I spoke. " Depending on what you decide Vince we'll explain what the go is, but for now you are better off in the dark, no offence." I said.

"None taken Steve, I........." the chopper pilot replied, but was interrupted by Winfrey who
smiling spoke up, "Even though I'm on orders, you know I'm always here for you buddy," he said.

"Nice speech mate, but no way I'm letting you go into the great unknown with this Yankee puppy. Stop trying to protect us. We are all over eighteen and we wouldn't let you face an enemy without us." Tiger laughed.

I turned to Vince, the chopper pilot, who had met me less than an hour ago and was much older than us three. As though he was reading my mind.

"I realise I don't know you, and you just met me but I'm not stupid. I'm just a bit long in the tooth compared to you blokes. I can still put a chopper on a dinner plate, so let's start with that. If something comes up that we all think Grandpa can handle, I'm up for that," the Vietnam Veteran said. We could all see that he hadn't lost any of his courage and was probably enjoying the excitement.

"OK, enough talk. I can't tell you guys what that means to me. I've never gone into harm's way with a better crew," I said, a little more emotionally than I had anticipated.

"Let's go before he starts crying and wants us all to hug each other." Tiger said, slapping me on the back as he headed for the helo.

As we walked, Vince added, "Anyway, like I said, as long as you're not knocking over the banks in Roma, I'll fly the Sortie." The Pilot easily back into fly-boy lingo, using the usual term for a helo mission.

"OK, Vince, for your protection, I haven't tell you everything. However, I assure you that this is official; the American and Australian Governments are aware of this mission and have supported it in various ways. I can tell you that it only involves one H.V.T., but an incredibly dangerous Target. That's why a small team with a low-profile attack is the go. That's probably all I can tell you," I said with a new level of respect and inclusion.

"That's good enough for me. Even though Tiger spun me a yarn, I still know I can trust him. I also know him well enough to be sure that you guys must be OK. He's a dumb grunt, but if he's willing to saddle up with you two. I'm in." Vince said with a big smile.

CHAPTER 30

We get into the Adventure Tour Industry.

Our plan was simple. We had identified three priority target RVs. They had been designated names Alpha, Bravo and Charlie. All of them were big enough for a long-term stay, parked as far away from the other campers as possible. The other noteworthy feature was the isolation factor. They were set up with a three-sixty-degree clear field of view or a round field of fire if it got loud.

"Now, all three fit the criteria, but two have done so without any sinister indicators. How are we going to do this," Winfrey asked as we readied ourselves to climb aboard.

"Step one, we need some wheels; I'm hoping there's a stray vehicle we can hire or, if we have to, knock it off. The first two, Alpha and Bravo RVs, are one side of the fifty acres, and we have Charlie nearly all the way over to the other boundary," I said.

Although Vince the Pilot hadn't been part of the conversations, he chipped in. "That will work; I've known that tourist operator for years. I used to sub for them now and then when they went on holiday. They'll lend me their 4WD, no prob," He said.

"OK, transport sorted, then we go into a classic two up, kickin' in the door, one back on overwatch from a distance," I said. "With only the three of us, I think that's the best we can do."

Winfrey shook his head. "Steve, two are just happy campers, so is kicking in the door or knocking the way to go? How about we make out we are from the park H.Q., checking on something passing on a weather warning or a welfare check or something," he suggested.

"I've got a better idea; we are in the Helo Tours 4WD, right? We knock and say we are there to pick up our next party of tourists. Of course, the people will say, no, not us. That will give us a chance to check them out. This Assassin we are hunting will look different, and he will react differently," Tiger offered.

"That's a great plan. Let's lock that in. But, I still want that overwatch; we don't know what the Target will do, and this guy is sharp," I said.

We talked while the Pilot did his final checks and rearranged our bags to balance the load. "Anyway, I've kicked the tyres and lit the fires, like we used to say. So let's get going. Anything else we can talk about on the way," the Vietnam Vet said, looking more relaxed than he had been since we had arrived.

Sitting in the civvy chopper, we appreciated the comfortable seats not normally found in Military Helos. This helo was quieter than the open-side Black Hawks we were all used to. We were about halfway to the L.Z. at Sandstone Park when my Sat-Phone vibrated in my pocket. I could see it was a call coming in from Colonel Goodrich.

"What's your SITREP Steve?" he asked

"Hi Sir, on plan, but it's still a chopper. I'll need you to shout a bit," I yelled over the rotors.

We both knew that the Sat -Phone was not secure, so automatically, we switched to careful mode. "Steve, I see you're on the way," Our gear bags had ADS-B transponders, which meant we were being tracked by Satellite so it was no mystery why how the Colonel was so well informed.

Colonel Goodrich continued, "I have an update on the Intel re the three Target RVs. The latest Satellite pass picked up some new photos. You're going to love this. Reference Target Charlie, the one out all by itself. The latest pass showed two adults and two children all running around the RV as naked as when they came into the world. My guess is they are not your guy," The Colonel laughed, so did I.

"Sir that's great news; you just reduced the risk by a third," I shouted.

"OK, I'll leave it to you Steve. I'll need a SITREP, but get it done first. I won't say take care, because I know you can't promise that. Thoughts and prayers are with you and yours. Out," The Colonel signed off.

Every helo seems to have David Clark Noise Cancelling Helicopter Headsets and Microphones, and this one was no different. I clicked the mike and told the crew the good news about Tango Charlie being eliminated from our search. Everyone agreed that was an absolute bonus. We had another look at the Satellite photos of RV Alpha and Bravo. We could see that they were both hugging the park's western boundary. Set up in a line, they were still a good two hundred metres apart.

Tiger came on the internal radio system, "Guys, I was just thinking about how might we might roll up and knock on the door of these RVs. Remember how bare that country is surrounding both campsites. The way I see it is this. We visit the first camper, and if the other camper is super vigilant like we would expect our Target to be, he will see us. Now, he might go either way. Fight or flight comes to mind; you get the picture. I think I have a solution. Instead of hiding behind the first RV, we drive around to the side where the second RV is camped. We park the 4WD so the second camper can see all the sign-writing. We hide in plain sight," Tiger said.

"That sounds like a good plan in my books. Don't forget we might be lucky and find him in the first RV. That brings its own set of variables and potential to go pear shape," I said through the system.

Vince, the Pilot, had heard all this and joined in saying, "So, I don't know the nitty gritty you guys are getting into, but a fourth gun, or maybe just a Driver, might help by the sound of it. I never thought getting old would be of benefit in a balls-to-the-wall Op, but I've had a thought, too. Using the RV as a blind, I drop two of you off at the first RV we get to and then, like Einstein here worked out, I drive the Helo Tour ute out into the open. If your Tango happens to be looking, he sees a grey-haired old bloke, not a young fit fella who can't help looking like Military," the Viet Vet suggested.

"Wow, for someone who is just flying this Bird, you just bought into the game fast," Winfrey said easily.

I could feel this spinning out of control, and we hadn't even reached the Landing Zone or L.Z. "I think we have a bit of a committee meeting when we land and talk all that through. It shouldn't take long. Let's rest up for the rest of the flight," I said, closing everyone down.

Attacking a known Enemy Loc comes with enough surprises. We all love Intel and especially the recently received info. We all know most of it turns out to be wrong. Lots of people, including Chris, struggled with my trust issues, but I have my reasons. I joke with my friends that it all started when my old man told me his twelve-gauge shotgun didn't kick. Nowhere is safe; nowhere is without risks.

One of the funniest things to observe when you know what you're looking at is when a group of us go out for dinner or a drink. Everyone wants to sit with his back to a wall that gives you the best view of any entries or exits. It's also a big Tell that someone has been in the Military if you know what to look for. As we drifted through the cloudless sky, I wondered whether we could trust Vince. What he had suggested was a great idea, but he had to be seventy-something and although he had said that could be an advantage, he was an unknown quantity to us. I would never doubt a Vet, but being a brave pilot is not quite the same as being down in the mud, face-to-face. Would he be ready to bite the bullet without hesitation?

We would soon find out. We were all pushed to the starboard side as the helo banked and flared as Vince prepared to land. The privately run airport or Landing Zone was really a cow paddock with a square of bitumen that doubled as the car park with a white circle marked as an L.Z. for the family business tourist chopper. The circle was vacant at the moment, however, our Pilot landed off to one side of the tar.

A pretty female came out of the small hangar that sat at the other end of the tarmac. She was dressed in jeans, boots and a tee shirt with a helo emblem on the front. Shading her eyes against the sun, she began to stride west towards our helo as the blades began to slow. She walked over confidently, already aware that we were coming because Vince had called ahead the night before.

"Thanks for landing her over there, Vince; Robby will be back any minute." She said as she shook hands with Vince.

"Oh Janeen, you know us old Rotorheads. We understand who gets the first pick of an L.Z." our Pilot said, laughing.

Introductions were made all around as we unloaded our gear. We were now way out west, so the sight of gun cases and camo bags was nothing new to the tour operator who had lived in the area all her life, growing up on a cattle property just down the road.

"You guys still want to borrow the four-by?" she asked.

"If it's still OK with you, that would be great," I said, realising she was probably talking to Vince, who she knew, not the blow-in she had just met. We had asked Vince to be vague about us. To her, we were just another group of tourists looking for different activities, with Vince as our guide. I figured we wouldn't tread on any toes as long as that didn't include a helo tour. Not for the first time, the strangeness of this Op struck me. You're usually all camed up, 'Full Battle-Rattle', what every grunt going outside the wire had. A flak jacket and protective plates, Kevlar vest, helmet, minimum of one-hundred-and-eighty-rounds of ammo, water, rations and, of course, your weapon. Here we were making polite conversation with this nice lady as though we were on holidays and about to take in all the scenic beauty Carnarvon Gorge offers.

"That's no worries. We need to wait for Robby and then, if you don't mind I'll get you guys to drop us off at home. It's way too far to walk, and we only have the one vehicle. He shouldn't be long. I was talking to him as you flew in," she said casually, not realising the various emotions all four of us were experiencing as we mentally prepared for the possible imminent battle.

CHAPTER 31

We go door to door looking for a Special Customer.

We talked about the landscape being flat, featureless, and pretty well devoid of any vegetation, let alone a nice stand of trees a Sniper could overwatch from. We had worked out that Winfrey was the man for that job, as I wanted to be up close and personal for several reasons. Getting into a suitable hide was going to be even more challenging than usual. Sniper School trains us to inch our way in if the land is flat or cleared of vegetation. One of the core skills is patience. It might take four or five hours to slowly crawl into place. However, we didn't have that sort of time. Once again, we decided that stopping the 4WD and using it as a shield while Winfrey slid out the opposite side was a go. He would then decide if he needed to slowly inch into a better lie. We would do our best. If we spotted an ant nest, a fallen log or perhaps a small mound, then we would attempt to drop him there. However, everything looks different when you're lying on the ground looking through a telescopic sight. All four of us had been here before, with a level of trained anticipation, and a flood of adrenaline. We were ready. This last little stall was taxing all of us.

Finally, Robby descended from the heavens in a shiny red helo; he landed precisely and without any bounce in the LZ circle. After introductions, we all piled into their 4WD and, with Janeen driving, headed for their home. While the wait had been a little wearing, this trip was no burden. Of course, we appreciated the ability to borrow the four-by, but the bonus was that where they lived was on the way to the two remaining Targets; RVs Alpha, Bravo. We arrived at their home, a low, sprawling bungalow oasis with lots of well-developed trees and gardens and even a nice front lawn. The house and yard were well-fenced to keep the 'roos and emus out of the grass and plants.

"Now, would you blokes like to come in for a cuppa tea or maybe a beer?" Robby asked sincerely.

Impressed by this bush hospitality, which was just a part of life in a hard land, we were all thinking we didn't want to offend our hosts. However, Vince came to the rescue.

"Oh mate, normally that would be great, but these fellas are on a bit of a short schedule. They are up working on the gas pipeline, and they've just pushed some fun into what time they could spare," he said with a smile.

Janeen and Robby gave a knowing smile. They understood tourism. You did what the customer wanted, pretty much the way they wanted it. And you grabbed anything that came your way because it was a fickle industry at the mercy of two unpredictable forces: politics and weather. They waved us goodbye at the gate, and we headed off.

'OK, Vince, stop under those Casuarina trees. We'll get our kit organised, and then the fun begins, I said, feeling relieved to be finally on our way.

It took no time at all to tool up. As we worked I confirmed the order and details of the plan. Tiger and I would knock on the door, so we stayed in our casuals, with the addition of our Glocks. We set them in the small of our backs so as to be out of sight from in front of us but still accessible for a quick draw if needed. We issued our Viet Vet with a Glock as well; I was hoping he wouldn't have to use it.

The floor of the 4WD was stacked with M4s, the rifle most used by SAS. We liked them for the same reason the Regiment did; it's lightweight, easily sourced ammo 5.56 X 45mm. And it has a fast rate of fire and ranges out to about six hundred metres. For Winfrey, he needed a bit more bang. Colonel Goodrich had kindly sent up the Sniper Rifle issued by the Australian Army, an SR98, in 7.62mm Calibre for a bit more push through and knockdown. His weapon was scoped with the latest Schmidt and Bender Variable with 3 to 12 X 50 magnification, pushing the range out to one Klick or even more. The fold-down stock was great for transporting as well.

CARNARVON GORGE
QUEENSLAND

Up ahead, a dirt devil spiralled towards the sun carrying dust, leaves and twigs. The warriors sitting in the 4WD drive were silent, each one of us in our own thoughts and prayers.

"Now, I know we have said all this before, but just to make sure. This isn't easy.

We are coming up against a top-class enemy who we have to assume is well armed and has had time to set booby traps and have numerous exfil plans," I said to my motley band of volunteers.

"That would normally be bad enough, but we can't kill this guy. In addition to this, we can't put any rounds into that RV if Chris is in there somewhere. He is the only person on earth who knows where Chris is. I'm sorry, guys, we don't have any Tasers or beanbag shot. It's cowboy stuff, but we need to subdue him in whatever way we can. Winfrey, I know it's a big ask, but aim low if it goes noisy, and we need you to shoot." I said, knowing my request was close to impossible as any hit from the long gun would do a lot of damage.

"Everyone else, we need to overpower him as best and as quickly as we can. If one of us has his attention, as in we are locked in a brawl, the other waits and then steps in, maybe slugging him or holding him. I have learned to respect this guy based on everything he has done. Don't underestimate his ability or his commitment. You guys have done it all before. Eyes on, heads on a swivel, and act without hesitation, and we get him," I said.

We were all trained and experienced in K.N.R. But usually, the target was not an Assassin who would probably be on alert 24/7.

"If Chris is not in that RV we will have to interrogate him," I said calmly.

The first RV, Target Alpha, loomed in the shimmering heat; we stopped about three hundred yards out, scoping the area. There was a small collapsed termite mound that Winfrey could use for cover and a place to rest his rifle's bipod. We worked out his line of fire and made sure we were careful not to get in his way if he had to take a shot.

He was also aware that his primary target was any armed response to our knocking on the door of the RV. Winfrey's secondary objective was to make sure no one got the motorhome mobile and attempted an escape.

Continuing on, Vince slowed the 4WD between the RV and the ant-bed without stopping entirely. The CIA Operative slithered out of the FWD and took up his position as overwatch. We kept rolling towards the first RV, focused on the potential target. Silence filled the cabin. We had entered a combat zone before, and although this mission was somewhat unique, we knew it could all turn pear-shaped in a blink of an eye. The first one was set up, providing us a barrier between it and the next RV.

"OK, Vince, we don't need you to block our presence on this site, so stay at the wheel, ready for a quick exit if needed," I said without taking my eyes from the first target as we got closer.

"Roger that, Steve," the old Viet Vet replied, clearly on edge as he approached the RV. It was too late to second guess whether he was still up for it. He slowly drove past the RV's door and eased the vehicle to a gentle stop. Even taking it easy, a cloud of dust engulfed the 4WD.

"Wait for the dust to blow past before we get out. Otherwise, Winfrey won't be able to see us," I said.

I shook my head to chase all my thoughts about whether Chris could be inside this RV away. Or was she long dead? I had to concentrate, or I shouldn't have been there. A good breeze took care of our dust cloud, and we casually exited the vehicle. We felt a little naked, having to depend on our side arms, but we figured that it was a better plan to leave our automatics out of site until we had confirmed who was inside the RV. We had to be low-key. The metal RV door reverberated as I knocked on it. Due to its size, it didn't take long for a response. As casually as possible, we both placed our hands on the pistol hidden on our belts in the small of our backs. I felt a rush of adrenalin, my body preparing for the perceived threat I took a deep breath. Yet, I had to control myself as this was a knock on the door rather than the usual kick-in followed by a Flashbang grenade. The woman who opened the door was dishevelled, dressed in a bikini with a short tee shirt covering part of it. Still, she projected no distress or concern that could suggest guilt. Instead, she was a camper who had clearly, understandably, not been expecting visitors. In my most friendly tone, I explained that we were from the Helicopter Tours, thumbing over my shoulder at the signed 4WD.

"Good morning. I am so sorry. We are here to pick up some folks who are booked for the Helicopter Tour. Somehow, we didn't get the full details," I said with a smile that would charm a bird out of a tree.

"You sure scared me. We don't usually get any visitors out here," she said through the screen door. "Well, I am sorry, too, because this isn't the right place, I know that for sure. No tourists here," She answered with a friendly laugh.

"Once again, my apologies. We are sorry to have disturbed you," I said as we backed away and headed towards the 4WD.

When we were all in, Vince drove to where Winfrey was set up. We slowed once again, blocking all view of his hide. As he climbed in, he said, "She looked pretty good through the scope, but obviously no sign of anything." the CIA Operative said.

"Nothing for us there, although the smoke coming outta that screen door was definitely wacky tobaccy. I said. "She probably thought we were Coppers; no wonder we scared her when we showed up."

"OK, Steve, did the cover plan seem to work for you? It was fine from my standpoint," Tiger asked.

"I think it was good; having this sign written Helitour four-by makes it look legit," I agreed.

Without further discussion, we circled towards Target Bravo, the motorhome about three hundred yards from the RV we had just left.

"OK, same again. I guess we are all thinking the same thing. Every time we kick a door in, are we relieved to find no baddies? Probably. But this knocking on the door like an insurance salesman is even more hyper. Head on a swivel guy's, fingers on the trigger." I said, noticing the others didn't say anything, but they were all nodding.

It was probably the same for every one of us. The adrenaline flooded our systems, and training, whether back in Nam seventies style or more recently, kicked in.

This time there wasn't an obvious hide for our over watch. He had his Ghillie suit and could flick it over his head and shoulders. It wasn't perfect, but at least he wouldn't be hung out there like the proverbial. Our Viet Vet took a left curve to place Winfrey in about the best position available. This time, his gut said that we shouldn't come to a complete stop. The elderly warrior somehow knew this was going to be different.

"OK, pretty boy, roll out this one; we'll pick you up on the other side. Our

Pilot cum Driver called out above the noise of the 4WD.

The ute door opened without any effort, and Winfrey was gone. Changing down a gear, Vince headed for the RV, our Target Bravo.

Roza couldn't maintain a 24/7 watch; it was impractical when alone, but the threat didn't demand it either. Roza was bored, but that didn't translate into complacency. Not much surprised him, but this Wallace guy had done so. The Australian was clearly a switched-on operator, but Roza couldn't understand why Wallace wasn't searching far and wide for his kidnapped bride. Roza had initially thought he could exact his revenge quickly with a baited trap at the old Meatworks. The bait was high value; for Wallace, Chris, his primary goal, capturing him the bonus, Roza the high-value second bait. But no, our 'hero' wallowed in self-pity and inaction.

Meanwhile, Roza was stuck in this sweltering motorhome, wondering whether to move on and count his losses. That was until today. He had lived here in near isolation since the kidnapping and had studied every track, dry creek and rocky feature.

I am unsure whether it was Vince's actions or my own Soldier's intuition, but something inside me was on alert. Tiger and I got out of our vehicle and headed for the door of the big motorhome.

We didn't want to look too switched on or aggressive, so we laughed about a nonexistent joke as we went. One thing about RVs and motorhomes is that the majority only have one front door or entrance. This one was no different, and, like our first Target, the door, while solid and secure, shook with each knock Tiger delivered.

CHAPTER 32

We find who we are looking for, but it costs in blood.

BANG, Tiger collapsed, his lower legs shattered where the nine mm balls of the SG twelve gauge round hit home. Well before the second shot, I had dived to the left. Clearly, the shots had come from under the RV, or at least from the other side fired under the chassis. I had gone left because the front tyres were there and they would provide me some cover. I hid behind the wheel on my side and peered under the RV to get a glimpse of the shooter, nothing. This scenario was very different to a suburban setting, where, by now, the guy who was shooting would have been two blocks away. Our guy had nowhere to go, but in the back of my head was the fact that he was no ordinary criminal.

BANG, BANG. I looked around in time to see our 4WD spare tyre explode and a handful of window glass fall into the red dust. I could only assume that our brave Viet Vet had copped a load of shot and was spread bleeding on the front seat. It was time to regain some control. I hadn't heard a shot from overwatch. Our Target was constantly moving and using the motorhome as cover.

He may not have known that Winfrey was out there waiting for a shot, but we had come from that side, and clearly, he was fighting from the opposite side of the RV. It had been too long since I had moved, so I hit the deck, hoping to glimpse a leg or ankle. Nothing. This guy was great, keeping a wheel between me and him while staying hidden from Winfrey. I turned slightly and prayed that Winfrey was watching. I signalled right in an agitated fashion. Winfrey responded, putting down a burst of rounds all over the rear of the RV, walking them to the far side and cleverly ricocheting the projectiles off the sun-baked ground. If my plan had worked, our Assassin should have been running around the front or heading towards the Driver's side door. As Winfrey started shooting, I flew up from where I had been squatting and ran around the front from my side of the motorhome. I hesitated for a fraction and leapt into where I hoped our Target would be sprinting towards.

My timing was near perfect. He was right in front of me. Roza knowing he couldn't get his shotgun muzzle down in time, performed a classic rifle sweep to the left, followed by an equally strong uppercut with the butt. I saw it coming and pulled my head back, feeling the breeze as the black shotgun stock passed close to my chin.

I concentrated on disarming him because the short barrel 12-gauge shotgun was specially designed for close-quarters fighting. Even without firing a shot, it made a worthy club.

Success came when I reversed from trying to grab the shotgun away from him to pulling him along the side of the RV. As agile as he was, this had taken him by surprise. I sensed that he was about to regain control of his movement. However, that millisecond of thought must have taken his eyes away from where we were heading.

Moving backwards, I ducked under the large side-view mirror; his extra height working against him. Using my grip on the shotgun's barrel, I dragged the Assassin towards the mirror. The only way for him to avoid smashing his face into the mirror was to let go of the 12 gauge and jump to the side. Finally, I had the shotgun, but only for a moment. This was no rent-a-cop or door guard. I was in the fight of my life.

Again and again, we pommelled each other, and neither gave an inch. I knew it was wearing me down, and I hoped it had to be the same for him. He hit my bicep as though he was swinging a baseball bat. The force of his blow caused the shotty to fly out of my hands as the nerves in my arm and hand lost all control. The Assassin grabbed my numbed hand and swung me around one eighty degrees, slamming my face and chest into the RV. I clawed at him, hanging on to him as I sagged to the ground. My eyes filled with stars as I began to lose consciousness. I dug deep, and somehow, my legs locked, stopping me from collapsing. I spun towards him, and the battle started again.

He was living up to his past performances. It was like fighting on the top of a cliff. Death was breathing down my neck from this skilled Assassin. And he still had enough tactical awareness to stay out of Winfrey's sights. I became aware that he was choreographing our blows and blocks to keep behind the RV. There was no way he could have known about us having an overwatch. But he continued to demonstrate his talent for thinking through every strategy. He would have placed an overwatch if it was him attacking, so he would set up his defence with this threat in mind. He had at least four inches on me. He wasn't overly muscular, but I could tell he was super fit. My blows to his stomach were met with an iron wall of muscle. Blocks were deflected from the hard chords of arm muscles. Punch after punch, kicks thrown in, it didn't matter what I tried. He was as quick as a cat, trained in multiple forms of Martial Arts and very confident in his skills.

We separated after a few minutes of intense probing, attack and counterattack. Knowing the true professional that he was, this may have been a pause to enable him to recover or reassess the situation. He didn't waste the opportunity.

"Your beautiful bride kept me company these last few weeks. We became......I suppose you could say close friends, better still intimate friends. I'm sure she wondered where her hero was. Where were you, Steve? Oh, that's right, you were hiding in a bottle," Roza said with a slight puffing as he recovered his breath.

Inside I was filled with rage, like molten lava, ready to erupt at any minute, but I couldn't show it, no, not to him. I was too exhausted to rationalise his words and see them for what they were.

He was clever. Deep within me I was rattled. Whether Chris had been abused was a close second to whether she was still alive. I decided not to respond, unsure that I could successfully hide the impact his words had made on me. When you are a sniper, whatever the mission, the first thing they teach you is simple. If you can't take a shot, get somewhere you can. I prayed Winfrey was thinking that now. I had set him a terrible mission, shoot to wound, but don't kill. This was hard enough to do with smaller calibres. It was really challenging for a sniper rifle designed for only one reason: to damage the human body at extreme ranges to result in death, even from a hit to a non-vital organ.

We continued back and forth for what seemed an hour at least but was in reality only a few minutes. The conflict produced no clear winner, but I was sure this was on a knife edge and could change in a blink. One punch or kick landing on target would do it. A buckled knee, a broken arm or leg. A strike that finally reached the throat, crushing the windpipe. Any lapse in concentration or a slower reaction brought on by exhaustion and this duel was over. As the Marines say, when you have tried everything, and it's still not working, try something else.

Although he was taller and heavier, I decided to rush him. I dug in my back foot and ploughed at him with all the speed and force I could muster. It worked to an extent, with him landing hard on his back. I fell on top of him, raising my knee and driving my knee into his solar plexus. I heard the air explode from his lungs, and landed two good punches to his head.

The Assassin was relentless; he had to be oxygen-deprived, sore everywhere and exhausted. So, how did he keep coming back at me with powerful elbow strikes? Always, valuable weapons up close. I blocked as many as I could but still copped a big hit above my left eye.

I had forced him onto his back, and I was still under attack. As I rolled off him, I dropped my own elbow into his stomach and stood up. I had no spring left; I was like an old man climbing to his feet. He followed me, by rolling onto his side. He kicked out, sweeping me off my feet. I was nearly done. He loomed over me, and I knew he was about to stomp on me, groin, stomach, throat or head. I had nothing left; he could finish this now. I saw him raise his foot and willed myself to tense whichever muscle group he chose to attack. BANG! In the middle of the strike, he threw himself backwards away from me. I didn't think he had been shot, but he wasn't sticking around for a second chance.

Where had the shot come from? Had Winfrey finally got a target opportunity? I looked under the RV and knew the answer. Tiger, although wounded had recovered enough to take the shot. He had missed, but it had still probably saved my life. I turned back, expecting the onslaught to continue. However, the Assassin was nowhere to be seen.

CHAPTER 33

An Apple Travel Gadget saves the day.

There was a roar of a motor from the rear of the RV, and an ATV flew away, its tyres scrabbling for purchase in the pebbles and dust. I stood there beyond exhaustion, admitting to myself that this Assassin was always a step ahead of the game.

Tiger yelled that he would be alright.

"Keep going, mate, I can wait for Medivac. Just get him," Tiger screamed.

I ran round to our 4WD. Thank God, Vince had done exactly what he needed to do by throwing himself onto the floor. He was ready to jump up when it seemed safe and take up his position behind the wheel. By the time I reached the 4WD he was ready to get us out of trouble or to chase whatever rabbit came out of the hole.

"Vince, we're leaving Tiger. I need you to swing around, pick up Winfrey and then we'll get after that Assassin," I said calmly as I swung into the front seat.

He was too experienced to waste time or energy on stupid questions.

"Sure thing Steve." The vehicle fishtailed momentarily as he expertly spun the wheel to aim the 4WD at Winfrey's hide.

Vince drove as well as he flew his helicopter; he made his final approach head-on. At the last moment, he touched the brakes and turned the steering wheel, so we slid towards Winfrey, who was now standing. Vince did a slick racing change that was enough to make the sliding 4WD nearly stop, but not quite. I reached across and opened the back door. Both man and machine timed it perfectly, and Winfrey flew/fell across the back seat. By the time I reached over and shut the back door, Vince had flattened the accelerator, and the

Toyota was screaming for a higher gear. We headed towards the RV, scooting around the front bull-bar. There was nothing but dirt and sky, no ATV, not even a dust cloud.

"OK, Steve, we are going, but I sure don't know where. I couldn't see anything from where I was parked. Which way did he go?" The Viet Vet yelled over the 4WD's engine and the constant pinging of the rocks thrown up by our tyres.

"Have we lost him? Oh, man, he's hard to pin down," Winfrey said as he searched the horizon for our Assassin.

"Keep going, Vince. We might not be able to see him, but he definitely went this way," I said confidently.

"I didn't have time to keep you guys up to speed, but I went all James Bond on him," I said with a smug look on my face.

The boys both wore question-mark faces. I enjoyed the moment and then explained.

"Well, I don't have a scientist called 'Q'. But I do have an APPLE AIR TAG. I don't know if you have used one, but they are small discs you register and then put in your suitcase. An App on your phone tracks where your bag is, literally from where you got on the plane and shows when your bag is coming to bag collection, in real-time. That's how accurate they are." I said. Vince interrupted not being able to wait for me to explain fully.

"Yeah, but what has that got to do with us?" He demanded.

Winfrey had caught on. "Are you telling us that you planted a tracker on him?" Winfrey asked.

"I wasn't sure I was going to come out on top. He was flogging me on points, and in the end, I was right. If Tiger hadn't distracted him with that shot, I'm pretty sure I would have been a goner," I paused as that truth hit me.

Physically, I shrugged my shoulders to rid myself of the thought of how death had breathed down my neck yet again.

"Anyway, I dropped my AIR TAG into his pocket during one of our clinches. Let's see where he is," I said, dragging my phone out of my pocket. There it was. A strong, steady signal was out to our right.

"Vince, take us outback at about two o'clock," I asked.

The small disc was continuing to send a strong signal. It wasn't designed for this and would have been useless in a city or busy highway. However, in the open outback, it served us well. We sped over the clear, stony terrain, Vince expertly dodging ant nests and the rare boulder. He maintained a chase speed faster than one would usually traverse this country with, but we had a catch-up to make. The AIR TAG gave us a general direction. Fortunately, there was nowhere for the Assassin to turn off or hide. If we had been in thick bush or a suburb we would never have seen him again.

Suddenly, there he was.

The ATV was making good time, but we were going even faster. The turbocharged 4WD was powerful and heavier than the ATV. This meant we rode lower and faster over the rough terrain, at least if he kept travelling in a straight line. We were constantly restricted by our goal of capturing the Assassin. Normally, we would just blitz the vehicle we were chasing, killing the occupants at best or at least taking out the ATV's tyres. I had a sinking feeling that I knew where he was heading.

Both the rabbit and the dog were avoiding the well-used tracks for the entire chase.

However, I knew we had crossed over two tracks and were now running parallel with the main dirt road that led towards the little private airstrip. The lovely young couple who had lent us their Helo Tour helicopter lived beside it. He may not have expected us to recover so quickly when he jumped into the ATV after our fight. He hadn't looked over his shoulders since we caught up and I could see him astride the vehicle. I had to make a decision that could cost me everything. This guy was ruthless; collateral damage meant nothing to him, especially when his escaping or not may hang in the balance. I wasn't going to let him take the couple hostage or kill them.

My decision was made. "Vince, roll him now, take him out," I yelled over the Toyota's screaming engine.

Again, Vince obeyed the orders without hesitation or discussion. We were already flying, but he found some more speed. Our vehicle came up level with him, and Vince moved our nose slightly to the left. The Viet Vet brought our 4WD bull-bar just past the rear of the Assassin's ATV's rear bush guard. The shock was apparent on the Assassin's face when he finally noticed us alongside. He was at max speed but had just started to turn away from our vehicle. CRASH! Metal on metal, the light ATV spun out of control, rolling three times before coming to a dusty stop back on its four wheels.

I was out of my seat before we had come to a halt. My Glock was in my right hand as I swooped onto the bloodied body of the Assassin, Chris's Kidnapper, my enemy to the death.

We had finally caught a break; his face was covered in blood from multiple facial wounds and a badly broken nose. I could see a glimpse of his radius bone, where the shattered bone had broken through his skin.

He was in a bad way, but this guy was world-class; he would recover quickly, whereas an average person would be in shock and be disabled for hours. He was also cunning and skilled, so I was not about to relax in case he was playing possum. It wouldn't be the first time an enemy had played dead only to cause casualties to nearby troops who had begun to switch off. I sensed Winfrey beside me, covering the inert Assassin from behind his seat. I checked for a pulse and thanked God he was still alive. Reaching in, I unbuckled his full harness belt, which had probably saved his life. Still no movement, not even a groan or grimace.

The next part was the tricky bit; getting him out of the vehicle meant I had to virtually hug him. If he was uninjured, this would be akin to hugging a grizzly. My compassion level for this guy was negative five on a nice day. I grabbed the compound fracture. I knew these were so painful that no one could fake being unconscious, with even a little movement. Nothing.

The owners of the Helo Tour business had heard the loud metallic clash. They had rushed out expecting to see some horrific traffic accident where there was no traffic.

"Are you guys OK?" he asked with a worried look on his face.

"I am really sorry to bring trouble to your door, but I need you both to go back inside. Forget what you have just seen; don't phone the Police or anyone else. One day soon, Vince will explain," I said in a serious tone which brooked no further discussion.

"We are the good guys, but we can't explain more than that, I'm sorry," I continued with as friendly a look on my face as I could muster. I realised I must look like a boxer who has gone fifteen rounds and I probably made them feel more concerned than not.

Vince tried to help as well. "Guys, what he just said is all true. Today, we can't give you all the information you deserve, but, like he said, we are the good guys in this," Vince stated confidently.

The tour operator was thinking about challenging the situation and then thought better of it. They turned and walked back into their house.

"OK, guys, we have him; there's no time for high fives, but it's definitely a job well done. We have to get back to Tiger and Medivac him to Roma Base Hospital. I'm sorry to sound uncaring, but the other pressing matter is getting this guy to tell me what I need to know," I said, feeling selfish when my mate Tiger was lying back there with wounded legs. The solution came from our Viet Vet chopper pilot, cum Driver.

"It's always been a sort of an urban myth if that's what you can call a rumour from Vietnam." Vince changed from talking generalities and maybes to definite certainty.

"OK, in Nam, we would question captured VC by taking them on a chopper ride. If there were two VCs, we would ask a question, and when no answers came, we would throw one out. The remaining VC would usually sing like a bird," The older man said without pride or shame.

"Obviously, we only have one to interrogate, one shot at this. But, if we do what Vince is saying and maybe dangle him by his ankles, it might just work," I said.

Everyone agreed; Vince had done it all before, and Winfrey knew what was at stake. I was totally invested, and even without the personal angle, this guy was a dead man walking whichever way it went. I had always been mission-focused, orders my fallback, but this had gone way past that. This professional Assassin who lay on the ground before me had made it personal. He had kidnapped my bride and beheaded my best mate,

Jake, my Border Collie, he'd tried to kill me at least twice, not counting our run-in at his RV. But, and it was a huge but. There were two huge questions we needed answers to. Who had sent him to kill the American President and our Prime Minister? The other question that was being raised in every Security and Police Department around the world; Was this the Assassin who had attempted to kill POTUS the same man who had Assassinated the Russian President and the Canadian Prime Minister?

I have given all of my adult life to serving my country. I have done my duty, my share and maybe even a bit more. For me to know I wasn't going to transport this prisoner to an official facility rang warning bells. I was not as logical or rational as usual. But this killer had taken the love of my life in one way or another. The tightness in my chest nearly buckled my knees. This ended here and now.

"OK, Winfrey, you have the prisoner. Vince, we follow your plan. Once in the air, Winfrey and I will take turns questioning and managing him physically.

Turning to Winfrey, i continued, "Mate, I know that he is a High-Value Target for your Boss. To be honest, he is with mine as well as a heap of agencies around the world. So this is the plan. I don't think I can make it by asking him about Chris. So this is how it will go, or at least this is the plan,"

I went on to outline that I would hammer him about the assassinations; we would

ask, dangle and pull him back in. Then, repeat it again. "Mate, you're free to ask anything when we are working together on the two biggies; who ordered and paid for the hits, and did he kill the Russian and Canadian VIPs?" I said, as cold as ice. The kidnapper started to come around. Winfrey and I had been around too long to fall for anything, and we had seen him in action. We were in near awe of this international Assassin's skills, and we definitely had professional respect. I splashed some water on his bloodied face. He shook his head, attempting to clear it and make sense of what he had woken to.

Credit where credit is due, he played his first card.

"Who are you? Why did you attack me? Is someone calling the Police?" he said it in an innocent tone, using a mix of soft European and Australian accent.

"Nice try, mate, we might not know your real name or much else but we know you are the Assassin the whole world is looking for. Now, have a drink; and take it slow; we wouldn't want you to drown or something," I said calmly.

"We are all going for a helicopter ride, so relax, and things will be easier for everyone." Winfrey said in a friendly manner.

"He is American. Where am I, who is he? No, I don't want to go for a ride; I need to go to the hospital," he said, holding up his broken arm.

Ignoring his questions we bundled him into the chopper. He noticed that Vince had removed one of the doors, although it was a civilian aircraft and commented on this but neither of us responded. He could work it out himself or be surprised. Either way, we didn't care. We both buckled up but held him between us on the floor. Here before us was the lone wolf, a world-class operator who had survived in a profession that few last very long. Keeping him trussed up and lying on the hard floor of the chopper told him that his reputation didn't impress us.

He had recovered from being hit; his injuries, while not life-threatening, would have to have been hurting him beyond most people's ability. However, he had evaluated the situation accurately.

"OK, what is it you want. If you were going to kill me, I'd be dead already. If you wanted to torture me, we all know a child could exert enough pain on this compound fracture for me to confess to anything. So what's it going to be?" he asked, attempting to regain control.

Winfrey and I had the same understanding and attitude about this lethal weapon sitting between us. We were aware of the psychological games you played when captured, but this guy was impressive. We both laughed. The effect was immediate.

The Assassin's blood and dust-streaked face registered a flicker of anger at our laughing at his speech. It was quickly replaced by perhaps concern or at least deep thought. I had asked Vince to head back towards the Assassin's RV so we could pick up our fallen comrade, Tiger. Any air and any hard ground would work so we could ask our questions on the way back.

Taking the lead I began, "Well, you are wrong about everything, so this is how it's going to go. We will ask you some questions, and you will answer them. Now I am so sick of you and talking. I need to warn you my patience is nil; you understand? Zero," I said menacingly, the game was on. We had no fixed agenda, just three questions, three answers.

Winfrey took over, "Now, don't bother with denials; we know a lot. We just want to know more. Question one is simple; did you Assassinate the Russian President and the Canadian Prime Minister?"

"You're going to kill me anyway; why should I tell you anything?" the kidnapper asked smugly.

"Because this is Australia, not Russia or somewhere in darkest Africa, where you're used to working for some crazy dictator. We don't have the death penalty here, mate. You starting to see the light at the end of the tunnel yet?" I said as sincerely as I could. Hoping he wouldn't realise that if we didn't have Capital Punishment, then torture would be off the table as well.

"How long do you think I would keep what's left of my reputation? I'd never work again if it gets around that I answered your questions," the Assassin spat angrily.

"Well, we won't tell anyone, and as far as work goes, we don't hang killers anymore, but the likes of you, we will lock up forever," I said.

"Enough chatter, you have three questions to answer, no more sob stories, no philosophical discussion like we are talking about someone else.

Question one; simple. Did you assassinate the Russian President and the Canadian Prime Minister?" Winfrey demanded as he grabbed Roza by the front of his shirt and dragged him towards the open Helo door. He did it well. He was clearly committed but did not overplay it. He was too clever to leave himself nowhere to go if the Assassin refused to answer.

"OK, I'll deal," he said without any sign of giving in, this was simply a negotiation to end all this.

"DEAL, DEAL!!!!! You have nothing to deal with. Sure, we want answers, but you will tell us one way or another," I stated trying with all I had to not lose control, my face just inches from his. "Let's show him the view." I yelled to Winfrey over the noise of the chopper.

Winfrey and I grabbed him by an arm and a leg each and put most of him outside the chopper. The wind ripped at his clothes, and his mouth was distorted as it filled with wind. After a few moments, I nodded to Winfrey, and we pulled him back in. Windblown, his eyes were watering, his hair was all over the place and his shirt buttons were gone.

"You.......You can't do this; I am a prisoner; I have rights," he said, sounding close to crying.

Although it may have been a ploy, I was surprised at this. He had consistently displayed intelligence, courage and determination. Just maybe we had stumbled upon his weakness, a fear of heights. At the top of his profession, he wasn't scared of dying, so this was different.

"Now, one more time. Did you kill those two High-Value Targets?" Winfrey screamed.

Taking his time, appearing totally in control, Roza answered. "OK, yes, yes I did. The Russian one, you should thank me, the other, who cares, hey? Now, can we stop all this?" Roza said as calmly as if he had just said he picked up dinner on the way home. He was a stone-cold killer, that was for sure.

"You're not finished yet. Who were you working for? Who took out these contracts? We need his name," Winfrey demanded, placing his hands on the Assassin's shirt to remind him just how close the open door was.

"If I tell you that, I'm a dead man. Just shoot me now to save time," Roza stated calmly but with a certainty that left no room for challenge.

"OK, I know you are bright enough to realise that you are never getting out of jail, but a few good words from us can make your life just that bit easier. Over the years to come, even a little help is huge. OK, now mate we are listening," I said in a friendly manner that I hoped would encourage him to sing.

"I need it in writing, then I will tell you everything," the Assassin stated as he sat up straight, his way of regaining some control.

"Now, buddy, you have been watching too many TV shows. Surprise, surprise we haven't got any paper. Look around. We are in a chopper, not some interrogation cell or office," Winfrey said, with a smile that didn't reach his eyes.

"Well, I'm being straight with you. I hope you will be the same with me," Roza, the international murderer, said.

He went on to name the Russian K.S.V. Director. We had no choice; if he was lying, our Intel was rubbish. If he was telling us the truth, some other team, under another control would take this guy out in cold retribution. Vince's voice came into the headset speaker I had kept on my left ear.

"Guys, we are 10 Mikes out from picking up Tiger. We are quickly running out of empty country. We need to DIDDY MOU," He said, reverting back to his Vietnam sayings.

With everything that was going on, I couldn't help myself as a thought raced through my mind; *Piloted by a Vietnam Vet on today's mission was like a scene from 'Apocalypse Now'. I suppose in a way, it was.*

My nod to Winfrey said that I was bowing out. It was time to ask about Chris. It was as though my heart stopped. Was she still alive? Had she been dead since our wedding day? I needed to know like I needed my next breath. But a part of me didn't really want to know the truth. Not knowing was torture, but knowing and accepting the reality was more terrifying than any foe I had ever faced. Winfrey knew what he had to do.

"One last question, and you can relax. Where is Chris, the bride you kidnapped?" He demanded.

"You will never find out. I had a lot of fun with her though, and now she's just where I put her," Roza said with a self-satisfied look.

"Same deal, man. Info, for security in jail, info for luxury where soap is gold, give me something," Winfrey said remaining deadly calm. I nodded to Winfrey, gesturing towards the open door. He picked up on it and, grabbing an arm and a leg each, we again put the Assassin outside the Helo cabin. This time, we left him dangling longer than last time. After a few minutes, I heard him screaming. I knew killers; they were the real deal, so posing wasn't a factor.

However, for an Operative, having the poker face, the thousand-yard stare, was a part of their genes. He was clearly terrified, which would have been a nearly unique experience for him but to actually show his fear by screaming must be doing his head in. I nodded to my CIA friend.

"OK, last chance, the rest of your life out of the main population with a few other amenities. Your choice, now, is a once-only offer. You decide. If not, there will be no special treatment for the rest of your days of hard time in gen-pop," Winfrey said calmly.

I appreciated his quality efforts.

With a cruel laugh, the Assassin said, "I know you're asking to assuage your own guilt, Wallace. You failed to protect her, and that is going with you to the grave. Here's my answer for you.

You killed her, not me. You killed her when you met her, and when you messed with me. You are the only person to have ever hurt me. And now I have returned the favour. Out of a thousand Marines and Secret Service and who knows what, it was you. You cost me millions. You cost me a reputation of success that took years to build. You took my world," Roza said passionately, his words chilled me to the core.

"Enough with the big speeches. Where is Chris?" Winfrey demanded, his voice full of threat and anger.

Ignoring Winfrey's threats, Roza continued, "Wallace, you have been a worthy opponent, but the fight is over. The game has no more moves. You have overpowered me. I am your prisoner. But I have something you will always want and never have. To know whether she lives or is dead, whether she is chained to a post somewhere or buried in a creek bed off some dirt track. All my life, I have killed without a thought of the Target as a human with friends or family, of dreams and plans. I only have a future in some jail, somewhere, and I can only hope that you will keep your promises. Revenge is a new thing for me. But I am caught; revenge is about all I have left," the international Assassin said, making sure that each word or phrase cut me like a well-honed knife.

I nodded to Winfrey again, and we swung the Assassin out of the chopper again. As we were holding him, a thousand thoughts bombarded my mind. Roza was right. We would never make him tell us what he had done with Chris. This was a heartbreaking, terrifying situation in which a man, driven by revenge, held all the cards. It has always amazed me that often the most powerful statements can sometimes be just one or two words, maybe three.

I called to Winfrey. "I've got him." Winfrey understood immediately. He released his grip on the Assassin's arm and leg and turned away from us.

"You killed my woman and my dog," I said with righteous tears of fury. I let go of his arm and leg and watched him spin away from us. He didn't struggle or scream.

It was over for us all.

CHAPTER 34

I beat the Champ, but did he win the game?

During the rest of the flight, I stayed where I was sitting when I had thrown the garbage out, where I had executed him. We would never know his real name or what I needed so much to know, where Chris was. There was no second-guessing on my part; he may have had a slight weakness for heights, but he was always going to be a top-class professional Assassin. He was clearly motivated by the hatred for me, his need to hurt me in a way that kept on hurting forever. I would always wonder if he ever really believed we would look after him after he had answered the questions. It didn't matter; in his sick twisted mind, he may have continued to string me along. He wanted me to think he was going to cooperate to reveal Chris's well-being.

He had been playing with me. Another demonstration of his world-class status as an Assassin, able to bend a victim's mind to a place that suited his plans or agenda. His game would have gone on forever. Knowledge is power, and he wanted to exert his power to destroy me, to inflict as much pain as possible. He had been so angry that he wanted to keep hurting me until I was dead. Every fibre of my being wanted Chris to be alive. I dreamed of finding her, taking her home to our sleepy little cottage in Roma. But, deep down under my love, beneath my imagination, I knew I had been in denial since my destroyed wedding day. I was only sure of two things.

He had murdered the Limo Driver, and he had beheaded my dog. There was no way for him to know the depth of the grief he dumped on me. But, it had hit me hard. Chris was my soulmate, and Jake, my Border Collie, was my best friend. He had taken my whole world from me in one action. I took his entire life with one of my own. These were the thoughts I had been struggling with for weeks since he destroyed my wedding day and my life. I had masked my own need for revenge in the hunt for this unknown Assassin who had tried to kill the American President and our own Prime Minister on my watch. Sure, we had been successful in robbing him of his prize. He had employed a devious and brazen escape plan by sacrificing a young Australian as a decoy.

Like the seasoned hunter he was, he had sat tight until he could make his escape.

He was an impressive foe. Up to that point, I could nearly call it just business. Sure, he was the enemy, but even though we did not know each other personally when we fought, it was just him and me.

Not personal or professional, but two seasoned warriors locking horns. But instead of leaving Australia, he stayed uncharacteristically. Unbeknown to me or anyone else at the time, it had become personal. The Assassin, driven by revenge, somehow found out my details as the one who had cost him so dearly on the Tortilla Flats USMC Base in the Northern Territory. He had murdered and kidnapped; he had to be caught and face the system for his crimes. Technically, I had executed him without a trial. There would be hell to pay if the media ever got wind of it.

Even my strongest supporter, Colonel Goodrich, would have let me fight that battle alone. I knew the guys with me, saw it my way; they would never speak of it again.

We had completed an off-the-books mission, so other than the outcome, my report could be carefully written, omitting the incriminating events.

The Police didn't rate a thought. Did I feel guilty? Had I become no better than him? The honest answer was that I felt nothing. Sure, some lounge chair expert would scream that I was a psychopath or a Soldier who had gotten carried away. But they would never know what happened out there that day. Thankfully, we got back to Tiger in time; he had lost a lot of blood, but the tough old Soldier was OK. We flew him to Roma Base Hospital with a hunting accident story. The med staff bought our account of the accident, it was still the hospital's SOP to report any wounds related to firearms to the Police. Vince saved the day again being from nearby Chinchilla and a local businessman.

Even his age made him the perfect one to talk to the Coppers.

"Vince, you've done so much already, but I need to ask you something more. The local Cops and I aren't exactly best mates. This will not go well if I am even in the vicinity. Mate, can you handle it? The usual hunting scenario should work. Sorry, you might have to play the; 'I must be getting old card, or something to explain how old mate got blasted," I asked. As I looked over his shoulder I saw the Police 4WD pull into the Emergency parking lot.

Vince didn't miss a beat, not bothering to answer me. I wouldn't have heard him any way I was out of there. A quick phone call that wouldn't allow him any questions and I would let Senior Sergeant Townsend know it was all over. No details, 'You understand National Security and everything' should satisfy him. But not right now, not face to face. I stood, hiding around the corner with Winfrey feeling slightly ridiculous, like two schoolboys smoking behind the shed.

"Vince has been gold, hasn't he? He hasn't complained once, mate, but we couldn't have done that without him. I hate to say it, but I thought taking him on was a mistake. That was so wrong; old Soldiers should never be written off. The guy is a legend," the CIA Operative said seriously.

"Between you and me, I wondered if I had been stupid for letting him onto the team. Same as you, he taught me how dumb that was," I said, thanking God that I had ignored the second-guessing.

"If you boys are finished hiding from the teacher I'll fly us all back to Chinchilla. Now they have him in the hospital, the Doctors think that Tiger will be fine. Turns out he lost some calf muscle but amazingly, except for a tiny chip that buckshot missed his leg bones," Vince said with obvious relief.

"That's great news; remembering what his bloodied legs looked like, that's nothing short of a miracle. I thought he might lose both of them or end up a bit shorter by the time the docs cleaned him up," I said, smiling. My relief was not only as a friend but he had been wounded doing me a favour. I was so grateful that he hadn't died; now it looked like he would probably have close to a full recovery.

EPILOGUE

WE WON, WE WON; I've lost everything.

It was a short flight from Roma back to Chinchilla. Of course, I expressed my gratitude to Vince, the Helicopter Pilot, Driver, and backup Soldier, who could not have performed any better. As sincere as they were, my words sounded inadequate as I delivered them. But, I had learned long ago that when you go through life and death situations that few comprehend, let alone experience, words neither succeed nor are needed.

I was very unpopular with Tiger's wife, but that was understandable. Once again, I was so glad the news wasn't any worse than it was. Winfrey and I returned to our comrade's Motel. However, it was clear that our family-level welcome was gone.

"Well, Winfrey, except for some spectacular vehicle mounts and dismounts, you didn't have much to do on this gig." I said, smiling, my words dripping with friendly sarcasm.

"But, seriously, mate, you know how much it means that you're always willing to watch my six. You know I can never repay you except to pledge the same willingness," I said sincerely.

"You know Steve, you are right, but that's how we are, two weapons in different armies, but thankfully, they are on the same side. Someone has to keep you safe," the CIA Operative said, smiling, looking more like a surfer than a skilled killer. "Where to now, mate, you OK?" he asked.

"I'm not sure; since we left Tiger in the hospital, I have thought about nothing but the future. Like you, it's a strange feeling, but our work always looks after the future. You go where they need you; it's simple, and there's no choice. Now my personal life, all my future plans with Chris, well obviously, they are smoke," I had to turn away so he couldn't see my eyes had teared up. Winfrey was pretty sensitive for such a tough warrior.

"Surely you don't have to make all those decisions right now. Colonel Goodrich seems about as good as it gets as Ops Control. He'll understand," Winfrey said encouragingly.

I interrupted, sounding a little more angry than I meant to show, "Yeah, you're right. He's a great Boss but I can't be one of those lame ducks. Next thing, I'll be on a desk in Canberra.

"Like I said, after everything that has happened, now is not the time to make life-changing decisions you may regret. We will fly down to your HQ and do our reports, and then we can both grab some leave. You need some RnR, a change in scenery. Maybe go to Thailand, one of those resorts where the only decision to make is which cocktail to try next," He said.

"Yeah, well, the first part is a given. The rest we'll see.

Colonel Goodrich was just as Winfrey had described; he was considerate but didn't smother me in condolences or treat me like a shattered human. Winfrey and I made our reports uniform in what happened, individually describing our respective roles and actions. Because the Op was Off the Books, I knew I couldn't get a medal for Vince or Tiger. In any case, neither of them was that way inclined. I implored the Colonel to reimburse them more than their expenses as a reward cum compensation.

I could just imagine some admin clerk Corporal freaking out because there were no dockets. They both deserved so much more. The Colonel got it; he promised to sort something out, and knowing I could trust him, I knew he would sort it.

I reeled out of his office and crashed through the Men's Room. I collapsed onto the mirror over the sink, sobbing and shaking, each taking turns. Walking towards Goodrich's office, I had realised I had nowhere to go. Our little cottage in Roma was 'our' place, not mine. It was still in Chris's name, so I could walk away emotionally and financially. It didn't matter anyway; I couldn't face all those memories of her and Jake. It was the same out at my mate's cattle property. The memories were too strong, and the ghosts too vivid, day or night. I couldn't face the Senior Sergeant, who grieved nearly as much as I did over her death. I couldn't even go back to my Motel room in Chinchilla. I wasn't welcomed or comfortable anywhere. I had no one.

I was on empty; even though nearly every part of me was bruised and cut, I felt nothing. Every tank was dry. I don't know if it is biologically possible, but that's how I felt. I wouldn't have been surprised if my body was so worn out it would refuse to make adrenaline. I couldn't think; now, the grief was like a battleship crushing my chest. Before, it had been pressing the air in a vague, undefined force. I made my mind up. I wanted to be alone so much. I couldn't put on a brave face any longer, or the face of a warrior even though it was what was expected of me. I was no longer that man, the cold professional Agent. Maybe I was no different to the unnamed Assassin I had executed. I was no better.

I don't remember a thing Colonel Goodrich had said; vaguely, I remember Winfrey agreeing to something. Like a patient heading for post-op or a guy drunker than his mates, as in a fog I had floated out of the Colonel's office. I was numb and dumb, but just like that drunk, I knew my friend was somehow looking after me. I would have gone anywhere I was led. In a blurry world, I said words that would set my destiny.

My phone's ring tone began to play 'The Good The Bad and The Ugly' Theme song.

It was an unknown number, I was about to disconnect thinking it was probably a telemarketer when something deep inside stopped me.

"Hi, whatever you're peddling I'm not interested," I said sarcastically.

"Ah....... I don't understand, is the phone of Mr Steven Wallace?" A Middle Eastern accented voice asked.

Realising my initial assumption was off target, I pulled myself together and replied, "Yes Steve Wallace speaking."

"Sir I have His Excellency Crown Prince Abdul Al Sattar's, wanting to speak with you. Will you take His Excellency's call?" The cultured voice enquired.

"Yes, yes, please forgive my rudeness," I said humbly.

Crown Prince Abdul Al Sattar's and I had met in Abu Dhabi after I had rescued his son from a gang of kidnappers. This had led to him proving me with assistance on an operation to take down a network of ISIS smugglers. We hadn't had any contact since then.

"Mr Wallace, thank you for taking my call," the Crown Prince said like I was doing him a massive favour.

"Please Your Excellency, call me Steve, and forgive me for not connecting more rapidly." I said. "Sir it is good to hear your voice again."

"Thank you Steve, a little like the last time we met I find myself embarrassed at what has happened to you." The deep western educated voice stated sincerely.

"Your Excellency, please we are friends that have shared troubles and come through them closer than we started. I can't think of anything that would cause embarrassment between us." I said calmly.

"Steve please hear me out as you say. It is true I am in your debt again, one of my people has betrayed you. I only hope this warning is in time to minimise any harm to you," he said, sadness softening his words, he continued.

"I am not very knowledgeable regarding such things, however, I am informed that Faishal, my Personal Assistant has betrayed both you and me by one action. I had to let him go when I discovered that he was using Cocaine on a regular basis while in my service. Apparently, about a month after he left my employ there was an enquiry on the Dark Web. Someone had offered Five Hundred Thousand Dollars for information regarding you. A lot of general information was posted, the enquirer seeking your name, address etc. It appears Faishal saw the advertisement and immediately thought it was about you. I pray he was wrong, my friend," a slight pleading entering his normal assertive voice.

"Sir, did he have my details? How would he?" I asked.

I immediately knew how. After I had refused a reward from the Crown Prince for saving his son, a canary yellow Lamborghini had been delivered to our little cottage in Roma. At the time I had marvelled at the reach the Prince had in finding me so far from Abu Dhabi.

I held my breath and thought it through.

"Yes, I assume during that hesitation that you just worked out how he had all your details. I am so sorry Steve. Faishal has now met with a fatal accident. However, I fear it was too late." Crown Prince Abdul Al Sattar said quietly.

"Your Excellency, I would never blame you for what has occurred. I thank you for acting so quickly to avenge his betrayal of both of us. However, the last two months have been hell on earth. I am unable to tell you the details. As I said you are innocent of any wrong doing. No one could have foreseen what Faishal's evil work has caused. As close as a Crown Prince and an Australian Soldier can be we will always be friends your Highness." I said as I disconnected the call.

"You know Winfrey, you're right. Thailand sounds good."

THE END

TO MY READERS.

Thank you for reading **TERROR in MY HEART,** my third book in the Steve Wallace Action Thriller sagas.

I hope you enjoyed it as much as I did as I wrote it.

If you haven't read **TERROR in OUR HOMELAND** or **TERROR in PARADISE** don't worry. They can be read as a stand alone story, or in sequence.

PLEASE WRITE A REVIEW.

I know reviews take a little of your time, however they are incredibly valuable to Authors.

Reviews help other readers find books they may like and assist me to strive for excellence in my writing.

I really appreciate reviews, whether positive or negative. Please take a couple of minutes to post your review where ever you purchased, thanks.

Thanks

Dave.

ABOUT THE AUTHOR

David Adams spends as much time as possible in the Australian bush, camping, gold and treasure fossicking, hunting feral animals throughout Australia. He served as an Officer in the Australian Army Reserve during the post-Vietnam era. Dave has trained alongside members of the United States Marine Corps and Special Air Services SAS. Serving his last two years in the A.D.F as a Platoon Commander Military Police provided him with exposure to law enforcement working closely with his civilian counterparts in the Queensland Police Service. Dave relies on this real-life experience to provide him with authentic characters, settings, and a knowledge of military equipment and procedures. He continues to travel the world in search of exciting settings and characters that he hopes will transport his readers to these exotic places while adding a reality to his books.

www.ingramcontent.com/pod-product-compliance
Lightning Source LLC
Chambersburg PA
CBHW030359030726
47497CB00002B/402